MW01138198

ROBIN HOOD THE OUTLAW

by Alexandre Dumas

Translated by Alfred Allinson

The Reginetta Press, 2020
www.ReginettaPress.com

Cover design by
Donnie Light & Celia Jones

ISBN 13: 978-0-9823714-7-3
ISBN 10: 0-9823714-7-0

REGINETTA
PRESS

Tales of Robin Hood by Alexandre Dumas:

THE PRINCE OF THIEVES
1872

ROBIN HOOD THE OUTLAW
1873

Ho for the good green wood!
Ho for brave Robin Hood!

The adventures that flowed from the pen of Alexandre Dumas are well loved. Less known today are his tales of Robin Hood. It is our pleasure to provide these two old works to a new public: readers of the 21st Century. English versions of *The Prince of Thieves* and *Robin Hood the Outlaw* have virtually disappeared from bookshelves; they are now edited, corrected, and made accessible to the world in print and e-formats, by the Reginetta Press.

This volume continues the story begun in *The Prince of Thieves*. Read more of Robin and Marian's romance, and learn of Robin's unlucky betrayal by a woman; of Robin's valiant leadership of the Merrie Men including Little John, Will Scarlett, and Friar Tuck; their battles against the Sheriff of Nottingham — and the craven Prince John. Outwitting crafty ecclesiastics along the way, Robin at last bows to King Richard Coeur-de-Lion.

Retold in Alfred Allinson's lush translation from the original French, the hero's adventure winds to a stirring conclusion.

The Reginetta Press

Alexandre Dumas

ROBIN HOOD
THE OUTLAW

CHAPTER I

In the early hours of a beautiful day in the month of August, Robin Hood, with a light heart and a song on his lips, was strolling down a narrow glade in Sherwood Forest. Suddenly a strong voice, whose capricious tones evidenced a profound ignorance of the rules of music, took up the amorous ballad Robin Hood was singing.

"By'r Lady!" muttered the young man, listening attentively to the stranger's song, "what an extraordinary thing. Those words are mine own composition, dating from my childhood, and I have never taught them to a soul."

Reflecting thus, Robin glided behind the trunk of a tree, to wait until the traveller had passed. The latter soon appeared. As he came opposite the oak tree at the foot of which Robin was sitting, he stopped and gazed into the depths of the wood.

"Ha! ha!" he said, perceiving through the thicket a magnificent herd of deer, "there are some old acquaintances; let us see whether mine eye is still true and my hand sure. By St. Paul! I shall give myself the pleasure of sending an arrow into yonder lusty fellow pacing along so stately."

Saying which, the stranger took an arrow from his quiver, and, adjusting it to his bow, aimed at the deer, wounding him mortally.

"Well done!" cried a laughing voice; "that was a right clever shot."

The stranger, taken by surprise, turned abruptly.

"Think you so, master?" said he, looking Robin up and down.

"Yea, you are most dexterous."

"Indeed!" added the other in a scornful tone.

"Never a doubt of it, and especially so for one little used to shoot at deer."

"How know you that I am not practised in this exercise?"

"By your fashion of holding the bow. I would wager what you will, Sir Stranger, that you are better versed in overthrowing a man on the field of battle than in stretching out the deer in the green wood."

"Excellently answered," laughed the stranger. "Is it permissible to ask the name of one whose eye is so penetrating as to judge by a single shot the difference betwixt the action of a soldier and that of a forester?"

"My name boots little in the question before us, Sir Stranger, but I can tell you my qualifications. I am one of the chief keepers of this Forest, and I do not intend to allow my helpless deer to be exposed to the attacks of any who take it into their heads to kill them, merely to try their skill."

"I care not much for your intentions, fair keeper," rejoined the stranger in a deliberate tone, "and I defy you to prevent me from shooting mine arrows as best me seemeth. I will kill the deer, I will kill the fawns, I will kill what I please."

"That will be easy, an if I do not oppose you, because you are a right good bowman," Robin replied. "And now I will make you a proposition. Hear me! I am chief of a band of men, stout-hearted, clear-witted, and well skilled in all the exercises of their trade. You seem to me a good fellow: if your heart be honest, if you be of a calm and conciliatory spirit, I shall be happy to enroll you in my company. Once you are one of us, you may hunt the deer; but if you refuse to join our brotherhood, I must ask you to quit the Forest."

"Truly, master keeper, you speak in a mighty overbearing tone. Come now, hear me in your turn. If you do not speedily show me your heels, I will give you such counsel as—with no grand phrases—will teach you to weigh your words; which counsel, pretty bird, will be a volley of blows from a cudgel plied pretty briskly."

"*You* beat me!" cried Robin, scornfully.

"Yea, I!"

"My lad," replied Robin, "I would fain not lose my temper, for thou wouldst find it would go ill with thee then; but if thou dost not at once obey my order to quit the Forest, thou wilt be first vigorously chastised; thereafter we will e'en try the compass of thy neck and the strength of thy body on the highest branch of a tree in this Forest."

The stranger began to laugh.

"Beat me and hang me," said he; "that would be curious, if it were not impossible. Let us see, then. Get to work; I am waiting."

"I do not trouble myself to cudgel with mine own hands all the rogues I encounter, my friend," returned Robin. "I have those who fill that useful office in my name. I will summon them, and thou canst explain thyself to them."

Robin raised a horn to his lips, and was about to sound a vigorous call, when the stranger, who had quickly fitted an arrow to his bow, shouted—

"Hold, or I kill you!"

Robin dropped his horn, seized his bow, and leaping towards the stranger with incredible nimbleness, cried—

"Madman! Dost not see with what a power thou wouldst strive? Before thou couldst strike me, I should have already smitten thee, and the death thou wouldst aim at me would have recoiled upon thyself. Be reasonable; we are strangers to each other, and for no good cause we treat each other as enemies. The bow is a murderous weapon: replace the arrow in thy quiver, and, since thou wilt play with the quarter-staff, so be it. I accept thy challenge."

"The quarter-staff then!" repeated the stranger; "and let him who is able to knock the other on the head, be not only the victor, but also free to rule the fate of his adversary."

"So be it," Robin returned. "Take heed of the consequences of the compact thou proposest; if I make thee cry for mercy, I shall have the right of enrolling thee in my band."

"Agreed!"

"Very well; and may the best man win the day."

"Amen!" said the stranger.

The trial of strength commenced. The blows, liberally administered on both sides, soon overwhelmed the stranger, who did not succeed in hitting Robin once. Indignant and breathless, the poor youth flung down his weapon.

"Cease!" he cried. "I have had enough of this."

"You own yourself beaten?" asked Robin.

"No; but I see you are much stronger than I am. You are accustomed to wield a cudgel, which gives you too great an advantage; the match should be as equal as possible. Can you use a sword?"

"Yea," replied Robin.

"Will you continue the struggle with that weapon?"

"Certainly."

They drew their swords. Each was an expert swordsman, and when they had fought for a quarter of an hour, neither had succeeded in wounding the other.

"Stop!" cried Robin, suddenly.

"You are tired?" asked the stranger, with a smile of triumph.

"Yea," Robin replied frankly; "since to me the sword is not a pleasant weapon. The quarter-staff is the thing; its blows are less dangerous and offer some sport; the sword hath something savage and cruel about it. My fatigue, though real," Robin went on, scrutinising the face of the stranger, whose head was covered by a cap which partly concealed his forehead, "is not my sole reason for seeking a truce. Since I have stood facing thee, memories of my childhood have surged up within me; the look of thy large blue eyes is not unfamiliar to me. Thy voice recalls that of a friend, my heart is irresistibly attracted towards thee. Tell me thy name; if thou art he whom I love and long for with all the yearning of a tender friendship, thou art welcome a thousand times. I will love thee for thyself and for the dear memories thou dost recall."

"You speak with a goodnature which attracts me, Sir Forester," replied the stranger, "but, to my great sorrow, I cannot grant your reasonable request. I am not at liberty to do so; my name is a secret which prudence counsels me to guard with care."

"You have nothing to fear from me," replied Robin; "I am one of those whom men call outlaws. Moreover, I am incapable of betraying the confidence of one who trusts me, and I despise the baseness of him who would reveal even a secret involuntarily surprised. Tell me your name?"

The stranger still hesitated.

"I will be your friend," added Robin, with an air of frankness.

"Agreed," replied the stranger. "I am called William Gamwell."

Robin uttered a cry.

"Will, Will—merry Will Scarlett?"

"Yea."

"And I am Robin Hood!"

"Robin!" cried the young man, as he fell into the arms of his friend; "what joy!"

The two young men embraced each other heartily; then, with looks of unspeakable delight, they gazed at each other with an affecting wonder.

"And I threatened thee!" said Will.

"And I did not recognise thee!" added Robin.

"I wished to kill thee!" cried Will.

"And I cudgelled thee!" continued Robin, breaking into a laugh.

"Bah! think no more of that. Give me news quick of...Maude."

"Maude is well, very well."

"Is she...?"

"Always a charming girl, who loves thee, Will, and only thee in all the world. She hath kept her heart for thee; she will give thee her hand. She hath mourned thy absence, the dear creature; thou hast suffered much, my poor Will, but thou wilt be happy, if thou dost still love the good and beautiful Maude."

"*If* I love her! How can you question it, Robin? Ah! yes, I love her, and God bless her for not having forgotten me! I have never ceased thinking of her for a single moment; her dear image was ever in my heart, and gave it strength. It was the courage of the soldier on the field of battle, and the consolation of the prisoner in the dark dungeon of the State prison. Maude, dear Robin, hath been my thought, my dream, my hope, my future. Through her I have been able to bear the most cruel privations, the most grievous hardships. God implanted in my heart an unshakeable confidence in the future. I felt sure of seeing Maude again, of becoming her husband, and of spending the last years of my life with her."

"That patient hope is on the point of being fulfilled, dear Will," said Robin.

"Yea, I trust so, or rather, I am certain of it. To prove to thee, friend Robin, how much I thought of the dear child, I will tell thee a dream I had in Normandy—a dream which lingers still in my thoughts, though it dates back nearly a month. I was in the depths of a prison, my arms bound, my body loaded with chains, and I saw Maude a few paces from me, pale as death and covered with blood.

The poor girl held out supplicating hands toward me, and her mouth, with its blood-stained lips, murmured plaintive words, the sense of which I could not comprehend, but I saw that she suffered cruelly and was calling me to her aid. As I have just said, I was bound with chains. I rolled upon the ground, and in my helplessness I bit the iron bands which gripped my arms; in a word, I made superhuman efforts to drag myself to Maude. Suddenly the chains which entwined me slackened gently, then fell off. I leapt to my feet and ran to Maude. I took the poor bleeding girl to my heart; I covered with burning kisses her wan, white cheeks, and little by little the blood, arrested in its course, began to circulate, slowly at first, then regularly and naturally. Maude's lips gained colour, she opened her great black eyes, and cast upon my face a look, at once so grateful and so tender that I was touched to the quick; my heart leapt within me, and a deep groan escaped my burning bosom. I suffered, but at the same time I was very happy. Awakening soon followed this deep emotion, and I leapt from my bed with the firm resolution of returning to England. I longed to see Maude again—Maude who must be unhappy—Maude who must be in need of me. I went at once to my Captain; he had been my father's steward, and I thought I had some interest with him. To him I disclosed, not the reason of my desire to return to England, for he would have laughed at my fears, but the desire alone. He refused harshly to give me leave. This first rebuff did not deter me. I was like a man possessed, mad to see Maude once more. I besought this man to whom I had once given orders; I entreated him to grant my wish. You will pity me, Robin," added Will, blushing; "no matter, I will tell you all. I threw myself on my knees before him; my weakness made him smile, and, with a brutal kick, he threw me on my back. Then, Robin, I rose. I was wearing my sword; I drew it from its scabbard and, without hesitation or reflection, I slew the wretch. Ever since I have been pursued, but I hope my trail is lost. That is why, dear Robin, taking you for a stranger, I would not give you my name; but thank Heaven for leading me to you! Now tell me about Maude; does she still live at Gamwell Hall?"

"At Gamwell Hall, my dear Will?" repeated Robin. "Then thou dost not know what hath happened?"

"I know nothing. But what *hath* happened? Thou dost frighten me!"

"Nay! never be uneasy; the trouble which befell thy family hath been partly repaired. Time and resignation have effaced all traces of a painful deed; Gamwell village and Hall have both been destroyed."

"Destroyed!" cried Will. "Holy Virgin! And my mother, Robin; my father and my poor sisters?"

"Are all safe and sound; do not be alarmed! Thy family are now living at Barnsdale. Later on I will tell thee the fatal story in detail; for the present let it suffice that this cruel destruction, which was the work of the Normans, hath cost them dear. We killed two-thirds of the troops sent by King Henry."

"By King Henry!" exclaimed William. Then he added hesitatingly, "Thou art, thou sayest, Robin, chief keeper of the Forest, and naturally in the service of the King."

"Not quite, fair cousin," returned the young man, with a smile. "It is the Normans who pay me for my supervision—at least, those who are rich, for I take naught from the poor. I am indeed keeper of the Forest, but on my own account and that of my jolly companions. In a word, William, I am lord of Sherwood Forest, and I will maintain my rights and privileges against all pretenders."

"I do not understand thee, Robin," said Will, in utter amazement.

"I will explain myself more clearly." Saying which, Robin lifted his horn to his lips and blew three piercing blasts.

Scarce had the depths of the wood been stirred by the strident notes, ere William saw issue from brake and glade, to right and left, a hundred men all clad alike in a neat garb, whose green colour well became their martial forms.

These men, armed with bows and arrows, shields and short swords, ranged themselves silently around their leader. William stared in amaze, and looked at Robin with an air of stupefaction. The young man amused himself for a moment in watching the astonishment and surprise his cousin displayed at the respectful attitude of the men summoned by the blast of his horn, then, laying a muscular hand on Will's shoulder, he said laughingly—

"My lads, here is a man who made me cry mercy in an encounter with swords."

"*He!*" cried the men, examining Will with marked curiosity.

"Yea, he beat me; and I am proud of his victory, for he hath a sure hand and a brave heart."

Little John, who seemed less delighted by William's prowess than Robin had been, advanced to the middle of the circle, and said to the young man—

"Stranger, if thou hast made the valiant Robin Hood ask for quarter, thou must be of superlative strength; natheless, it shall not be said that thou hast had the glory of beating the chief of the merry foresters without having been thrashed by his lieutenant. I am a good hand with the quarter-staff—wilt play me? If thou canst make me cry, 'Hold, enough!' I will proclaim thee the best blade in all the country side."

"My good Little John," said Robin, "I wager a quiver of arrows against a bow of yew that this brave lad will be victor once again."

"I take the double stake, master," replied John; "and if the stranger bears off the prize, he shall be known not only as the best blade, but as the most skillful cudgel-player in all merry England beside."

On hearing Robin Hood address the tall swarthy young man before him as "Little John," Will felt his heart beat quickly, though he showed no emotion. He composed his face, pulled down the cap which covered his head on to his brows, and, answering with a smile the signals Robin was making him, he saluted his adversary gravely, and, armed with his quarter-staff, awaited the first onslaught.

"What! Little John," cried Will, as the young man was about to begin the contest, "wouldst fight with Will Scarlett—with 'merry William,' as thou wast wont to call him?"

"Good Lord!" exclaimed Little John, as he let fall his quarter-staff. "That voice! That look!"

He took a few steps forward, and, staggering, leant on Robin's shoulder for support.

"Well! that voice is mine, Cousin John," cried Will, throwing his cap on the grass; "look at me!"

The long red locks of the young man clustered in silky curls around his cheeks, and Little John, after gazing in silent joy at the laughing face of his cousin, threw himself upon him, clipping him fairly in his arms, as he said, with an expression of unutterable tenderness—

"Welcome to merry England, Will, dear Will; welcome to the land of thy fathers—thou who, by thy return, bringest it happiness and content. To-morrow the inhabitants of Barnsdale will make merry; to-morrow their arms will be around him they believed lost for ever. The hour which brings thee back to us is an hour blessed of Heaven, beloved Will; and I am glad to...to...see thee again. Thou must not think that because thou seest tears on my face, that I am chicken-hearted, Will. No, no; I am not weeping—I am happy, very happy."

Poor John could say no more; he clasped Will convulsively in his arms and continued to weep silently.

William shared in the affecting delight of his cousin, and Robin Hood left them for a moment in each other's arms.

Their first emotion calmed, Little John gave Will, as briefly as possible, the details of the frightful catastrophe which had driven his family from Gamwell Hall. The tale finished, Robin and John conducted Will to the different hiding-places which the band had made for themselves in the Forest, and, at the young man's request, he was enrolled in the troop with the title of lieutenant, which placed him in the same rank as Little John.

Next morning, Will expressed a wish to go to Barnsdale. Robin perfectly understood this very natural desire, and he at once prepared to accompany the young man, as did Little John also. For two days previously Will's brothers had been at Barnsdale, preparing a feast to celebrate Sir Guy's birthday, and by William's return this would be made a scene of great rejoicings.

After giving some orders to his men, Robin Hood and his two friends took the road to Mansfield, where they would find horses. They started blithely on their way, Robin singing pretty ballads in his true and tuneful voice, while Will, intoxicated with joy, danced along beside him, taking up at random the refrain of his songs. Little John even ventured on a wrong note sometimes, whereat Will shouted with laughter, and Robin joined in his mirth. If a stranger had seen our friends, he would certainly have taken them for the guests of a too-generous host, so true is it that intoxication of the heart can resemble closely the intoxication of wine.

At a short distance from Mansfield their high spirits received a sudden check. Three men in the garb of foresters emerged from behind a group of trees and placed themselves across the road, as if determined to bar their way.

Robin Hood and his companions stopped for an instant. Then the young man scrutinised the strangers, and asked imperiously—

"Who are ye, and what do ye here?"

"I was just about to put the same questions," replied one of the three men, a sturdy, square-shouldered fellow, who, armed with quarter-staff and dagger, seemed quite prepared to stand any attack.

"Verily?" replied Robin. "Ah, well! I am very glad to have spared you the trouble; for had you permitted yourself to ask me anything so impertinent, it is probable that I might have responded in such fashion as to make you regret your audacity for ever and a day."

"Thou speakest proudly, my lad," replied the Forester, in a mocking tone.

"Less proudly than I should have acted, had you been so impertinent as to question me; I do not reply, I question. Therefore I ask, for the last time, who are ye, and what are ye doing here? One would think, by your haughty mien, that Sherwood Forest belonged to you."

"God be praised, my lad, but thou hast a good tongue. Ah! thou dost me the favour of promising me a thrashing, if I question thee in turn? 'Tis bravely boasted! Now, jovial stranger, I am about to give thee a lesson in courtesy and to reply to thy request. That done, I will make known to thee how I chastise fools and impudent rascals."

"Done!" returned Robin, gaily. "Tell me thy name and title; then beat me, an thou canst; I should like it."

"I am the keeper of this part of the Forest; my rights of supervision extend from Mansfield as far as a wide cross-road about seven miles from hence. These two men are my assistants. I hold my commission from King Henry, and by his orders I protect the deer against ruffians like you. Dost take me, sirrah?"

"Perfectly; but if you are keeper of the Forest, what am I and my companions? Up to this present I was thought to be the only man possessing the rights of that title. True it is, I do not hold them by the kindness of King Henry, but entirely of my own will, which is all-powerful here, because it is called the right of the strongest."

"Thou the chief keeper of Sherwood Forest!" replied the Forester, scornfully. "Thou art joking; art a common rogue and vagabond—no less."

"My good friend," Robin returned quickly, "you seek to overawe me with your own importance; but you are not the keeper whose name you are attempting to assume. I know the man it belongeth to of rights."

"Ho! ho!" laughed the keeper; "canst tell me his name?"

"Certainly. He is called John Cockle, the fat miller of Mansfield."

"I am his son, and bear the name of Much."

"You are Much? I do not believe it."

"He speaks truly," put in Little John. "I know him by sight. He hath been pointed out to me as one well skilled in handling a cudgel."

"Thou hast not been misinformed, forester, and, if thou knowest me, I can say the same of thee. Hast a face and figure 'tis impossible to forget."

"You know my name?" queried the young man.

"Yea, master John."

"As for me, I am Robin Hood, Keeper Much."

"I suspected as much, my good fellow, and I am delighted to meet thee. A handsome reward is offered to him who can lay hands on thy person. I am naturally ambitious, and the reward, which is for a large amount, would be quite to my taste. To-day I have the opportunity of catching thee, and I do not mean to let it escape me."

"You are quite right, gallows purveyor," replied Robin, in a tone of contempt. "Come, off with your jacket, draw your sword. I am your man."

"Stop!" cried Little John. "Much is more expert in handling a cudgel than in drawing a sword; let us fight all against all. I will take Much; Robin and you, William, take the others, and 'twill be an equal match."

"Done," replied the keeper, "for it shall never be said that Much, the miller of Mansfield's son, ran away from Robin Hood and his merry men."

"Well answered," cried Robin. "Come, Little John, take Much, as you wish to have him for your foe; and I will take this lusty rascal. Art willing to fight me?" Robin asked the man whom chance had given him as opponent.

"Right willing, brave outlaw."

"To work, then, and may the Holy Mother of God give the victory to them that deserve her aid."

"Amen," said Little John. "The Holy Virgin doth never desert the helpless in the hour of need."

"She doth forsake no one," said Much.

"No one," said Robin, making the sign of the cross.

Preparations for the contest being cheerfully completed, Little John cried aloud:—

"Begin!"

"Begin!" repeated Will and Robin.

An old ballad, which has preserved the memory of this combat, describes it thus:—

> "Robin and Will and Little John
> Had fought from eight till noon,
> All on a lovely summer day
> In the leafy month of June,
> And never gave the foemen chance
> To injure them with sword or lance."

"Little John," panted Much, after asking for quarter, "I had long heard tell of thy skill and gallantry, and I desired to match myself against thee. I have had my wish; thou hast beaten me, and thy victory will teach me a salutary lesson in modesty. I considered myself a worthy adversary, and thou hast e'en taught me I am but a blundering fool."

"Thou art an excellent jouster, friend Much," replied Little John, shaking the hand held out to him by the keeper, "and well deservest thy reputation for valour."

"I thank thee for thy compliment, forester," returned Much, "but I consider it more polite than sincere. Thou supposest, perhaps, that my vanity would suffer under an unexpected defeat, but thou mayest undeceive thyself; I am not mortified at having been beaten by a man of thy worth."

"Bravely spoken, valiant miller's son!" cried Robin, cheerily. "Thou givest proof that thou dost possess the most enviable of all riches—a good heart and a Saxon soul. Only an honest man would accept cheerfully and without the least bitterness a wound to his self-esteem. Give me thy hand, Much, and forgive the name that I called thee when thou madest me the confidant of thy covetous ambition. I did not recognise thee, and my slight was directed not at thy person but at thy words. Wilt take a glass of Rhine wine? We will drink to our lucky meeting and future friendship."

"Here is my hand, Robin Hood; I offer it with all my heart. I have often heard thy praises sung; I know that thou art a noble outlaw, and that thou dost extend a generous protection to the poor. Thou art even the friend of those that should hate thee worst, thine enemies the Normans. They speak of thee with esteem, and I have never heard any one seriously blame thine actions. Thou hast been stripped of thy possessions; thou hast been banished; honest men should hold thee dear, because misfortune hath been a guest in thy home."

"I thank thee for those words, friend Much; I will not forget them, and I hope that thou wilt give me the pleasure of thy company as far as Mansfield."

"I am with thee, Robin," replied Much.

"And I too," said the man who had fought with Robin.

"I say the same," added Will's adversary.

Arm in arm they took their way together toward the town, laughing and conversing as they went.

"My dear Much," asked Robin, as they entered Mansfield, "are thy friends discreet?"

"Why do you ask?"

"Because their silence is necessary for my security. As thou mayst well believe, I am here disguised; and if my presence at a Mansfield inn were to be made known by an indiscreet word, the dwelling of mine host would promptly be surrounded by soldiers, and I should be obliged to fight or fly, neither of which would suit me to-day. I am expected in Yorkshire, and I want not to delay my departure."

Alexandre Dumas

"I can answer for the discretion of my comrades. As to mine own, how canst doubt it? but I think, good Robin, thou dost exaggerate the danger; the curiosity of the citizens of Mansfield is the only thing to fear. They will dog thy steps, so anxious are they to see with their own eyes the celebrated Robin Hood, the hero of all the ballads the maidens sing."

"The poor outlaw, you mean to say, Master Much," replied the young man, bitterly. "Fear not to call me so; the shame of that name falls not on me, but rather on the head of him who pronounced a sentence as cruel as it was unjust."

"Very good, my friend; but whatever the name added to thine own, they love and respect it."

Robin wrung the honest fellow's hand.

Without attracting any attention, they reached an inn a little way out of the town, and installed themselves at a table, which the host quickly covered with half a dozen long-necked bottles full of that good Rhine wine which loosens the tongue and opens the heart.

The bottles succeeded each other rapidly, and the conversation became so unreserved and confidential that Much experienced a wish to prolong it indefinitely. Consequently he proposed to join Robin Hood's band; and his companions, enchanted by the delightful descriptions of a life of freedom under the great trees of Sherwood Forest, followed the example of their leader, and engaged themselves with heart and lip to follow Robin Hood. He accepted the flattering offer made to him, and Much, who wished to start at once, asked his new chief for permission to bid his family good-bye. Little John was to await his return, conduct the three men to the hiding-place in the Forest, instal them there, and once more take the road to Barnsdale, where he would find William and Robin. These several arrangements concluded, the conversation took another turn.

Some minutes before the hour of their departure from the inn, two men entered the room in which they sat. The first of the men glanced rapidly at Robin Hood, looked at Little John, then fixed his attention on Will Scarlett. This attention was so intense and so tenacious that the young man noticed it himself, and he was about to question the new-comer, when the latter, perceiving that he had roused a feeling of uneasiness in the young man's mind, turned away his eyes, swallowed a glass of wine at a gulp, and left the room with his companion.

Entirely absorbed in the delight caused by the hope of seeing Maude before nightfall, Will neglected to inform his companions of what had occurred, and mounted horse and rode away with Robin Hood without giving it another thought. As they went on their way, the two friends concocted a plan for Will's entry into the castle.

Robin wished to appear there alone, and prepare the family for Will's return; but the impatient youth would not allow this.

"My dear Robin," said he, "do not leave me alone; my emotion is such that it would be impossible for me to remain silent and tranquil a few steps from my father's house. I am so much altered, and my face bears such visible traces of a hard life, that it is not to be feared my mother will recognise me at a first glance. Present me as a stranger—as a friend of Will's; I shall thus have the happiness of seeing my dear parents the sooner, and of making myself known when they have been prepared for my arrival."

Robin acceded to Will's wishes, and the two young men presented themselves at Barnsdale Castle together.

The whole family was assembled in the hall. Robin was received with open arms, and the Knight extended to the stranger—as he took him to be—a cordial and affectionate hospitality.

Winifred and Barbara seated themselves near Robin, and overwhelmed him with questions, for he was usually an echo of the news of the outer world to the young girls.

The absence of Maude and Marian put Robin at his ease, and after answering his cousins' questions, he rose and said, turning to Sir Guy—

"Uncle, I have good news for you—news which will make you very happy."

"Your visit alone is a great joy to my old heart, Robin Hood," replied the old man.

"Robin Hood is a messenger from heaven," cried pretty Barbara, shaking her clustering blonde tresses coquettishly.

"At my next visit, fair Barbara," Robin returned gaily, "I will be a messenger of love, for I will e'en bring you a husband."

"And I will welcome him right gladly, Robin," replied the girl, laughing merrily.

"You will do well, cousin, for he will be worthy of your kindest welcome. I will not draw his portrait, but will content myself with saying that, so soon as ever your pretty eyes light upon him, you will say to Winifred, 'There, sister, there is the right man for Barbara Gamwell.'"

"Are you quite sure of that, Robin?"

"Perfectly sure, little witch."

"Well, to decide that, we must know all about the matter, Robin. Though you might not think it, I am very particular, and the young man will have to be *very* nice to please me."

"What do you mean by 'very nice'?"

"Like you, cousin."

"Little flatterer!"

"I say what I think, and I cannot help it, if you call it flattery. And I do not only require my husband to be as handsome as you are, but he must have your good heart too and kindly ways."

"You approve of me, then, Barbara?"

"Certainly; you suit me exactly."

"I am both pained and pleased to have such luck, cousin mine; but, alas! if you are nourishing the secret hope of winning me, allow me to lament your folly. I am already pledged, Barbara—pledged to two people."

"I know those two people, Robin."

"Really, cousin?"

"Yea, an if I liked to name them."

"Ah! I beseech you not to betray my secret, Mistress Barbara."

"Never fear, I will spare your blushes. But to return to me, dear Robin; I consent, if you will graciously grant me this favour, to be the third of your lady-loves, or even the fourth, for I presume that there are at least three other damosels awaiting the felicity of bearing your illustrious name."

"You little scoffer," said the young man, laughing, "you do not deserve the affection I feel for you. Nevertheless, I will keep my promise, and within a few days I will bring you a charming young man."

"If your friend be not young, lively, and handsome, I will have never a word to say to him, Robin; remember that."

"He is all that you could wish for."

"Very well; now let us hear the news that you were on the point of telling my father, ere you bethought you to offer me a husband."

"Mistress Barbara, I was about to tell my uncle, my aunt, and you too, dear Winifred, that I had news of some one very dear to your hearts."

"Of my brother Will?" said Barbara.

"Yea, cousin."

"Ah, what joy! Well?"

"Well, that young man who is looking at you so shyly, delighted as he is to be in the presence of so charming a girl, saw William only a few days agone."

"Is my boy well?" asked Sir Guy, in trembling tones.

"Is he happy?" questioned Lady Gamwell, clasping her hands.

"Where is he?" added Winifred.

"Why does he stay away from us?" said Barbara, fixing her eyes, which were full of tears, upon the face of Robin's companion.

Poor William was unable to speak a word for the lump in his throat and the beating of his heart. A minute's silence followed these searching questions. Barbara continued to gaze pensively at the young man, then suddenly she uttered a cry, threw herself upon the stranger, putting her arms around him, as she sobbed out—

"It is Will, it is Will! I know him! Dear Will, how glad I am to see you!"

And dropping her head upon her brother's shoulder, she began to weep convulsively.

Lady Gamwell, her sons, and Winifred and Barbara, pressed round the young man, while Sir Guy, though he tried to appear calm, sank into an armchair and wept like a child.

Will's young brothers seemed intoxicated with joy. After giving vent to a terrific hurrah! they picked William up in their strong arms and hugged him until he was nearly stifled.

Robin took advantage of the general attention being taken off himself to leave the room, and went to look for Maude. Mistress Lindsay was in very delicate health, requiring the greatest care, so that it might have been dangerous to announce William's return too suddenly to her.

As he crossed the apartment adjoining Maude's, Robin met Marian.

"What is a-foot in the Castle, Robin dear?" asked the girl, when her lover's tender greeting was over. "Just now I heard what methought were shouts of joy."

"And so they were, dear Marian, to celebrate the return of one ardently longed for."

"Whose return?" asked the girl, tremulously—"not my brother's?"

"Alas! no, dear Marian," returned Robin, taking the girl's hand; "as yet God hath not sent Allan back to us; but Will—you remember Will Scarlett, merry William?"

"Of course I do, and I am right glad to hear that he is back again safe and sound. Where is he?"

"With his mother; when I left the hall his brothers were fighting to embrace him. I am looking for Maude."

"She is in her room. Shall I tell her to come down?"

"No, I must go to her, for the poor child must be prepared for William's visit. My mission is not easy to fulfil," Robin went on with a laugh, "for the labyrinths of Sherwood Forest are much better known to me than the mysterious recesses of a woman's heart."

"Why so modest, Master Robin?" replied Marian, gaily. "You know better than any one how to set about fathoming a woman's heart."

"Really, Marian, I do believe that my cousins, you and Maude, are all in league to try and make me vain; you vie with one another in showering compliments upon me."

"There is no doubt about it, Master Robin," said Marian, shaking her finger at the young man. "You lay yourself out to make Winifred and Barbara fond of you. What? you are trying to break your little cousins' hearts? Very well, then, I am delighted to hear it, and I will in my turn try the effect of my eyes on handsome Will Scarlett."

"I give my consent, dear Marian, but I warn you that you will have a dangerous rival. Maude is devotedly loved, she will defend her own honour; and poor Will will blush sorely when he finds himself betwixt two such charming women."

"If William cannot blush better than you do, Robin, I need not be afraid of causing him that embarrassing emotion."

"Hah! hah!" laughed Robin, "you mean, Mistress Marian, that I know not how to blush?"

"Nay! I mean that you have forgotten how, which is quite a different matter. Once upon a time, I remember, a brilliant scarlet tinted your cheeks."

"When did that memorable event take place?"

"The day when first we met in Sherwood Forest."

"May I tell you why I blushed, Marian?"

"I am afraid to say yea, Robin, for I see a twinkle in your eye and the outline of a wicked smile on your lips."

"You dread my reply, but at the same time you await it impatiently, Marian."

"Not at all."

"That's a pity, for I thought I should please you by divulging the secret of my first and last blush."

"You always please me when you talk about yourself, Robin," said Marian, with a smile.

"That day when I had the happiness of taking you to my father's house, I had the greatest desire to behold your face, which was hidden within the folds of a great hood, leaving visible only the limpid brightness of your eyes. Walking shyly beside you, I said to myself, 'If yonder wench's face be as sweet as her eyes, I will e'en be her lover.'"

"What, Robin, at sixteen you dreamt of making a woman love you?"

"I did i' faith; and just as I was contemplating devoting my whole life to you, your adorable face, shaking off the sombre veil which had hidden it from mine eyes, appeared in all its radiant splendour. So ardently did I gaze upon you that your cheeks became suffused with blushes. Something within me cried, 'This maid shall be thy wife.' The blood which had rushed to my heart mounted to my face, and I felt that I must love you. There, dear Marian, that is the story of my first and last blush. Since that day," Robin went on after a moment of affecting silence, "this hope, heaven-born promise of a happy future, hath been the consolation and support of mine existence. I hope and I believe."

Sounds of merriment from the Great Hall below reached the room above, where hand-in-hand the two young people continued to exchange tender whispered confidences.

"Quick, dear Robin," said Marian, pressing her lovely forehead to the young man's lips, "go to Maude; I must go to welcome Will, and tell him that you are with his betrothed."

Robin soon reached Maude's room, and found the girl within.

"I felt almost sure I heard the shouts of joy which announced your arrival, dear Robin," she said, as she offered him a seat. "Excuse me for not having come down to the withdrawing room, but I feel ill at ease and almost an intruder amongst the general rejoicings."

"How is that, Maude?"

"Because I am the only one for whom you never have any good news."

"Your turn will come, dear Maude."

"I have lost courage, Robin, and I am filled with a feeling of deadly sadness. I like you with all my heart, I am very glad to see you, and yet I give you no proof of my affection, nor do I convey to you how agreeable your presence is; sometimes, dear Robin, I even try to avoid you."

"To avoid me?" cried the young man, in a tone of surprise.

"Yea, Robin, for when I hear you giving Sir Guy news of his sons, or giving a message from Little John to Winifred, or one from her brothers to Barbara, I say to myself, 'I am always forgotten; I am the only one to whom Robin never brings anything.'"

"Never anything, Maude?"

"Oh, I am not speaking of the charming presents which you bring, and a very large proportion of which you always give to your sister Maude, thinking thus to compensate her for the lack of news. Your kind heart wishes to console me, dear Robin, but alas! I cannot be comforted."

"You are a naughty little girl," said Robin, in a bantering tone. "What, do you complain that you never receive from any one tokens of friendship or remembrance? Ungrateful girl, do I not bring you news from Nottingham at each of my visits? Who was it, who, at the risk of losing his head, paid frequent visits to your brother Hal? Who, at the still greater risk of losing his heart, exposed himself bravely to the murderous fire of two beautiful eyes? In order to please you, Maude, I brave the danger of a *tête-à-tête* with the lovely Grace, I submit to the charms of her gracious smile, I suffer the touch of her pretty hand, I even kiss her beautiful brow; and for whom, I ask you, do I thus endanger my peace of mind? For you, Maude, and for you alone."

Maude began to laugh.

"I must indeed be of an ungrateful nature," said she, "for the pleasure I feel in hearing you speak of Halbert and his wife doth not satisfy the desire of my heart."

"Very well, then, Madam, I will not tell you that I saw Hal last week, that he charged me to kiss you on both cheeks; nor will I tell you that Grace loves you with all her heart, and that her little daughter Maude—an angel of goodness—wishes her pretty godmother a very good day."

"Thank you a thousand times, dear Robin, for your charming manner of telling me nothing. I am quite content to remain thus in ignorance of what is happening at Nottingham; but, by the way, have you told Marian of the attention you paid to Halbert's charming wife?"

"What a spiteful question, Maude! Well, to give you a proof my conscience hath naught to reproach itself withal, I will tell you that I have confided to Marian but a small part of my appreciation of the charms of the beautiful Grace. However, as I have a great admiration for her eyes, I was very careful not to be too expansive upon the subject."

"What! you deceived Marian? It would serve you right were I to go at once and reveal to her the full extent of your wickedness."

"We will go together presently, and I will offer you my arm; but before we go to Marian, I wish to talk to you."

"What have you to tell me, Robin?"

"Something very nice, and which, I am sure, will give you great pleasure."

"Then you have news of...of..." And the young girl looked at Robin with questioning eyes and an expression of mingled doubt, hope, and joy, while the blood rushed into her face.

"Of whom, Maude?"

"Ah! you are teasing me," said the poor girl, sadly.

"No, dear little friend, I really have something very good to tell you."

"Tell me quick, then."

"What do you think of a husband?" asked Robin.

"A husband? What a strange question!"

"Not at all, if that husband were..."

"Will! Will! You have heard news of Will! For mercy's sake, Robin, never play with my heart; it beats with such violence as to pain me. I am listening. Speak, Robin; is dear William sound and well?"

"Without a doubt, since he wishes to call you his dear little wife at the earliest possible moment."

"You have seen him? Where is he? When will he be here?"

"I have seen him; he will soon come."

"Holy Mother of God, I thank thee!" cried Maude, clasping her hands and raising her tearful eyes to heaven. "How glad I shall be to see him!" added the girl. "But..." continued Maude, as her eyes turned irresistibly towards the door, on the threshold of which stood a young man, "it is he! it is he!"

Maude, with a cry of intense delight, threw herself into William's arms and swooned away.

"Poor dear girl!" murmured the young man, in a trembling voice, "the emotion hath been too much for her, too sudden; she hath fainted. Robin, hold her up a little; I am weak as a child, I can hardly stand."

Robin took Maude gently from William's arms and carried her to a couch. As for poor William, with his head hidden in his hands, he wept bitterly. Maude soon came to herself, and her first thought was for Will, her first look for him. He knelt at her feet, and, putting his arms round her waist, murmured tenderly the name of his beloved—

"Maude! Maude!"

"William! dear William!"

"I want to speak to Marian," said Robin, smiling. "Good-bye; I will leave you together. Do not quite forget others who love you."

Maude held out her hand to the young man, and William looked gratefully at him.

"Here I am, back at last, dear Maude," said Will. "Are you glad to see me?"

"How can you ask, William? Oh yes, I am glad, and, more than that, I am happy, very happy."

"You don't want me to go away again?"

"Did I ever want you to?"

"No; but it depends on you alone whether I stay here for good or only as a visitor."

"What do you mean?"

"Do you remember the last conversation we had together?"

"Yea, William dear."

"I left you with a heavy heart that day, dear Maude; I was in despair. Robin noticed my distress, and, urged by his inquiries, I told him everything. I thus learned the name of him you once loved...."

"Do not let us speak of my girlish follies," interrupted Maude, twining her arms round William's neck; "the past belongs to God."

"Yea, dear Maude, to God alone, and the present to us, is it not so?"

"Yea, to us and to God. Perhaps it might be as well for your peace of mind, dear William," added the young girl, "to have a clear, frank, and decided idea of my relations with Robin Hood."

"I know as much as I desire to know, dear Maude; Robin told me all that had passed betwixt you."

A delicate pink flooded the girl's face.

"If your departure had been less hurried," she replied, hiding her blushing face on the young man's shoulder, "you would have learnt that, deeply touched by the patient tenderness of your love, I longed to return it. During your absence I got into the habit of regarding Robin as a brother, and to-day I ask myself, Will, if my heart ever beat for any one but you."

"Then it is quite true that you love me a little, Maude?" said William, clasping his hands, and with tears in his eyes.

"A little! No; but very much."

"Oh, Maude, how happy you make me! You see, I was right to hope, to wait, to be patient, to say to myself, 'The day will come when I shall be loved.' We are going to be married, are we not?"

"Dear Will!"

"Say yea, or say, rather, 'I want to marry my good William.'"

"'I want to marry my good William,'" repeated the girl, obediently.

"Give me your hand, dear Maude."

"Here it is."

William kissed the little hand of his betrothed passionately.

"When shall our wedding be, Maude?" he asked.

"I do not know, my dear—some day."

"Of course, but it must be settled; suppose we say to-morrow?"

"To-morrow, Will! You don't mean it; 'tis impossible."

"Impossible! Why impossible?"

"Because it is too unexpected, too soon."

"Happiness never comes too soon, dear Maude; and could we be married at this very moment, I should be the happiest of men. As we must wait until to-morrow, why, I resign myself to it. But it is settled, is it not, that to-morrow you will be my wife?"

"To-morrow!" cried the girl.

"Yea; and for two reasons, the first being that we shall keep my father's seventy-sixth birthday, the second that my mother wishes to celebrate my return with great rejoicings. The merrymaking would be quite complete, if still further brightened by the accomplishment of our mutual desires."

"Your family, dear William, are not prepared to receive me as one of their number, and your father would perhaps say..."

"My father," interrupted Will—"my father will say that you are an angel, that he loves you, and that you have long been his daughter. Ah, Maude! you do not know the good and kind old man, if you doubt his joy at the happiness of his son."

"You have such a gift of persuasion, my dear Will, that I agree with you entirely."

"Then you consent, Maude?"

"I suppose I must, dear Will."

"You are not forced to do so, Madam."

"Really, William, you are very difficult to please; probably you would prefer to hear me reply, 'I consent with all my heart.'"

"To marry you to-morrow," added Will.

"'To marry you to-morrow,'" repeated Maude, laughing.

"Very well; I am content. Come, dear little woman, let us go and announce our approaching marriage to our friends."

William look Maude's arm, drew it through his own, and, kissing the girl, he led her towards the Great Hall, where the whole family was still assembled.

Lady Gamwell and her husband gave Maude their blessing, Winifred and Barbara greeted her by the sweet name of sister, and Will's brothers embraced her enthusiastically.

The preparations for the wedding now occupied the ladies, who, all animated by the same desire of ministering to the happiness of Will and to the beauty of Maude, set themselves at once to make a charming dress for the young girl.

The morrow came slowly, as do all impatiently expected to-morrows. From early morning the courtyard of the Castle had been furnished with innumerable casks of ale, which, festooned with garlands of leaves, were to wait patiently until their presence was discovered. A splendid banquet was in preparation, armfuls of flowers strewed the halls, the musicians tuned their instruments, and the expected guests came thronging in.

The hour fixed for the celebration of the wedding of Mistress Lindsay and William Gamwell was about to strike; Maude, dressed with exquisite taste, awaited William's arrival in the Great Hall, but William did not come.

Sir Guy sent a servant to look for his son.

The servant looked all over the pleasaunce, searched the Castle, called the young man, and got no reply, save the echo of his own voice.

Robin Hood and Sir Guy's sons mounted their horses and searched the neighbourhood; they could find no trace of the bridegroom, nor hear any tidings of him.

The guests divided into parties, and explored the country in other directions, but their search was equally futile.

At midnight, the whole family gathered round Maude, who had been unconscious for the last hour.

William had disappeared.

CHAPTER II

As we have already mentioned, Baron Fitz-Alwine had brought his beautiful and charming daughter, the Lady Christabel, back with him to Nottingham Castle.

Some days before the disappearance of poor Will, the Baron was sitting in one of his apartments opposite to a little man, splendidly dressed in a robe laden with golden embroidery.

If it were possible to be rich in ugliness, one would have said that Lord Fitz-Alwine's guest was immensely rich.

Judging by his face, this old beau should have been much older than the Baron, but he did not seem to recall the antiquity of his birth himself.

With wrinkled and grimacing faces, like two old monkeys, the men talked together in low voices, and it was evident that they were trying to obtain from one another, by dint of cunning and flattery, a definite conclusion to some important business.

"You are too hard on me, Baron," said the hideous old man, wagging his head.

"Faith, no," replied Lord Fitz-Alwine, briskly. "I wish to secure my daughter's happiness, that is all, and I challenge you to discover any ulterior motive in me, my dear Sir Tristan."

"I know that you are a good father, Fitz-Alwine, and that the happiness of Lady Christabel is your only thought....And what dowry intend you to give this dear child?"

"I have told you already, five thousand pieces of gold on her wedding day, and the same amount later."

"The date must be stated precisely, Baron; the date must be precisely stated," grumbled the old man.

"Let us say in five years, then."

"The delay is long, and the dowry you give your daughter is very small."

"Sir Tristan," said the Baron, dryly, "you put my patience to too great a trial. I pray you to remember that my daughter is young and beautiful, and that you yourself no longer possess the physical advantages you may have had fifty years ago."

"There, there, don't get angry, Fitz-Alwine; my intentions are good. I can place a million beside your ten thousand pieces of gold. What am I saying? One million, probably two."

"I know you are rich," interrupted the Baron. "Unhappily, I am not on a level with you there, and yet I would fain place my daughter in the rank of the greatest ladies in Europe. I want the Lady Christabel's position to be equal to that of a queen. You are aware of this paternal desire, and yet you refuse to entrust me with the money necessary to realise it."

"I cannot understand, my dear Fitz-Alwine, what difference it can make to the happiness of your daughter, an I keep the half of my fortune in mine own hands. I will settle the income of a million, of two millions even, on the Lady Christabel, but I must retain the control of the capital. Do not distress yourself, my wife shall lead the life of a queen."

"That is all very well, in words, my dear Sir Tristan; but permit me to remind you that when there is a great disparity in the ages of husband and wife, misunderstanding is apt to be their guest. It might happen that the caprices of a young woman would become unbearable to you, and you would take back what you had given. If I kept half your fortune in mine own hands, I should be satisfied as to the future happiness of my daughter; she would have nothing to fear, and you might e'en quarrel with her to your heart's content."

"Quarrel? You are joking, my dear Baron; never could such a misfortune occur. I am too fond of the pretty little dove to wish to annoy her. For twelve years I have aspired to the honour of her hand, and yet you think me capable of reproving her caprices; she may have as many as e'er she please, for she will be rich and able to satisfy them."

"Permit me to remark that, if you still refuse to accede to my demands, I shall distinctly retract the promise I have given you."

"You are too hasty, Baron, much too hasty," grumbled the old man. "Let us discuss the matter a little longer."

"I have already said all there is to say; I have come to a decision."

"Do not be obstinate, Fitz-Alwine. What if I were to place fifty thousand pieces of gold in your hands?"

"I should ask whether you intended to insult me."

"To insult you, Fitz-Alwine? What a poor opinion you must have of me! If I said two hundred thousand pieces of gold?"

"Sir Tristan, this must end. I know your immense fortune, and the offer you make me is a mere mockery. What am I to do with your two hundred thousand pieces of gold?"

"Did I say two hundred thousand, Baron? I meant to say five hundred thousand—five hundred, do you understand? Now, isn't that a noble sum, a very noble sum?"

"True," replied the Baron, "but you have just told me that you could lay two million beside my daughter's ten thousand pieces of gold. Give me one million, and my Christabel shall be your wife to-morrow if you wish it, my dear Sir Tristan."

"A million! You want me to give you a million, Fitz-Alwine! Truly your demand is absurd. I cannot in conscience place half my fortune in your hands."

"Do you doubt my honour and good faith?" cried the Baron, irritably.

"Not in the least, my good friend."

"Do you imagine that I have any motive other than my daughter's happiness?"

"I know that you love the Lady Christabel, but..."

"But what?" thundered the Baron. "Decide quickly, or I annul for ever the promises I have made."

"You do not give me time for reflection."

At this moment a serving-man knocked softly at the door.

"Come in," said the Baron.

"My Lord," said the man, "a messenger from the King hath brought urgent news, and awaits your Lordship's good pleasure to announce them."

"Bring him hither," replied the Baron. "Now, Sir Tristan, one last word. If you do not accede to my wishes before the entry of the messenger, who will be here in two minutes, you shall not have the Lady Christabel."

"Hear me, Fitz-Alwine, pray hear me."

"I will hear nothing. My daughter is worth a million; besides, you told me that you loved her."

"Tenderly, very tenderly," mumbled the hideous old man.

"Well, then, Sir Tristan, you will be very unhappy, for you are about to be separated from her for ever. I know a young lord, as noble as a king, rich, very rich, and good-looking, who only awaits my permission to lay his name and fortune at my daughter's feet. If you hesitate a second longer, to-morrow—note well, *to-morrow*—the maiden you love, my daughter, the beautiful and charming Christabel, will be the wife of your more fortunate rival."

"You are pitiless, Fitz-Alwine!"

"I hear the messenger. Answer yes or no."

"But, Fitz-Alwine..."

"Yea or nay?"

"Yea, yea," stammered the old man.

"Sir Tristan, my good friend, only think of your happiness; my daughter is a treasure of grace and beauty."

"It is true she is very beautiful," said the amorous old man.

"And that she is worth a million pieces of gold," added the Baron, with a sneer. "Sir Tristan, she is yours."

Thus did Baron Fitz-Alwine sell his daughter, the beautiful Lady Christabel, to Sir Tristan Goldsborough for a million pieces of gold.

As soon as he was announced, the messenger informed the Baron that a soldier who had killed the captain of his regiment had been pursued as far as Nottinghamshire. The King's orders to Baron Fitz-Alwine were to have this soldier seized and hanged without mercy.

The messenger dismissed, Lord Fitz-Alwine wrung the trembling hands of his daughter's future husband, excusing himself for leaving him at this happy moment, but the King's commands were peremptory, and must be obeyed without the least delay.

Three days after this most honourable bargain had been struck between the Baron and Sir Tristan, the fugitive soldier was taken prisoner and thrown into a dungeon of Nottingham Castle.

Robin Hood still continued an active search for William, who was, alas! the poor soldier seized by the Baron's men.

In despair at the ill success of his investigations throughout the county of Yorkshire, Robin Hood sought the Forest once more, hoping to hear something from his followers, who, posted on the roads leading from Mansfield to Nottingham, might perchance have discovered some traces of the young man.

About a mile from Mansfield, Robin Hood met Much, the miller's son, who, mounted like himself on a spirited horse, was galloping at full speed in the direction from which Robin had just come.

On seeing his young leader, Much uttered a cry of joy, and drew rein.

"How glad I am to meet you, friend!" said he. "I was going to Barnsdale. I have news of the lad who was with you the first time we met."

"Have you, indeed? We have been seeking him these three days past."

"I have seen him."

"When?"

"Last evening."

"Where?"

"At Mansfield, whither I returned, after spending eight and forty hours with my new companions. As I drew near my father's house, I perceived at the door a troop of horse, on one of which sat a young man with his arms tightly bound. In him I recognised your friend. The soldiers, who were refreshing themselves, had left their prisoner guarded by the cords which bound him to the horse. Without attracting their attention, I was able to convey to the poor lad that I would at once hasten to Barnsdale and inform you of the misfortune which had overtaken him. This promise revived the courage of your friend, and he thanked me with an expressive look. Without losing a moment I called for a horse, and as I mounted asked a soldier some questions as to the fate in store for their prisoner; he replied that by order of Baron Fitz-Alwine they were taking the young man to Nottingham Castle."

"I thank you for the trouble you have taken to help me, my good Much," replied Robin. "You have just told me everything I wanted to know, and we shall be unlucky indeed an we do not succeed in preventing the cruel intentions of his Norman Lordship. To horse, good Much. Let us hasten to the heart of the Forest; there I will take measures for a successful expedition."

"Where is Little John?" asked Much.

"He is making his way to our retreat by another road; by separating, we each hoped to obtain news. Fortune hath favoured me, since I had the luck to meet you, brave Much."

"The luck is on my side," replied Much, cheerily; "my actions are governed by your will alone."

Robin smilingly acknowledged the compliment, then set off at a gallop, followed closely by his companion.

On arriving at the general rendezvous, Robin and Much found Little John already there. After giving the latter the news Much had brought, Robin ordered him to assemble the men scattered through the Forest, form them into one troop, and take them to the verge of the wood near Nottingham Castle. There, concealed in the covert of the trees, they were to await a summons from Robin, and hold themselves ready to fight. These arrangements concluded, Robin and Much mounted again, and set off at full gallop on the way to Nottingham.

"Friend," said Robin, when they had reached the edge of the Forest, "here we are at the end of our journey. I must not enter Nottingham; my presence in the town would be known at once, and its motive (which I wish to conceal) discovered. You understand, don't you? If William's enemies became aware of my sudden appearance, they would be on their guard, and, in consequence, it would be more difficult for us to set our friend at liberty. You must go alone into the town, and then make your way to a cottage lying on the outskirts of the place. There you will find a good friend of mine, by name Halbert Lindsay; in the event of his absence, his comely wife, who well deserves her pretty name of Grace, will tell you where to find him. You will seek him out and bring him to me. Is that quite clear?"

"Perfectly."

"Very well, then go! I will stay here to keep a look-out!"

Left alone, Robin hid his horse in the thicket, stretched himself beneath the shade of an oak, and set to work to devise a plan of campaign for poor Will's successful deliverance. While bringing all his inventive faculties to bear upon this subject, the young man kept a careful watch on the road.

Presently he saw in the distance a richly dressed young knight approaching the Forest from the direction of Nottingham.

"By my faith!" said Robin to himself, "if this gay traveller is of Norman blood, he does well to choose this direction for his country walk. Dame Fortune appears to have treated him so kindly, that it will be a pleasure to relieve his pockets of the price of the bows and arrows which will be broken to-morrow in William's honour. His habit is sumptuous, his gait haughty; of a truth, this gallant is well met. Come along, my fine gentleman, you will be all the lighter when we have become acquainted."

Rising quickly from his recumbent position, Robin placed himself in the traveller's way. The latter, expecting, doubtless, some token of politeness, stopped courteously.

"Welcome, Sir Knight," said Robin, putting his hand to his cap. "The sky is so dark that I took your glorious appearance for a messenger from the sun. Your smiling countenance brightens the landscape, and if you would remain a few minutes longer on the verge of the old Forest, the very flowers hidden beneath its shade would take you for a ray of light."

The stranger laughed gaily.

"Do you belong to Robin Hood's band?" he asked.

"You judge by appearances, Sir," replied the young man, "and because you see me clothed in the garb of the foresters, you presume that I must belong to Robin Hood's band. You are wrong. All the inhabitants of the Forest do not follow the fortunes of the Outlaw Chief."

"That's like enow," returned the stranger, in a tone of manifest impatience. "I thought I had met a member of the company of Merrie Men. I was wrong, that is all."

The traveller's reply excited Robin's curiosity.

"Master," said he, "your countenance betokens a hearty frankness, which, despite the profound hatred I have borne against the Normans these many years past..."

"I am no Norman, Sir Forester," interrupted the traveller, "and I might imitate you in saying that you, too, judge by appearances. My dress and the accent of my speech lead you into error. I am Saxon, though there are a few drops of Norman blood in my veins."

"A Saxon is a brother to me, Master, and I am happy to be able to give you a proof of my confidence. I do belong to Robin Hood's band. As you are doubtless aware, we use a less disinterested fashion of making ourselves known to Norman travellers."

"I know that fashion, at once courteous and productive," replied the stranger, laughingly. "I have often heard of it, and I am on my way to Sherwood solely that I may have the pleasure of meeting your leader."

"And what if I were to tell you that you were now in the presence of Robin Hood?"

"I would offer him my hand," replied the stranger, quickly, accompanying the words with a friendly gesture. "And I would say to him, 'Friend Robin, have you forgotten Marian's brother?'"

"Allan Clare! You are Allan Clare!" exclaimed Robin, gleefully.

"Yea, I am Allan Clare. And the recollection of your expressive countenance, my dear Robin, was so deep graven on my heart that I recognised you at the first glance."

"How glad I am to see you, Allan!" replied Robin Hood, shaking the young man by both hands. "Marian doth not expect the happiness which your return to England will give her."

"My poor dear sister!" said Allan, with an expression of deep tenderness. "Is she well? Is she happy?"

"Her health is perfect, Allan, and she hath no other sorrow than that of being separated from you."

"I have returned, never to quit my native land again. My good sister will then be quite happy. Did you hear, Robin, that I was in the service of the King of France?"

"Yea. One of the Baron's men, and the Baron himself in a burst of confidence produced by fear, made known to us your position about the King's person."

"A lucky chance enabled me to render the King of France a great service," continued the Knight, "and in his gratitude he deigned to acquaint himself with my desires, and took a great and friendly interest in me. His Majesty's kindness emboldened me, and I made known my troubles to him. I told him how my goods had been confiscated, and I besought him to allow me to return to England. The King was so gracious as to grant my prayer; he gave me a letter to King Henry on the spot, and, without losing a moment, I started for this country. At the request of the King of France, Henry II. restored to me my father's property; and the King's Treasury will have to give me back in good golden crowns the revenue produced by mine estates since their confiscation. Beside which, I have realised a large sum, which, once placed in the hands of Baron Fitz-Alwine, is to win me the hand of my dear Christabel."

"I have heard of the bargain," said Robin. "The seven years given you by the Baron are on the point of expiring, are they not?"

"Yea. To-morrow is my last day of grace."

"Well, then, you had best hasten to see the Baron, for the delay of an hour would be your loss."

"How did you learn of the existence of this contract and its conditions?"

"From my cousin, Little John."

"Sir Guy of Gamwell's gigantic nephew?" asked Allan.

"The very same; then you remember the worthy fellow?"

"Of course I do."

"Well, he is now bigger than ever, and stronger even than he is tall. It was from him that I learnt of your arrangement with the Baron."

"Lord Fitz-Alwine took him into his confidence, then?" said Allan, with a smile.

"Yea, Little John threatened his Lordship, and interrogated him at the point of the dagger."

"Then I can quite comprehend the Baron's expansiveness."

"My good friend," replied Robin, gravely, "beware of Lord Fitz-Alwine. He bears you no love, and if he can find a means of breaking his oath, he will not hesitate to do so."

"Should he attempt to dispute with me over Lady Christabel's hand, I swear to you, Robin, I will make him repent it bitterly."

"Have you any especial means of making the Baron fear your threats?"

"Yea; and beside, were I unable to obtain the fulfilment of his promise, I would lay siege to the Castle sooner than give up my Christabel."

"An you want help, I am entirely at your service, good Allan; I can immediately place at your disposal two hundred men, fleet of foot and strong of arm. They are equally well skilled in the use of bow, sword, lance and buckler; say but one word, and at my command they will be with us."

"A thousand thanks, dear Robin. I expected no less from your good friendship."

"And you were right; but tell me how learned you that I dwelt in Sherwood Forest?"

"Having concluded my business in London," replied the Knight, "I came to Nottingham. There I heard of the Baron's return, and of Christabel's presence at the Castle. Being assured of the existence of my beloved, I repaired to Gamwell. Imagine my astonishment on entering the village and finding only the ruins of the good Knight's noble dwelling. I returned to Mansfield with all haste, and an inhabitant of that town told me what had occurred. He sang your praises to me, and informed me that the Gamwell family had retired secretly to their Yorkshire lands. Tell me of my sister Marian, Robin Hood; is she much changed?"

"Yes, Allan, she is indeed changed."

"My poor sister!"

"She is of a perfect beauty now," continued Robin, laughing, "for each spring hath added to her graces."

"Is she married?" asked Allan.

"Nay, not yet."

"So much the better. Do you know if she hath given her heart to any one, or if her hand is promised?"

"Marian shall answer that question," said Robin, blushing slightly. "How hot it is to-day!" he added, passing his hand over his flushed brow. "Do let us go into the shade of the trees; I am expecting one of my men, and meseemeth his absence is unduly prolonged. By the way, Allan, do you recall one of the sons of Sir Guy—William, surnamed Scarlett, by reason of the something vivid hue of his locks?"

"A well-favoured lad with large blue eyes?"

"The same. The poor fellow, sent to London by Baron Fitz-Alwine, had been enrolled in a regiment that formed part of the army which still occupies Normandy. One fine day William was taken with an unconquerable desire to see his family again; he asked for leave, which he could not obtain, and, beside himself at the persistent refusal of his Captain, he killed him. Will succeeded in reaching England, a lucky chance brought us together, and I took the lad to Barnsdale, where his family live. The day after his return all the household were rejoicing, for they were not only celebrating the return of the wanderer, but also his marriage and Sir Guy's birthday."

"Will going to be married? To whom?"

"To a charming damosel whom you know—Mistress Lindsay."

"I do not recollect the lady you name."

"What, you have forgotten the existence of the companion, friend, and devoted follower of the Lady Christabel?"

"I know, I know," returned Allan Clare. "You are speaking of the merry daughter of the Keeper of Nottingham, of the sprightly Maude?"

"That's it; Maude and William have loved each other for a long time."

"Maude loved Will Scarlett! What are you saying, Robin? It was you, my friend, who had won the girl's heart."

"Nay, nay, you are mistaken."

"Not at all, not at all; I remember now that, if she did not love you, which I doubt, at least she took a deep and tender interest in you."

"I had then, and have still, a brotherly affection for her."

"Really?" questioned the Knight, slyly.

"On my honour, yea!" replied Robin. "But to finish William's story. This is what happened to him. An hour before the celebration of his marriage, he disappeared, and I have just learnt that he hath been carried off by the Baron's soldiers. I have collected my men—in a few minutes they will be within call—and I am relying on my skill, supported by their aid, to deliver William."

"Where is he?"

"Without the least doubt he is in Nottingham Castle. I shall soon be certain of it."

"Do not be too rash, my good Robin; wait till to-morrow. I shall see the Baron, and I will bring to bear all the influence which entreaties or threats can have on him to obtain the release of your cousin."

"But if the old miscreant acts summarily, should I not all my life regret having lost several hours?"

"Have you reason to fear it?"

"How can you ask me such a question, Allan, when you know the cruel answer to it better than I do myself? You know well, do you not, that Lord Fitz-Alwine is without pity and without feeling? If he dared to hang Will with his own hands, be assured he would do it. I must hasten to drag William from the lion's jaws, an I would not lose him for ever."

"Belike you are right, dear Robin, and my prudent counsel would be dangerous to follow in that case. I shall present myself at the Castle this very day, and, once inside, I may possibly be able to help you. I will question the Baron; an he will not answer, I shall address myself to the soldiers, who will, I hope, be open to the temptation of a heavy bribe. Rely on me; but an if my efforts be fruitless, I will let you know, and you must act with the greatest promptitude."

"That is understood. Here is my man coming back; he is accompanied by Halbert, Maude's foster brother. We shall now learn something of poor Will's fate."

"Well?" asked Robin, after having greeted his friend.

"I have very little to tell you," replied Halbert; "I only know that a prisoner hath been carried to Nottingham Castle, and Much tells me that the unfortunate wretch is our poor friend Will Scarlett. If you wish to try and save him, Robin, you must lose no time; a monk, a pilgrim on his way through Nottingham, hath been sent for to the Castle to shrive the prisoner."

"Holy Mother of God, have pity on us!" cried Robin, in a trembling voice. "Will, my poor Will, is in danger of his life; we must rescue him; it must be done at any cost. You know naught else, Halbert?" he added.

"Naught relating to Will; but I have learnt that the Lady Christabel is going to be married at the end of the week."

"Lady Christabel to be married?" repeated Allan.

"Yea, master," replied Halbert, looking at the Knight with an air of surprise. "She is to marry the richest Norman in all England."

"Impossible! Quite impossible!" exclaimed Allan Clare.

"It is perfectly true," returned Halbert, "and great preparations are on foot at the Castle to celebrate the happy event."

"The happy event!" repeated the Knight, bitterly. "What is the name of the scoundrel who thinks to marry the Lady Christabel?"

"Are you a stranger to these parts, Master?" continued Halbert, "since you are unaware of the immense delight of the Baron Fitz-Alwine? His Lordship hath manœuvred so well that he hath succeeded in securing a colossal fortune in the person of Sir Tristan Goldsborough."

"Lady Christabel to be the wife of that hideous old man?" cried the Knight, completely taken aback. "Why, the creature is half dead! He is a monster of ugliness and sordid avarice. The daughter of Baron Fitz-Alwine is my betrothed, and so long as there is breath in my body, none other save I shall have a right to her."

"Your betrothed, master! Who, then, are you?"

"Sir Allan Clare," said Robin.

"The brother of the Lady Marian! The Lady Christabel's dearest friend?"

"Yea, Halbert," said Allan.

"Hurrah!" cried Halbert, throwing up his cap. "Here's a piece of good luck! Welcome to England! Your presence will change the tears of your beautiful betrothed into smiles. This odious marriage is to be solemnised at the end of this week, and i' faith you have no time to lose, an you wish to prevent it."

"I will go and see the Baron this instant," said Allan. "An he thinks he can still play with me, he is wrong."

"You may count on my help, Sir Knight," said Robin; "and I will engage to put an all-powerful obstacle in the way of the accomplishment of this misfortune, to wit force allied with cunning. We shall carry off the Lady Christabel. My idea is that we should all four go to the Castle together; you will enter alone, while I await your return with Much and Halbert."

The young men soon reached the approach to the Castle. As the Knight went towards the drawbridge, a noise of chains was heard, the bridge was lowered, and an old man in the garb of a pilgrim emerged from the postern.

"Yonder comes the Confessor summoned by the Baron for poor William," said Halbert. "Question him, Robin; perhaps he can tell you what fate is destined for our friend."

"I had the same idea, good Halbert, and I feel that our meeting with this holy man is an omen of Divine favour. May the Holy Virgin protect you, good Father!" said Robin, respectfully saluting the old man.

"Amen to thy kind prayer, my son," replied the pilgrim.

"Have you come far, Father?"

"From the Holy Land, where I have made a long and wearisome pilgrimage to expiate the sins of my youth. Now, worn out with fatigue, I have returned to die beneath the sky of my native land."

"God hath vouchsafed you a long life, Father."

"Yea, my son, I shall soon be ninety years old, and my life seems but a dream."

"I pray the Virgin may give you calm repose in your last hours."

"So be it, my child. I, in my turn, pray Heaven to shower blessings on thy young head. Thou art good and a believer, be thou also charitable, and give a thought to those who suffer, to those about to die."

"Explain yourself, Father; I do not understand," said Robin, in a broken voice.

"Alas! alas!" returned the old man, "a soul is about to ascend to heaven, its last home. The body which it animates can scarce count thirty years. A man of your age is about to die a terrible death. Pray for him, my son."

"Hath this man made his last confession to you, Father?"

"Yea. In a few hours more he will be violently removed from this world."

"Where is the unfortunate man?"

"In one of the dark dungeons of this stately pile."

"Is he alone?"

"Yea, my son, alone."

"And this unhappy creature is to die?" questioned the young man.

"To-morrow morning at sunrise."

"You are quite sure, Father, that the execution will not take place before daybreak?"

"I am quite certain. Alas! is it not soon enough? Thy words grieve me, my son; dost desire a brother's death?"

"No, holy man, no; a thousand times no! I would give my life to save him. I know the poor lad, Father; I know and love him. Know you to what death he is condemned? Have you heard whether he is to die within the Castle?"

"I learnt from the gaoler of the prison that the unhappy youth is to be put to death by the hangman of Nottingham. Orders have been given for a public execution in the market-place of that town."

"God keep us!" murmured Robin. "Kind, good Father," he went on, taking the old man's hand, "will you render me a service?"

"What wouldst thou, my son?"

"I desire, I pray, Father, that you will of your kindness return to the Castle and beg the Baron to grant you the favour of accompanying the prisoner to the foot of the gallows."

"I have already obtained that permission, my son; I shall be near thy friend to-morrow morning."

"Bless you, holy Father, bless you! I have one last word to say to the condemned man, and I would charge you to give it him. To-morrow morning I will be here, near this clump of trees; will you be so good as to confess me before entering the Castle?"

"I will meet thee punctually, my son."

"Thank you, holy Father; until to-morrow, then."

"To-morrow. And may the peace of our Lord go with thee."

Robin bowed reverently, and the Palmer, with his hands crossed on his breast, went on his way praying.

"Yea, to-morrow," repeated the young man. "We shall see to-morrow an if Will is to be hanged."

"It will be needful," said Halbert, who had listened to Robin's conversation with the prisoner's Confessor, "to place your men within a short distance from the place of execution."

"They will be within sound of call," said Robin.

"How will you screen them from view of the soldiers?"

"Do not be uneasy, my good Halbert," replied Robin. "My merry men have long possessed the art of making themselves invisible, even on the high-road; and, believe me, their doublets will not graze the Baron's soldiers, nor will they make their appearance, save at a prearranged signal from me."

"You seem so certain of success, my dear Robin," said Allan, "that I begin to wish I could be as hopeful about mine own affairs."

"Sir Knight," returned the young man, "first let me set William free, and put him safe in the hands of his dear little wife at Barnsdale, then we will think about the Lady Christabel. The projected marriage will not take place for several days; we have time to prepare for a serious struggle with Lord Fitz-Alwine."

"I will go into the Castle," said Allan, "and by hook or by crook I will get to the bottom of this business. If the Baron hath thought fit to break an engagement which he should, in honour, have held sacred, I shall consider myself justified in waiving all respect, and, willy-nilly, Lady Christabel shall be my wife."

"You are right, my friend. Present yourself at once to the Baron; he doth not expect you, and very like in his surprise he will deliver himself into your hands bound hand and foot. Speak him boldly, and make him understand you intend to use force, if need be, to win the Lady Christabel. Whilst you are taking these important measures with Lord Fitz-Alwine, I will go and seek out my men and prepare for the successful accomplishment of the expedition I have planned. If you should need me, send without delay to the place where we met a few minutes since; there you are sure of finding one of my brave companions at any hour of the day or night. If it is necessary for you to have a talk with your faithful ally, you will be conducted to my retreat. But are you not afraid lest, once inside the Castle, it may be impossible for you to leave it again?"

"Lord Fitz-Alwine would not dare to treat a man like me with violence," replied Allan; "he would be exposing himself to too great a risk. Beside, an if he really intend to give Christabel to this hateful Tristan, he will be so eager to get rid of me that I fear he may refuse to receive me at all, rather than that he will wish to keep me near him. Farewell, then, for the present, my good Robin; I shall surely see you again before the end of the day."

"I shall expect you."

Whilst Allan Clare made his way towards the postern of the Castle, Robin, Halbert, and Much hastened to the town.

Introduced without the least difficulty into the apartment of Lord Fitz-Alwine, the Knight soon found himself in the presence of the terrible Castellan.

If a spirit had risen from the tomb, it could scarce have caused the Baron more dismay and terror than he experienced at sight of the handsome young man who stood before him with proud and dignified mien.

The Baron threw at his serving-man so withering a glance that the latter escaped from the room with the utmost speed his limbs were capable of.

"I did not expect to see you," said his Lordship, bringing back his wrathful eyes to the Knight.

"That may well be, my Lord; but here I am."

"So I see. Happily for me, you have broken your word—the term which I had allotted you expired yesterday."

"Your Lordship is in error; I am punctual to the rendezvous you gave me."

"I can hardly take your word for it."

"I am sorry, because you will oblige me to force you to do so. We undertook a formal engagement, and I am in the right in exacting its fulfilment."

"Have you fulfilled all the conditions of the agreement?"

"Of a truth have I. They were three: I was to obtain re-possession of my estates; I must possess one hundred thousand pieces of gold; and I must return in seven years to claim the hand of the Lady Christabel."

"Do you really possess one hundred thousand pieces of gold?" asked the Baron, enviously.

"Yea, my Lord. King Henry hath restored me mine estates, and I have received the revenue arising from my patrimony since the day of its confiscation. I am rich, and I insist on your giving me the Lady Christabel to-morrow."

"To-morrow!" cried the Baron; "to-morrow! and if you were not here to-morrow," he added, sombrely, "the contract would be annulled?"

"Yea; but hearken to me, Lord Fitz-Alwine. I advise you to renounce all thoughts of consummating the diabolical schemes you are meditating at this moment. I am within my rights; I am here at the hour appointed me, and naught in all the world (it is useless to dream of resorting to force)—naught in all the world will constrain me to renounce her I love. If in desperation you resort to fraud and cunning, I will take—of that you may sure—a terrible revenge. I know of a dark secret in your life, which I will reveal. I have sojourned at the court of the King of France; I have been initiated into the secret of an affair which doth very narrowly concern you."

"What affair?" questioned the Baron, uneasily.

"It is useless for me to enter into long explanations with you just now; let it suffice that I have learnt and keep a note of the names of the miserable Englishmen who have offered to place their country under the yoke of the stranger."

Lord Fitz-Alwine became livid.

"Keep the promise you have made me, my Lord, and I will forget you have been a coward and a traitor to your King."

"Sir Knight, you insult an old man," said the Baron, assuming an indignant air.

"I speak truth, and no more. One more refusal, my Lord, one more lie, one more subterfuge, and the proofs of your patriotism will be sent to the King of England."

"It is lucky for you, Allan Clare," said the Baron, blandly, "That Heaven hath bestowed upon me a calm and equable temper; if I were of an irritable and hasty nature, you would pay dearly for your audacity, for I would have you thrown into one of the Castle moats."

"That would be a great mistake, my Lord, for it would in no wise save you from the Royal vengeance."

"Your youth excuses the impetuosity of your words, Sir Knight; I would rather show indulgence where it would be easy for me to punish. Why speak threateningly, ere you know whether I really intend to refuse you the hand of my daughter?"

"Because I have learnt for certain that you have promised the Lady Christabel to a miserable and sordid old man—to Sir Tristan Goldsborough."

"Indeed, indeed! And from what silly gossip learnt you this foolish story?"

"That matters not; the whole town of Nottingham hath heard rumours of the preparations for this rich and ridiculous marriage."

"I cannot be responsible, Sir Knight, for the stupid lies which circulate around me."

"Then you have not promised the hand of your daughter to Sir Tristan?"

"I must beg to decline to answer such a question. Until to-morrow I am at liberty to think and wish what I please; to-morrow is yours. Come then, and I will give you a full satisfaction of your desires. Farewell, Sir Allan Clare," added the old man, rising; "I wish you a very good day, and pray you to leave me."

"I shall have the pleasure of seeing you again, Baron Fitz-Alwine. Remember that a gentleman hath only one promise."

"Very well, very well," grumbled the old man, turning his back on his visitor.

Allan left the Baron's apartment with a heavy heart. He could not hide from himself that the old Lord meditated some perfidy. His menacing looks had accompanied the young man to the threshold of the room; then he had retired to the embrasure of the window, disdaining to respond to the Knight's parting salute.

As soon as Allan had disappeared (the young man went to seek Robin Hood) the Baron rang a small handbell on the table violently.

"Send Black Peter to me," said the Baron, gruffly.

"Anon! my Lord."

Some minutes later the soldier in question appeared before Lord Fitz-Alwine.

"Peter," said the Baron, "thou hast under thee brave and trustworthy fellows that will execute, without comment, any orders given them?"

"Yea, my Lord."

"They are courageous, and know how to forget the services they are able to render?"

"Yea, my Lord."

"That is well. A knight, elegantly clad in a red tunic, hath just left here; follow him with two good men, and see that he is no longer able to trouble any one. Dost understand?"

"Perfectly, my Lord," replied Black Peter, with a frightful leer, and half drawing a huge dagger from its sheath.

"Thou shalt be well rewarded, brave Peter. Go without fear, but act secretly and with prudence. An if this butterfly take the road through the wood, let him get well under the trees, and there you will have it all your own way. After he hath been despatched to another world, bury him at the foot of some old oak, and cover the spot with leaves and brushwood, so that his body is not likely to be discovered."

"Your orders shall be faithfully executed, my Lord; and when you see me again, the Knight will sleep beneath a carpet of green grass."

"I shall look out for thee. Now up and follow yonder impertinent fop without delay."

Accompanied by two men, Black Peter left the Castle, and soon found himself on the track of the young Knight.

The latter, with pensive brow, his mind absorbed and his heart heavy with sorrow, paced slowly along the borders of Sherwood Forest. On seeing the young man enter under the covert of the trees, the assassins following him trembled with sinister joy. They hastened their steps, and took hiding behind a bush, ready to throw themselves upon the young man at an opportune moment.

Allan Clare looked about for the guide promised by Robin Hood, and whilst he searched he reflected on the means necessary for tearing Christabel from the hands of her unworthy father.

A sound of hurried footsteps roused the Knight from his sad reverie. Turning his head, he beheld three men with evil faces advancing toward him, sword in hand.

Allan set his back against a tree, drew his sword from the scabbard, and said in a firm voice—

"Ho, caitiffs! what would you have?"

"We would have thy life, thou gaudy butterfly!" cried Black Peter, throwing himself upon the young man.

"Back, rogue!" said Allan, striking his aggressor in the face. "Back all!" he continued, disarming with incomparable skill the second of his adversaries.

Black Peter redoubled his efforts, but he could not succeed in touching his adversary, who had not only rendered one of the assassins powerless by sending his sword up into the branches of a tree, but had likewise broken the skull of the third.

Disarmed and mad with rage, Black Peter uprooted a young tree and again rushed upon Allan. He hit the Knight on the head with such violence that the latter let fall his weapon and fell senseless to the ground.

"The quarry is pulled down!" Peter cried exultingly, as he assisted his wounded companions to their feet. "Get ye along to the Castle, and leave me alone; I will finish this fellow. Your presence here is a danger, and your groanings weary me. Begone; I will myself dig the hole in which to bury the young Lord. Give me the spade you brought."

"'Tis here," said one of the men. "Peter," added the wretched varlet, "I am half dead, I cannot walk."

"Begone, or I will finish thee," replied Peter, brutally.

The two men, overcome with pain and fright, dragged themselves painfully out of the Forest.

Left alone, Peter set to work; he had half finished his dreadful task when he received upon the shoulder a blow from a stick, so vigorously delivered that he fell full length at the edge of the hole.

When the violence of the pain was a little spent, the wretch turned his eyes towards the dealer of this very just retribution. He then perceived the rubicund visage of a robust fellow arrayed in the garb of a Dominican Friar.

"How now, profane rascal with the black muzzle!" cried the Friar, in stentorian tones, "dost knock a gentleman on the head, and then, to hide thine infamy, bury thy victim? Answer me, robber, who art thou?"

"My sword shall speak for me," said Peter, leaping to his feet. "It shall send thee to another world, where thou mayest have leisure to ask Satan the name thou dost desire to know."

"I shall not need to give myself that trouble; an I have the bad luck to die before thee, insolent rogue, I can read on thy face thine infernal parentage. Now let me counsel thy sword to keep quiet, for an it attempt to wag its tongue, my cudgel will impose an eternal silence on it. Get thee hence, that is the best thing thou canst do."

"Not until I have shown thee that I know how to use a sword," said Peter, striking at the Monk.

The blow was so rapid, so violent, and so adroitly aimed that it struck the Brother on the left hand, cutting three fingers almost to the bone. The monk uttered a cry, fell upon Peter on the instant, and crushing him in his powerful embrace, applied a volley of blows from his cudgel.

Then a strange sensation overcame the miserable assassin; he lost his sword, his eyes grew dim, his senses failed him, and he lost all power of defending himself. When the Brother ceased beating him, Peter fell dead.

"The knave!" muttered the Monk, spent with pain and weariness, "the damned knave! Did he imagine that the fingers of poor Tuck were made to be cut about by a Norman dog? I think I have given him a good lesson; unfortunately, he will not derive much benefit from it, since he hath breathed his last breath. So much the worse; 'twas all his fault, not mine. Why did he kill this poor boy? Ah!" cried the good Brother, placing his sound hand on the Knight's breast, "he still breathes, his body is warm and his heart beats, feebly 'tis true, but enow to show that there is still life in him. I will bear him on my shoulders to the retreat. Poor lad, he is no great weight! As for thee, vile assassin," added Tuck, pushing away Peter's body with his foot, "lie there, and if the wolves have not yet dined, thou wilt serve them for a meal."

Saying which, the Monk took his way with a firm and rapid step in the direction of the retreat of the merry men.

*　　*　　*　　*　　*

A few words will suffice to explain Will Scarlett's capture.

The man who had seen him in company with Robin Hood and Little John in the Inn at Mansfield was under orders seeking the fugitive. Perceiving the young man accompanied by five strong fellows who might lend him a helping hand, the wary scout determined to await a more favourable moment to effect the capture. Quitting the Inn, he sent to Nottingham to ask for a company of soldiers, and these, guided by the spy, repaired to Barnsdale at midnight.

Next morning a strange fatality led Will outside the Castle; the poor youth fell into the hands of the soldiers, and was carried off without being able to offer the smallest resistance.

At first he was seized with utter despair; but the meeting with Much gave him some hope. He understood instantly that, once made aware of his unhappy plight, Robin Hood would do everything in the world to come to his aid, and if he could not succeed in saving him, at least he would allow no obstacle to deter him from avenging his death. He knew, moreover—and this afforded some relief to his heavy heart—that many tears would be shed over his cruel fate; he knew, too, that Maude, so happy in his return, would weep bitterly at the destruction of their mutual happiness.

Imprisoned in his dark dungeon, Will awaited in agonies of fear the time fixed for his execution, and every hour brought him both hope and anguish. The poor prisoner listened with straining ears for every sound from without, hoping always to hear the echo of Robin Hood's horn.

The first streak of dawn found Will at his prayers; he had confessed piously to the good pilgrim, and with strengthened spirit, and confident in him whose succour he still expected, he made ready to follow the guards who came to seek him at sunrise.

The soldiers set Will in their midst, and took the road to Nottingham.

On entering the town, the escort was soon surrounded by a large concourse of the inhabitants, who, since dawn, had been on the look-out for the melancholy procession.

However great the young man's hopes might be, he felt his spirits fail at seeing around him not one single face he knew. His heart sank, and the tears, though manfully repressed, wetted his eyelashes; nevertheless, he still hoped, for a voice within him seemed to say, "Robin Hood is not far away, Robin Hood will come."

When they reached the hideous gallows erected by the Baron's orders, William became livid; he had not expected to die so infamous a death.

"I wish to speak to Lord Fitz-Alwine," said he.

In his capacity of Sheriff the latter was obliged to assist at the execution.

"What dost want of me, wretch?" asked the Baron.

"My Lord, may I not hope for pardon?"

"No," replied the old man, coldly.

"Then," said William, in a firm voice, "I implore a favour which it is impossible for a generous soul to refuse me."

"What favour?"

"My Lord, I belong to a noble Saxon family, whose name is the synonym of honour, and never yet hath one of its members merited the scorn of his fellow-citizens. I am a soldier and a gentleman; I deserve the death of a soldier."

"Thou wilt be hanged," said the Baron, brutally.

"My Lord, I have risked my life on the field of battle, I do not deserve to be hanged like a thief."

"Ah, indeed!" sneered the old man. "And in what fashion, then, dost wish to expiate your crime?"

"Give me but a sword, and command your soldiers to pierce me with their spears or pikes; I would die as dies an honest man, with free arms and face upturned to Heaven."

"Dost think I am fool enough to risk the life of one of my men to satisfy thy fancy? Not at all, not at all! Thou wilt be hanged."

"My Lord, I conjure you, I beseech you to have pity on me. I will not even ask for a sword, I will not defend myself, I will let your men hack me in pieces."

"Vile wretch!" said the Baron; "thou hast killed a Norman, and thou dost ask pity from a Norman. Art mad? Back, I say! Thou shalt die upon the gallows; and shalt soon have company, too, I trust—the robber who with his band of rascals doth infest Sherwood Forest."

"An if he you speak of with such scorn were within earshot, I would laugh at your boasts, cowardly poltroon that you are! Remember this, Baron Fitz-Alwine, if I die, Robin Hood will avenge me! Beware of Robin Hood! Ere this week be gone, he will be at the Castle of Nottingham."

"Let him come, and eke his whole band with him! I will have two hundred gallows erected. Hangman, do you duty," added the Baron.

The hangman put his hand on William's shoulder. The poor youth threw a glance of despair around him, and seeing only a silent and pitying crowd, commended his soul to God.

"Stay," said the trembling voice of the pilgrim—"stay; I have one last benediction to give to my unhappy penitent."

"Your duties toward the wretched creature are ended," cried the Baron, in a furious tone. "It is useless to retard his execution longer."

"Ungodly man," cried the pilgrim, "would you deprive this young man of the succour of religion?"

"Hurry, then," said Lord Fitz-Alwine, impatiently; "I am aweary of all these delays."

"Soldiers, stand back a little," said the old pilgrim; "the prayers of a dying man must not fall upon profane ears."

At a sign from the Baron the soldiers fell back a little way from the prisoner, and William was left alone with the pilgrim at the foot of the gallows.

The hangman was listening respectfully to some orders from the Baron.

"Do not move, Will," said the pilgrim, leaning towards the young man; "I am Robin Hood, and I am going to cut the cords which fetter your movements. Then we will dash into the midst of the soldiers, and sheer surprise will rob them of their wits."

"Bless you, dear Robin, bless you!" murmured poor William, choking with joy.

"Stoop down, William, and pretend to talk to me. Good! the cords are cut. Now take the sword which hangs beneath my gown. Can you feel it?"

"Yea! here it is," murmured Will.

"Very well; now, put your back against mine, and we will show Lord Fitz-Alwine that you did not come into this world to be hanged."

With a movement quicker than thought, Robin Hood dropped his pilgrim's gown, and revealed to the amazed gaze of the assembled crowd the well-known costume of the renowned outlaw.

"My Lord," cried Robin, in a firm and thrilling voice, "William Gamwell is one of our band of merry men. You took him from me. I am come to reclaim him, and in exchange I will send you the corpse of the rogue who had your orders foully to destroy the good Knight Allan Clare."

"Five hundred pieces of gold to the man who arrests this robber," bellowed the Baron; "five hundred pieces of gold to the valiant soldier who will secure him."

Robin Hood flashed a glance at the crowd, who stood stupefied with fear.

"I do not advise any one to risk his life," said he; "my comrades will rally round me."

As he finished speaking, Robin blew his horn, and instantly a large body of foresters issued from the Forest, their bows ready strung in their hands.

"To arms!" cried the Baron, "to arms, faithful Normans; exterminate these bandits!"

A volley of arrows poured upon the Baron's company. The latter, seized with terror, threw himself on his horse, and urged it with loud cries in the direction of the Castle. The citizens of Nottingham, distracted with fright, followed in the steps of their lord; and the soldiers, carried away by the terror of the general panic, took to their heels in headlong flight.

"Ho for the good green wood! Ho for brave Robin Hood!" shouted the merry men, as they chased their foes before them with great shouts of laughter.

Citizens, foresters, and soldiers dashed through the town, helter-skelter, the first dumb with fright, the second laughing, the last with rage in their hearts. The Baron was the first to gain the interior of the Castle, whither the others followed him, all except the merry men, who on arriving there took leave of their faint-hearted adversaries with shouts of derision.

When Robin Hood, accompanied by his band, had again taken the Forest road, the citizens who had suffered no hurt or loss through this strange encounter, sang the praises of the young Chief and his readiness to succour any in distress.

The maidens blended their sweet voices in this chorus of eulogy, one of them even declaring she thought the Foresters appeared such kind and merry gentlemen, she would never more fear to cross the Forest alone.

CHAPTER III

Having assured himself that Robin Hood had no intention of besieging the Castle, Lord Fitz-Alwine, with aching body and mind torn by a thousand projects, each more impossible than the other, retired to his own apartments in the Castle.

There the Baron reflected on the strange audacity of Robin Hood, who in broad daylight, with no other weapon save an inoffensive sword (for he had only drawn it from the scabbard to cut the prisoner's bonds) had enough strength of mind to hold a large body of men in check. Remembering the shameful flight of his soldiers, and forgetting that he had been the first to set them the example, the Baron cursed their cowardice.

"What craven terror!" he cried; "what silly panic! What will the citizens of Nottingham think of us? *Their* flight was permissible, for they had no means of defence, but well-disciplined soldiers, armed to the teeth! My reputation for valour and courage will be gone for ever by this unheard-of behaviour!"

From this reflection, so humiliating to his self-esteem, the Baron passed to another train of thought. So greatly did he exaggerate the shame of his defeat, that he ended by making his soldiers entirely responsible for it; he imagined that instead of having shown the way for their stampede, he had covered their mad flight, and that with no protection save his own courage, he had cut a way through the ranks of the outlaws. Utterly confounding fact and fancy, this last thought brought the Baron's indignation to a head; he dashed from his room and burst headlong into the Courtyard, where his men, gathered in little groups, were talking over their pitiful defeat, for which they blamed their noble lord. The Baron fell like a thunderbolt into the midst of the troop, and ordered them to form up around him, whilst he read them a lecture on their infamous cowardice. After this, he cited imaginary examples of senseless panics, adding that never in the memory of man had such cowardice been known as that which they had just exhibited. The Baron spoke with such vehemence and indignation, and adopted such an air of invincible and unappreciated courage, that the soldiers, influenced by the feeling of respect in which they held their Chief, at last came actually to believe that they alone were really guilty. The Baron's rage appeared to them a righteous indignation;

they bowed their heads, and fully believed that they were no better than poltroons frightened by their own shadows. When the Baron had terminated his pompous discourse, one of the men proposed to pursue the outlaws to their Forest retreat. This proposition was hailed with acclamation by the entire troop, and the soldier with whom had originated this bellicose notion, begged the valiant orator to put himself at their head. But the latter, little disposed to accede to this ill-timed demand, replied that though he was gratified at such a token of high esteem, it seemed to him for the moment far wiser to remain at home.

"My brave fellows," added the Baron, "prudence counsels us to await a more favourable opportunity of seizing Robin Hood; it will be wiser, I think, to abstain from any precipitate measures, at any rate, for the present. Patience now, and courage in the hour of battle, is all I ask of you."

Having thus said, the Baron, who feared that his men might insist more strongly, hastily left them to their dreams of victory. His mind at ease concerning his military reputation, the Baron forgot Robin Hood and turned his attention to his personal affairs, and the aspirants to his daughter's hand. It is unnecessary to add that Lord Fitz-Alwine relied entirely on the proved skill of Black Peter for the realisation of his dearest hopes, and imagined that Allan Clare no longer existed. It is true that Robin Hood had informed him of the death of his blood-thirsty emissary, but it was of little consequence to the Baron that Peter had paid with his life the services rendered to his lord and master. Allan Clare disposed of, no obstacle could come between Christabel and Sir Tristan, and the latter was so near his grave that the young wife might exchange in a day her bridal veil for a widow's weeds. Young and passing fair, free of all bonds, enormously rich, Lady Christabel might then make a marriage worthy of her beauty and her immense fortune. "But what marriage?" asked the Baron of himself; and, fired by an overpowering ambition, he sought for a husband who should fulfil his highest hopes. The elated old man had glimpses of the splendour of the Court, and he dreamt of the son of Henry II. At that moment of incessant strife between the two parties which divided the kingdom of England, necessity had made a great power of wealth, and the elevation of the Lady Christabel to the rank of Princess Royal was not quite impossible of realisation. The exciting hope which Lord Fitz-Alwine had conceived began to take the shape of a project on the eve of execution; already he looked upon himself as the father-in-law of the King of England, and he wondered to what nation it would be most advantageous to unite his grandsons and great-grandsons, when Robin's words recurred to his mind, and shattered this castle in the air. Perhaps Allan Clare was still alive! "I must make certain of it at once," cried the Baron, almost beside himself at the mere supposition. He rang the hand-bell, placed within his reach night and day, violently, and a servant appeared.

"Is Black Peter in the Castle?"

"No, my Lord, he went out yesterday with two men, who returned alone, one grievously wounded, the other half-dead."

"Send the one who is able to get about to me."

"Yea, my Lord."

The man required soon made his appearance, his head enveloped in bandages and his left arm in a sling.

"Where is Black Peter?" inquired the Baron, without even bestowing a look of pity on the poor creature.

"I know not, my Lord; I left Peter in the Forest digging a hole in which to hide the body of the young Lord whom we had killed."

The Baron's face became purple; he tried to speak, confused words rushed to his lips; he turned his head away, and signed to the assassin to leave the room. The latter, who wished for nothing better, went out, supporting himself by the wall.

"Dead!" murmured the Baron, with an indefinable feeling. "Dead!" he repeated; and, pale as death, he continued to stammer in a feeble voice, "Dead! dead!"

Let us leave Lord Fitz-Alwine a prey to evil conscience, and seek his daughter's destined husband.

Sir Tristan had not left the Castle; and indeed his sojourn there was to be prolonged until the end of the week.

The Baron wished his daughter's marriage to be celebrated in the Castle Chapel; but Sir Tristan, who feared some sinister attack on his person, preferred to be married openly at Linton Abbey, about a mile from the town of Nottingham.

"My good friend," said Lord Fitz-Alwine, in a peremptory tone, when this question was broached, "you are a stubborn fool, for you do not understand either my good faith or your own interests. You must not imagine that my daughter will be overjoyed to be yours, nor that she will walk gladly to the altar. I cannot tell you the reason, but I have a presentiment that at Linton Abbey some great disaster may occur. We are in the neighbourhood of a troop of bandits who, led by an audacious chief, are quite capable of surrounding and plundering us."

"I should be escorted by my servants," replied Sir Tristan; "they are numerous and of tried courage."

"As you please," said the Baron. "If any accident occur, you will only have yourself to blame."

"Never be uneasy; I will take the responsibility of the fault upon myself, if it be a fault, my choice of the place for celebrating the wedding."

"By the way," said the Baron, "do not forget, I beg, that on the eve of the happy day you are to give me a million pieces of gold."

"The chest containing that amount is in my room, Fitz-Alwine," said Sir Tristan, fetching a deep sigh, "and it will be carried into your apartment on the day of the wedding."

"On the eve," said the Baron—"the eve, so it was agreed."

"On the eve, then."

With this the old men parted, the one going to pay his court to the Lady Christabel, the other returning to his dreams of greatness.

At Barnsdale Hall the gloom was profound. Old Sir Guy, his wife and their daughters, passed the hours of the day in mutual consolation and the nights in weeping over the death of poor Will.

The day after the lad's miraculous deliverance, the Gamwell family was assembled in the great hall, talking sadly over Will's strange disappearance, when the joyous sound of a hunting-horn was heard at the gate ot the Hall.

"It is Robin!" cried Marian, rushing to the window.

"He must be bringing good news," said Barbara. "Come, dear Maude, hope and courage, William is coming back."

"Alas, my sister! may you prove right," said Maude, weeping.

"I am right! I am right!" cried Barbara. "Here are Will and Robin with a young man, doubtless a friend of theirs."

Maude flew to the door, and Marian, who had recognised her brother (for Allan Clare had only been stunned, and, after lying unconscious for a few hours, was now quite recovered), threw herself, like Maude, into the young men's outstretched arms. Maude, nearly delirious with joy, could only murmur fondly, "Will! Will! dear Will!" whilst Marian, with her arms around her brother's neck, was unable to utter a word. We will not attempt to depict the joy of this now happy family, to whom God had sent back safe and sound him they had mourned as lost for ever.

Laughter soon drove away their tears, and both beloved children were strained to the maternal bosom with the same fond kisses and caresses. Sir Guy gave his blessing to Will and to his son's deliverer, while Lady Gamwell, radiant with joy, pressed the charming Maude to her heart.

"Was I not right in maintaining that Robin was bringing good tidings?" said Barbara, kissing Will as she spoke.

"Of a truth, you were right, dear Barbara," replied Marian, pressing her brother's hand.

"I should like," said saucy Barbara, "to pretend that Robin was Will, and hug him with all my might."

"Such a mode of expressing your gratitude would set us a very bad example, Barbara dear," laughed Marian; "for we should all feel constrained to imitate you, and poor Robin would succumb beneath the weight of so much happiness."

"My death would be an easy one, at any rate. Think you not so, Lady Marian?"

Marian blushed, and an almost imperceptible smile hovered on Allan Clare's lips.

"Sir Knight," said Will, approaching the young man, "you see what an affection Robin hath inspired in my sisters' hearts; but he well deserves it. In recounting our troubles to you, Robin never told how he had rescued my father from death; he said nothing of his devotion to Winifred and Barbara; he spoke not of his affectionate care—that of the best of friends—for Maude, my affianced bride. When giving you tidings of Lady Marian, Robin added not, 'I have watched over her happiness when you were far away; in me she had a faithful friend, a devoted brother.' He did not..."

"William, I beseech you," interrupted Robin, "spare my blushes; for though Lady Marian avers that I cannot blush, my face doth verily feel afire."

"My dear Robin," said Allan, visibly affected, as he wrung the young man by the hand, "I have long been greatly in your debt, and at length I am happy in being able to repay you. It did not need Will's word to assure me that you had nobly fulfilled the delicate mission confided to you; the loyalty of all your deeds was a sure guarantee of that."

"Oh, brother," said Marian, "if you only knew how good and generous he hath been to us all! If you only knew how praiseworthy his conduct toward me hath been, you would honour him and you would love him as...as..."

"As thou dost thyself—is it not so?" said Allan, with a tender smile.

"Yea, as I do myself," replied Marian, her face radiant with a smile of unutterable pride, and her sweet voice tremulous with emotion. "I fear not to openly avow my love for the generous man who hath shared the sorrows of my heart. Robin loves me, dear Allan; his love for me is as deep and hath endured as long as mine for him. My hand is promised to Robin Hood, and we only awaited thy presence to ask of God His holy benediction."

"I am ashamed of my selfishness, Marian," said Allan; "and my shame forces me to admire the more Robin's gallant behaviour. Thy natural protector was far from thee, and thou didst not deem it fitting to be happy until he returned. Forgive me both for abandoning you so cruelly; Christabel will plead my cause to your tender hearts. Thank you, dear Robin," added the Knight, "thank you; no words can express to you my sincere gratitude. You love Marian and Marian loves you; I am proud and happy to give you her hand."

As he finished speaking, the Knight took his sister's hand, and with a smile placed it in that of the young man, who, straining Marian to his bursting heart, kissed her passionately. William seemed quite intoxicated with the joy he saw around him, and with the object of suppressing the violence of his emotion, he took Maude round the waist and kissed her neck again and again, uttering some incoherent words and finishing with a triumphant "Hurrah!"

"We will be married on the same day, won't we, Robin?" cried Will, joyously, "or rather we will be married to-morrow. Oh no! not to-morrow; it is unlucky to put off till to-morrow what can be done to-day—we will be married to-day. What say you, Maude?"

The girl laughed.

"You are in a tremendous hurry," cried the Knight.

"A hurry! It is easy for you, Allan, to criticise; but an if, like me, you had been torn from the arms of your beloved when you were on the point of giving her your name, you would not say I was in too great a hurry. Am I not right, Maude?"

"Yea, William, you are right; but our marriage cannot take place to-day."

"Why not? I should like to know, why not?" repeated the lad, impatiently.

"Because it is necessary for me to leave Barnsdale in a few hours, friend Will," replied the Knight, "and I must certainly be present at your wedding and at my sister's. I for my part hope to have the happiness of marrying the Lady Christabel, and our three weddings could then be celebrated on the same day. Wait a little longer, William; in one week from to-day all will be settled to our mutual satisfaction."

"Wait another week?" cried Will. "It is impossible!"

"But, William," said Robin, "a week is soon gone, and you have a thousand reasons for patience."

"Well, I resign myself," said the young man, dismally. "You are all against me, and I have never a soul to speak up for me. Maude, who of rights should add the eloquence of her sweet voice to mine, remains silent, so I will hold my tongue too. I suppose, Maude, we ought to talk of our future home. Come, let us go round the garden; that ought to take a good two hours at least, and it will be so much subtracted from the eternity of a week."

Without awaiting the girl's consent, Will took her hand, and laughingly led her out under the shady trees of the park.

A week after the interview between Allan Clare and Lord Fitz-Alwine, the Lady Christabel was alone in her room, seated, or rather crouching, in an armchair. The silken folds of a beautiful white satin dress draped the girl's cowering form, and a veil of English point covered her blonde tresses. A deathly pallor overspread her delicate and perfect features, her colourless lips were closed, and her large eyes, with their listless look, were fixed in a terrified stare on a door opposite.

From time to time a large tear rolled down her cheeks, and this tear, a pearl of sorrow, was the only sign of life her enfeebled body gave.

Two hours passed in a dreadful waiting. Christabel was hardly conscious; her mind, steeped in happy memories of a past beyond recall, regarded with unspeakable horror the approaching sacrifice.

"He hath forgot me," wailed the poor girl, suddenly, wringing her hands, whiter than the satin of her dress; "he hath forgot her whom he said he loved, whom alone he loved; he hath forgot his vows—he is married to another. Oh, God! have pity on me; my strength fails me, for my heart is broken. I have suffered so much already! For him have I borne bitter words, the loveless looks of the father I should love and respect! For him I bore ill-treatment without complaint, even the sombre solitude of the cloister! I believed in him and he hath deceived me!"

A convulsive sob escaped her, and the tears gushed from her eyes. A light tap at the door aroused her from her painful thoughts.

"Come in," she said in a stifled voice.

The door opened, and the wrinkled face of Sir Tristan appeared before the eyes of the unhappy girl.

"Sweet lady," said the old man, with a leer, which he fondly imagined was an enchanting smile, "the hour of our departure is about to strike. Prithee allow me to offer you my arm; the escort awaits us, and we shall soon be the happiest couple in England."

"My Lord," stammered Christabel, "I cannot go downstairs."

"How say you, dear love—you cannot go downstairs? I do not well understand; you are quite ready, and they wait for us. Come, give me your dear, dainty hand."

"Sir Tristan," replied Christabel, as she rose with burning eyes and trembling lips, "hear me, I beseech you, and if there be a spark of pity in you, you will save the poor girl, who thus implores you, from this terrible ceremony."

"Terrible ceremony!" repeated Sir Tristan, in astonishment. "What means this, my Lady? I do not comprehend you."

"Spare me the pain of an explanation," Christabel answered, with a sob, "and I will bless you, Sir, and ever remember you in my prayers."

"You appear agitated, my pretty dove," said the old man in honeyed accents. "Calm yourself, my love, and this evening, or to-morrow, if you prefer it, you shall make your little confidences to me. At present we have no time to lose, but when we are married it will be different; we shall have plenty of leisure, and I will listen to you from morn till eve."

"In the name of pity, Sir, hear me now. If my father hath deceived you, I will not buoy you up with false hopes. My Lord, I do not love you; my heart is given to a young Lord who was my childhood's earliest friend. At the very moment when I am about to bestow my hand upon you, I am thinking of him. I love him, my Lord, I love him, and my whole soul is his, and his alone."

"You will soon forget this young man, fair lady. Once my wife, believe me, you will think of him no more."

"Never shall I forget him; his image is indelibly graven on my heart."

"At your age we think we shall love for ever, my dear love; then time creeps on and effaces in his march the tenderly cherished image. But come, we will speak of all this another time, and I will help you to set the hope of the future betwixt the past and the present."

"You have no pity, Sir?"

"I love you, Christabel."

"God have pity on me!" sighed the poor girl.

"God will certainly have pity," said the old man, taking Christabel's hand. "He will send you resignation and oblivion."

Sir Tristan kissed the cold hand in his with a respect mingled with tenderness and sympathy.

"You will be happy, fair lady," he said.

Christabel smiled sadly.

"I shall die," she thought to herself.

At Linton Abbey great preparations were being made for the wedding of the Lady Christabel and old Sir Tristan.

Ever since daybreak the Chapel had been hung with magnificent hangings, and sweet-smelling flowers diffused the most fragrant perfumes throughout the sanctuary. The Bishop of Hereford, who was to perform the marriage ceremony, stood at the Church door, with Monks in white vestments around him, awaiting the nuptial procession. Shortly before the arrival of Sir Tristan and the Lady Christabel, a man bearing in his hand a small harp presented himself before the Bishop.

"My Lord," said the new-comer, making a respectful genuflexion, "are you not about to celebrate a High Mass in honour of the bride and bridegroom?"

"Yea, friend, I am," returned the Bishop. "But why dost thou ask?"

"My Lord," answered the stranger, "I am the best harpist in France or England, and usually in much request at all feasts. Having heard of the intended marriage betwixt the rich Sir Tristan and Baron Fitz-Alwine's only daughter, I am come to offer his Lordship my services."

"An thy talent match thy vanity and assurance, thou art welcome."

"I thank you, my Lord."

"The sound of the harp pleaseth me much," the Bishop continued, "and I should love to hear thee play before the wedding party arriveth."

"My Lord," replied the stranger, haughtily, drawing the folds of his long cloak around him with a majestic air, "an I were a wandering minstrel, like those you are wont to hear, I would fall in with your wishes; but I play only at stated seasons and in suitable places. By-and-by I hope to give you complete satisfaction."

"Insolent varlet," replied the Bishop, in an angry voice, "I command thee to play to me this very instant."

"I will not touch a string until the escort arrive," said the stranger, imperturbably; "but when it doth come, you will hear sounds which will astonish you. Of that rest assured."

"We shall be able to judge of thy merits," replied the Bishop, "for here they come."

The stranger stepped back a few paces, while the Bishop advanced to meet the procession.

As she was about to enter the Church, Christabel turned half fainting to Baron Fitz-Alwine.

"Father," she said in a faltering voice, "have pity on me; this marriage will be my death."

A severe look from the Baron silenced the poor girl.

"Sir Knight," added Christabel, laying her trembling hand on Sir Tristan's arm, "be not merciless; you can still restore me to life. Have pity on me!"

"We will speak of that later," said Sir Tristan; and he signed to the Bishop to enter the Church.

The Baron took his daughter's hand, and was about to conduct her to the altar, when a loud voice cried "Stay!"

Lord Fitz-Alwine uttered a cry; Sir Tristan tottered, and had to lean for support against the great doorway of the Church. The stranger took the Lady Christabel's hand in his.

"Presumptuous caitiff!" said the Bishop, recognising the minstrel, "who gave thee permission to lay thy mercenary hands on this noble lady?"

"'Tis Providence sends me to succour her in her helplessness," replied the stranger, haughtily.

The Baron threw himself upon the minstrel.

"Who are you?" he asked; "and why come you here to disturb a holy ceremony?"

"Villain!" cried the stranger, "call you this shameful union of a young maiden with an old man a holy ceremony? My Lady," he added, bowing respectfully to the Lady Christabel, who was half dead with anguish, "you are come into the House of the Lord to receive the name of an honest man, and that name you shall receive. Take courage! Divine Providence yet watcheth over your innocence."

The minstrel loosed with one hand the girdle which confined his robe, while with the other he raised to his lips a hunting-horn.

"Robin Hood!" cried the Baron.

"Robin Hood! the friend of Allan Clare!" murmured the Lady Christabel.

"Yea, Robin Hood and his Merrie Men," replied our hero, indicating by a glance a number of foresters, who had stolen up silently and surrounded the escort.

At the same moment an elegantly clad young knight threw himself at the feet of Lady Christabel.

"My Lord," said Robin Hood, respectfully approaching the Bishop with bared head, "you were about to unite, contrary to all human and social laws, two beings never destined by Heaven to dwell beneath one roof. Behold this young maiden; look at the husband whom the insatiable avarice of her father would have given her. Since earliest childhood the Lady Christabel hath been betrothed to the Knight Allan Clare. Like herself he is young, rich, and noble; he loves her, and we are come to humbly beg you to bless their union."

"I formally oppose the marriage!" cried the Baron, striving to break from the grasp of Little John, to whom had fallen the lot of guarding him.

"Peace, inhuman man!" cried Robin Hood. "Dost dare to raise thy voice on the threshold of this holy place, and give the lie to the promises thou hast made?"

"I have made no promises," roared Lord Fitz-Alwine.

"My Lord," continued Robin Hood, addressing the Bishop, "will you unite these young people?"

"I cannot do it without the consent of Lord Fitz-Alwine."

"Which consent I will never give."

"My Lord," continued Robin, taking no notice of the vociferations of the old man, "I await your final decision."

"I cannot take it upon me to do as you wish," replied the Bishop; "the banns have not been published, and the law doth require..."

"We will obey the law," said Robin. "Friend Little John, confide his Lordship to the care of one of our men, and do you publish the banns."

Little John obeyed. Three times he announced the marriage of Allan Clare and the Lady Christabel Fitz-Alwine, but the Bishop again refused to give the young people his blessing.

"Your decision is final, my Lord?" asked Robin.

"It is," replied the Bishop.

"So be it. I had foreseen such an event, and am accompanied by a holy man, who hath the right to officiate. My father," continued Robin, addressing an old man, who had remained unnoticed, "I pray you enter the Chapel; the young couple will follow you."

The pilgrim, the same who had connived at Will's escape, advanced slowly.

"I am here, my son," he said; "I go to pray for the unfortunate and to beseech God to pardon the wicked."

Guarded by the merrie men, the party entered the Chapel quietly, and the ceremony began at once. The Bishop disappeared, Sir Tristan groaned dismally, and Lord Fitz-Alwine muttered deep oaths of vengeance.

"Who giveth this woman?" asked the old palmer, laying his palsied hands on Christabel's head, as she knelt before him.

"Will you be so good as to answer, my Lord?" said Robin Hood.

"Father, I pray you!" besought the girl.

"No, no! a thousand times, no!" cried the Baron, beside himself with rage.

"Since her father hath refused to keep the solemn promise he gave," said Robin, "I will take his place. I, Robin Hood, do give the Lady Christabel as wife to the good Knight Sir Allan Clare."

The ceremony proceeded without further obstacle. Hardly were Allan Clare and Christabel wedded ere the Gamwell family appeared on the threshold. Robin Hood advanced to meet Marian, and led her to the altar, William and Maude following them. As he passed close to Robin, who knelt at Marian's side, Will whispered—

"At length, Rob, the happy day hath arrived. Look at Maude; how beautiful she is, and her dear little heart is beating fast, I warrant you."

"Silence, Will; God is listening to us at this moment."

"Yea, I know, and I am going to pray with my whole soul," replied the happy youth.

The palmer blessed the new couples, and, raising his hands to Heaven, implored the divine mercy upon them.

"Maude, dear Maude," said William, as soon as he was able to lead the girl from the Church, "at last you are my wife—my dear wife! Fate hath set so many obstacles in the way of our happiness, 'tis difficult for me now to realise its full extent. I am mad with joy; thou art mine, and mine alone. Hast prayed, Maude, my darling? Hast asked the Holy Virgin to grant us for ever the same radiant joy she doth bestow on us this day?"

Maude smiled and wept together, so full was her heart of love and gratitude to William.

Robin's marriage threw the band of merrie men into transports of delight, and on issuing from the Church they uttered deafening cheers.

"The brawling ruffians," growled Lord Fitz-Alwine, reluctantly following the form of Little John, who had politely requested him to leave the Chapel.

A few minutes after the Chapel was deserted. Lord Fitz-Alwine and Sir Tristan, deprived of their horses, dolefully supporting each other, and in a state of mind which baffles description, set out for the Castle with halting steps.

"Fitz-Alwine," said the old man, stumbling as he spoke, "you will give me back the million pieces of gold which I confided to your care?"

"Nay, i' faith! Sir Tristan, for it was not my fault that misfortune befell you. Had you followed my counsels, this disaster would never have occurred. By holding the wedding in the Castle Chapel, our mutual desires would have been assured; but you preferred broad daylight to obscurity, and behold the result! This rascal hath carried off my daughter; I must have compensation, therefore I keep the gold."

Returning to Nottingham in as sorry a plight as their masters, the servants of the two noblemen followed them at a distance, laughing behind their backs at the strange events of the day.

The wedding party, escorted by the merrie men, soon gained the depths of the wood. The old Forest had decked itself out to receive the happy couples, and the trees, refreshed by the morning dew, bowed their green branches over the visitors. Long garlands of flowers and foliage were wreathed from tree to tree, and bound together secular oaks and sturdy elms and slender poplars. Here and there appeared in the distance a stag crowned with flowers like a classic god. A fawn, bedecked with ribbons, bounded across the path, or a deer, wearing its festive collar too, darted like an arrow along the greensward. In the midst of a wide clearing in the woods a table was spread, a dancing-green levelled, and sports prepared—in short, all the pleasures that could add to the satisfaction of the guests were disposed around them. Most of the fair maids of Nottingham had come to grace with their presence the feast of Robin Hood, and the most frolic gaiety prevailed in the happy gathering.

Maude and William, arm in arm, with smiling lips and joyous hearts, were wandering apart down a green avenue near the dancing-green, when Friar Tuck appeared before them.

"Halloa, good Tuck, merry Giles, my fat brother," cried Will, laughing, "art come to share our stroll? Welcome! Giles, my very good friend, and do me the honour to look at the treasure of my soul—my cherished wife, my most precious possession; look at this angel, Giles, and tell me if there doth exist beneath the skies a more charming being than my beautiful Maude. But methinks, friend Tuck," added the young man, looking more closely at the Monk's anxious face—"methinks thou art ill at ease; what is it? Come, confide thy troubles to us; I will endeavour to cheer thee. Maude, my darling, let us be kind to him. Come, what is it, Giles? First, I will hear thy confidences, then I will speak to thee of my wife, and thine old heart will be young again in sympathy with mine."

"I have no confidences to make thee, Will," replied the Monk, in a somewhat broken voice, "but I rejoice to know that all thy desires are fulfilled."

"That doth not prevent me, friend Tuck, from remarking with real sorrow the sad expression of thy countenance. Come, what is it?"

"Naught," replied the Monk, "naught, unless it were an idea which crossed my mind, a will o' the wisp which burns into my brain, an elf which plagues my heart. Well, Will, I know not whether I should tell thee, but for many years I had hoped that the little witch whom thou dost hold so tenderly to thee would be my sunbeam, the joy of my existence, my dearest and most precious jewel."

"What, poor Tuck, until now thou hast loved my pretty Maude?"

"Yea, William."

"If I am not wrong, thou hast known her longer than Robin?"

"Than Robin? Yea, indeed."

"And hast loved her?"

"Alas, yea!" sighed the Monk.

"Could it be otherwise?" said Will, in a tender voice, kissing his wife's hand. "Robin loved her at first sight, I adored her from the first, and now, Maude, thou art mine."

Silence followed Will's passionate exclamation. The Monk bowed his head, and Maude blushed and smiled at her husband.

"I do hope, friend Tuck," continued William, in a tone of affection, "that my happiness is not thy pain; if I am happy to-day, it is by great tribulation that I have succeeded in making Maude my well-beloved wife. Thou hast not known the despair of rejected love; thou hast not known exile; thou hast not languished far from thy beloved; thou hast not lost thy strength, thy health, thy peace of mind."

As he enumerated the last of his sorrows, Will cast his eyes upon the rubicund countenance of the Monk, and a loud laugh burst from him. Friar Tuck weighed at least fifteen stone, and his expansive figure resembled a full moon. Maude, who had understood the cause of Will's sudden laughter, shared in his mirth, and Tuck joined in unaffectedly.

"I am quite well," he said, with a charming good nature; "but that makes no odds....Well, no matter, I quite understand; and by'r Lady, good friends," he added, taking the clasped hands of the young people in his own large ones, "I wish you both perfect happiness. 'Tis true, sweet Maude, your fawn-like eyes turned my head long ago; but there, it will not bear much thought. I have found a good moral to that chapter; I sought for a consolation in my cruel sorrow, and I found it."

"Found it!" cried William and Maude together.

"Yea," replied Tuck, with a smile.

"A black-eyed maid?" asked the coquettish Maude; "a young girl who can appreciate your good sterling qualities, Master Giles?"

The Monk began to laugh.

"Yea, truly," he said, "my consolation is a lady with brilliant eyes and ruby lips. You ask me, sweet Maude, if she appreciates my merits? That is a question difficult to resolve, for my consoler is truly a thoughtless creature, and I am not the only one to whom she renders kiss for kiss."

"And yet thou lovest her?" said Will, in a tone full at once of pity and reproach.

"Yea, I love her," replied the Monk; "albeit, as I have just told you, she is very free with her favours."

"But she must be a horrid woman," cried Maude, flushing.

"What, Tuck," added Will, "as brave a heart and as honest a soul as thine to be caught in the toils of such an infatuation! As for me, sooner than bestow my love on such a creature, I..."

"Tut! tut!" interrupted the Monk, mildly; "be careful, Will."

"Careful—why?"

"Because it ill becomes thee to speak evil of one whom thou hast oft embraced."

"You have embraced this woman!" cried Maude, in a reproachful voice.

"Maude, Maude, it is a lie!" said Will.

"It is not a lie," replied the Monk, tranquilly; "thou hast embraced her not once, but ten times, twenty times."

"Will, Will!"

"Never listen to him, Maude, he is deceiving you. Now, look here, Tuck, tell the truth. I have embraced the maid of thy love?"

"Yea, and I can prove it."

"You hear him, Will," said Maude, ready to weep.

"I hear him, but I do not understand him," replied the young man. "Giles, in the name of our good friendship, I adjure you to confront me with this maid, and we will see whether she hath the effrontery to sustain your imposture."

"I ask naught better, Will, and I wager that not only wilt thou be constrained to confess the affection thou dost bear her, but thou wilt eke give her fresh proofs of it, and thou wilt even embrace her."

"I do not wish him to do so," said Maude, twining her arms round Will; "I do not wish him to speak to this woman."

"He will speak to her and he will embrace her," replied the Monk, with strange persistency.

"'Tis impossible," said Will.

"Quite impossible," added Maude.

"Show me thy beloved, Master Giles. Where is she?"

"What mean you, Will?" said Maude. "You cannot desire her presence, and beside...and beside, Will, methinks the person of whom you speak would not be a proper acquaintance for your wife."

"Thou art right, dear little wife," said Will, kissing Maude's brow; "she is not worthy to look at thee for a moment. My dear Tuck," he continued, "thou wilt oblige me by ceasing a pleasantry which is so disagreeable to Maude. I have neither desire nor curiosity to see thy beloved, wherefore let us speak of her no more."

"But 'tis necessary for the honour of my word, Will, that thou shouldest be confronted with her."

"Not at all, not at all!" said Maude. "William doth not desire this meeting, and it would be too painful for me."

"I wish thee to see her," replied the obstinate Giles; "and here she is!" Saying which, Tuck drew from his robe a silver flask, and raising it to William's eyes, he said, "Look at my pretty bottle, my sweet consolation, and dare to say again that thou hast ne'er embraced her."

The two young people laughed merrily.

"I do confess my sin, good Tuck," cried Will, taking the bottle, "and I ask my dear little wife's permission to implant a kiss of friendship on the ruby lips of this old friend."

"Thou hast my consent, Will; drink to our happiness and the merry Monk's prosperity."

Will sipped the rosy fluid and returned the flask to Tuck, who in his enthusiasm drained it completely. The three friends then strolled about with linked arms until at a call from Robin they rejoined the assembly.

Robin had presented Much to Barbara, saying that this handsome young man was the long-promised husband. But Barbara had shaken her fair curls, saying that she did not want to marry yet.

Little John, who was not of a very expansive nature, was quite amiable that day. He showered attentions on his cousin Winifred, and it was easy to see that the two young people had many secrets to confide to each other, for they conversed in whispers, danced together all the time, and seemed unconscious of everything going on around them.

As for Christabel, her sweet face was radiant with happiness, but she was still so much affected by her abrupt separation from her father, so much enfeebled by her recent sufferings, that it was impossible for her to mix in the games. Seated near Allan Clare beneath a canopy, upon a little hillock strewn with flowers, she looked like a young Queen presiding over a Royal feast given to her subjects.

Marian, tenderly supported by the arm of her husband, was walking on the dancing-green with him.

"I am coming to live near you, Robin" said the young wife, "and until the happy moment when you are restored to favour, I shall share the vicissitudes and loneliness of your existence."

"It were wiser, my dearest, to live at Barnsdale."

"No, Robin, my heart is with you, and I cannot leave my heart."

"I am proud to accept thy courageous devotion, dear wife, my sweet love," replied the young man with emotion, "and I will do all ever I can for thy satisfaction and happiness in thy new life."

In truth Robin Hood's wedding day was one of happiness and joy.

CHAPTER IV

Marian kept her word, and, despite Robin's mild objections, took up her abode under the great trees of Sherwood Forest. Allan Clare, who owned, as we have already said, a large house in the valley of Mansfield, could not prevail upon his sister to come and live in it with Christabel; for Marian was firmly resolved not to leave her husband.

Immediately after his wedding, the Knight had offered to sell his Huntingdonshire estates to King Henry II. at two-thirds of their value, on condition of his marriage with Lady Christabel Fitz-Alwine being confirmed by letters patent. The King, who always seized with avidity any opportunity of acquiring the richest domains in England for the Crown, accepted the offer, and, by a special act, confirmed the marriage of the two young people. Allan Clare had made his application with such adroitness and promptitude, and the King was so eager to close the bargain, that all was completed by the time the Bishop of Hereford and Baron Fitz-Alwine arrived at Court.

It is hardly necessary to remark that the Bishop and the Norman Baron stirred up the Royal anger against Robin Hood to the utmost. At their urgent request, Henry gave the Bishop leave to seize the person of the hardy outlaw, and to put him to death without delay or mercy.

Whilst the two Normans were conspiring thus against Robin Hood, the latter, at the height of his bliss, was living quietly and without a care beneath the good green trees of Sherwood Forest.

Will Scarlett was the happiest man in all the world, in the possession of his well-beloved Maude. Gifted with a vivid imagination, Will had imagined eternal bliss as consisting in a wife like Maude, and in his eyes she was endowed with all the charms of an angel. Maude was aware of this flattering affection, and she strove to remain upon the pedestal to which her husband's love had elevated her. Following the example set by Robin Hood and Marian, Will and his wife had made their home in the Forest, and they all lived there together in the greatest harmony.

Robin Hood loved the fair sex, firstly from natural inclination, and secondly out of regard for the charming creature who bore his name. Robin Hood's companions shared his feelings of respect and veneration towards women; and thus the maidens of the neighbourhood were able to traverse the Forest paths without fear of molestation. If by chance they encountered any of the band, they were asked to partake of refreshment, and afterwards they were given an escort through the wood, and no cause for complaint had ever arisen. When the kindly courtesy of the Foresters became known, its renown travelled afar, and many a bright-eyed maiden with light heart and tripping feet had ventured among the dells and glades of Sherwood.

On Robin's wedding day, a number of these young maidens joined in the festivities, and gazed admiringly at the handsome couple. As they danced, these fair daughters of Eve cast furtive glances at their gallant swains, and were only surprised to think that they had ever feared them for a single moment, whispering to each other that it must be very delightful to share the adventurous loves of the hardy outlaws. In the innocence of their young hearts they allowed these secret wishes to appear, and the enraptured Foresters, making the best use of their time, the beautiful maidens of Nottingham found that the language of Robin Hood's Merrie Men was no less irresistibly eloquent than their eyes.

The result of all this was that Friar Tuck became overwhelmed with work, being occupied from morning to night in solemnising marriages. Very naturally the good Monk was anxious to discover whether these multiple unions were not an epidemic of a peculiar character, and how many people would still succumb to it. But his question remained unanswered. Having attained its zenith, the rage for marriages abated, and the cases became fewer. Nevertheless, it is curious to observe that the symptoms are still as violent, and that they continue even to our own day.

The little colony in the Forest lived very merrily. The cave of which we have spoken had been divided into cells and rooms which served only for bedchambers, the vast glades serving as drawing and dining-rooms, and it was only in winter that they had recourse to their subterranean retreat. It is difficult to imagine how quiet and peaceful was the life these men led. Nearly all were of Saxon origin and attached to one another like members of one family; most of them had suffered cruel oppression at the hands of the Norman invaders.

Robin Hood's band levied tribute most particularly upon two classes of society: the rich Norman nobles and the clergy. On the first because they had robbed the Saxons of their titles and patrimony, and on the second because they were continually augmenting their already considerable riches at the expense of the people. Robin Hood levied imposts on the Normans, and though such contributions were heavy, they were exacted without combat or bloodshed. The orders of the young Chief were strictly carried out, for disobedience meant death. The severity of this discipline had earned an excellent reputation for Robin Hood's band, whose loyal and chivalrous character was well known. Many expeditions were undertaken vainly to try and oust the Merrie men from their retreat; but the authorities, wearied at last by their fruitless endeavours, ceased to harass them, and Henry II.'s indifference finally compelled the Normans to submit to the dangerous vicinity of their enemies.

Marian found her forest life even more agreeable than she had dared to hope; she was born (as she laughingly said) to be Queen of this merry tribe. The respectful homage, affection, and devotion lavished on Robin were extremely flattering to Marian, and she was proud to depend on the valiant young man's protecting arm. If Robin Hood knew how to gain and keep the affection of his followers by showing towards every man a consistent kindness and sincere friendship, he could also exert absolute authority over them.

The beautiful Forest held a thousand pleasures for Marian. Now she wandered with her husband through the picturesque windings of the wood, anon she found amusement in the sports and games then in vogue. Thanks to Robin's care, she possessed a rare and valuable flock of falcons, and she learnt to fly them with a tried and skilful hand. But the sport which Marian loved best was archery; with indefatigable patience Robin initiated his young wife into all the mysteries of the art. Marian attended carefully to the lessons given her, and never was pupil more apt. She thus became in a short time an archer of the first rank. It was a pleasing site to Robin and his Merrie Men to watch Marian, bow in hand, clad in a tunic of Lincoln green, her majestic and supple figure slightly bent, her left hand holding the bow, while her right, curving gracefully, drew the arrow to her ear. When Marian had mastered all the secrets of the art which had made Robin so famous, she acquired a like renown. The young woman's inimitable skill roused the admiration and respect of the inhabitants of the Forest to the utmost, and the allies of the band and the citizens of the towns of Mansfield and Nottingham came in crowds to witness her prowess.

A year slipped by—a year of joy, happiness, bliss. Allan-a-Dale (we will now speak of the Knight by the name of his property) had become a father; Heaven had blessed him with a daughter. Robin and William each rejoiced in a handsome son, and a round of dances and general rejoicings celebrated these happy events.

One morning Robin Hood with Will Scarlett and Little John met beneath a tree called the "trysting-tree," because it served as the rallying-point of the band, when they heard a faint sound in the distance.

"Hark!" said Robin, quickly. "'Tis a horse I hear in the clearing; go see whether we may expect a guest. You take me, Little John?"

"Perfectly. And I will bring back the rider, an he prove worthy to share your repast."

"He will be twice welcome," laughed Robin, "for I begin to feel the pangs of hunger."

Little John and Will glided through the thicket toward the road taken by the traveller, and soon came near enough to distinguish him.

"By the holy Mass, the poor devil hath a sorry look, and I dare swear his fortune causeth him but little embarrassment."

"I must e'en avow the Knight doth wear a grievous air," replied Little John; "but perchance the poverty of his outer man is but a clever artifice. The traveller trusteth to his seeming misery to traverse the Forest with impunity. We will teach him that, an he incline to trickery, we are his match in cunning."

Though habited in the garb of a Knight, the traveller at a first glance inspired a feeling of pity. His clothes hung on him anyhow, as though adversity had made him careless of appearances; the hood of his cloak hung round his neck; and his head, bowed in thought, bore evidence of extreme wretchedness. The deep bass voice of Little John roused the stranger suddenly from his reverie.

"Good day, Sir Stranger!" cried our friend, advancing to meet the traveller; "art welcome to the green wood. Thou hast been anxiously awaited."

"Awaited?" asked the stranger, fixing his sad gaze upon John's broad countenance.

"Yea, Sir Knight," replied Will Scarlett; "our master bade us seek thee, and for three hours he hath awaited thine arrival, ere commencing his meal."

"No one doth expect me," replied the stranger, with a troubled air. "You are mistaken; I am not the guest whom your master expects."

"I ask pardon, Master, but 'tis indeed thou. He had learnt thou wouldst be coming through the Forest to-day."

"Impossible, impossible," repeated the stranger.

"We speak the truth," returned Will.

"May I ask the name of one who shows such courtesy toward a poor traveller?"

"It is Robin Hood," replied Little John, hiding a smile.

"Robin Hood, the famous outlaw?" questioned the stranger, in evident surprise.

"Himself, Master."

"I have long heard tell of him," added the stranger, "and his noble conduct hath inspired in me a true regard for him. I am much pleased to have a chance of meeting Robin Hood; he hath a loyal and faithful heart. I will accept his kind invitation with pleasure, though I am at a loss to understand how he was aware of my journey through his domains."

"He will be glad to inform thee of that himself," replied Little John.

"As you will, brave Forester. Lead the way; I will follow in your steps."

Little John took the traveller's horse by the bridle, and conducted him into the path leading to the cross-road where Robin still remained. Will followed as rear-guard.

Little John did not doubt for a single moment but that this semblance of grief and poverty was a mask to serve as passport in case of an unwelcome encounter, whilst Will divined, more correctly perhaps, that the traveller was really and truly a poor man from whom they would obtain no other satisfaction than that of seeing him eat a right good dinner.

The stranger and his guides soon found Robin Hood. The latter saluted the new-comer, and, struck by his dejected appearance, watched him narrowly, whilst the other strove to readjust in some measure his poor clothing. An air of the greatest distinction accompanied all his movements, and Robin soon arrived at the same conclusion as Little John, that the stranger affected this careworn melancholy and these tattered garments as a safeguard to his purse.

Nevertheless, the young Chief received the dejected stranger with great kindness, offering him a seat, while he ordered one of his men to look after his guest's horse.

A delicious repast was spread upon the green turf, which is thus described in the words of an old ballad:—

> "And then with wine and manchet bread
> And mumbrils of the roe,
> They feasted, while the Malmsey wine
> Around the board did flow.
> And many a sylvan guest was there,
> With feathered minstrels of the air."

As we have remarked, despite the miserable appearance of his guest, Robin did not fail in hospitality toward him. If sorrow sharpens the appetite, we must say that the stranger was full of woe. He attacked the dishes with all the ardour of a stomach that has been empty for twenty-four hours, and the meats disappeared with great draughts of wine which bore witness to the excellence of the liquid, or to the weakening effect of sorrow.

After the repast Robin and his guest stretched themselves beneath the majestic shade of the great trees, and conversed without reserve. The Knight's opinions of men and matters raised him high in Robin's estimation, and, notwithstanding his miserable bearing, the young Chief could not believe in the sincerity of his apparent misery. Of all vices Robin most disliked dissimulation; his frank and open nature hated cunning. Therefore, in spite of the real esteem with which the Knight inspired him, he resolved to make him pay heavily for his repast. An opportunity for putting this determination into effect soon presented itself, for, after having railed against human ingratitude, the stranger added—

"I have so great a scorn for this vice that it doth no longer astonish me; but I can affirm that never in all my life have I been guilty of it myself. Allow me, Robin Hood, to thank you with all my heart for your friendly reception of me, and if ever a lucky chance should lead you into the neighbourhood of St. Mary's Abbey, forget not that at the Castle of the Plain you will ever find a loving and cordial hospitality."

"Sir Knight," replied the young man, "those whom I receive in the Forest never undergo the danger of a visit from me. To those who are really in need of a good meal I willingly give a place at my table;

but I am less generous toward travellers who have the wherewithal to pay for my hospitality. I fear to wound the pride of a man favoured by fortune, an if I give him of my venison and wine for naught. I find it more pleasant both for him and myself to say, 'This Forest is an inn, I am the host, my Merrie Men the servants. As noble guests, pay liberally for your refreshment.'"

The Knight began to laugh.

"That is," said he, "a mighty pleasant way of looking at things, and an ingenious fashion of levying tribute. I heard tell, not many days agone, of the courteous way in which you eased travellers of their superfluous wealth, but I have never had so clear an explanation as this."

"Well, Sir Knight, I am about to complete the explanation," saying which Robin took up a hunting horn and raised it to his lips. Little John and Will Scarlett appeared in answer to his summons. "Sir Knight," Robin Hood went on, "the hospitality comes to an end; be so good as to pay the shot, my manciples stand ready to receive it."

"Since you consider the Forest as an inn, the charges are no doubt in proportion to its extent?" said the Knight, in a calm voice.

"Just so, Master."

"You receive knights, barons, dukes, and peers of the realm at the same price?"

"Yea, at the same price," replied Robin Hood, "and it is but just. You would not wish, I imagine, that a poor peasant like myself should entertain gratuitously an emblazoned knight, an earl, a duke, or a prince; it would be contrary to all rules of breeding."

"You are perfectly right, good host, but you will have but a sad opinion of your guest, when he tells you that his entire fortune consists in ten pistoles."

"Permit me to doubt that assertion, Sir Knight," replied Robin.

"My dear host, I invite your companions to prove the truth of my statement by searching me."

Little John, who rarely allowed an opportunity of demonstrating his social position to escape him, hastened to obey.

"The Knight speaks truth," he cried, with a disappointed air; "he hath but ten pistoles."

"And that small sum doth represent all my fortune at present," added the stranger.

"Have you, then, consumed your inheritance?" asked Robin, with a laugh, "or was that inheritance of so little value?"

"My patrimony was considerable," replied the Knight, "and I have not squandered it."

"How, then, are you so poor? for you will own that your present situation looks hopeless enow."

"Appearances sometimes err, and to make you understand my misfortunes it would be necessary to recount to you a very sad story."

"Sir Knight, I will give you my best attention, and should it be in my power to help you, make use of me."

"I am aware, noble Robin Hood, that you generously extend your protection to the oppressed, and that they have claims on your warm sympathy."

"Spare me, Master, I pray you," interrupted Robin, "and let us concern ourselves with your affairs."

"My name is Richard," continued the stranger, "and my family is descended from King Ethelred."

"You are a Saxon, then?" said the young man.

"Yea, and the nobility of my birth hath been the cause of much misfortune."

"Suffer me to shake a brother's hand," replied Robin, with a merry smile on his lips. "Saxons, rich or poor, are freely welcome to the Forest of Sherwood."

The Knight responded cordially to his host's hand-clasp, and continued thus:—

"I was given the surname of Sir Richard of the Plain from the situation of my Castle in the centre of a vast moorland about two miles from St. Mary's Abbey. While still quite young I was married to a maid whom I have loved from my earliest childhood. Heaven blessed our union and sent us a son. Never did parents love their child as we loved our little Herbert, and never was child more love-worthy. Our proximity to the Abbey had led to frequent intercourse, and a great intimacy had sprung up betwixt the Brothers and myself. One day a Brother toward whom I had shown much sympathy asked me for a few minutes' conversation, and taking me aside spoke thus:—

"'Sir Richard, I am about to take irrevocable vows. I am about to quit the world for ever. Beside her mother's tomb I leave a poor orphan, defenceless and penniless. I am for ever dedicated to God, and I trust that the austerity of the Cloister will give me the courage to support the burden of life a few years longer. I come to ask you in the name of Divine Providence to have pity on my poor little daughter.'

"'My dear brother,' said I to the unhappy man, 'I thank you for your confidence, and since you have placed your trust in me, that trust shall not be betrayed; your daughter shall become mine.'

"The Brother, moved to tears by what he called my generosity, thanked me warmly and, at my request, sent for his little daughter.

"I have never experienced any emotion like that produced by the sight of this child.

"She was twelve years old, with a willowy, graceful figure, and long blonde tresses covered her pretty shoulders with their silken curls. On entering the room where I was waiting, she greeted me prettily, fixing upon me two large blue eyes full of sadness. As you may imagine, good host, this charming little maid quite won my heart; I took her hands in mine, and implanted on her brow a fatherly kiss.

"'You see, Sir Richard,' said the Monk, 'this sweet child is worthy of affection.'

"'Yea, truly, Brother, and I avow that never in my life have mine eyes rested upon so charming a being.'

"'Lilas is very like her mother,' replied the Monk, 'and the sight of her adds to my sorrow; she takes my mind from heavenly things and carries back my thoughts to the sweet creature sleeping yonder within the cold tomb. Adopt my sweet child, Sir Richard; you will never regret your charitable action. Lilas doth possess excellent qualities and a good temper; she is pious, sweet, and good.'

"'I will be a father to her, a tender father,' I replied with emotion.

"The poor little girl heard us with an air of surprise, and looking anxiously from her father to me with her large blue eyes, she said—

"'Father, you wish...'

"'I only wish your happiness, my darling child,' replied the Monk. 'Our separation hath become imperative.'

"I will not attempt to depict the painful scene which followed or the long explanations given by the Monk to his heart-broken child. He wept with her, until, at a sign from the unhappy man, I took Lilas in my arms and bore her from the Monastery.

"During the first days after her arrival, at the Castle, Lilas was sad and troubled, then time and the companionship of my son Herbert appeared to calm her sorrow. The two children grew up together, and when Lilas had attained her sixteenth, and Herbert his twentieth year, I could plainly see that they loved each other with a more tender love.

"'These young hearts,' I said to my wife, after having made this discovery, 'have never known sorrow; let us protect them against its attacks. Herbert adores Lilas, and on her part Lilas loves our dear son passionately. What matters it to us that Lilas is of lowly birth? Though her father was once only a poor Saxon peasant, he is now a holy man. Thanks to our care, Lilas possesses all the qualities which are an appanage of her sex; she loves Herbert, and will make him a good wife.'

"My wife consented with all her heart to the marriage of her two children, and we betrothed them that same day.

"The day fixed for the happy union was approaching, when a Norman Knight, owner of a small fief in Lancashire, came to pay a visit to the Abbey of St. Mary. This Norman had seen and admired my house, and was seized with a desire to possess it himself. Without disclosing this covetousness, he learned that I had under my paternal care a pretty girl of marriageable age; and rightly supposing that a portion of my wealth would be given to Lilas as her dowry, the Norman appeared at my gate, and under pretext of visiting the Castle, he managed to gain an entrance into our family circle. As I told you, Robin, Lilas was very beautiful, and the sight of her fired my guest's imagination; he repeated his visit, and confided to me his love for my son's betrothed. Without rejecting the Norman's honourable proposal, I told him of the engagement already made by the maiden, adding at the same time that Lilas was free to bestow her hand where she would.

"He then spoke to the girl herself. Lilas' refusal was kind but firm; she loved Herbert.

"The Norman left the Castle in a rage, swearing to have his revenge for what he called our insolence.

"At first we only laughed at his threats, but we learnt by experience how serious they were. Two days after the departure of the Norman, the eldest son of one of my vassals came to tell me that he had met, some four miles from the Castle, the stranger who had lately been my guest, carrying in his arms my poor unhappy child. This news caused us terrible distress. I could hardly believe it, but the young man gave me irrefutable proofs of the calamity.

"'Sir Richard,' he said to me, 'my words are only too true, and it was thus that I became assured that Mistress Lilas had been abducted. I was seated at the side of the road when a horseman, bearing before him a weeping woman and followed by his squire, stopped a few paces from me. The harness of his horse was broken, and with angry threats he called me to his assistance. I approached; Mistress Lilas wrung her hands. 'Arrange this bridle,' said the Knight, gruffly to me. I obeyed, and without being perceived, I cut the girths of the saddle; then, whilst pretending to examine the horse's shoes, I managed to slip a pebble into his hoof. Having done which, I fled to warn you.'

"My son Herbert could tarry to listen to no more, but away to the stables, saddled a horse, and set off at topmost speed.

"The young peasant's trick had been successful. When Herbert overtook the Norman, he had dismounted. Then there was a terrible fight between the villain and my son, in which right conquered, and my son killed the ravisher.

"Soon as ever the Norman's death became known, a troop of soldiers was sent to arrest Herbert. I hid him and sent a humble petition to the King. I made known to His Majesty the Norman's infamous conduct; I pointed out to him that my son had fought with his enemy, and had killed him while exposing himself to a like fate. The King made me buy my son's pardon at the price of a considerable ransom. Only too happy to obtain mercy, I hastened to satisfy the King's demands. My coffers emptied, I appealed to my vassals, and sold my plate and furniture. My last resources exhausted, I still required four hundred gold crowns. The Abbot of Saint Mary's then offered to lend the required sum on mortgage, and it is hardly necessary to add that I gladly accepted his kind offer. The conditions of the loan were as follows: A pretended sale of my estates would give him the rents for one year. If on the last day of the twelfth month of this year I do not repay him the four hundred gold crowns, all my goods will remain his. That is my position, good host," added the Knight—"the day of reckoning approaches, and my whole fortune consists of ten pistoles."

"Do you think that the Abbot of Saint Mary's will not give you time to free yourself?" asked Robin Hood.

"I am unfortunately but too sure that he will not give me an hour, a minute. If he be not reimbursed to the last crown, my estates will remain in his hands. Alas! I am indeed in a sorry plight; my beloved wife will have no home, my children no food. Could I suffer alone, I should take courage; but to watch the sufferings of those I love is too great a trial of my strength. I have asked help from those who called themselves my friends in the day of prosperity, and have received an icy refusal from some, indifference from others. I have no friends, Robin Hood; I am alone."

As he finished speaking, the Knight hid his face in his trembling hands, and a convulsive sob escaped him.

"Sir Richard," said Robin Hood, "your story is a sad one; but you must not despair of God's goodness; He watcheth over you, and I believe you are on the point of obtaining heavenly succour."

"Alas!" sighed the Knight, "could I but obtain a delay, I might be able to pay off the debt. Unfortunately the only security I can offer is a vow to the Virgin."

"I will take that security," replied Robin Hood; "and, in the revered name of the Mother of God, our holy patroness, I will lend you the four hundred golden crowns you lack."

The Knight uttered a cry.

"You, Robin Hood! Ah! bless you a thousand times. I swear with all the sincerity of a grateful heart loyally to repay the money."

"I will count on it, Sir Knight. Little John," Robin added, "you know where to find our horde, since you are treasurer of the Forest; go seek me four hundred crowns. As for you, Will, go look in my wardrobe and see whether there be not a garment worthy of our guest there."

"In truth, Robin Hood, your goodness is so great..." cried the Knight.

"Peace, peace," interrupted Robin, laughingly. "We have just entered upon an agreement, and I must honour you as the envoy of the Holy Virgin. Will, add to the clothes some ells of fine cloth; put new harness on the grey horse which the Bishop of Hereford committed to our care; and, Will, my friend, add to these modest gifts all that your inventive mind can think of as necessary to a Knight."

Little John and Will hastened to accomplish their mission.

"Cousin," said John, "thy hands be nimbler than mine, count the money whilst I measure the cloth; my bow will serve for yard measure."

"Certes," replied Will, with a laugh, "the measure will be good."

"It will, as thou shalt see."

Little John took his bow in one hand, unrolled the piece of cloth with the other, and set himself to measure, not by ells, but exactly by bow lengths.

Will burst out laughing.

"Go on, friend John, go on; wilt soon come to an end of the whole piece, an thou go on giving three yards for one. Well done!"

"Hold thy tongue, thou prating fool. Dost not know that Robin would give even more, an he were in our place?"

"Then will I add a few crowns," said William.

"A few handfuls, cousin; we will recover it from the Normans."

"Well, I have finished."

When Robin saw the generosity of John and Will, he smiled, and thanked them by a look.

"Sir Knight," said Will, putting the gold into the Knight's hand, "each roll contains one hundred crowns."

"But there are six rolls, my young friend."

"You are mistaken, Sir Guest; there are but four. And, after all, what matter? Put the money in your purse, and say no more on't."

"When shall I repay it?" asked the Knight.

"One year from this, day for day, an that will suit you, and I am still of this world," said Robin.

"Agreed."

"Beneath this tree."

"I will attend punctually, Robin Hood," replied the Knight, as he wrung the young Chief's hand with effusive gratitude. "But ere we part, let me tell you that all the praises lavished on you cannot equal those which fill my heart; you have saved more than my life; you have saved my wife and children."

"Master," replied Robin Hood, "you are a Saxon, and that name alone doth give you a claim upon my friendship; beside which, you have another interest for me—that of distress. I am what men call a robber, a thief—so be it! But an I extort money from the rich, I take naught from the poor. I detest violence, and I shed no blood; I love my country, and the Norman race is odious to me because to usurpation they have added tyranny. Nay, never thank me; I have done but my duty; you had naught, and I gave to you—'tis only just."

"Say what you will, your conduct toward me is noble and generous; you, a stranger, have done more for me than all they which call themselves my friends. May God bless you, Robin, for you have brought joy to my heart. At all times and in every place I shall be your debtor, and I pray Heaven to enable me to prove my gratitude some day. Farewell, Robin Hood! farewell, true friend! In one year I will return to pay my debt."

"Farewell, Sir Knight," replied Robin, shaking his guest warmly by the hand; "and should fate bring me to a pass where I need your help, believe me, I shall not fail to ask it without compunction or reserve."

"May God hear you! My greatest hope is that I may be able to assist you."

Sir Richard wrung the hands of Will and Little John, and bestrode the Bishop of Hereford's dapple grey. The Knight's own mount, laden with Robin Hood's presents, was to follow its master.

As Robin Hood watched his temporary guest disappear at a bend of the road, he said to his companions, "We have made a man happy; the day hath been well spent."

CHAPTER V

Marian and Maude had been living at Barnsdale Hall for a month past, and they could not return to their old mode of life until their health was quite re-established, for it must not be forgotten that the young women had become mothers.

But Robin Hood could not endure the prolonged absence of his beloved companion, and one day, carrying with him part of his band, he took up his abode in Barnsdale Forest. William, who had naturally followed his young chief, soon declared that the subterranean dwelling, constructed hastily in the neighbourhood of the Hall, was infinitely preferable to that in the great Forest of Sherwood; or, at least, if it wanted certain things to complete the well-being of the troop, the proximity of Barnsdale Hall was a very agreeable compensation.

Robin and William were enchanted at their change of abode, and two young people of our acquaintance shared in their unreserved satisfaction for the same reason; these two young men were Little John and Much Cockle, the miller's son. Robin soon perceived that Little John and Much were absent at all hours of the day without apparent motive. These absences became so frequent that Robin wished to know the cause of them. He made inquiries, and learnt that his cousin Winifred, being very fond of walking, had asked Little John to show her the most noteworthy parts of the Forest. "Good!" said Robin. "So much for Little John; now for Much." He was told that Barbara, sharing her sister's curiosity as to the beauties of the country, had wished to accompany her in these woodland rambles; but that Little John, with praiseworthy prudence, had told the young girl that the responsibility of looking after the one lady was already very great, and that it was impossible for him to accept her company and the extra responsibility involved thereby. Consequently, Much offered his protection to Mistress Barbara, and she accepted it. So the two couples wandered among the trees and into the most mysterious and gloomy recesses of the woods, talking the while of no one knows what. They forgot to look at the objects they had come to see; and the old gnarled oaks, the beeches with their graceful boughs, the secular elms, passed before their eyes without attracting the least attention. Then a coincidence, stranger even than this indifference to the beauties of nature, always led them to remote paths, and they never met till they came to the gate of the Hall as the stars began to peep out.

These walks, repeated daily, sufficiently explained to Robin the absence of his two companions.

It was the evening of a scorching day, and a warm zephyr fanned the air, when Marian and Maude, leaning on the arms of Robin and William, set out from the Hall to take a long walk in the fragrant glades of the forest. Winifred and Barbara followed the two young couples, while Little John and his inseparable friend Much shadowed the two sisters.

"Here I can breathe," said Marian, holding up her pale face to the breeze. "There seems no air in a room, and I long to return to the Forest once again."

"Then life in the woods is very pleasant?" questioned Mistress Barbara.

"Yea," replied Marian; "there is so much sunshine, light, shade, flowers, and foliage."

"Much told me yesterday," continued Barbara, "that Sherwood Forest doth surpass Barnsdale in beauty; but if that is so, it must contain all the marvels of creation, for here we have the most bewitching spots."

"You think Barnsdale Wood very pretty, then, Barbara?" said Robin, concealing a smile.

"It is charming," replied the girl, vivaciously; "there are such beautiful views in it."

"Which part of the wood particularly attracts your attention, cousin?"

"I cannot well reply to your question, Robin; but I think I prefer a valley, which I am certain hath not its equal in old Sherwood Forest."

"And where is this valley?"

"Some distance from here. But you can imagine nothing fresher, more still, or more fragrant than that little spot. Picture to yourself, cousin, a large lawn with sloping sides, on the summit of which all kinds of trees grow in profusion. The different varieties of leaves lit up by the sunshine take on marvellous aspects; now you see before you a curtain of emeralds, anon a veil of multitudinous colours unrolls itself beneath your gaze. The turf which covers this dell is like a large green carpet without a wrinkle to break its smooth surface. Scatter flowers of purple and gold and all the colours of the rainbow over the declivities beneath the trees, imagine a slender thread of water rippling through the shady ravine, and you will have before you the oasis of Barnsdale Forest. And then," continued the girl, "the stillness is so great in this delicious spot, the air one breathes so pure, that the heart swells with joy—in very truth I have never in all my life seen so ravishing a place."

"And where is this enchanted valley, Barbara?" asked Winifred, innocently.

"Oh! then you do not always walk about together?" interrupted Robin, with a smile.

"Yea," added Winifred; "only we always lose each other—no, I mean to say very often—at least sometimes. I mean to say that Little John loses the way, and then we get separated; we seek for each other, but I do not know how it happens that we never meet until we arrive at the Hall. This continual separation is quite accidental, I assure you."

"Yea, truly; quite accidental," Robin returned mockingly; "and no one supposes the contrary. Then why blush, Barbara? Why look down, Winifred? Look at John and Much, neither of them is embarrassed; they know so well that you get lost in the wood without meaning it."

"Yea, i' faith!" answered Much; "and knowing Mistress Barbara's fancy for quiet and retired spots, I took her to the little valley which she hath just described."

"I am forced to believe," said Robin, "that Barbara doth possess a great talent for observation to have been able to take in at one glance all the charming details which she hath just depicted. But tell me, Barbara, did you not find in this oasis of Barnsdale—as you call the vale discovered by Much—something still more charming yet than the trees with varied green, the verdant sward, the murmuring stream and the many-hued flowers?"

Barbara blushed.

"I do not know what you mean, cousin."

"Oh, indeed! Much will understand better than you, I hope. Come now, Much, answer frankly: Hath not Barbara forgotten to tell us of some charming episode connected with your visit to this terrestrial paradise?"

"What episode, Robin?" asked the young man, with the shadow of a smile.

"My discreet friend," replied Robin, "have you never known two young people, attracted by one another, go alone to this delicious retreat, the memory of which is engraved on Barbara's heart?"

Much blushed painfully.

"Well," continued Robin, "two young people, intimate acquaintances of mine, visited your terrestrial paradise a few days ago. Arrived on the flowering banks of the little stream, they seated themselves side by side. At first they admired the landscape, listened to the song of the birds; then for some minutes they remained blind and dumb; then the youth, emboldened by the solitude, the stirring silence of his trembling companion, took her two little hands in his. The maiden did not raise her eyes, but she blushed, and this blush spoke for her. Then, in a voice which to the girl sounded sweeter than the sound of birds, more melodious than the murmur of the breeze, the young man said to her, 'There is no one in all the world I love so much as you; I would rather die than lose your love; and if you will be my wife, you will make me the happiest of men.' Tell me, Barbara," added Robin, with a smile, "do you know whether the maiden granted her lover's fervent prayer?"

"Make no reply to such a very indiscreet question, Barbara!" cried Marian.

"Speak for Barbara, Much," said Robin.

"You ask us such strange questions," replied the young man, strongly inclined to believe that Robin had overheard his *tête-à-tête* with Barbara, "that it is impossible to gather what they mean."

"I' faith, Much," said William, "meseemeth Robin speaks truth, and, judging by your abashed looks and the brilliant colour which o'erspreads my sister's face, you are the lovers of the vale. Upon my word, Barbara, if they call me Will Scarlett because of my ruddy locks, they might e'en call thee Barbara Scarlett, for thy face is well-nigh purple. Is't not so, Maude?"

"Master William," said Barbara, with an air of displeasure, "if thou wert within reach of mine hand, I would have much pleasure in pulling out a handful of thine ugly locks."

"Thou mightest well behave so, an those same locks grew on any head save mine," said William, throwing a look at Much; "but thy brother's head is unassailable. It hath its own particular tyrant—eh, Maude?"

"Yea, Will; but I never pull your hair out."

"That will come, little wife."

"Never," said Maude, with a laugh.

"Then, Much, thou wilt not tell me what answer the maiden gave thee?"

"If you should e'er meet that maiden, you can ask her yourself, Robin."

"I will not fail. And you, Little John, do you know any youth who loves a *tête-à-tête* with a charming lady?"

"Nay, Robin, but if you wish to know these lovers, I will strive to discover them for you," replied Little John, naively.

"I have just thought of something, John," cried Will, bursting out a-laughing. "These lovers of whom Robin speaks are not unknown to thee, and I dare wager what thou wilt that the young man in question might be called my cousin, while the maiden is a sweet lady of this neighbourhood."

"Art wrong, Will," answered John, "it is naught to do with me."

"Certes, I am on the wrong track," returned Will, with a smile; "it could not have been thou, for thou hast never been in love."

"I beg thy pardon, Will," replied the giant, tranquilly. "I love with all my heart, and have long done so, a beautiful and charming maid."

"Ha! ha!" cried Will. "Little John in love; here's something new!"

"And why should not Little John be in love?" asked the youth, good-humouredly. "I ween there is naught extraordinary in that."

"Naught at all, my good friend. I like to see all the world happy, and love is happiness; but, by St. Paul! I should very much like to see thy lady love."

"My lady love!" exclaimed the other. "But who could that be save thine own sister Winifred, Cousin Will? Thy sister, whom I have loved from childhood as you love Maude, or Much loves Barbara."

A general shout of laughter greeted John's frankness, and Winifred, overwhelmed with congratulations, threw a look of tender reproach at the young giant.

"Ah, ha! Much," Robin resumed, "sooner or later truth will out. I hit the mark in fixing upon thee as the hero of the little scene enacted in Barnsdale Wood."

"You witnessed it, then?" asked Much.

"Nay; but I guessed it, or, rather, I recalled mine own impressions. The same thing happened to me a year agone; Marian had enticed me..."

"What, *I* enticed you?" cried the young wife. "I would have you remember that it was *you*, Robin, and had I foreseen then how you would treat me after our marriage..."

"What would you have done in that case?" interrupted Barbara.

"I should have married all the sooner, dear Barbara," replied the young wife, smiling at her husband.

"There, I hope that is an answer which will encourage the confidence of which you have already given secret proof, saucy Barbara. Come, make a clean breast of it; we are all one family. Tell us that you love Much, and Much on his part will avow the same."

"Yea, I will avow it," cried, Much, with deep emotion. "I will cry aloud, 'I love Barbara Gamwell with all my strength.' I will say to all who will listen, 'Barbara's eyes are the light of my day, her sweet thrilling voice echoes in mine ears like the harmonious notes of singing birds; I prefer the company of my dear Barbara to the pleasures of the feast and the elation of the dance beneath the green leaves of spring; I would rather a tender look from her eyes, a smile from her lips or the pressure of her little hand, than all the riches of the world. I am entirely devoted to Barbara, and sooner than do anything to annoy her, I would e'en ask the Sheriff of Nottingham to send me to the gallows.' Yea, good friends, I love the dear maid, and I call down all the holy blessings of Heaven upon her fair head. If she will give me the happiness of protecting her with my name and life, she shall be happy and very, very tenderly beloved."

"Hurrah!" cried Will, throwing his cap into the air, "'tis right well spoken. Dry your eyes, little sister, and I give you permission to present your pink—nay, scarlet—cheeks to this brave wooer. If, instead of being a lusty lad, I were but a feeble maiden, and I had heard such sweet things said, I should have already given my hand and heart to my lover. Would you not have done the same, Maude? You know you would."

"Nay, Will, modesty..."

"We are a family party, there is no need to blush at so natural an action. I am assured, Maude, that you are of mine own opinion. If I were Much and you were Barbara, you would be already in mine arms, and I should embrace you with all my heart."

"I am on William's side," said Robin, smiling a little maliciously. "Barbara must give us a proof of her affection for Much."

Thus called on, the maiden advanced to the centre of the merry group, and said timidly—

"I sincerely believe in the love which Much doth bear me, and I am very grateful to him for it. In return I must avow that...that..."

"That you love him as much as he loves thee," added Will, quickly. "Your speech is slow to-day, little sister. I assure you it took me much less time to make Maude understand that I loved her with my whole heart, did it not, Maude?"

"That is true, Will," replied the young wife.

"Much," continued William, more seriously, "I give thee sweet Barbara to wife; she doth possess all the qualities of a true heart, and thou wilt be a happy husband. Barbara, my love, Much is a good man, a brave Saxon, true as steel. He will never disappoint thy tender hopes; he will love thee for ever."

"For ever and ever," cried Much, taking the hands of his betrothed in his.

"Embrace thy future wife, friend Much," said Will.

The young man obeyed, and, despite Mistress Gamwell's pretended resistance, he touched her crimson cheeks with his lips.

The Knight gave his consent to the marriage of his daughters, and the date of the double wedding was fixed forthwith.

Next morning Robin Hood, Little John, and Will Scarlett were gathered, with about a hundred of their Merrie Men, beneath the old trees of Barnsdale Forest, when a young man, who appeared to have come from a distance, presented himself before Robin.

"Noble master," said he, "I bring you good tidings."

"Very good, George," replied the young man. "Let us hear them quickly. What is it all about?"

"It is about a visit of the Bishop of Hereford. His Lordship, accompanied by a score of his servants, will traverse Barnsdale Wood this very day."

"Bravo! This is indeed good tidings. Dost know at what hour my Lord Bishop will give us the honour of his company?"

"About two o'clock, Captain."

"Good. How didst learn of his Lordship's journey?"

"From one of our men, who, in passing through Sheffield, learnt that the Bishop of Hereford proposed paying a visit to St. Mary's Abbey."

"Art a good lad, George, and I thank thee for thy kind thought in putting me on my guard. My sons," added Robin, "pay heed to my words, and we will have a merry jest. Will Scarlett, take with thee a score of men, and go guard the road near thy father's house. Thou, Little John, go with a like number of companions to the path leading to the north of the Forest. Much, thou wilt post thyself at the eastern side of the wood with the rest of the band. I will take up my position on the high-road. We must not give his Lordship an opportunity of escaping, for I am fain to invite him to take part in a right royal feast; he will be treated nobly, but he must pay for it. As for thee, George, thou wilt choose a deer of good growth and a fine fat roe, and thou wilt prepare two joints to receive the honours of my table."

When his three lieutenants had set out with their little band of men, Robin ordered those who were left to dress themselves as shepherds (the outlaws kept every kind of disguise in their stores), and himself donned a modest smock-frock. This transformation complete, they planted sticks in the ground, to which they suspended the deer, and the flames of a goodly fire, fed with dry branches, soon began to lick the savoury venison.

Towards two o'clock, as George had announced, the Bishop of Hereford and his suite appeared at the end of the road, in the middle of which sat Robin and his men disguised as shepherds.

"The prey approaches," said Robin, with a laugh. "Come, merry friends, baste the meat; here is our guest."

The Bishop, accompanied by his suite, moved quickly, and the noble company soon came up with the shepherds.

At the sight of the gigantic spit turning slowly above the fire, the Prelate gave vent to an outburst of violent anger.

"How is this, rogues? what means...?"

Robin Hood raised his eyes to the Bishop, and looked at him stolidly, but made no reply.

"Do ye not hear me, villains?" repeated the Bishop. "I ask for whom do ye prepare this noble feast?"

"For whom?" repeated Robin, with an admirably affected expression of simplicity.

"Yea, for whom? The deer of this Forest belong to the King, and I deem you mighty insolent varlets in daring to lay hands upon it. Answer my question. For whom is this repast prepared?"

"For ourselves, my Lord," replied Robin.

"For you, fool? for you? What a jest! Never think to make me believe that this profusion of food is for your repast."

"My Lord, I speak truth; we be hungry men, and since the roast is cooked to a turn, we will e'en sit down to it."

"To what estate do ye belong? Who are ye?"

"Simple shepherds who guard our flocks. To-day we wished to seek repose from our labours and to amuse ourselves a little, with which idea we killed the two fine roes you see before you."

"Of a truth, ye wished to amuse yourselves! This is but an artless answer. Come, say, who gave you permission to hunt the King's game?"

"No one."

"No one, varlet! and think ye to calmly enjoy the product of so shameless a theft?"

"Of a surety, my Lord; but an if your Lordship would take your share, we should hold ourselves highly honoured."

"Thine offer is an insult, insolent shepherd; I decline it with scorn. Art not aware that poaching is punishable by death? Peace; enough of these useless words. Prepare to follow me to prison, from whence ye will all be conducted to the gallows."

"The gallows!" cried Robin, with an air of despair.

"Yea, my lad, to the gallows."

"I have no wish to be hanged," groaned Robin Hood, in doleful accents.

Alexandre Dumas

"Of that I am very sure, but it matters little; thou and thy companions deserve the noose. Come, fools, prepare to follow me; I have no time to waste."

"Pardon, my Lord, a thousand pardons. We have sinned in ignorance; be merciful to poor wretches who are more deserving of pity than of blame."

"Poor wretches who eat such good roast meat are not to be pitied. Ah, my fine fellows, you feed yourselves on the King's venison; it is well—very well! Together will we go into the presence of His Majesty, and we shall see if he will grant you the pardon which I refuse."

"My Lord," continued Robin, in a supplicating voice, "we have wives and children; be merciful, I implore you, in the name of their weakness and their innocence. What would happen to the poor creatures without our support?"

"What care I for your wives and children?" returned the Bishop, harshly. "Seize the varlets," he added, turning to his followers, "and if they attempt to escape, slay them without pity."

"My Lord," said Robin Hood, "allow me to give you some good advice. Take back your unjust words; they breathe of violence, and are lacking in Christian charity. Believe me, it were wiser for you to accept the offer I have just made you, to partake of our dinner."

"I forbid you to address another word to me," cried the Bishop, furiously. "Soldiers, seize the robbers!"

"Stand back!" cried Robin, in a voice of thunder, "or, by Our Lady, you will repent it!"

"Have at the vile serfs roundly," repeated the Bishop, "and spare them not."

The Bishop's servants hurled themselves upon the group of Merrie Men, and the *mêlée* threatened to become a bloody one, when Robin wound his horn, and instantly the rest of the band, who, warned of the Bishop's presence, had stolen up quietly, made their appearance.

The first task of the new-comers was to disarm the Bishop's escort.

"My Lord," said Robin to the Prelate, who had fallen dumb with terror on finding into whose hands he had fallen, "you have shown yourself pitiless; we will show no pity neither. What is to be done to the man who would have sent us to the gallows?" asked Robin of his companions.

"His dress must mitigate the severity of his sentence," replied John, quietly; "he must not be made to suffer."

"Your speech is that of an honest man, good Forester."

"Think you so, my Lord?" replied John, quite unconcerned. "Well, I will further disclose to you my peaceful intentions. Instead of torturing you, both body and soul, and killing you by slow degrees, we will simply cut off your head."

"Simply cut off my head!" groaned the Bishop, in a voice of despair.

"Yea," replied Robin; "you must prepare for death, my Lord."

"Robin Hood, have pity on me, I do beseech you!" besought the Bishop, clasping his hands. "Grant me a few hours; I would fain not die without confession."

"Verily, your erstwhile haughtiness hath given place to very great humility, my Lord," responded Robin, coldly; "but this humility doth naught affect me. You are condemned out of your own mouth, therefore prepare your soul to appear before God. Little John," he added, making a sign to his friend, "see to it that the ceremony lacketh naught of due solemnity. Will you follow me, my Lord? I will lead you to the Court of Justice."

Half paralysed with fear, the Bishop dragged himself along, tottering, in the wake of Robin Hood.

When they were arrived at the trysting-tree, Robin made his prisoner sit down on a grassy hillock, and bade one of his men bring some water.

"Will you be pleased, my Lord, to lave your hands and face," asked the young Chief, politely.

Although very much surprised at receiving such a suggestion, the bishop condescendingly acquiesced. This done, Robin added—

"Will you do me the honour of sharing my repast? I am about to dine, for I cannot administer justice fasting."

"I will dine, if you insist upon it," replied the Bishop, in a tone of resignation.

"I do not insist, my Lord; I pray you."

"Then I yield me to your prayer, Sir Robin."

"Good, my Lord; to dinner, then."

With these words, Robin led his guest to the banqueting hall—that is to say, towards a green sward spangled with flowers, where the meal was already set out.

The festive board, laden with dishes, presented a pleasing spectacle, and its appearance seemed to lighten the Prelate's dismal forebodings. Having fasted since the night before, the Bishop was hungry, and the stimulating odour of the venison mounted to his head.

"These," he said, sitting down, "are admirably cooked viands."

"And of a delicious flavor," added Robin, helping his guest to a choice morsel.

By the middle of the feast the Bishop had forgotten his fears; by the time dessert came, he looked upon Robin only as an amiable companion.

"My excellent friend, he said, "your wine is delicious, it warms my heart. A while agone I was cold, I was ill, sorrowful, anxious; now I feel quite light-hearted."

"I am very happy to hear you say so, my Lord, for you praise my hospitality. My guests are generally enchanted at the good cheer they are welcomed here withal. However, there comes a bad quarter of an hour with them when it comes to the settlement of the account. They are very happy to receive, but they are very loth to give; it really seems quite disagreeable to them."

"True, very true," replied the Prelate, not knowing in the least what he meant by this approval. "Yea, truly, such is the case. Give me another bumper, an it please you; meseemeth there is a fire in my veins. Ah! mine host, do you know you lead a very happy life here?"

"That is why we are called the Merrie Men of the Forest."

"That is right, that is right. Now, Sir—I do not rightly know your name—allow me to bid you farewell; I must continue my journey."

"Naught could be more reasonable, my Lord. I pray you, pay your reckoning, and prepare to drink the stirrup-cup."

"Pay my reckoning!" grumbled the Bishop. "Am I, then, in an inn? I believed myself to be in Sherwood Forest."

"My Lord, you are in an inn; I am master of the house, and these men around us are my drawers."

"How say you, all these men are your drawers? But there are at least one hundred and fifty or two hundred."

"Yea, my Lord, not counting the absentees. You must see, then, that with such a following I am bound to make my guests pay as heavily as may be."

"Give me my account," said he, "but treat me in a friendly spirit."

"As a great Lord, Sir Guest, as a great Lord," replied Robin, gaily. "Little John!" he called. The latter ran up. "Make out the charges for my Lord the Bishop of Hereford."

The Prelate looked at John, and began to laugh.

"Well indeed, little, little! they call you little, and you might be a young tree! Come, gentle treasurer, give me my score."

"That is scarce needful, my Lord; only tell me where you keep your money, and I will pay myself."

"Insolent varlet!" said the Bishop, "I forbid you to poke your long fingers into my purse."

"I would spare you the trouble of counting, my Lord."

"The trouble of counting! Think you I am drunk? Go seek my valise and bring it me; I will give you a piece of gold."

Little John hastened to obey the Prelate's command; he opened the valise and found a leathern bag. John emptied it; it contained three hundred pieces of gold.

The Bishop of Hereford, with half-closed eyes, heard John's triumphant exclamations without comprehending them, and when Robin said to him—

"My Lord, we thank you for your generosity," he only closed his eyes completely and muttered some confused words, of which Robin caught the following only—

"Saint Mary's Abbey at once..."

"He is fain to set forth," said John.

"Order his horse to be brought up," added Robin.

At a sign from John one of the Merrie Men brought up the horse ready saddled and with its head garlanded with flowers.

The Bishop was hoisted half asleep into his saddle, and tied on to prevent a fall, which might prove serious; then, followed by his little company, enlivened by the wine and good cheer, he took the road to St. Mary's.

A band of the Merrie Men, mingling in a friendly way with the Prelate's escort, accompanied the cavalcade to the gates of the Abbey.

It need scarce be added that after ringing the porter's bell the Foresters hasted away as fast as their horses could carry them.

We will not attempt to depict the surprise and horror of the reverend brothers when the Bishop of Hereford appeared before them with a red face, staggering gait, and disordered garments.

On the morrow of this fatal day the Bishop was mad with shame, rage, and humiliation. He passed long hours in prayer, asking God to pardon his faults, and imploring the Divine protection against that rogue and villain Robin Hood.

At the request of the outraged Prelate the Prior of St. Mary's armed fifty men and placed them at the disposal of his guest. Then, his blood boiling with rage, the Bishop led his little army in pursuit of the famous outlaw.

That very day Robin, desiring to see for himself how Sir Richard of the Plain was faring, went alone along a forest path leading to the main road. The sound of an approaching cavalcade attracted his attention; he hastened his steps in the direction of the sound, and found himself face to face with the Bishop of Hereford.

"Robin Hood!" cried the Bishop, recognising our hero. "It is Robin Hood! Traitor, surrender yourself!"

As may be well imagined, Robin Hood had no desire to comply with this request. Surrounded on all sides, unable to defend himself or even to call his Merrie Men to his aid, he slipped daringly between two horsemen, who made as if to block his passage, and darted with the swiftness of a deer towards a little house standing about a quarter of a mile away.

The Bishop's men started in pursuit of the young man, but, being forced to make a *détour*, they could not reach as soon as he did the house in which he sought shelter.

Robin Hood found the door of the house open, and entering, he barricaded the windows, without paying any heed to the cries of the old woman within seated at her spinning-wheel.

"Have no fear, good mother," said Robin, when he had finished closing the doors and windows; "I am no thief, but a poor unfortunate man, to whom you can render a service."

"What service? What is your name?" demanded the old dame, in very uneasy tones.

"I am an outlaw, good mother; I am Robin Hood. The Bishop of Hereford pursues me to take my life."

"Eh, what? You are Robin Hood?" said the peasant dame, clasping her hands—"the noble and generous Robin Hood! God be praised for enabling a poor creature like myself to pay her debt of gratitude to the charitable outlaw! Look at me, my son, and search the memory of your good deeds for the features of her who speaks with you now. It is two years agone. An ungrateful woman would say you came in here by chance; I say you were sent by Divine Providence. You found me quite alone. I had just lost my husband; there was naught left for me but death. Your sweet and consoling words gave me back courage, strength, and health. The next day a man, sent by your orders, brought me food, clothing, and money. I asked him the name of my generous benefactor, and he answered me, 'He is called Robin Hood.' Since that day, my son, I have always remembered you in my prayers. My house and my life are yours; do as you will with your servant."

"I thank you, good mother," replied Robin Hood, cordially pressing the woman's trembling hands. "I crave your help, not through fear of danger, but to avoid useless shedding of blood. The Bishop is accompanied by fifty men, and, as you see, a struggle between us is impossible—I am but one."

"If your enemies discover your retreat they will kill you," said the old woman.

"Be not uneasy, good mother. They shall not accomplish their end. We will invent a plan for saving ourselves from their violence."

"What plan, my son? Speak; I am ready to obey you."

"Will you exchange your garments for mine?"

"Exchange our garments!" cried the old dame. "I fear, my son, that would be but a useless trick. How could you transform a woman of my age into a gay young gentleman?"

"I will disguise you so well, good mother," replied Robin, "that it will be quite possible to deceive the soldiers, to whom my face is probably unknown. You must feign to be drunk, and my Lord of Hereford will be so anxious to seize my person that he will look only at your dress."

The transformation was quickly effected. Robin put on the old woman's grey gown; then he helped her to dress herself in his hose, tunic, and buskins.

This done, Robin hid the peasant's grey hair under his elegant cap, and attached his weapons to her belt.

The double disguise was just completed when the soldiers arrived at the door of the cottage.

First they knocked repeatedly; then a solider proposed that he should make his horse kick in the door.

The Prelate received the proposition favourably, whereupon the horseman, turning his horse round, backed it against the door, at the same time pricking it up with his lance. This produced an effect contrary to that expected by the soldier, for the animal reared and threw his rider to the ground.

This accident to the poor soldier, who shot through the air with the rapidity of an arrow, had a disastrous effect. The Bishop, who had come up to see the door fall in and to prevent Robin Hood from escaping, was struck violently in the face by the soldier's spurs.

The pain caused by this blow so exasperated the old man that, without thinking of the unjust cruelty of his rage, he raised the mace which he carried in his hand as a token of his rank, and unmercifully beat the unlucky wretch, who lay half dead under the hoofs of the plunging horse.

In the midst of this valiant proceeding the cottage door opened.

"Close your ranks!" cried the Bishop, in a tone of command; "close your ranks!"

The soldiers pressed in confusion around the cottage.

The Bishop dismounted, but as he touched the ground, he stumbled over the body of the soldier, where it lay weltering in blood, and fell head foremost through the open doorway.

The confusion caused by this ludicrous accident served Robin Hood's turn admirably. Stunned and breathless, the bishop saw, without examining closely, a figure standing motionless in the darkest corner of the room.

"Seize the rogue!" cried his Lordship, pointing out the old woman to his soldiers. "Gag him, bind him to a horse. You are answerable for his safe keeping with your lives, for if ye let him escape, ye shall all hang without mercy."

The soldiers rushed upon the person indicated by their leader's furious outcry, and in default of a gag they muffled up the old woman's face in a large handkerchief which happened to be handy.

Bold to rashness, Robin Hood in a trembling voice implored mercy for the prisoner; but the Bishop thrust him aside and left the cottage, after enjoying the intense satisfaction of seeing his enemy bound hand and foot on the back of a horse.

Sick and half blinded by the wound which had gashed his face, his Lordship remounted and ordered his men to follow him to the Trysting Tree of the outlaws. It was upon the highest branch of this that the Bishop proposed to hang Robin. The worthy man was determined to give the outlaws a terrible warning of the fate in store for them, if they continued to follow their worthless leader's mode of life.

No sooner had the cavalcade disappeared into the depths of the wood, than Robin Hood left the cottage and ran towards the Trysting Tree.

He had just entered a glade when he perceived Little John, Will Scarlett, and Much at some little distance.

"See there in the centre of the clearing," said Little John to his two friends, "what a strange creature approaches; it looks like an old witch. By'r Lady, if I thought the vixen had evil intentions, I would let fly an arrow at her."

"Thine arrow could not touch her," replied Will, laughing.

"And wherefore, I pray thee? Dost doubt my skill?"

"Not the least in the world; but an if, as thou dost suppose, this woman is a witch, she could arrest the flight of thine arrow."

"By my faith!" quoth Much, who had kept his attention fixed on the strange figure, "I share Little John's opinion. This doth seem a very extraordinary old dame; her figure is gigantic, and, moreover, she doth not walk like a woman, she covers the ground with prodigious strides. Verily she affrighteth me; and if you will suffer it,

Will, we will e'en prove the power of the sorcery she seems so richly endowed withal."

"Act not so rashly, Much," replied Will. "The garments this poor creature wears claim our respect; and for me, you know I could not hurt a woman. Beside, who knows whether this strange creature be verily a witch? One must not judge by appearances, for ofttimes it happens that an ugly rind doth enclose an excellent fruit. In spite of her ridiculous looks, the poor old dame is, mayhap, a good wench and an honest Christian. Be kind to her, and, to make the indulgence easier, call to mind Robin's orders, which do straitly forbid any hostile or even disrespectful doings toward women."

Little John made as if to bend his bow and take aim at the supposed witch.

"Hold!" cried a deep and sonorous voice.

The three men uttered a cry of surprise.

"I am Robin Hood," added the person who had puzzled the Foresters so sorely, and while declaring his name, Robin tore off the head-dress which covered his head and part of his face. "I was quite unrecognisable, then?" asked our hero, as he joined his comrades.

"You are very ugly, my good friend," replied Will.

"Why did you assume such an unbecoming disguise?" asked Much.

Robin related to his friends as briefly as possible the mishap which had befallen him.

"Now," he continued, having ended his tale, "we must think about defending ourselves. First of all, I must have clothes. You, good Much, will do me the service of hastening to the store-house and bringing me thence some suitable garments. Meanwhile, Will and Little John will assemble all the men who are in the Forest round about the Trysting Tree. Hasten, my lads; I promise you compensation for all the trouble caused us by my Lord Bishop of Hereford."

Little John and Will dashed off into the Forest in different directions, while Much went in search of the garments required by Robin.

An hour later Robin, arrayed in an elegant hunting-suit, arrived at the Trysting Tree.

John brought sixty men, and Will had collected forty.

Robin dispersed his men among the thickets which formed an impenetrable background to the clearing, and seated himself at the foot of the great tree designed by his Lordship to serve as a gallows.

Scarce were these arrangements completed, ere the ground echoed with the sound of the approaching cavalcade, and the Bishop arrived, followed by his escort.

When the soldiers had made their way to the middle of the clearing, the blast of a horn rang through the air, the foliage of the young trees stirred, and from every side emerged men armed to the teeth.

A cold shudder ran through the Bishop at sight of the Foresters' formidable appearance. The latter ranged themselves in battle array at a sign from their Chief, who had not yet been perceived by the Prelate; he threw a glance of dismay around him, and discovered a young man clad in a scarlet tunic, with words of command on his lips, directing the band of outlaws.

"Who is this man?" demanded the Bishop of a soldier standing beside the prisoner, who was bound to a horse.

"That man is Robin Hood," replied the prisoner, in trembling tones.

"Robin Hood!" quoth the Bishop. "And who, then, art thou, wretch?"

"I am but a woman, my Lord—a poor old woman."

"Woe be to thee, malignant hag!" cried the infuriated Bishop, "woe be to thee! Come, my men," continued his Lordship, beckoning to his men, "charge down the glade. Fear nothing; force a road with your swords through the ranks of these rogues. Forward, my brave lads, forward!"

Doubtless the brave lads thought that if the order to attack the bandits was easy enough to give, it was more difficult to carry out, for they did not stir.

At a signal from Robin, the Foresters adjusted their arrows, lifting their bows with admirable uniformity; and their reputation for skill was so widely known and so renowned that the Bishop's soldiers, unable to remain inactive, stooped in their saddles as one man.

"Down with your arms!" cried Robin Hood. "Unbind the prisoner."

The soldiers obeyed the young man's orders.

"My good mother," said Robin, leading the old woman beyond the glade, "go home now, and to-morrow I will send you a reward for your kind action. Go quick. I have no time to thank you now, but forget not that my gratitude is great."

The old dame kissed Robin Hood's hands, and went her way, accompanied by a guide.

"O Lord, have pity on me!" cried the Bishop, wringing his hands.

Robin Hood drew nearer to his enemy.

"Welcome, my Lord," said he, in a wheedling tone, "and permit me to thank you for your visit. My hospitality, I see, proved so attractive that you could not resist the desire of once more partaking its delights."

The Bishop gazed despairingly at Robin, and a deep sigh escaped him.

"You appear downcast, my Lord," Robin continued. "What troubles you? Are not you pleased to meet with me again?"

"I cannot well say that I am pleased," replied the Bishop, "for, indeed, the plight in which I find myself renders that impossible. You can readily guess my intention in coming here, and your conscience will acquit you if you avenge yourself on me, for you will be striking an enemy. However, let me say this much. Let me go free, and never, under any circumstances whatever, will I seek to harm you. Let me go with my men, and your soul will not have to answer to God for a mortal sin, for such it would surely be, were you to attempt the life of a high priest of the Holy Church."

"I detest murder and violence, my Lord," replied Robin Hood, "as mine actions do daily prove. I never attack; I am content to defend my life and the lives of my brave followers, who trust in me. Did I cherish in my heart the least sentiment of hate or rancour toward you, my Lord, I would inflict on you the same death which you had intended for me. But it is not so. I bear you no ill will, and I take no vengeance on those who have not succeeded in harming me. Therefore I will set you free, but on one condition only."

"Speak, Sir," said the Bishop, graciously.

"You must promise to respect my independence and the liberty of my men; you must swear that at no future period and under no circumstances whatever will you lend a hand to any attempt upon my life."

"I have willingly promised to do you no harm," replied the Bishop, suavely.

"A promise is not binding on an unscrupulous conscience, my Lord. I must have an oath."

"I swear by St. Paul to let you live as you please."

"Very good, my Lord; you are free."

"I thank you a thousand times, Robin Hood. Will you be so good as to give an order to my men to assemble; they have dispersed, and are fraternising with your companions."

"I will do as you wish, my Lord; in a few minutes the men will be in the saddle. In the mean time will you accept some slight refreshment?"

"Nay, nay! I wish for naught," the Bishop answered hastily, terrified at the mere mention of the word.

"You have been long fasting, my Lord, and a slice of pasty..."

"Not a morsel, good host—not a mouthful even."

"A cup of good wine, then?"

"Nay, nay, a hundred times nay!"

"You will neither eat nor drink with me, my Lord?"

"I am neither hungry nor thirsty. I wish to depart, that is all. Do not seek to detain me longer, I pray you."

"As you please, my Lord. Little John," added Robin, "his Reverence wishes to leave us."

"His Reverence is at perfect liberty," growled John. "I will give him his bill."

"My bill!" repeated the Bishop, in surprise. "What do you mean? I have neither eaten nor drunken."

"Oh! That boots not," replied Little John, calmly; "from the moment you enter the hostelry, you must share its expenses. Your men are hungry; they ask for food. Your horses are satisfied already; nor must we be the sufferers by your abstemiousness, and receive naught, because it doth not please you to accept of anything. We demand largess for the servants who have had the trouble of entertaining man and beast."

"Take what you will," answered the Bishop, impatiently, "and let me go."

"Is the money still in the same place?" asked Little John.

"It is here," replied the Bishop, showing a little leathern bag attached to his saddle-bow.

"It feels heavier than at your last visit, my Lord."

"I should well think so," responded the Bishop, making a desperate effort to appear cool and calm; "it contains a much larger sum."

"You shall watch me take it away, my Lord; and may I ask how much there is in this elegant saddle-bag?"

"Five hundred pieces of gold..."

"Admirable! What generosity to come here with such a treasure!" said the young man, ironically.

"This treasure," stammered the Bishop—"shall we not divide it? You dare not utterly despoil me—rob me of so large a sum?"

"Rob you!" repeated Little John, disdainfully. "What do you mean by such a word? Do you not comprehend the difference between robbing and taking from a man what is not his? You have obtained this money on false pretences; you took it from those who needed it, and I shall return it to them. Thus you see, my Lord, I do not rob you."

"We call our way the woodland philosophy," said Robin, with a laugh.

"The legality of such philosophy is doubtful," returned the Bishop; "but having no means of defence, I must submit to anything you may exact. Therefore, take my purse."

"I have another request to make, my Lord," Little John continued.

"What is it?" questioned the Bishop, anxiously.

"Our spiritual adviser," replied Little John, "is not at Barnsdale just now, and as it is long since we have profited by his pious instructions, we would beg of you, my Lord, to say a Mass for us."

"What profane request is this you dare make to me?" cried the Bishop. "I would liever die than do aught so impious."

"Nevertheless, it is your duty, my Lord," replied Robin, "to help us at all times to adore the Lord. Little John is right; for long weeks we have not been able to take part in the Holy Office of the Mass, and we would not lose this fortunate opportunity; I pray you, therefore, be so kind as to prepare yourself to satisfy our very proper demands."

"It would be a mortal sin, a crime, and I should expect to be struck by the hand of God, did I commit this unworthy sacrilege!" replied the Bishop, purple with rage.

"My Lord," continued Robin, gravely, "we reverence with the most Christian humility the divine symbols of the Catholic faith, and, believe me, you will never find, even within the walls of your vast Cathedral, a more attentive or more select congregation than the Outlaws of Sherwood Forest."

"Can I put any faith in your words?" asked the Bishop, doubtfully.

"Yea, my Lord, and you will soon recognise the truth of them."

"Then I will believe you. Conduct me to the Chapel."

"This way, my Lord."

Robin, followed by the Bishop, made for an enclosure at a short distance from the Trysting Tree. There, in the centre of a declivity appeared an altar of earth embellished with a thick layer of moss sprinkled with flowers. All the vessels necessary for the celebration of the Holy Sacrifice were disposed on the high altar with exquisite taste, and His Reverence marveled at the beauty of this natural shrine.

It was a touching spectacle to see the band of 150 or 200 men kneeling in prayer with bared heads.

After Mass the Merrie Men testified their gratitude to the Bishop, and he had been so astonished at their respectful attitude during the celebration of the Holy Office that he could not resist putting a host of questions to Robin as to his manner of life beneath the trees of the old Forest.

Whilst Robin responded with a charming courtesy to the Bishop's questions, the foresters placed before the soldiers a substantial repast, and Much looked after the preparation of the most delicate feast that had ever been served in the greenwood.

Led insensibly toward the merry revellers by Robin, the Bishop watched them with an envious eye, and the sight of their gaiety dissipated the last vestiges of his bad temper.

"Your men employ their time well," said Robin, pointing out the most voracious group amongst them.

"They certainly eat with a good appetite."

"They must be hungry, my Lord; it is two o'clock, and I myself feel the need of something. Will you play your part in a little unceremonious dinner?"

"Thank you, my dear host," replied the Bishop, trying to remain deaf to the repeated appeals of his stomach; "I wish for nothing, absolutely nothing, although I *am* a little hungry."

"You should never disregard the calls of nature, my Lord," replied Robin, gravely. "Mind and body alike suffer thereby, and the health is injured. Come, let us take our places on this green turf; they will bring us something, and you need only eat a little bread, an if you be afraid of retarding your departure."

"Am I obliged to obey you?" said the Bishop, with a vainly dissimulated expression of joy.

"You are not constrained, my Lord," said Robin, maliciously, "and if you are not pleased to taste of this delicious venison pasty or the exquisite wine contained in this bottle, abstain, I pray you; for it is even more dangerous to force the stomach to receive food than to deprive it of all nourishment for several hours."

"Oh, I do not force my stomach," replied the Bishop, laughing. "I am endowed with an excellent appetite, and as I have been long fasting, why, I think I will e'en accept your kind invitation."

"To table, then, my Lord, and a good appetite!"

The Bishop of Hereford dined well. He was fond of the bottle, and the wine Robin Hood poured out for him was so heady that at the end of the repast the Bishop was quite drunk, and towards evening he returned to St. Mary's Abbey in a condition of mind and body which drew forth fresh cries of horror and indignation from the pious Monks of that Monastery.

CHAPTER VI

"I should much like to know how the Bishop of Hereford finds himself to-day," said Will Scarlett to his cousin Little John, who, followed by Much, was accompanying Will to Barnsdale.

"The poor Prelate's head must be a little heavy," replied Much, "though one would think that his Lordship was accustomed to the abuse of wine."

"Your observation is very just, my friend," replied John; "my Lord of Hereford doth possess the faculty of drinking heavily without losing his senses."

"Robin treated him right pleasantly," said Much. "Does he act thus toward every Ecclesiastic he encounters?"

"Yea, when these same Ecclesiastics, like the Bishop of Hereford, do abuse their spiritual and temporal power to rob the Saxon people; it hath even happened to Robin not only to await the arrival of these pious travellers, but eke to go out of his own way to put himself in theirs."

"What do you mean by 'go out of his way'?" said Much.

"I will tell you a story as we go along which will explain my words. One morning Robin Hood learned that two Black Friars, carrying a large sum of money to their Abbey, would traverse a part of Sherwood Forest. This was good news for Robin, as our funds were on the decline, and the arrival of the money would be most opportune. Without a word to any one (the waylaying of two Monks was but a small affair), Robin, dressed in a long pilgrim's robe, posted himself in the road the two Friars must take. He had not long to wait, for the Monks soon appeared, two large men sitting squarely in their saddles.

"Robin advanced to meet them, bowed to the ground, and, seizing as he rose the bridles of the two horses, which were pacing side by side, said in pitiable accents, 'Bless you, holy brethren, and let me tell you how glad I am to have met you; 'tis a great happiness for me, and one for which I humbly give thanks to Heaven.'

"'What means this deluge of words?' asked one of the Monks.

"'It expresseth my joy, Father. You are the representatives of the God of goodness, you are the reflection of Divine mercy. I need help, I am unhappy, I am hungry; brothers, I die of hunger, give me the charity of some food.'

"'We have no provisions with us,' replied the Monk who had first spoken, 'therefore cease your useless demands, and let us pursue our way in peace.'

"Robin Hood, who still held the bridles of the horses in his hands, prevented the Monks from escaping him.

"'Brothers,' he went on in a still sadder and weaker voice, 'have pity on my misery, and as you have no bread to give me, give me instead a small piece of money. I have wandered in this wood since yesterday morning, and have neither eaten nor drunk. Good brothers, in the name of the Holy Mother of Christ, give me, I conjure you, this small charity.'

"'See here, foolish babbler, let go of our bridles; leave us in peace; we do not wish to waste our time with a witless loon like you.'

"'Yea,' added the second Monk, repeating word for word the speech of his companion, 'we do not wish to waste our time with a witless loon like you.'

"'For mercy's sake, good Monks, a few pence to keep me from dying of hunger.'

"'Even supposing that I were fain to give you an alms, thick-headed mendicant, 'twould be impossible, for we do not possess a farthing.'

"'All the same, brothers, you have not the appearance of men deprived of all resources; you are well mounted, well equipped, and your jovial faces shine with good cheer.'

"'We had some money a few hours agone, but we have been despoiled by robbers.'

"'They have not left us a penny piece,' added the Monk, whose mission seemed to be to repeat the words of his superior like an echo.

"'I verily believe,' said Robin, 'that ye both lie with a rare impudence.'

"'Thou dost dare to accuse us of falsehood, thou miserable rogue?' cried the fat Monk.

"'Yea, first because ye have not been robbed, for there are no robbers in the old Forest of Sherwood; and then ye tried to deceive me in saying that ye had no money. I hate falsehood, and I love to know the truth. So you will see it is but natural I should assure myself by mine own investigations of the falseness of your words.'

"As he finished speaking, Robin let fall the bridles of the horses and put his hand on a bag which hung from the first Monk's saddle-bow, who, startled, put spurs to his horse and made off at a gallop, closely followed by his companion. Robin, who, as you know, is fleet as a deer, overtook the travellers, and at a stroke unhorsed them both.

"'Spare us, worthy mendicant,' murmured the fat Monk; 'have pity on your brethren. I assure you we have neither money nor food to offer you, wherefore it is a sheer impossibility to exact immediate help from us.'

"' We have naught, worthy mendicant,' added the Father Superior's echo—a poor lean devil, now livid with fear. 'We cannot give you what we have not ourselves!'

"'Well, Fathers,' Robin continued, 'I would fain put faith in the sincerity of your words. Therefore will I point out to you both a means of obtaining a little money. We will all three kneel down and ask the Holy Virgin to help us. Our Lady hath never abandoned me in the time of my need, and I am sure she will hearken favourably to my supplications. I was engaged in prayer when ye appeared at the end of the road, and, thinking that Heaven had sent you to my assistance, I put my modest request to you. Your refusal hath not discouraged me. Ye are not the emissaries of Providence, that is all; but ye are—or should be—holy men: we will pray, and our united voices will the better carry our invocations to the feet of the Lord.'

"The two Monks refused to kneel, and Robin Hood could only constrain them to do so by threatening to search their pockets."

"What," interrupted Will Scarlett, "they all three fell on their knees to ask Heaven to send them money?"

"Yea," replied the story-teller, "and they prayed, by Robin's orders, aloud and in an audible voice."

"It must have made a funny picture," said Will.

"Very funny indeed. Robin had enough self-control to remain serious, and listened gravely to the Monks' prayers. 'Holy Virgin,' said they, 'send us some money to save us from harm.' It is unnecessary to tell you that the money came not. The Monks' voices took every minute sadder and more lamentable accents, so that at length Robin could control himself no longer, but broke into a hearty peal of laughter.

"The Monks, reassured by this transport of mirth, attempted to rise, but Robin raised his staff and asked, 'Have ye received any money?'

"'No,' they replied, 'none.'

"'Then pray once more.'

"The Monks bore this wearisome torture for an hour; then they began to wring their hands in despair, to tear their hair and weep with rage. They were spent with fatigue and humiliation, but they still protested that they possessed nothing.

"'The Holy Virgin hath never abandoned me,' quoth Robin, to console them. 'I have not the proofs of her goodness as yet, but I shall not have much longer to await them. Therefore, my friends, be not disheartened, but, on the contrary, pray the more fervently.'

"The two Monks groaned so dismally that at length Robin got tired of listening to them.

"'Now, my dear brothers,' he said to them, 'let us see how much money Heaven hath sent us.'

"'Not a farthing,' cried the fat Friar.

"' Not a farthing?' repeated Robin. ' How is that? My good brothers, tell me, could ye be quite sure I had no money, even though I did affirm the emptiness of my pockets?'

"'No, certainly we could not be quite sure,' said one of the Monks.

"'There is always a means of ascertaining.'

"'What is that?' asked the fat Monk.

"'It is quite simple,' replied Robin; 'you would have to search me. But it doth not concern you greatly whether I have money or no, that question interesting myself alone. Now I am e'en going to take the liberty of searching your pockets.'

"'We cannot submit to such an outrage,' cried both Monks with one voice.

"'It is not an outrage, my brothers; I only wish to prove to you that if Heaven hath heard my prayers, it hath sent me succour through your holy hands.'

"'We have nothing, nothing!'

"'It is of that I wish to assure myself. Whatever sum of money hath fallen to you jointly, we will divide, one part for you and the other for myself. Search yourselves, I pray you, and tell me what you possess.'

"The Monks obeyed mechanically; each put a hand into his pocket, but brought nothing whatever out.

"'I see,' said Robin Hood, 'that you would fain give me the pleasure of searching you myself; so be it, then.'

"The Monks objected strenuously, but Robin Hood, armed with his terrible staff, threatened so seriously to beat them unmercifully that they resigned themselves to a close search. After seeking for some minutes, Robin got together 500 golden crowns. In despair at the loss of all this pelf, the fat Monk asked Robin, anxiously, 'Will you not share the money with us?'

"'Do you really think it was sent you by Heaven since we have been together?' replied Robin, looking at the Monk sternly. The Monks were silent. 'You have lied; you protested that you had no money when you carried in your pockets the ransom of a good man; you refused an alms to one who said that he was famished and dying. Do you think, either of you, this was the conduct of a Christian? However, I pardon you. I will keep the promise I made you; here are fifty gold crowns for each of you. Go, and if upon your way ye should meet with a poor beggar, remember that Robin Hood hath left you the means of helping him.'

"At the name of Robin Hood the Monks trembled, and gazed stupidly at our friend. Without taking any notice of their affrighted looks, Robin saluted them and disappeared into the glade. Hardly had the sound of his footsteps died away, ere the Monks threw themselves upon their horses and fled without a glance behind."

"Robin must have been very skilfully disguised not to have been recognised by the Monks," said Much.

"Robin Hood is wonderfully clever at that, as you have seen for yourself in the way he counterfeited the old woman. I could cite hundreds of examples in which he was disguised and not recognised, and I assure you it was a merry jest he played upon the Town-Reeve of Nottingham."

"Yea," said Much, "it was a pretty jest, and it made a noise; every one laughed at the Reeve and applauded Robin's audacity."

"What was that?" asked William. "I have never heard of it."

"What, know you not of Robin's adventure as a butcher?"

"Nay; but tell me the tale, Little John."

"Willingly. About four years agone a great dearth of meat was felt in Nottinghamshire. The butchers kept the price of meat so high that only the rich could furnish their tables withal. Robin Hood, who is always on the look-out for news, learned of this state of things, and resolved to find a remedy for the sufferings of the poor. One market day he lay in wait upon the road through the Forest to be taken by a cattle-dealer, who was the chief purveyor to the town of Nottingham. Robin met his man mounted upon a thoroughbred and driving before him an immense herd of cattle, and he at once bought the herd, the mare, the butcher's consent and his secrecy, and as a guarantee of the last purchase, he confided the man to our care until his own return to the Forest.

"Robin, who intended to sell his meat at a very low price, thought that if he neglected to procure protection—for instance, that of the Reeve—the butchers might combine against him, and defeat his good intentions toward the poor. The Reeve kept a large Inn, where the dealers of the neighbourhood met together when they came to Nottingham. Robin knew this, and to prevent any strife betwixt himself and the other dealers, he took his beasts to the Market Place, picked out the fattest animal, and led it to the Town Reeve's Inn.

"The latter was standing at his door, and was much struck by the appearance of the young bullock Robin was leading. Our friend, delighted at the great man's welcome—which was, perhaps, somewhat interested—told him he possessed the finest drove in the Market, and that he would be well pleased an if the Reeve would accept a bullock as a present.

"The Reeve protested modestly against so rich a gift.

"'Sir Reeve,' continued Robin, 'I am ignorant of the customs of this country. I do not know my fellow dealers, and I greatly fear me they may seek to fasten a quarrel upon me. I should therefore be obliged if you would extend your protection to one who is only too anxious to please you.'

"The Reeve swore (for the moment his gratitude equalled the bullock in size) that he would hang any man who should dare to molest our friend; and he declared further that Robin was a good fellow, and the best butcher who had ever sold him meat.

"With mind at rest on this important point, Robin returned to the Market Place, and when the sales began, a crowd of poor people came to ask the price of the meat; but, unhappily for their small purses, the price was still very high. When he saw the prices fixed, Robin offered as much meat for a penny as his neighbours were selling for three.

"The news of this extraordinary cheapness spread rapidly through the town, and the poor flocked in from all sides. Robin then gave them for a penny about as much as his neighbours could give for five. Soon it was known in every corner of the Market that Robin sold only to the poor. Thus they formed an excellent opinion of him, while his fellow-dealers, who were not disposed to follow his example, looked upon him as a prodigal who, in an access of generosity, was squandering the best part of his wealth; so acting on this supposition, they sent to Robin all those to whom they could sell nothing.

"Towards mid-day the cattle-dealers consulted together, and with one accord decided that they must make the acquaintance of the new-comer. One of them, detaching himself from the rest, approached Robin, and said—

"'Good friend and brother, your conduct seems passing strange; for, by your leave, it quite ruins the trade. But, on the other hand, as your intentions are excellent, we can only congratulate you heartily, and give warm praise to so admirable a sentiment of generosity. My companions, enraptured with your goodness of heart, charge me to present their compliments and to invite you to dinner in their names.'

"'I accept their invitation with the greatest pleasure,' replied Robin, gaily, 'and I am ready to follow wherever you are pleased to lead me.'

"'We usually meet at the Town Reeve's Inn,' answered the butcher, 'and if that house is not out of your way...'

"'Why, certainly not,' interrupted Robin. 'On the contrary, I shall be most happy to be in the company of a man whom you honour with your confidence.'

"'In that case, Master, we will end the day right merrily.'"

"Were you with Robin then?" asked Much, surprised to hear the narrator enter into so much detail.

"Of course. Do you think I could have allowed Robin to expose himself alone to the danger of being recognised? He had ordered me to keep aloof; but I did not consider myself bound to obey his order, and I was almost at his side. All at once he became aware of my presence, and, seizing my hand, he angrily reproached me for my disobedience. In a low voice I explained my motive for disregarding his orders. He calmed down at once, and regarding me with that sweet smile you know so well, he said—

"'Mingle with the crowd, John, and while keeping an eye on me, look to thine own safety also.' I obeyed him, and disappeared in the crowd. When Robin and the gay band of butchers set out for the Reeve's Inn, I followed in their wake, and entered the dining-hall along with him.

"Ordering a good meal, I took my place in the embrasure of a window.

"Robin was very merry that day, and toward the end of dinner he invited them to drink of the best wine in the cellar, adding that he would bear this last expense. As you may imagine, Robin's generous offer was received with acclamation; the wine went round the room, and I had my share with the rest.

"When the merriment was at its height, the Reeve appeared in the doorway.

"Robin invited him to take a seat. He accepted, and as Robin seemed to be the guest of honour, he asked him for news of Robin Hood.

"'Tis a cunning rascal!' cried one of the butchers; 'a fine blade, a rare wit, and a good lad.'

"Then the Reeve perceived me. I was not drunk, and my sober face inspired him with a desire to question me.

"'That young man,' said he, indicating Robin by a glance, 'is doubtless a prodigal who, having sold lands, house, or castle, intends to squander his money foolishly.'

"'It may well be so,' I replied with indifference.

"'Maybe he doth still possess some wealth,' continued the Reeve.

"'That is very likely, Master.'

"'Do you think he would be disposed to sell his remaining cattle cheap?'

"'I do not know; but there is one very simple way of finding out.'

"'What is that?' asked the Reeve, innocently.

"'Why, to ask him thyself.'

"'You are right, Sir Stranger.' Saying which the Reeve approached Robin, and, after paying him some pompous compliments on his generosity, he congratulated him on the noble use to which he was putting his fortune. 'My young friend,' added the Reeve, 'have you not some cattle to sell? I will find you a purchaser, and, while rendering you this service, permit me to remark that a man of your rank and appearance cannot well become a cattle-dealer without compromising his dignity.'

"Robin perfectly understood the true motive of this crafty speech; he began to laugh, and answered the obliging Reeve that he possessed a thousand head of cattle, and that he would dispose of them willingly for five hundred golden crowns.

"'I will offer you three hundred,' said the Reeve.

"'At present prices,' Robin continued, 'my beasts are worth, taking one with another, two crowns a head.'

"'If you will consent to sell the whole herd, I will give you three hundred crowns; and I might remark, my gallant gentleman, that three hundred gold crowns in your purse would be worth more than one thousand beasts in your pastures. Come, decide; the bargain will be for three hundred gold crowns.'

"'Tis too little,' replied Robin, throwing a furtive look at me.

"'A liberal heart like yours, my Lord,' replied the Reeve, trying to flatter, 'should not haggle over a few crowns. Come, let us strike a bargain. Where are your cattle? I should like to see them all together.'

"'All together!' repeated Robin, laughing at an idea which struck him.

"'Certainly, my young friend; and if the pasture of this magnificent herd is not very far from here, we could ride over and conclude the bargain there. I will take the money, and if you are reasonable, the matter can be settled before we return to Nottingham.'

"'I possess a few acres about a mile from the town,' replied Robin; 'my beasts are penned there, and there you may see them at your ease.'

"'A mile from Nottingham!' replied the Reeve—'some acres....I know the neighbourhood, and I cannot quite make out the situation of your property.'

"'Silence!' whispered Robin, leaning toward the Reeve. 'I desire for private reasons to conceal my name and quality. A word of explanation as to the whereabouts of my cattle would betray a secret required in mine own interest. You take me, do you not?'

"'Perfectly, my young friend,' replied the Reeve, winking slyly; 'friends are to be feared, the family dreaded. I understand, I understand.'

"'You possess an admirable penetration of mind,' said Robin, mysteriously, 'and I am tempted to believe that we understand each other wonderfully. Well, an if you like, we will profit by the inattention of the butchers, and make off secretly. Are you ready to follow me?'

"'How now! 'tis I who wait for you. I will have our horses saddled with all haste.'

"'Go, then; I will rejoin you immediately.'

"The Reeve left the room, and at Robin's orders I went to seek our companions, whom I had posted, in case of misadventure, within sound of his horn, and announced the Town Reeve's visit to them.

"A few minutes after my departure the latter took Robin up to his private lodging, presented him to his wife, a pretty woman of some twenty years, and begging him to take a seat, said he would go and count his money.

"When the Reeve returned to the room in which he had left Robin alone with his wife, he found the young man at the feet of the lady.

"This sight greatly irritated the touchy husband, but his hope of gulling Robin enabled him to control his anger. He only bit his lips, and said, 'I am ready to follow you, fair Sir.'

"Robin threw a kiss to the pretty lady, and, to the great indignation of the scandalised husband, announced to her his speedy return.

"Soon after, the Reeve and Robin set out on horseback from Nottingham.

"Robin led his companion by the most deserted woodland paths to the cross-road where we were to meet him.

"'This,' said Robin, pointing to a delightful valley, 'is part of my land.'

"'You speak absurdly and falsely,' replied the Reeve, who thought it was all a hoax. 'This Forest, with all it contains, is the property of the King.'

"'Possibly,' returned Robin; 'but as I have taken possession of it, it belongs to me.'

"'To you?'

"'Certainly, and you shall soon learn in what manner.'

"'We are in a lonely and dangerous part,' said the Reeve. 'The wood is infested by robbers. God keep us from falling into the hands of that wretch, Robin Hood! Should such a misfortune befall us, we should very soon be stripped of all we possess.'

"'We shall see what he will do,' replied Robin, with a laugh, 'for I could wager a thousand to one that we shall be face to face with him immediately.'

"The Reeve turned pale, and cast affrighted glances into the underwood.

"'I wish,' said he, 'that your estates were less evilly situated; and had you warned me of the dangers surrounding them, I would certainly never have come.'

"'I assure you, my dear sir,' replied Robin, 'that we are on my land.'

"'What mean you? Of what land do you speak?' asked the other, anxiously.

"'My words seem plain enow to me,' replied Robin. 'I show you these glades, valleys, cross-roads, and I say, "Behold my estates." When you speak of your wife, do you not say "my wife"?'

"'Yea, yea, without doubt,' stammered the Reeve. 'And I pray you, what is your name? I am anxious to know the name of so rich a landlord.'

"'Your very proper curiosity shall soon be gratified,' laughed Robin Hood.

"At that moment a large herd of deer crossed the road.

"'Look, look, Master, to your right; there are an hundred beasts. How say you, are they not fat and well to look upon?'

"The poor Reeve trembled in all his limbs.

"'I would I had never come here,' said he, gazing into the depths of the wood with terror.

"'Why?' asked Robin, 'I assure you old Sherwood is a charming dwelling-place; besides, what have you to fear? Am I not with you?'

"'That is just what doth alarm me, Sir Stranger. For some moments past I own that your companionship hath ceased to be agreeable to me.'

"'Happily for me, there are very few people of that opinion, Sir Reeve,' replied Robin, laughing; 'but since, to my distress, you are of that number, it is useless to prolong our interview.'

"As he said this, Robin bowed ironically to his companion, and raised his hunting-horn to his lips.

"(I forgot to tell you, my friends, that we had followed the travellers step by step.) At his first call we ran forward. The terrified Reeve very near fell flat upon the neck of his horse.

"'What do you desire, noble Master?' said I to Robin. 'Give me your orders, I beg, that I may execute them instantly.'"

"Do you always speak thus to Robin, Little John?" asked Will Scarlett.

"Yea, Will, for it is a duty and a pleasure," replied the young giant, good-humouredly.

"'I have brought hither the puissant Town Reeve of Nottingham,' replied Robin. 'His Lordship wishes to see my cattle and share my supper. See to it, my good lieutenant, that our guest is treated with the style and splendour due to his position.'

"'He shall be served with the choicest viands,' I replied, 'for I know he will pay very generously for his dinner.'

"'Pay!' cried the Reeve. 'What mean you by that?'

"'Explanations will follow in their turn, Master,' replied Robin. 'And now permit me to answer the question you did me the honour to put as we entered the Forest.'

"'What question?' muttered the Reeve.

"'You asked my name.'

"'Alack!' groaned the Inn-keeper.

"'They call me Robin Hood, Master.'

"'So I see,' said the Reeve, looking round at the Merrie Men.

"'As to what we mean by paying, it is this. We keep open house for the poor, but we re-imburse ourselves largely by the guests who are fortunate enow to possess well-furnished purses.'

"'What are your conditions?' asked the Reeve, in a doleful voice.

"'We have none, nor any fixed price; we take the whole of our guests' money without counting it. For example, you have three hundred gold crowns in your pocket.'

"'Lord, Lord!' muttered the Reeve.

"'Your expenses will be three hundred gold crowns.'

"'Three hundred crowns!'

"'Yea, and I advise you to eat as much as possible and drink as much as you can, so as not to have to pay for what you have not consumed.'

"An excellent repast was served upon the green turf. The Reeve was not hungry, and ate but little, though, to make up for it, he drank heartily. This boundless thirst we supposed to be a result of his despair.

"He gave us three hundred golden crowns, and no sooner was the last crown in my purse than he manifested an ardent desire to quit our company. Robin ordered his horse to be brought, helped him into the saddle, wished him good luck, and begged earnestly to be remembered to his charming wife.

"The Reeve made no reply to our farewells; he was in such haste to leave the Forest that he put his horse to a gallop, and set off without saying one word. Thus ended Robin's adventure with the Town Reeve of Nottingham."

"I should much like," said Will Scarlett, "to prove my cleverness in disguising myself one day. Have you ever tried it, Little John?"

"Yea, once, in obedience to Robin's orders."

"And how did you fare?" asked Will.

"Well enough for the occasion," replied John.

"And what was the occasion?" asked Much.

"'Twas thus. One morning Robin Hood wished to pay a visit to Halbert Lindsay and his pretty little wife; but I pointed out to him the danger of going openly into the town after what had happened with the Reeve about the sale of the cattle, for we feared serious reprisals. Robin Hood laughed at my fears, and replied that, in order to deceive everybody, he would go disguised as a Norman. To that intent he assumed a magnificent knight's dress, paid a visit to Halbert, and from his abode made his way to the Town Reeve's Inn. There he spent much money, complimented the host's pretty wife upon her good looks, and chatted with the Reeve, who overwhelmed him with attentions. Then, a few minutes before quitting the house, he took the man aside, and said to him with a laugh, 'A thousand thanks, good host, for your courteous entertainment of Robin Hood.'

"Before the Reeve could recover from the astonishment caused by Robin's words, the latter had vanished."

"Good," said William; "but this fresh proof of Robin's ability doth not tell us in what manner you were disguised, Little John."

"I dressed myself as a beggar."

"But wherefore?"

"To carry out, as I told you, an order from Robin. Robin wished to put my ability to the test, and desired to know whether I was capable of seconding his wonderful adroitness. The choice of disguise was left to me, and having learnt of the death of a rich Norman whose estates lay in the neighbourhood of Nottingham, I resolved to mingle with the beggars who usually accompany the funeral procession. On my head was an old hat adorned with cockle-shells; I wore a pilgrim's dress, and carried a mighty staff, a sack of provisions, and a purse destined for gifts of money. My garments were so wretched, and I so much resembled a real beggar that even our merry companions were tempted to offer me an alms. About a mile from our retreat I fell in with several beggars who, like myself, were on their way to the Castle of the deceased noble. One of these rogues was apparently blind, another limped painfully, the others bore no distinctive signs beyond miserable rags and tatters.

"'Here,' I said to myself, regarding them out of the corner of mine eye—'here are fellows who will serve me for models. I will accost them, so as to be able to take a leaf out of their book.'

"'Good day, brothers,' I cried heartily. 'I am right glad to meet you. Which way are you going?'

"'We are going along the road,' dryly replied the man whom I had more particularly addressed.

"The jester's companions eyed me with suspicion from head to foot.

"'Might not this fellow be taken for the Tower of Linton Abbey?' quoth one of the beggars, stepping back a step or two.

"'I might be taken for a man who fears no one,' I replied in a menacing tone.

"'Come, come, peace!' growled another of the beggars.

"'So be it,' I replied. 'But what is there to devour at the end of this road, that I see surging from all directions our holy fraternity of rags? Why do the bells of Linton Abbey toll so mournfully?'

"'Because a Norman hath just died.'

"'Are ye, then, going to his burial?'

"'We are going to take our share of the largess which they distribute among poor devils like us on the occasion of a funeral; you are at liberty to accompany us.'

"'I trow I am, and I owe you no thanks for the permission,' I replied scornfully.

"'Long handle of a dirty broom,' cried the lustiest of the beggars, 'if that be so, we are not disposed to bear with thy foolish company any longer. Thou dost appear a very sorry rogue, and thy presence is distasteful to us. Go, and take as a parting gift this blow on thy pate.'

"As he said these words, the tall ragamuffin dealt me a blow on the head.

"This unexpected onslaught made me furious," continued Little John. "I fell on the rascal, and rained a volley of blows upon him.

"He was soon incapable of defending himself, and cried for mercy.

"'Here's at you, lying dogs!' I cried, menacing the other miscreants with my staff.

"You would have laughed, I am sure, good friends, to have seen the blind man open his eyes and fearfully watch my movements, and the lame man run at the top of his speed toward the woods.

"I silenced the brawlers, who were shouting fit to deafen a man, and laid my staff soundly and well across their broad shoulders. A wallet, broken open by my blows, let fall some pieces of gold, and the rogue to whom they belonged fell on his knees upon his treasure, hoping, doubtless, to conceal it from me.

"'Oho!' I cried, 'this puts another appearance on the matter, miserable ragamuffins, or rather thieves, that ye are. Give me instantly, to the last groat, all the money you possess, or I will beat you all into a pulp.'

"The cowards again sued for mercy, and as my arm was beginning to get tired of beating, beating, beating, I was merciful.

"When I left the beggars with my pockets full of their spoils, they could scarce stand up. I quickly took my way to the Forest, delighted with my prowess, for there is a certain justice in plundering thieves.

"Robin Hood, surrounded by his Merrie Men, was practising at archery.

"'Well, Little John,' he cried as I appeared, 'are you back already? Had you not the courage to carry out your beggar's part to a finish?'

"'Pardon me, dear Robin, I have done my duty, and my quest hath been productive. I bring back six hundred gold crowns.'

"'Six hundred golden crowns!' he cried. 'Then you have plundered a Prince of the Church.'

"'Nay Captain, I gleaned that sum from members of the beggar tribe.'

"Robin looked grave.

"'Explain yourself, John,' he said to me. 'I cannot believe that you have robbed the poor.'

"I recounted the adventure to Robin, observing that beggars with pockets full of gold could only be professional thieves.

"Robin was of my opinion, and smiled again."

"That was a good day's work," laughed Much—"six hundred golden crowns at one haul."

"That very evening," continued John, "I distributed the half of my booty among the poor in the neighbourhood of Sherwood."

"Good John!" cried Will, wringing the young man's hand.

"Generous Robin! you should say, William, for in acting thus I only obeyed the orders of my Chief."

"Here we are at Barnsdale," said Much; "but the way hath not seemed long to me."

"I shall tell that to my sister," cried Will, laughing.

"And I will add," replied Much, "that I never ceased to think of her for a single instant."

CHAPTER VII

William, Much, and Little John had been staying at Barnsdale for a week, and the happy household was preparing to celebrate the wedding of Winifred and Barbara. By Will Scarlett's orders the park and gardens of the Hall had been transformed into dancing-greens; for the good-natured young man was constantly watching over the well-being of the world in general and the happiness of each in particular. Indefatigable in his efforts, he turned his hand to anything, busied himself over everything, and filled the house with his light-hearted mirth.

While working hard he talked and laughed, poking fun at Robin, tormenting Much. Suddenly a wild idea struck him, and he began to roar with laughter.

"What ails you, William?" asked Robin.

"My dear friend, I will leave you to guess the reason of my mirth," replied Will, "and I wager you will not succeed."

"It must be something very entertaining, seeing it doth amuse you so much that you laugh all by yourself."

"In sooth, 'tis highly entertaining. You know my six brothers? They are all built much on the same model—fair as corn, gentle, placid, brave, and honest."

"What is all this leading up to, Will?"

"To this: these good lads are unacquainted with love."

"Well?" asked Robin, smiling.

"Well," replied Will Scarlett, "an idea hath just struck me which might give us a good deal of amusement."

"What is it?"

"As you are aware, I have a great influence over my brothers, and this very day I will persuade them they ought all to marry."

Robin began to laugh.

"I will assemble them in a corner of the court-yard," Will went on, "and I will put into their heads the idea of taking each of them a wife on the same day as Much and Little John."

"It is impossible to do such a thing, my dear Will," responded Robin. "Your brothers are of too placid and phlegmatic a nature to be influenced by your words; besides, I know well they are not in love."

"So much the better; they will be obliged to pay their court to my sisters' young friends, and that will be a most pleasing sight.

Picture to yourself for one moment the appearance of Gregory, the steady, awkward, simple fellow—of Gregory striving to make himself agreeable to a young woman. Come with me, Robin, for there is no time to lose; we can only give them three days in which to make their choice. I will call my brothers together, and in a grave voice deliver a fatherly oration to them."

"Marriage is a serious thing, Will, and ought not to be lightly treated. If your brothers, persuaded by your eloquence, consent to marry, and then later on are rendered unhappy through a thoughtless choice, will you not keenly regret having helped to make their whole life miserable?"

"Have no fears on that score, Robin; I mean to find my brothers young maidens worthy of the most tender love both now and in the future. I know, for one, a charming little creature who loves my brother Herbert passionately."

"That is not enough, Will. Is this maiden worthy to call Winifred and Barbara her sisters?"

"Without a doubt; and, what is more, I am certain that she will make an excellent wife."

"And hath Herbert already seen this young damsel?"

"Certainly he hath; but the poor artless fellow little imagines that he could be the object of such a preference. Several times I tried to make him perceive that he was always welcome at Mistress Anna Meadows' house. 'Twas but wasted labour, for Herbert did not understand me; he is so young, in spite of his twenty-nine years. I have a great friendship for a charming damsel who would suit Egbert perfectly in every respect; then Maude was speaking to me to-day of a maiden in this neighbourhood who thinketh Harold a mighty fine fellow. Thus, as you see, Robin, we have already a part of what is needful to carry out my project."

"Unfortunately, Will, 'tis not sufficient, seeing you have six brothers to marry off."

"Never distress yourself; I will go seek, and I shall find three more maidens."

"Very good. But when you have found the damsels, do you think that your brothers will please them?"

"I am sure of it. My brothers are young and strong, fair to look upon—they resemble me in appearance," added Will, with a touch of self-conceit in his tone; "and if they be not so attractive as you are, Robin, if they are not exactly sweet-tempered or lively, at any rate there is naught in their looks to offend the eye of a wise and sensible girl—a girl who seeks a good husband. There is Herbert," he went on, turning towards a young man crossing a garden path; "I will call him. Herbert, come here, my lad."

"What dost want, Will?" replied the young man, as he came near them.

"I wish to speak with thee."

"I am listening, Will."

"That which I have to say doth concern thy brothers also; go seek them."

"I will do so at once."

Will remained thoughtful during the few moments which elapsed before Herbert's return.

The young men came running up, their faces wreathed in smiles.

"Here we are, William," said the eldest, joyfully. "To what must we set down thy wish to assemble us all around thee?"

"To a grave cause, my dear brothers. Will you allow me first to ask you all a question?"

The young men gave signs of assent.

"You love our father dearly, do you not?"

"Who dare doubt our love for him?" demanded Gregory.

"No one; that question is merely a preliminary. So, you love our father dearly. You have never seen him behave otherwise than as a man of honour, a true Saxon?"

"Certainly not," cried Egbert; "but, in the name of Heaven, Will, what do thy words signify? Hath some one slandered our father's name? Point out the wretch to me, and I undertake to avenge the honour of the Gamwells."

"The honour of the Gamwells is unsullied, dear brothers; and if it had been soiled by a lie, the stain would have been already washed out in the slanderer's blood. I wish to speak to you of something less grave, but still very serious; only you must not interrupt me, an if you wish to hear the last words of my harangue before nightfall. Show your approbation or disapprobation of my words by nodding or shaking your heads. Attend; I am about to begin again. The conduct of our father is that of an honourable man, and ought to serve as our guide and model."

"Yea," nodded the six fair heads with one accord.

"Our mother hath followed the same path," continued Will. "Her existence hath been the accomplishment of every duty, the example of every virtue?"

"Yea, yea!"

"How, then, have you been able to remain blind, with this picture of bliss before you? How can you be so ungrateful to Providence? How is it you refuse to accord to our parents a token of respect, tenderness, and gratitude?"

Will's brothers stared in astonishment, for they could make naught of his words.

"What mean you, William?" asked Gregory.

"I would say, Sirs, that, following the example of our father, you should marry, and by so doing prove your admiration of our father's conduct, who himself married."

"Oh, good Lord!" cried the youths, but little pleased.

"Marriage is happiness," Will continued. "Think how happy you will be when you have a dear little creature hanging on your arm like the flower on a vigorous plant, a dear little creature who will love you, think of you, and whose happiness you will be. Look around you, rogues, and you will see the sweet fruits of marriage. First of all, there are Maude and me, whom I am sure you must envy when we are playing with our dear little child. Then Robin and Marian. Think of Little John, and imitate that worthy lad's example. Do you want further proof of the happiness shed by heaven on young husbands and wives? Go and visit Halbert Lindsay and his pretty wife Grace; go down into the valley of Mansfield, and there you will find Allan Clare and the Lady Christabel. You are shockingly selfish to have never thought it was your duty to make a woman happy. Nay, do not shake your heads; you will never persuade any one that you are good and generous lads. I blush for the hardness of your hearts, and I am hurt by hearing everywhere: 'The sons of the old Knight have bad hearts.' I am resolved to put an end to such a state of things, and I warn you that I intend you to marry."

"Really!" said Rupert, defiantly. "Well, I want no wife. Marriage may be a very fine thing, but at present it doth in no wise concern me."

"Thou dost not want a wife?" replied Will. "Very possibly; but thou shalt take one, for I know a maiden who will make thee take back that opinion."

Rupert shook his head.

"Come now, speak freely; dost love any one woman more than another?"

"Yea," replied the young man, gravely.

"Bravo!" cried Will, quite taken aback at this unexpected confidence, for Rupert shunned the society of girls. "Who is she? Tell us her name."

"It is my mother," said the simple lad.

"Thy mother!" repeated Will, a little scornfully. "Thou dost teach us nothing new. I have long been aware that thou dost love, venerate, and respect our mother. I am not speaking of the filial affection which we have for our parents; I speak of another thing—of love, true love. Love is a sentiment which...a tender feeling that... well, a sensation which makes the heart leap toward a young woman. One can adore one's mother and cherish a charming maiden at the same time."

"I do not wish to marry, either," said Gregory.

"Dost think thou hast a will of thine own, my boy?" replied Will. "Wilt soon be shown thine error. Canst tell me thy reason for refusing to marry?"

"No," murmured Gregory, fearfully.

"Wilt live for thyself alone?"

Gregory remained silent.

"Hast thou the audacity to answer me," cried Will, with an affectation of indignation, "that thou dost share the opinion of the rascals who despise the society of women?"

"I did not say that, and still less do I think it; but..."

"There is no *but* which can hold good in the face of reasons so conclusive as those which I do give you all. Therefore, prepare to set up house, my lads; for you will be married at the same time as Winifred and Barbara."

"What," cried Egbert, "in three days? Thou art mad, Will; we have not time to find wives."

"Leave that to me; I will undertake to satisfy you better even than your natural modesty could dare to hope."

"As for me, I positively refuse to relinquish my liberty," said Gregory.

"I did not think to find such selfishness in a son of my mother's," said William, in a wounded tone.

Poor Gregory blushed.

"See here, Gregory," said Rupert. "Let Will do as he doth purpose; he only wishes our happiness, after all, and if he will have the kindness to seek me a wife, why, I will take her. Thou knowest well, brother, that resistance is useless; William hath always done what he would with us."

"Since William doth insist upon marrying us off," added Stephen, "I would as lieve wed in three days as in six months."

"I am of Stephen's opinion," said the timid Harold.

"I give way to force," added Gregory, "for Will is a very devil; he would surely end sooner or later in dragging me into his nets."

"Thou wilt soon thank me for having overthrown thy false allegations, and thy joy shalt be my reward."

"I will marry to oblige thee, Will," said Gregory, again; "but I hope that in return thou wilt give me a pretty little bride."

"I will introduce you one and all to young and charming maidens, and, if ye do not find them adorable, ye may spread it abroad that Will Scarlett doth not know a pretty face."

"I can spare thee the trouble of hunting about for me," said Herbert, "my wife is already found."

"Ha, ha!" laughed Will, "you will see, Robin, that my fine fellows are provided for, and their apparent distaste for marriage is but a merry jest. Who is thy beloved, Herbert?"

"Anna Meadows. We had arranged that our marriage should take place at the same time as my sisters'."

"Sly dog!" said Will, giving his brother a dig in the ribs. "I spoke to thee yesterday of the maiden, and thou hadst never a word to say."

"'Twas only this morning my dear Anna gave me a satisfactory reply."

"Very good; but when I alluded to her love for thee, thou didst make no response."

"I had none to make. Thou saidst to me, 'Mistress Anna is very pretty, she hath a good temper, she will make an excellent wife.' As I have long known all that, thy reflections were but an echo of mine own. Thou didst add further, 'Mistress Anna loveth thee well.' I believed it, thou didst think it; we were each as wise as the other, and consequently I had nothing to tell thee."

"Well answered, discreet Herbert; and I see, from my bothers' silence, that thou alone art worthy of mine esteem."

"I had already made up my mind to marry," said Harold; "Maude inspired me with the wish."

"Hath Maude chosen thy wife?" asked Will, with a laugh.

"Yea, brother; Maude said it was very agreeable to live with a charming little wife, and I agree with her."

"Hurrah!" cried Will, in delight. "My good brothers, will you consent willingly, with hand on heart, to be married on the same day as Winifred and Barbara?"

"We consent," answered the young men, who had no prospective wives.

"Hurrah for marriage!" cried Will, again, throwing his bonnet in the air.

"Hurrah!" repeated the six voices, with one accord.

"Will," said Egbert, "think of our brides; thou must haste to present us to them, for sure they would wish to converse a little with us before wedding us."

"That is very like. Come with me, all. I have a pretty maiden for Egbert, and I think I know three girls who would suit Gregory, Rupert, and Stephen admirably."

"My dear Will," said Rupert, "I wish for a fair, slim maiden; I would not care to marry too stout a wife."

"I know thy romantic taste, and I will deal with thee accordingly; thy betrothed is frail as a reed and pretty as an angel. Come, my lads, I will present you one after another; ye shall pay your court, and if ye do not know how to please a woman, I will advise you, or, better still, I will take your places beside your ladyloves."

"What a pity 'tis that thou canst not marry our future wives, brother Will; things would go so much more smoothly then."

William shook his fist at his brother, took Gregory by the arm, and set out from Barnsdale, accompanied by the procession of lovers.

The seven brothers soon reached the village, where Herbert separated himself from his companions to pay a visit to his beloved; Harold disappeared some moments later; and Will, accompanied by the rest of his brothers, made his way to the home of the maiden destined for Egbert.

Mistress Lucy opened the house-door herself. She was a charming girl with a rosy face and archly sparkling eyes. Her smile expressed goodness, and she was always smiling.

William presented his brother to Mistress Lucy, and told her of Egbert's good qualities. He was so eloquent and persuasive that the maiden, with her mother's consent, allowed Will to hope that his wishes would be accomplished.

Delighted at Mistress Lucy's complaisance, William left Egbert to continue his wooing alone, and went off with his brothers.

Hardly were they out of the house ere Stephen remarked to Will, "I wish I could speak with as much wit, animation, and grace as thou dost use in conversation."

"Nothing is easier than to speak gracefully to a woman, my dear lad. The words themselves are of little importance; it is quite enow to tell the truth, and that right heartily, without embellishing it with fine speeches."

"Is she whom thou hast chosen for me comely?"

"Let me know thy taste; tell me of the kind of beauty thou dost admire."

"Oh," replied Stephen, "I am not very hard to please; a wife like Maude would suit me well enow!"

"A wife like Maude would suit thee well enow!" repeated Will, overcome with astonishment. "That I can readily believe, and I would have thee know that thou art not at all moderate in thy desires. By St. Paul! Stephen, a wife like Maude is a rare thing to find—if not quite undiscoverable. Know well, poor ambitious lad, that there doth not exist on earth any one to be compared with my dear little wife!"

"Dost think so, Will?"

"I am certain of it," replied Maude's husband, in a peremptory tone.

"Indeed, I did not know it. You must excuse my ignorance, Will; I have not travelled yet," replied the young man, innocently. "But if thou couldst give me a wife whose beauty was of Maude's kind..."

"No one in the world doth possess one of Maude's perfections," replied Will, half irritated by his brother's desire.

"Very well, then, Will, choose a wife for me after thine own taste," replied Stephen, in a disconsolate tone.

"Then thou wilt be happy with her. First of all, I will tell thee her name; it is Minnie Meadows."

"I know her," said Stephen, smiling. "She is a young girl with black eyes and curly hair. Minnie was in the habit of making fun of me; she said that I was foolish and sleepy. However, I like her, in spite of her teasing. One day, when we were by ourselves, she laughingly asked me if I had ever kissed a maid in my life."

"What reply didst make to Minnie's question?"

"I answered that certainly I had kissed my sisters. Minnie went off into fits of laughter, and asked me again, 'Have you never kissed any other woman but your sisters?' 'By your leave, mistress,' I replied, 'I have kissed my mother.'"

"Thy mother, thou silly fool! Well, what did she say to thee after thy fine answer?"

"She laughed louder than ever. Then she asked me if I did not wish to kiss any other women besides my mother and sisters. I made answer, 'Nay, mistress.'"

"Thou great ninny! thou shouldest have kissed Minnie; that was the reply due to her questions."

"I never thought of it," answered Stephen, quietly.

"How did ye part after this pleasant conversation?"

"Minnie called me a gaby; then she ran away, laughing still."

"I thoroughly approve of the epithet applied to thee by thy future wife. Doth she really suit thee?"

"Yea, but what shall I say to her when we are alone?"

"Thou must say all sorts of pretty things to her."

"I understand. But tell me, Will, how must I begin a pretty sentence? It is alway difficult to think of the first word."

"When thou art alone with Minnie, thou wilt tell her thou dost wish to receive lessons in the art of kissing young maidens, and as thou art speaking, thou wilt kiss her. The first obstacle surmounted, thou wilt not find it difficult to continue the progress."

"I should never dare to be so bold," said Stephen, timidly.

"'I should never dare!'" repeated Will, in a mocking tone. "Upon my word, Stephen, if I were not sure that thou wert a brave and valiant forester, I should take thee for a girl dressed in man's clothes."

Stephen blushed.

"But," he said hesitatingly, "if the maiden should be distressed at my behaviour?"

"Well, thou wilt kiss her again, and say to her, 'Sweet mistress, adorable Minnie, I shall not cease from kissing you until you do forgive me.' Beside which, bear this in mind, and remember it on occasion, a girl never seriously objects to a kiss from the man she loves. But if her lover displeases her, the case is altered; then she defends herself, and she defends herself so well that you cannot begin again. Thou needst not fear a real refusal from Minnie. I have learnt from a good source that the little maid is friendly disposed toward thee."

Stephen plucked up courage, and promised William to get over his shyness.

Minnie was alone in the house.

"Good day, sweet Minnie," said Will, taking the extended hand of the maiden, who blushed prettily as she greeted him. "I have brought my brother Stephen, who hath something of importance to tell you."

"He!" cried the girl. "And what very important thing can he have to say to me?"

"I must tell you," responded Stephen, quickly, becoming pale with fright, "that I wish to take some lessons..."

"Hush! Hush!" interrupted Will. "Not so fast, my boy. Dear Minnie, Stephen will explain to you presently what he wishes you to grant him of your kindness. Meanwhile, allow me to announce my sisters' marriages."

"I have heard of the festivities which are on foot at the Hall."

"I hope, dear Minnie, that you will take part in our merrymakings."

"With pleasure, Will; the maidens of the village are all busied with their dresses, and I myself shall be overjoyed to dance at a wedding ball."

"You will bring your lover, will you not, Minnie?"

"Nay, nay," interrupted Stephen. "Thou dost forget, Will..."

"I forget naught," said Will. "Be so good as to hold thy tongue for a few minutes. You will bring your lover, eh, Minnie?" continued the young man, repeating his question.

"I have no lover," replied the maiden.

"Is that true, Minnie?" asked Will.

"It is quite true; I know not of any whom I could call lover."

"If you wish it, Minnie, I will be your lover," cried Stephen, taking the girl's hand in one of his own trembling ones.

"Bravo, Stephen!" said Will.

"Yea," continued the young man, encouraged by his brother's approbation, "yea, Minnie, I will be your lover; on the wedding day I will seek you, and we will be married at the same time as my sisters."

Astonished at this abrupt declaration, the maiden did not know how to answer.

"Listen to me, dear Minnie," said Will. "My brother hath long loved you, and his silence cometh not from his heart but from the extreme timidity of his nature. I assure you upon mine honour that Stephen speaks with the sincerity of love. You are not betrothed; Stephen is a fine lad, better still, he is a good and excellent lad, and will be a husband worthy of you. If we have your consent and that of your family, your marriage could be celebrated at the same time as my sisters'."

"Really, Will," replied the girl, looking down in confusion, "I was so little prepared for your proposal; 'tis so hasty and unexpected, I do not know how to reply."

"Reply thus: 'I take Stephen for my husband,'" said that youth, put quite at his ease by the pretty girl's sweet looks. "I have a very great affection for you, Minnie," continued he, "and I should be the happiest of men an if you would give me your hand."

"'Tis impossible for me to reply to your honourable proposal to-day," said the maiden, bowing gracefully and playfully to her timid lover.

"I will leave you alone, good friends," William continued. "My presence embarrasses you, and I am certain that if Minnie loves Winifred and Barbara, she will be glad to call them sisters."

"I love Winifred and Barbara with all my heart," replied the girl, softly.

"Then," said Stephen, "I may hope, mistress, that in consideration of your love for my sisters, you will treat me kindly?"

"We shall see," said the girl, coquettishly.

"Good-bye, charming Minnie," said William, with a smile. "I pray you be good and kind to the fine fellow who loves you so well, even though he doth not testify very eloquently to his love."

"You are too severe, Will," replied the maiden, gravely. "I do not think Stephen could possibly have expressed himself better."

"Well, I see that you are really a most excellent young woman, sweet Minnie," said Will. "Permit me to kiss your hand and to say once more, 'Good-bye, sister mine.'"

"Should I reply to William, 'Good-bye, brother mine?'" asked Minnie, turning to Stephen.

"Yea, dear lady, yea," cried Stephen, joyfully. "Say to him, 'Good-bye, brother,' so that he may go quickly."

"Thou dost make progress, my lad," laughed Will. "My lessons are evidently bearing fruit."

With which William kissed Minnie, and went on his way with Gregory and Rupert.

"Now 'tis our turn, is't not, Will?" said Gregory. "I am impatient to see my future wife."

"And so am I," added Rupert.

"Where doth she live?" asked Gregory.

"Shall I see my future bride to-day?" continued Rupert.

"Your very natural curiosity shall be satisfied," replied Will. "Your future wives are cousins, and are called Mabel and Editha Harrowfield."

"I know them both," said Gregory.

"I know them too," added Rupert.

"They are pretty girls," Will continued, "and I am not surprised that their charming faces have attracted your attention. I have hardly been eighteen months at Barnsdale, but there is not a maiden in the county, blonde or brunette, that I do not know. Like yourselves, mine attention hath already been attracted by Mabel and Editha."

"I never saw a fellow to equal thee, Will," said Gregory; "thou dost know all the women, and art always roving. Of a truth we resemble thee but little."

"Unhappily for yourselves, my lads; for did you resemble me the least bit in the world, I should not be obliged to seek wives for you, or have to teach you how to make love to them."

"Oh," replied Gregory, firmly, "it will not be difficult for us to make love to Mabel and Editha. Rupert thinks Mabel charming, and I am persuaded Editha is good creature, so I shall just ask her an if she will be the wife of Gregory Gamwell."

"Such a question must not be put abruptly, my good lad, or thou wilt run the risk of a refusal."

"Tell me, then, how I should explain mine intentions to Editha. I do not know the tricks of cunning. I wish to have her for wife, and I should think it but natural to say, 'Editha, I am ready to marry you.'"

"Thou wilt embarrass the maiden overmuch, an thou dost shoot such a declaration at her point blank."

"What must I do, then?" asked Gregory, in despair.

"Thou must gently lead the conversation in the way thou wouldst follow; speak first of the ball to be given at the Hall in three days' time, of the happiness of Little John and Much; make a skilful allusion to thine approaching marriage, and, in this connection, ask Editha, as I have asked Minnie, if she thinks of being married, and if she will come to the feast at Barnsdale with a lover."

"What if Editha reply, 'Yea, Gregory, yea, I will go to the ball with a lover'?"

"Well, then thou wilt say, 'Mistress, that lover is myself.'"

"But," Gregory ventured once again, "what if Editha doth refuse my hand?"

"Then you will offer it to Mabel."

"And what of me?" said Rupert.

"Editha will not refuse," answered Will; "therefore never be uneasy: each of you shall have the girl of his heart to wife."

The young men crossed the village green, and stopped before a pretty house, upon the doorstep of which stood two girls.

"Good morrow, fair Editha and Mabel," said Will, greeting the cousins. "My brothers and I are come to ask you to a wedding dance."

"Welcome, fair Sirs," said Mabel, in a voice as sweet as the song of a bird. "Do us the honour to enter and partake of some refreshment."

"A thousand thanks, charming Mabel," replied Will. "So kind and gracious an offer should not meet with a refusal. We will drink your health and happiness in a flagon of ale."

Editha and Mabel, who were kindhearted and sprightly maidens, received the brothers' compliments with much laughter; then, after an hour's merry conversation, Gregory summoned up his courage to ask Editha timidly whether she intended going to the Hall in the company of her lover.

"I shall not be accompanied by one lover alone, but by half a dozen merry lads," replied Editha, gaily.

This most unexpected answer threw poor Gregory into great confusion. He sighed, and turning to his brother, whispered him aside—

"'Tis all over with me; dost not think so? I cannot compete with half a dozen aspirants. Really, I have no luck, and must e'en remain a bachelor all my days."

"Since thou dost not wish to marry, that will suit thee," said Will, teasingly.

"I had not thought of it, that was all; but since the idea entered my mind, I have been tormented with the fear of not being able to find a wife."

"Thou shalt have Editha; let me manage it. Mistress Editha," said William, "our visit had a double object. First we wished to invite you to our family festivities, then I would present to you, not a gallant for the dance, an adorer for four and twenty hours—you have six of those, and the seventh would cut a sorry figure—but an honest lad, steady, good, rich, and one who will be proud and happy to offer you his heart, his hand, and his name."

Mistress Editha looked pensive.

"Are you speaking seriously, Will?" she asked.

"Quite seriously. Gregory loves you; however, he is here himself, and if you close your eyes to the eloquence of his looks, pray be so kind as to give heed to the sincerity of his words. I will leave to him the pleasure of pleading a cause which is, I believe, half won already," added the young man, interpreting in his brother's favour the joyous smile which hovered on Editha's lips. William allowed Gregory to approach the maiden, and looked at Rupert to see whether he required any help, intending to go to his assistance, if it were necessary. But Rupert did not require his aid; he was talking to Mabel in a low voice and holding her hands as he knelt on one knee before her, apparently thanking her for some favour.

"Good," quoth Will to himself, "he can look after himself; I can leave him to his own resources."

He watched the lovers for a few minutes, and then, without attracting their attention, he left the room and ran back to the Hall.

There he met Robin, Marian, and Maude, to whom he related what had happened, depicting to them the timorous embarrassment of the prospective bridegrooms, but he ended in recognising that the young men had brought themselves out of their difficult positions very well.

Towards evening the brothers returned to the Hall radiant with joy. Their victory was complete, and they had one and all obtained the consent of their lady loves.

The parents of the maidens thought it a piece of folly to marry with such precipitation, but the honour of entering the noble family of Gamwell removed all their scruples.

Sir Guy, cleverly prepared by Robin to approve of his sons' choice, welcomed the six pretty girls with great kindness. The eight marriages were celebrated on one day with much pomp, and each was delighted at the happiness which had fallen to his share.

CHAPTER VIII

A month after the events just related, Robin Hood, his wife, and the whole of his band of Merrie Men were installed once again beneath the trees of Sherwood Forest.

About this time, a number of Normans, liberally paid for their military services by Henry II., came to take possession of the domains given them by the King's generosity. Some of these Normans, who were obliged to cross Sherwood Forest to reach their new estates, were constrained to pay their way liberally by the merry band of outlaws. The newcomers protested loudly, and carried their complaints to the authorities in the town of Nottingham. But these complaints were taxed with exaggeration, and received no reply, and the reason of this apathy on the part of the Reeve and other important personages was as follows.

Many of Robin Hood's men were related to the inhabitants of Nottingham, and quite naturally these latter used their influence with the civil and military authorities to prevent any rigorous measures being taken against the Foresters. These worthy men were terribly afraid that if, in consequence of a successful attack, the Merrie Men were driven from their green dwelling-place, they might some morning have the melancholy satisfaction of seeing one of their own kinsmen hanging by the neck from the town gallows.

However, as it was necessary to make a pretence of righteous indignation and justice, they doubled the reward promised to any one who should succeed in capturing Robin Hood. Whoever applied for it could at once obtain a warrant for arresting the famous Outlaw. Many men of great physical strength or of a determined spirit had made the attempt, but an unexpected thing happened— they had all become, by their own wish, members of the band of merry Foresters.

One morning Robin and Will Scarlett were strolling through the Forest when Much suddenly appeared before them, streaming with perspiration and panting for breath.

"What hath happened, Much?" asked Robin, anxiously. "Are you pursued? You are soaking with perspiration."

"Never fear, Robin," replied the young man, wiping his crimson face. "Thanks be to Heaven, I have had no dangerous encounter. I have only come from a bout with quarter-staves with Peaceful Arthur. Good Lord! the lad hath the strength of a giant in his arm."

"You speak truly, my dear Much, and 'tis indeed a rough job to fight with Arthur when he is in earnest..."

"Arthur always keeps cool," replied Much; "but as he is ignorant of the real rules of the game, he owes his success only to his tremendous muscle."

"Did he make you cry for quarter?"

"I should think so. But for that, he would have knocked all the breath out of me. At this moment he is trying a bout with Little John, but with such an adversary Arthur's defeat cannot be doubted, for when he begins to strike hard, Little John doth e'en lift his staff and give him some shrewd blows on the shoulders, to teach him to moderate the transports of his strength."

"For what reason did you engage with the indomitable Arthur?" asked Robin.

"Without rhyme or reason, simply to pass an hour agreeably and to give our limbs healthy exercise."

"Arthur is a terrible fighter," said Robin, "and one day he overcame me in a bout with quarter-staves."

"You!" cried Will.

"Yea, cousin, he treated me somewhat after the fashion in which he hath handled Much; the rascal used his oaken staff like a bar of iron."

"How was it that he beat you? Where did the bout take place?" asked Will, curiously.

"The match took place in the Forest, and this is how I made Arthur's acquaintance. I was walking by myself down a lonely path in the wood, when I saw the gigantic Arthur leaning upon an iron ferruled staff, with eyes and mouth wide open watching a herd of deer within a few feet of him. His gigantic appearance, the air of candid innocence which overspread his large face, made me wish to amuse myself at his expense. I glided dexterously behind him, and accosted him by a vigorous blow with the fist between his shoulders. Arthur started, turned his head, and glared at me wrathfully.

"'Who art thou?' said I to him, 'and what dost thou mean by wandering in the wood? Thou hast all the appearance of a robber going to steal the deer. Be so good as to clear off at once. I am the Keeper of this part of the Forest, and I will not suffer the presence of rascals of thy kind.'

"'Well,' he replied carelessly, 'try and remove me if thou dost wish it, but I do not intend to go. Call for help, if it be thy good pleasure; I will not oppose thee.'

"'I need call for no one to enforce the law or my wishes, my fine fellow. I am accustomed to trust to mine own resources, which, as thou mayst see, are worthy of respect. I have two good arms, a sword, and a bow and arrows.'

"'My little forester,' said Arthur, looking me up and down from head to foot disdainfully, 'if I gave thee a single blow on the fingers with my staff, thou wouldst not be able to use either sword or bow.'

ROBIN HOOD THE OUTLAW

"'Speak civilly, my lad,' I replied, 'an thou wish not to get a sound thrashing.'

"'How now, little friend, whip an oak with a reed! Whom dost take thyself for, then, young prodigy of valour? Learn that I care not for thee the least bit in the world. However, an if thou wish to fight, I am thy man.'

"'Thou hast no sword,' I observed.

"'I need none when I have my staff.'

"'Then I must take a staff of the same length as thine.'

"'So be it,' said he, putting himself on his guard.

"I immediately dealt him the first blow, and I saw the blood gush from his forehead and stream down his cheeks. Staggering under the blow, he made a step backward. I lowered my weapon, but seeing the movement, which no doubt appeared to him an expression of triumph, he set himself again to wield his staff with an extraordinary strength and cleverness. With such violence did he strike out that I had hardly strength to ward off his blows and keep my staff in my clenched hands. In leaping back to avoid a terrible attack, I neglected to keep up my guard, and he took advantage of it to deal me the most terrific crack on the skull I have ever received. I fell back as though pierced by an arrow, but I did not lose consciousness, and again sprang to my feet. The combat, suspended for an instant, began again; Arthur rained his blows upon me with such tremendous force, he scarce gave me time to defend myself. Thus we fought for nearly four hours. We made the echoes of the old wood ring with our blows, revolving round one another like two wild boars when they fight. At length, thinking there was not much use in continuing a struggle in which there was little to gain, not even the satisfaction of thrashing my adversary, I threw down my staff.

"'Enow,' I said to him; 'let us finish the quarrel. We might knock each other about until to-morrow and both be ground to powder without winning aught thereby. I give thee the free run of the Forest, for thou art a brave lad.'

"'Gramercy for that great favour,' he replied disdainfully. 'I have purchased the right to go my own way by the aid of my staff; therefore it is to that rather than to thee my thanks are due.'

"'That is true, my brave lad, but thou wouldst have found it difficult to defend thy right with thy staff alone to enforce it. Thou wouldst find some doughty opponent in the green wood, and thou couldst only preserve thy liberty at the cost of broken crowns and aching limbs. Believe me, life in the town even would be preferable to that which thou wouldst lead here.'

"'However,' replied Arthur, 'I am fain to dwell in the old Forest.'

"My valiant adversary's answer made me consider," continued Robin. "I looked at his tall figure, the amiable frankness of his face, and I told myself that the attachment of such a young blade as this might be to the advantage of our community.

"'Then thou dost not like living in the town?' I asked him.

"'Nay,' he replied, 'I am aweary of being the slave of these cursed Normans. I am tired of hearing myself called "dog, knave,

112

serf." My master hath applied to me this morning some of the worst epithets in his vocabulary, and, not content with baiting me with his viperish tongue, wished to strike me. I did not wait for the blow. I found a stick within reach of my hand, and used it, giving him a blow over the shoulders that knocked him senseless. That done, I fled.'

"'What is thy trade?' I asked him.

"'I am a tanner,' he answered, 'and I have lived for several years in the county of Nottingham.'

"'Well, my fine friend,' I said to him, 'if thou have not too great a liking for your trade, canst say good-bye to it, and come and live here. I am Robin Hood. Is the name known to thee?'

"'For sure it is; but are you Robin Hood? You told me just now that you were one of the Keepers of the Forest.'

"'I am Robin Hood, I give thee my word of honour,' I replied, holding out my hand to the poor lad, who was overcome by surprise. 'Upon my soul and conscience!'

"'Then I am very glad to have met you,' added Arthur, joyfully, 'for I came to seek you, generous Robin Hood. When you told me that you were one of the Keepers of the Forest I believed you, and should not have dared to tell you my reason for coming to Sherwood. I wish to join your band, and if you will accept me as a companion you will have no more devoted or more faithful follower than Peaceful Arthur, the tanner of Nottingham town.'

"'Thy frankness pleaseth me, Arthur,' I answered him, 'and I consent gladly to admit thee as one of the Merrie Men who form my band. Our laws are few and simple, but they must be observed. On every other point thou shalt have complete liberty, and in addition to that thou wilt be well clothed, well nourished, and well treated.'

"'My heart swells as I listen to you, Robin Hood, and the thought of being one of your band makes me very happy. I am not quite the stranger you might imagine, for Little John is a kinsman of mine. My maternal uncle married John's mother, who was a sister of Sir Guy Gamwell. Shall I see Little John soon? I am all impatience to do so.'

"'I will bring him hither,' I said, and wound my horn.

"Some minutes later Little John appeared.

"At sight of our blood-bespattered faces and frightful bruises, Little John stopped short.

"'What is it, Robin?' he cried, startled. 'Your face is in a frightful state.'

"'I have been thrashed,' I replied calmly, 'and the culprit stands before thee.'

"'If that rascal hath beaten you, he must wield his staff very prettily,' cried Little John. 'Well, I will repay with interest the blows he hath given thee. Step forward, my fine lad.'

"'Stay thy hand, friend John, and give it to a faithful ally, to a cousin; this young man is called Arthur.'

"'Arthur of Nottingham, known as Peaceful Arthur?' questioned John.

"'The same,' replied Arthur. 'We have not met since our child-hood, but all the same I recognised thee, Cousin John.'

"'I cannot say as much,' said John, with his simple frankness. 'I do not recall thy features, but that matters little; thou art welcome, Cousin, and thou wilt find good and merry hearts in the green wood.'

"Arthur and John embraced each other, and the remainder of the day passed merrily."

"Have you ever striven against Arthur since that day?" Will asked Robin.

"I have had no opportunity of doing so as yet; but it is probable that I should be vanquished again, and that would be for the third time."

"What, for the third time?" cried Will.

"Yea, Jasper the Tinker gave me a sound drubbing."

"Really? When was that? Doubtless before he was enrolled in the band?"

"Yea," replied Robin. "I am in the habit of proving the courage and strength of a man for myself before putting my confidence in him. I do not wish for companions with weak heads and hearts. One morning I met Jasper the Tinker on the road to Nottingham. You know his vigorous broad-shouldered person, and I need give you no description of the jolly rascal; his looks pleased me, as he walked with a firm step, whistling a gay air. I advanced to meet him.

"'Good day, my friend,' said I to him. 'I see thou art a traveller. 'Tis said there is bad news abroad; is that true?'

"'What news dost speak of?' he asked. 'I know of none worth naming. I come from Bamborough, and am a tinsmith by trade, and I think only of my work.'

"'The news in question ought to interest thee all the same, my fine fellow. I have heard that ten of you Tinkers have just been put in the stocks for being drunk.'

"'Thy news is not worth a groat,' he replied; 'but if all who drank were put in the stocks, thou wouldst certainly take the first place there, for thou hast not the air of a man who despiseth good wine.'

"'In truth, I am no enemy to the bottle, and I do not think there is a jovial heart in all the world that despiseth wine. But what brings thee hither from Bamborough? For assuredly it was not the interests of thy trade.'

"'It was not my trade, in sooth,' responded Jasper. 'I am seeking a robber called Robin Hood. A reward of one hundred golden crowns is promised to anyone who can capture him, and I much desire to gain that reward.'

"'How thinkest to capture Robin Hood?' I asked the Tinker, for I was greatly surprised at the calm and serious way in which he made this strange confidence.

"'I have an order for his arrest, signed by the King,' Jasper made answer.

"'Is the order strictly in rule?'

"'Perfectly; it empowereth me to arrest Robin, and proposeth me the reward.'

"'Thou speakest of this arrest, already so often vainly attempted, as if it were the easiest thing in the world to accomplish.'

"'It will not be very difficult for me,' replied the Tinker. 'I am of solid build, I have muscles of iron, a tried courage, and much patience. Thus can I well hope to catch my man.'

"'Wert thou to meet accidentally, shouldst recognise him?'

"'I have never seen him; an if I knew his face, my task would be half accomplished. Art any wiser than I am in this respect?'

"'Yea, I have met Robin Hood twice, and perchance it would be possible for me to help thee in thine enterprise.'

"'My fine lad, an thou canst do that,' said he, 'I will e'en give thee a large share of the reward I shall gain.'

"'I will point out a place where thou couldst meet him,' I replied; 'but before going any further in our undertaking, I should like to see the order for his arrest; to be valid it must be drawn up according to rule.'

"'I am greatly obliged for thy precaution,' answered the Tinker, defiantly, 'but I shall confide the paper to no one. I know it is valid and in order; that satisfies me, and so much the worse for thee if thou dost not believe it. Robin Hood shall see the King's order when I have him in my power, bound hand and foot.'

"'Perchance thou art right, my good man,' I replied indifferently. 'I am not so anxious to assure myself of the value of thy permit as thou seemest to think. I am going to Nottingham as much from curiosity as from idleness, for I heard this morning that Robin Hood was going into the town, and if thou wilt come with me I will show thee the famous Outlaw.'

"'I will take thee at thy word, my lad,' said the Tinker, quickly, 'but an if, when we arrive at our destination, I see any sign of deceit on thy part, thou shalt make acquaintance with my staff.'

"I shrugged my shoulders in disdain. He saw the action, and began to laugh.

"'Thou wilt not regret having helped me,' said he, 'for I am not an ungrateful man.'

"When we arrived at Nottingham we stopped at Pat's Inn, and I asked the master of the house for a bottle of a special kind of beer. The Tinker, who had been on his feet since early morning, was literally dying of thirst, and the beer soon disappeared. After the beer I called for wine, and after the wine again for beer, and so on for an hour. Without perceiving it, the Tinker had emptied every bottle set before him, for I, being by nature averse to the immoderate use of wine, contented myself with a few glasses. I need hardly tell you that the worthy fellow became completely intoxicated. Then he began to regale me with a boastful account of all he would do to capture Robin Hood, and how, after taking the Chief of the Merrie Men prisoner, he would arrest the whole band, and take them all to London. The King would reward his bravery by giving him a fortune and the privileges of a grand dignitary of the State; but at the very moment when the illustrious conqueror was on the point of marrying an English Princess, he fell from his chair, and rolled, fast asleep, beneath the table.

"I took the Tinker's purse; it contained, besides money, the order for my arrest. I paid our expenses, and told the Innkeeper—

"'When this fellow awakes, you will ask him to pay for our refreshment; then, if he asks you who I am and where I am to be found, you will answer that I live in the Forest, and that my name is Robin Hood.'

"The Innkeeper, a worthy man, in whom I have every confidence, began to laugh gaily.

"'Be easy, Master Robin,' said he, 'I will faithfully carry out your orders; and should the Tinker wish to see you again, he will only have to seek you.'

"'You understand me, my good fellow,' I replied, picking up the Tinsmith's bag. 'And there is every reason to believe the good man will not let me wait his visit for long.'

"Saying which, I bade the Innkeeper farewell, and left the house.

"After sleeping for some hours, Jasper awoke. He soon became aware of my absence and of the loss of his purse.

"'Landlord,' he shouted, in a voice of thunder, 'I am robbed, I am ruined! Where is the thief?'

"'Of what thief do you speak?' asked the host, with the greatest coolness.

"'Of my companion. He hath plundered me.'

"'Well, that doth not suit me at all,' said the Innkeeper, with an appearance of anger, 'for you have here a long shot to settle.'

"'A shot to settle!' groaned Jasper. 'I have naught left, naught whatever; the wretch hath utterly despoiled me. I had in my purse a warrant of arrest under the King's hand; and by the help of that warrant I might have made my fortune, I might have captured Robin Hood. This thief of a stranger promised to help me, and was going to conduct me into the presence of the outlaw chief. Oh, the rogue! He hath abused my confidence and carried off my precious paper!'

"'How?' returned the Innkeeper. 'You confided to that young man the evil intentions that have brought you to Nottingham?'

"The Tinker threw a sidelong glance at his host.

"'It appears,' said he, 'that you would not lend a helping hand to the brave fellow who would wish to arrest Robin Hood?'

"'By my faith,' replied the Innkeeper, 'Robin Hood hath never done me harm, and his quarrels with the rulers of the land do not concern me. But how the devil,' continued the man, 'did you come to be drinking joyously with him, and showing him your little paper, instead of seizing his person?'

"The Tinker stared wildly at him.

"'What do you mean?' he asked.

"'I mean that you have lost an opportunity of capturing Robin Hood.'

"'How so?'

"'Oh, what a dolt you be! Robin Hood was here just now. You entered together, you drank together, and I thought you were one of his band.'

"'I drank with Robin Hood! I clinked glasses with Robin Hood!' cried the astounded Tinker.

"'Yea, a thousand times yea!'

"'This is too much!' exclaimed the poor man, seating himself heavily in a chair. 'But he shall never say that he tricked Jasper the Tinker with impunity. Oh, villain! Oh, thief!' bellowed the Tinker, 'wait, wait, wait while I seek thee out.'

"'I would fain see the colour of my money before you go,' said the Innkeeper.

"'What is the amount of your bill?' asked Jasper, wrathfully.

"'Ten shillings,' replied the host, overjoyed at the unhappy Tinker's furious countenance.

"'I have not a penny to give you,' returned Jasper, turning out his pockets; 'but as guarantee for the payment of this unlucky debt, I will leave my tools with you. They are worth three or four times what you claim. Can you tell me where to find Robin Hood?'

"'Not this evening, but to-morrow you will find your man hunting the King's deer.'

"'Well, then, to-morrow the robber shall be captured,' rejoined the Tinker, with an assurance which gave the Innkeeper food for thought; for," added Robin, "when recounting this to me, the host avowed that he greatly feared Jasper's rage against me.

"The next morning I started in quest, not of the deer, but of the Tinsmith, and I had not long to seek. As soon as he perceived me, he uttered a cry, and threw himself upon me, brandishing an enormous cudgel.

"'What clown is this,' I cried, 'who dares to present himself before me in so unseemly a manner?'

"'It is no clown,' replied the Tinker, 'but an ill-used man, resolved to take his revenge.'

"Saying this, he attacked me with his cudgel; but I placed myself beyond his reach and drew my sword.

"'Stop,' I said to him. 'We will fight with equal weapons; I must have a cudgel.'

"Jasper suffered me quietly to trim the branch of an oak tree, and then recommenced his attack.

"He held his staff in both hands, and hacked at me like a woodcutter at a tree. My arms and wrists were beginning to fail me, when I called for a truce; for there was no honour to be gained from such a contest.

"'I would fain hang thee on the nearest tree,' he said furiously, throwing down his staff.

"I leapt back and blew my horn; the fellow was strong enough to send me into another world.

"Little John and the Merrie Men ran up at my call.

"I was seated beneath a tree, spent with fatigue, and, without saying a word, I pointed out the reinforcement which had come to my assistance.

"'What is it?' asked John.

"'My lad,' I replied, 'here is a Tinker wight who hath given me a sound drubbing, and I recommend him to you, for he is worthy of your consideration. My good man,' I added, 'an if you will join our band, you will be very welcome.'

"The Tinker accepted forthwith, and from that time, as you are aware, he hath been one of us."

"I prefer a bow and arrows to all the cudgels in the world," said William, "whether as a game or taken as weapons of offence and defence. It is better, in my opinion, at least to be sent out of the world by one single blow than to go piecemeal; and the wound of an arrow is a thousand times preferable to the pain caused by a blow from a cudgel."

"My good friend," returned Robin, "the cudgel renders very good service where the bow hath no power. The effect doth not depend on whether your quiver is empty or full, and when you do not desire the death of an enemy, a good beating will leave him a sharper remembrance than the wound of an arrow."

The three friends were making their way to Nottingham as they conversed, and all at once they met a little girl dissolved in tears.

Robin hastened toward the weeping beauty.

"Why dost weep, my child?" he asked in a kindly tone.

The little girl broke into sobs.

"I want to see Robin Hood," she answered, "and if you have any pity in your heart, Master, take me to him."

"I am Robin Hood, my pretty child," replied the young man, gently. "Have my men been wanting in respect to thy youth and innocence? Is thy mother ill? Dost come to ask my help? Speak, I am entirely at thy disposal."

"Master, a great misfortune hath befallen us; three of my brothers, who belong to thy band, have been taken prisoners by the Sheriff of Nottingham."

"Tell me the name of thy brothers, my child."

"Adalbert, Edelbert, and Edwin the Merry-hearted," sobbed the little girl.

An exclamation of dismay escaped Robin.

"Good companions," said he, "these are the bravest and hardiest of all my troop. How did they fall into the Sheriff's hands, my little friend?"

"In rescuing a young man who was being taken to prison for having defended his mother against the insults of some soldiers. At this very moment, Sir, they are getting ready the gallows at the gate of the town, doubtless to hang my brothers thereon."

"Dry thy tears, pretty child," answered Robin kindly. "Thy brothers have naught to fear; there is not a man in all Sherwood Forest but would not be ready to give his life for these three good fellows. We will go into Nottingham; return to thy home, console thy father's afflicted heart by thy sweet voice, and tell thy mother that Robin Hood will give her back her children."

"I will pray Heaven to bless thee, Master," murmured the little girl, smiling amid her tears. "I had heard that thou wert alway ready to help the unfortunate and protect the poor. But, I beseech thee, Master Robin, haste thee, for my dear brothers are in sore danger of their lives."

"Trust me, dear child; I will arrive at the most propitious time. Hurry back to Nottingham, and tell no one of what thou hast done."

The child took Robin Hood's hands and kissed them warmly.

"I shall pray for thy happiness all my life, Master," said she, in a voice full of emotion.

"God bless thee, my child! Good-bye."

The little maid ran off down the road to the town, and soon disappeared beneath the shade of the trees.

"Hurrah!" said Will. "We shall have something to do now. I shall be amused. What are your orders, Robin?"

"Go to Little John, tell him to assemble as many of the men as he can find, and lead them—of course without being seen—to the outskirts of the wood nearest to Nottingham. Then at sound of my horn you will cut your way through to me, sword in hand and with bows bent."

"What do you purpose, then, to do?" asked Will.

"I shall go into the town and see whether there be any means whatever of delaying the execution. Forget not, friends, that you must act with extreme caution, for should the Reeve come to learn that I have been warned of the critical condition of my men, he would take care to prevent any attempt at deliverance on my part, and would hang our comrades within the Castle. So much for the prisoners. As for you, you are well aware that his Lordship hath loudly boasted that if ever we fell into his hands, he would hang us upon the town gallows. The Sheriff hath conducted the affair of the Merry Hearts so swiftly that he cannot fear that I have been warned of the fate in store for them; consequently, in order to instil a wholesome lesson into the citizens of Nottingham, he will hang our companions publicly. I will make all speed to the town; do you rejoin your men, and follow my instructions to the letter."

As he said this, Robin hurried off. Hardly had he left his companions ere he met a pilgrim of the Mendicant Order.

"What news from the town, good Father?" asked Robin.

"The news from the town, young man," replied the pilgrim, "is full of woe and lamentation. Three of Robin Hood's companions are to be hanged by order of the Lord Fitz-Alwine."

A sudden idea crossed Robin's mind.

"Father," said he, "I should like to be present at the execution of these poachers, without being known for one of the Keepers of the Forest. Wilt exchange thy clothes for mine?"

"Art joking, young man?"

"Nay, father, I simply desire to give thee my costume and to put on thy robe. If thou dost accept my proposition, I will give thee forty shillings, to use according to thy fancy."

The old man looked curiously at the author of this strange request.

"Thy clothes are handsome," said he, "and my robe is ragged. It is not possible to believe thou shouldst wish to change thy brilliant garb for these wretched rags. He who makes fun of an old man commits a great sin; he mocks both God and misfortune."

"Father," replied Robin, "I respect thy white hairs, and I pray the Virgin to take thee under her Divine protection. I put my request with no ill intent in mine heart; 'tis necessary for the accomplishment of a good work. Hold," added he, offering the old man twenty pieces of money, "Here is an earnest of our bargain."

The pilgrim looked covetously at the coins.

"Youth hath many foolish ideas," said he, "and if thou art in a paroxysm of fantastic mirth, I see not why I should refuse to let thee have thy way."

"Now, that is well said," returned Robin, "and if thou wilt disrobe....Thy hose are fashioned by events," continued Robin, gaily, "for, to judge by the innumerable pieces of which they are composed, they have gathered to them the materials of the four seasons."

The pilgrim began to laugh.

"My robe is like a Norman's conscience," he said, "'tis made up of odds and ends, while thy doublet is the image of a Saxon heart, strong and without blemish."

"Thy speech is golden, Father," said Robin, donning the old man's rags as fast as he was able, "and if I must do homage to thy wit, 'tis likewise my duty to accord praise to the manifest scorn I inspire in thee, for thy robe is of quite a Christian simplicity."

"Am I to keep thy arms?" asked the pilgrim.

"Nay, Father, for I shall want them. Now that our mutual transformation is complete, allow me to give thee some advice. Get thee hence from this part of the Forest, and above all, in the interests of thine own safety, beware of attempting to follow me. Thou hast my clothes upon thy back, my money in thy pocket, thou art rich and well clothed, go seek thy fortune some leagues away from Nottingham."

"I thank thee for thy advice, good lad; it doth accord well with mine own wishes. Take the benediction of an old man, and if thine enterprise be honest, I wish it immediate success."

Robin saluted the pilgrim gracefully and made off with all haste in the direction of the town.

At the moment when Robin, thus disguised, and bearing no weapon save an oaken cudgel, arrived at Nottingham, a procession of mercenaries left the Castle, and took the road toward the end of the town, where three gallows had been set up.

Suddenly an unexpected piece of news went round the crowd; the hangman was ill, and, being on the point of death himself, was quite unable to launch another into eternity. By order of the Sheriff, a proclamation was made; and a man was called for who would consent to fulfil the office of hangman.

Robin, who had placed himself at the head of the procession, advanced towards Baron Fitz-Alwine.

"Noble Lord," said he, in a snuffling voice, "what will you give me, an I consent to take the hangman's place?"

The Baron stepped back, as one who fears a dangerous contact.

"Methinketh," replied the noble Baron, looking Robin up and down, "that if I should offer thee a new assortment of clothing, thou shouldst be glad to accept such reward. Therefore, beggar, if thou wilt get us out of this difficulty, I will e'en give thee six new suits, and beside that the hangman's perquisite of thirteen pence."

"And what will you give me, my Lord, if I hang you into the bargain?" asked Robin, approaching the Baron.

"Keep thy distance, beggar, and repeat what thou hast just said; I did not understand it."

"You offered me six new suits and thirteen pence," returned Robin, "for hanging these poor lads. I ask what you would add to my reward an if I engage to hang you and a dozen of your Norman dogs."

"Shameless ragamuffin! What is the meaning of thine insolence?" cried the Baron, astounded at the pilgrim's audacity. "Dost know whom thou art addressing? Impertinent knave, one word more and thou wilt make the fourth bird hanging on the gallows-tree."

"Have you remarked," quoth Robin, "that I am a poor man, very miserably clad?"

"Yea, in truth, very miserably clad," replied the Baron, making a face of disgust.

"Well," continued our hero, "that outer misery hides within a large heart and a right sensitive nature. I am very sensible to an insult, and resent disdain and injury at least as much as you do, noble Baron. You do not scruple to insult my misery."

"Hold thy tongue, thou beggarly chatterbox. Dost dare compare thyself with me, the Lord Fitz-Alwine? Go to, thou art mad."

"I am a poor man," said Robin, "a very poor, miserable man."

"I did not come here to listen to the prating of one of thy sort," returned the Baron, impatiently. "If thou dost refuse my offer, get you gone; if thou dost accept it, prepare to fill thine office."

"I do not rightly know in what mine office consists," returned Robin, who was seeking to gain time for his men to reach the outskirts of the wood. "I have never acted as hangman, and I thank the Holy Virgin for it. Cursed be the infamous trade and the miserable wretch who doth practise it."

"How now? dost mock me?" roared the Baron, beside himself at Robin's insolence. "Hark thee, if thou dost not set about thy work at once, I will have thee soundly beaten."

"And would that help you on at all, my Lord?" returned Robin. "Would you the more readily find a man disposed to carry out your orders? No, you have just made a proclamation which all have heard, and yet I am the only man who hath offered to do your wishes."

"I know well enow what art driving at, base wretch," cried the Baron, overwhelmed with rage. "Thou wouldst have the sum promised thee for despatching these clowns into another world increased."

Robin shrugged his shoulders.

"Let them be hanged by whom you please," replied he, affecting complete indifference.

"Not at all, not at all," returned the Baron, in a milder voice; "thou shalt do the work. I will double the reward, and if thou dost not fill thine office exactly, I shall have the right to call thee the least conscientious hangman in the world."

"If I wished to put the unhappy creatures to death," replied Robin, "I should content myself with the reward you have already offered me, but I refuse point blank to soil my hands by contact with the gallows."

"What dost mean, wretch?" bellowed the Baron.

"Wait, my Lord; I will call for men who, at my command, will deliver you for ever from the sight of these terrible culprits."

As he finished speaking Robin blew a joyous flourish upon his hunting-horn, and laid his hands upon the terrified Baron.

"My Lord," said he, "your life hangs by a thread; if you make a movement, I plunge this knife into your heart. Forbid your servants to come to your assistance," Robin added, brandishing an immense hunting-knife over the old man's head.

"Soldiers, remain in your ranks!" cried the Baron, in a stentorian voice.

The sun glanced off the sparkling blade of the knife, and the shining reflection dazzled the old lord, and made him appreciate his adversary's power; so, instead of attempting an impossible resistance, he submitted with groans.

"What dost desire of me?" he said, trying to put a conciliatory softness into his voice.

"The life of the three men whom you would hang, my Lord," replied Robin Hood.

"I cannot grant thee that boon, my good man," returned the old man; "the unhappy creatures have killed the King's deer, which misdemeanor is punishable by death. The whole town of Nottingham knows of their crime and their sentence, and if, from a culpable weakness I grant thy prayer, the King would be informed of a compliance so entirely inexcusable."

At that moment at great tumult was observed among the crowd, and the whistling of arrows was heard.

Robin, who knew his men were come, gave a shout.

"Ah, you are Robin Hood," groaned the Baron.

"Yea, my Lord," replied our hero, "I am Robin Hood."

Protected in a friendly manner by the inhabitants of the town, the Merrie Men now appeared from all directions, and Will Scarlett with his brave fellows soon joined their companions.

The prisoners once free, Baron Fitz-Alwine saw plainly that the only means of getting himself safe and sound out of such a critical situation was to conciliate Robin Hood.

"Take the prisoners away quickly," said he. "My soldiers, exasperated by the remembrance of a recent defeat, might put obstacles in the way of the success of your project."

"This act of courtesy was dictated to you by fear," retorted Robin Hood, laughingly. "I do not dread any violence from your soldiers; the number and valour of my men render them invulnerable."

Saying which, Robin Hood saluted the old man ironically, turned his back on him, and ordered his men to hie them back to the Forest.

The Baron's livid features expressed rage and fear. He called his men together, remounted his horse, and rode off in all haste.

The citizens of Nottingham, who regarded poaching as hardly a blameworthy action, surrounded the Merrie Men, uttering shouts of joy. Then the chief men of the town, put at ease by the Baron's flight, testified their sympathy to Robin Hood, while the parents of the young prisoners embraced the knees of their sons' deliverer.

The humble and sincere thanks of these poor people appealed more to Robin Hood's heart than any lofty sentiments expressed in flowery rhetoric could have done.

CHAPTER IX

A whole year had slipped away since the day when Robin had so generously succoured Sir Richard of the Plain, and for some weeks past the Merrie Men had again taken up their abode in Barnsdale Forest. From the early morning of the day fixed for the Knight's visit Robin had been prepared to receive him, but the appointed hour did not bring the expected visitor.

"He will not come," said Will Scarlett, who, with Little John and Robin, was seated beneath a tree watching with some impatience the road which stretched before them.

"Sir Richard's ingratitude will give us a lesson," replied Robin. "It will teach us to put no trust in the promises of men; but for the sake of the human race I should not like to be deceived by Sir Richard, for I have never seen a man who bore in his countenance more visible imprints of loyalty and frankness; and I declare that if my debtor doth not keep his word, I shall no longer know by what external sign to know an honest man."

"I await the good Knight's coming with certainty," said Little John. "The sun is not yet hidden beyond the trees, and Sir Richard will be here before another hour hath passed."

"May God grant it, my dear John," replied Robin Hood, "for, like you, I would fain hope that the word of a Saxon is a pledge of honour. I will stay here until the first stars begin to peep out, and if the Knight come not, I shall mourn for him as for a friend. Take your arms, my lads, call Much, and patrol the road leading to St. Mary's Abbey. You may meet with Sir Richard, or, in default of that ungrateful man, some rich Norman, or even some half-famished devil. I wish to see some unknown face; go, seek some adventure, and bring me any guest whatsoever."

"That indeed is a strange way of consoling yourself, my dear Robin," laughed Will, "but it shall be as you wish. We will go in search of some passing distraction."

The two young men called Much, and on his appearance they all set off together in the direction indicated by Robin.

"Robin is very gloomy to-day," said Will, thoughtfully.

"Why?" asked Much, in a tone of surprise.

"Because he fears he hath been deceived in trusting Sir Richard of the Plain," replied Little John.

"I do not see why it should cause Robin such sorrow; we do not need money, and four hundred crowns more or less in our treasure-chest..."

"Robin doth not think of the money," interrupted John, almost irritably. "You are talking very foolishly, cousin. Robin is wounded at having helped an ungrateful soul, that is all."

"Stop," said Will. "I hear horses approaching."

"I will go and meet the travellers," cried Much, running off.

"If it is the Knight, call us," said John.

William and his cousin waited, and soon Much re-appeared at the end of the path.

"It is not Sir Richard," said he, as he came up to his friends, "but two Dominican friars accompanied by a dozen men."

"If these Dominicans have a cavalcade at their heels," said John, "you may be sure they are richly provided with gold, consequently they must be invited to partake of Robin's repast."

"Shall we call some of the Merrie Men?" asked Will.

"'Tis not needful; the cravens' hearts are in their legs and are so much the slaves of the latter that in the presence of danger their one thought is flight. But hold! here comes the monks. Remember, we absolutely must take them to Robin; he is dull, and 'twill be a pleasant distraction for him. Get ready your bows, and be prepared to bar the way of this fine cavalcade."

William and Much hastened to carry out his orders.

On turning a corner of the road, which wound at will among the trees, the travellers perceived the Foresters and the hostile position they had taken up.

The servants, terrified at the dangerous encounter, reined in their steeds, and the Monks, who occupied the front rank of the little column, tried to hide themselves behind their men.

"Do not attempt to move," cried John, commandingly, "or I will surely kill you."

The Monks grew pale, but, finding themselves at the mercy of the Foresters, they obeyed the order so roughly given.

"Fair stranger," said one of the Monks, grinning most amiably, "what do you desire from a poor servant of Holy Church?"

"I desire that ye bestir yourselves. My master hath awaited you this three hours, and the dinner groweth cold."

The Dominicans exchanged uneasy looks.

"Your words are a riddle to us, my friend. Be so good as to explain yourself," replied one of them in honeyed tones.

"I will say it once again, and it needs no explanation—my master awaits you."

"Who is your master, my friend?"

"Robin Hood," replied Little John, shortly.

A shudder of fear passed like an icy blast over the men who accompanied the Monks. They glanced fearfully around them, expecting, no doubt, to see more outlaws burst from the thicket.

"Robin Hood," repeated the Monk, in a voice more harsh than musical. "I know of Robin Hood; he is a robber by profession, on whose head a price is set."

"Robin Hood is no robber," replied Little John, furiously, "and I do not counsel any one to echo the insolent accusation you bring against my noble master. But I have no time to discuss so delicate a point with you. Robin Hood invites you to dinner; follow me without demur! As for your servants, I warn them to show me their heels, an if they wish to save their lives. Will and Much, bring down the first man who attempts to remain here against my wishes."

The Foresters, who had lowered their bows during the conversation between the Monk and Little John, raised them once more, and stood ready to discharge their arrows. Seeing the bows raised and turned against them, the Dominicans' men set spur to their steeds and saved themselves with a precipitation which spoke volumes for their prudence. The Monks were preparing to follow the example of their men when they were arrested by John, who constrained them to stop by seizing the bridles of their horses. Behind the Monks, John perceived a young groom who appeared to be in charge of a sumpter horse, and near the groom stood a boy, dressed as a page and dumb with fear.

More courageous than the men of the escort, the two youths had not deserted their posts.

"Keep an eye on those young rogues. I give them permission to follow their masters."

Robin had remained seated beneath the Trysting Tree, but when he saw John and his companions, he rose quickly, and, advancing to meet them, greeted the Monks with effusion.

"Never heed the insolent fellows, Robin," said John, irritated by the Monks' want of respect. "They are but ignorant fellows; they have never a kind word for the poor nor courtesy toward any one at all."

"No matter," replied Robin. "I know the Monks, and I expect from them neither good words nor gracious smiles; but I am a slave to politeness. Whom have you there, Will?" added Robin, looking at the two pages and the sumpter horse.

"The remainder of a troop consisting of a dozen men," replied the young man, with a laugh.

"What have you done with the main body of this valiant army?"

"Naught at all; the sight of our bent bows threw its ranks into confusion, and they fled without even turning their heads."

Robin began to laugh.

"But, worthy brothers," he continued, addressing the Monks, "you must be very hungry after so long a journey; will ye share my meal?"

The Dominicans regarded the Merrie Men, who had run up at the sound of the horn, with so terrified an expression that Robin said kindly to them, in order to calm their fears—

"Fear naught, good Monks; no harm shall befall you. Seat yourselves at the table, and eat your fill."

The Monks obeyed, but it was easy to see that they were but little reassured by the young Chief's kind words.

"Where is your Abbey?" asked Robin; "and what name doth it bear?"

"I belong to the Abbey of St. Mary," said the elder of the Monks, "and I am the Grand Cellarer of the Monastery."

"Welcome, Brother Cellarer," said Robin. "I am happy to receive a man of your worth. You shall give me your opinion on my wine, for you must be an excellent judge in such matters; though I dare hope you will find it to your taste, for, being myself difficult to please, I always drink wine of the best quality."

The Monks took heart; they ate with a good appetite, and the Cellarer acknowledged the excellence of the dishes and the full body of the wine, adding that it was a real pleasure to dine upon the turf in such joyous company.

"My good brothers," said Robin Hood, toward the end of the meal, "ye appeared surprised at being asked to dinner by a man whom ye did not know. I will explain the mystery of the invitation in a few words. A year ago I lent a sum of money to a friend of your Prior, and accepted as a guarantee the Holy Mother of Jesus, our sainted patroness. My unshakeable confidence in the Holy Virgin led me to believe firmly that at the expiration of the appointed term I should receive in some manner the money I had lent. Whereupon I sent three of my men to seek for travellers; they saw you, and brought you hither. You belong to a Monastery, and I can guess the delicate mission confided to you by the provident and generous benevolence of our Holy Patroness; you are come to repay me in Her name the money lent to the poor man. Be ye welcome!"

"The debt of which you speak is quite unknown to me, Master," returned the Monk, "and I do not bring you any money."

"You are mistaken, Father; I feel certain that the chests carried by that horse led by your page contain the amount due to me. How many pieces of gold have you in that pretty little leathern trunk attached so securely to the poor beast?"

The Monk, thunderstruck by Robin Hood's question, grew pale, and stammered out in an almost unintelligible voice—

"I have scarce anything, Master; at most but a score of gold pieces."

"Only twenty pieces of gold?" returned Robin, fixing a stern look upon the Monk.

"Yea, Master," replied the Monk, whose livid face became suddenly suffused with colour.

"If you are speaking the truth," said Robin, in a friendly tone, "I will not take one groat of your small fortune from you. Better still, I will give you as much money as you may need. But, on the other hand, if you have had the bad taste to lie to me, I will not leave you even a penny piece. Little John," continued Robin, "open the little trunk; if you find there but twenty pieces of gold, you may respect our guests' property, but if the sum is double or treble that amount, take it all."

Little John hastened to obey Robin's order. The colour faded from the Monk's cheeks; tears of rage coursed down his cheeks; he clasped his hands convulsively together, and a deep groan burst from him.

"Ho, ho!" said Robin, watching the Brother, "it appears that the twenty pieces of gold are in numerous company. Well, John," he asked, "is our guest as poor as he would fain make out?"

"I know not if he be poor," answered John; "but of one thing am I well assured, and that is that I have just found eight hundred gold pieces in the little trunk."

"Leave me the money, Master," said the Monk; "it is not mine, and I am responsible for it to my Father Superior."

"To whom bear you these eight hundred pieces of gold?" questioned Robin.

"To the Inspectors of St. Mary's Abbey, from our Abbot."

"The Inspectors abuse the generosity of your Prior, Brother, and it ill becomes them to repay themselves so heavily for a few words of indulgence. This time they shall have nothing, and you will tell them that Robin Hood, having need of money, hath carried off the sum they expected."

"There is yet another chest," said John; "shall I open it?"

"Nay," replied Robin; "I will content myself with eight hundred pieces of gold. Sir Monk, you are free to continue your journey. You have been treated with courtesy, and I hope I see you depart satisfied on all points."

"I do not consider a forcible invitation and an open theft very courteous," said the Monk, superciliously. "Here am I obliged to return to the Monastery, and what can I say to the Prior?"

"You will greet him from me," laughed Robin Hood. "He knows me, the worthy Father, and he will be very sensible of this token of good friendship."

The Monks mounted their horses, and, with hearts bursting with rage, galloped off along the road leading to the Abbey.

"The Holy Virgin be praised!" cried Little John; "she hath returned to us the money you lent Sir Richard, and if the latter have broken his word, we can still console ourselves in that we have lost nothing."

"I cannot so easily console myself in having lost confidence in the word of a Saxon," replied Robin, "and I should have preferred a visit from Sir Richard, poor and despoiled of everything, rather than be convinced that he is ungrateful and without honour."

"Noble Master," suddenly called a voice from the glade, "a Knight appeareth on the high-road, accompanied by an hundred men, all armed to the teeth. Shall we prepare to bar their way?"

"Are they Normans?" asked Robin, quickly.

"One seldom sees Saxons so richly clothed as these travellers," answered the lad who had announced the approach of the troop.

"Look alive, then, my Merrie Men," cried Robin. "To your bows and lurking-places. Get ready your arrows, but draw not ere you receive my order to attack."

The men disappeared, and the cross-road where Robin remained soon appeared completely deserted.

"You come not with us?" John asked Robin, who sat motionless at the foot of a tree.

"Nay," rejoined the young man; "I will await the strangers, and find out with whom we have to deal."

"Then I remain with you," said Little John, "to be alone might prove dangerous for you, an arrow is so quickly sped. If they strike you, I am at least here to defend you."

"I, too, will remain as body-guard," said Will, seating himself beside Robin, who had stretched himself carelessly on the grass.

The unexpected arrival of a body of men so formidable in proportion to the number of the Foresters, who were mostly scattered all about the wood, disquieted Robin slightly, and he did not wish to commence hostilities before being assured of victory.

The horsemen advanced rapidly along the glade. When they were an arrow's flight from where Robin lay, the man who seemed to be their chief cantered up to encounter Robin.

"It is Sir Richard," cried John gaily, as he looked at the approaching horseman.

"Holy Mother, I praise thee!" said Robin, springing to his feet. "A Saxon hath not broken his word."

Sir Richard leapt from his horse, ran toward Robin, and threw himself into his arms.

"God keep thee, Robin Hood," said he, giving the young man a fatherly embrace. "God keep thee in health and happiness to thy last day!"

"Be welcome to the green wood, gentle Knight," replied Robin, with emotion. "I am happy to see thee true to thy promise, and with a heart full of kindness to thy devoted servant."

"I should have come empty-handed even, Robin Hood, to have the honour of wringing thy hand; but, luckily for mine own satisfaction, I can return the money thou didst lend me with so much grace, kindness, and courtesy."

"Hast, then, recovered entirely the possession of thy property?" asked Robin Hood.

"Yea, and may God prosper thee in proportion to the happiness which I owe to thee."

Robin's attention was next attracted by the men, magnificently clad in the fashion of the day, who formed a glittering line behind Sir Richard.

"Doth this fine troop belong to thee?" asked the young man.

"It doth at present," answered the Knight, with a smile.

"I admire the bearing of the men and their martial figures," continued Robin, in a tone of some surprise; "they seem to be perfectly disciplined."

"Yea, they are brave and faithful, and all of Saxon origin, and their temper loyal—for I have proved all the qualities which I have described to thee. Thou wouldst do me a good service, dear Robin, if thou wouldst instruct thy men to entertain my companions; they have made a long journey, and will require some hours of repose."

"They shall learn the meaning of forest hospitality," replied Robin, heartily. "My Merrie Men," continued he to his band, who began to appear on all sides, "these strangers are brother Saxons, they are hungry and thirsty; I pray you show them how we treat the friends who visit us in the green wood."

The Foresters obeyed Robin's orders with a promptitude which should have satisfied Sir Richard, for before retiring with his host he beheld the turf covered with viands, pots of ale and bottles of good wine.

Robin Hood, Sir Richard, Little John, and Will sat down to a succulent repast, and when dessert was brought, the Knight began the following account of the events which had befallen him since his first encounter with our hero.

"I cannot depict to you, my good friends, with what sentiments of gratitude and infinite joy I quitted the Forest a year agone to-day. My heart leapt within me, and I was in so great a haste to see my wife and children once more, that I regained the Castle in less time than it would take to tell you all my story.

"'We are saved,' I cried, straining my beloved ones to my heart. My wife dissolved in tears, and almost fainted.

"'Who is the generous friend who hath come to our aid?' asked Herbert.

"'My children,' I replied, 'I knocked in vain at every door; in vain I implored the succour of those who called themselves my friends; and I received no pity save from one man to whom I was unknown. This benevolent man is a noble Outlaw, the protector of the poor, the support of the wretched, the avenger of the oppressed, and his name is Robin Hood.'

"My children knelt around their mother, and piously rendered to God the sincere thanks of a profound gratitude. This duty accomplished, Herbert entreated me to allow him to pay thee a visit, but I pointed out to him that such a step would give thee more pain than pleasure, since thou dost not love to hear thy good deeds spoken of."

"My dear Knight," interrupted Robin, "let us put aside this part of thy story, and tell us how thou didst arrange thy business with the Abbot of St. Mary's."

"Patience, good host, patience," said Sir Richard, with a smile. "I do not wish to praise thee. Be not afraid; I know thy admirable modesty on that point. Nevertheless, I must tell thee that sweet Lilas joined her prayers to Herbert's, and I was obliged to exert all my paternal authority to calm the impatience of their young hearts. I promised my children in your name, however, that they should have the happiness of seeing you at the Castle."

"Thou didst well, Sir Richard, and I promise thee that some day I will seek thy hospitality," said Robin, with emotion.

"Thank thee, good host; I will inform Herbert and Lilas of the engagement thou hast just made, and the hope of thanking thee in person will give them great satisfaction."

"On the morrow of my return," continued Sir Richard, "I presented myself at St. Mary's Abbey. I learnt later that at the very moment that I was making my way towards the Abbey, the Abbot and the Prior were together in the refectory and speaking of me in these terms—

"'It is a year to-day,' said the Abbot to the Prior, 'since a Knight whose domains adjoin the Monastery, borrowed from me four hundred pieces of gold; he was to repay me the money with interest, or leave me the free disposal of all his property. According to me, the time is up at mid-day, therefore I consider the moment for payment hath arrived, and I consider myself absolute master of all his hereditaments.'

"'Brother,' returned the Prior, indignantly, 'you are cruel; a poor man with a debt to discharge should in all justice have a final delay of four and twenty hours. It would be shameful of you to lay claim to property on which you had no rights. In acting thus you would ruin an unfortunate creature and reduce him to great misery, while as a member of Holy Church it is your duty to relieve as much as possible the burden which doth weigh upon our unfortunate fellow-creatures.'

"'Keep your counsels for those who need them,' replied the Abbot, angrily. 'I will do what meseemeth good without heeding your hypocritical reflections.'

"At this moment the Chief Cellarer entered the refectory.

"'Have you any news of Sir Richard of the Plain?' the Abbot asked of him.

"'Nay. But that matters not. All I know is that his property is now yours, Sir Abbot.'

"'The Chief Judge is here,' continued the Abbot; 'I will ask him whether I may now claim Sir Richard's Castle.'

"The Abbot went to find the Judge, and the latter, for due consideration received, replied to the Monk—

"'Sir Richard will not come to-day, therefore you may consider yourself entitled to all his estates.'

"This iniquitous judgment had just been given when I presented myself at the gate of the Monastery.

"In order to prove the generosity of my creditor, I had arrayed myself in mean garments, while the men who accompanied me were also very poorly accoutred.

"The porter of the Abbey came to meet me. I had been kind to him in the time of my prosperity, and the poor man had not forgotten it. He told me of the conversation which had taken place between the Abbot and the Prior. I was not surprised; I knew well that I had no reason to expect any grace from the holy man.

"'Be welcome,' continued the Monk; 'your arrival will be a very agreeable surprise to the Prior. My Lord Abbot will doubtless be less satisfied, for already he looketh upon himself as owner of your estates. You will find a large company in the Great Hall, several lords and gentlemen. I hope, Sir Richard, that you will put no confidence in the honeyed words of our Father Superior, and that you have brought the money,' added the porter, in tones of affectionate solicitude.

"I reassured the good Monk, and proceeded alone to the Great Hall, where the whole of the Community was assembled in solemn conclave, to make arrangements for informing me of the sequestration of my property.

"The exalted assembly was so disagreeably surprised at my appearance that I might well have been some phantom come from another world on purpose to snatch from their grasp some ardently coveted prey.

"I humbly saluted the honourable company and, with an air of false humility, I said to the Abbot—

"'You see, Sir Abbot, I have kept my promise and have come back.'

"'Have you brought the money?' demanded the holy man, sharply.

"'Alas! not one penny....'

"A pleased smile hovered on the lips of my generous creditor.

"'Then what doest thou here, an thou art not prepared to discharge thy debt?'

"'I am come to entreat you to give me yet a few days longer.'

"'It is impossible; according to our agreement, thou must pay this very day. If thou canst not do it, thine estates belong to me; besides which, the Judge hath so decided. Is that not true, my Lord?'

"'It is,' replied the Judge. 'Sir Richard,' he continued, throwing a contemptuous look at me, 'the lands of your ancestors are the property of our worthy Abbot.'

"I feigned a great despair and entreated the Abbot to have compassion upon me, to grant me three days longer. I depicted to him the miserable fate in store for my wife and children, an they were turned out of their home. The Abbot was deaf to my entreaties, he wearied of my presence, and imperiously commanded me to quit the Hall.

"Exasperated by this unmerited treatment, I held up my head proudly, and advancing to the middle of the great room, I laid upon the table a bag full of money.

"'Here are the four hundred pieces of gold you lent me. The dial doth not as yet show the hour of noon; I have therefore fulfilled all the conditions of our agreement, and, despite your subterfuges, my estates will not change owners.'

"You cannot conceive, Robin," added the Knight, laughing, "the Abbot's stupefaction, rage, and fury. He rolled his head from side to side and glared around him, muttering incoherently, and looking like a madman.

"After enjoying the spectacle of his dumb fury for a few seconds, I left the Hall and regained the Porter's lodge. There I arrayed myself in more suitable garments; my men also changed their clothes, and, accompanied by an escort worthy of my rank, I re-entered the Hall.

"The change in my outer appearance seemed to strike the company with astonishment; deliberately I advanced to the Judge's chair.

"'I address myself to you, my Lord,' I said, in a loud firm voice, 'to ask in the presence of this honourable company whether, having fulfilled all the conditions of my bond, the lands and Castle of the Plain are not mine?'

"'They are yours,' replied the Judge, reluctantly.

"I acknowledged the justice of this decision and left the Monastery with a light heart.

"On the way home, I met my wife and children.

"'Rejoice, my dear ones,' I said, as I embraced them, 'and pray for Robin Hood; for without him we should be beggars. And now let us try to show generous Robin Hood that we are not insensible of the service he hath rendered us.'

"We set to work the very next day, and my estates, with proper cultivation, soon realised the value of thy loan. I bring thee five hundred pieces of gold, my good Robin, one hundred bows of the finest yew, with quivers and arrows, and besides that, I make thee a present of the troop of men whose fine appearance thou didst but now admire. The men are well armed and each one hath a good horse to ride. Accept them as followers, they will serve thee with gratitude and fidelity."

"I should hurt mine own self-esteem an I were to accept so rich a gift, my dear Knight," replied Robin with emotion. "Nor can I take the money which thou dost bring. The Chief Cellarer of St. Mary's Abbey broke his fast with me this morning and his expenses here have put eight hundred pieces of gold into our coffers. I do not take money twice in one day; I have taken the monk's gold in place of thine, and thou art out of thy debt. I know, my dear Knight, that the revenues of thy property have been impoverished by the King's exactions, and they must be carefully managed. Think of thy children. I am rich; the Normans crowd into these parts with their pockets full of money. Never speak of service or gratitude betwixt us, unless I can be useful in furthering the fortunes or the happiness of those whom thou dost love."

"Thou dost treat me in so noble and generous a manner," replied Sir Richard, greatly moved, "that I feel I should be indiscreet to force upon thee a gift which thou dost refuse."

"Yea, Sir Knight, let us speak no more of it," said Robin gaily. "But tell me how it is thou didst come so late to keep thine assignation."

"On my way hither," replied Sir Richard, "I passed through a village where all the best yeomen of the West Country were gathered together, occupied in trying feats of strength against one another. The prizes destined for the victor were a white bull, a horse, a saddle and bridle studded with gold nails, a pair of gauntlets, a silver ring, and a cask of old wine. I stopped awhile to watch the sport. A yeoman of ordinary size gave such proofs of strength that it was evident the prizes would be his, and, indeed, having felled all his adversaries, he remained master of the field. They were about to give him the objects he had earned so well, when he was recognised as one of thy band."

"Was he in truth one of my men?" asked Robin, quickly.

"Yea, they called him Jasper the Tinker."

"Then he gained the prizes, brave Jasper?"

"He gained them all; but under pretext of his being one of the band of Merrie Men, they disputed his right to them. Jasper defended his cause valiantly. And then two or three of the other combatants set to calling thee evil names. Thou shouldst have seen the vigour of lungs and muscles with which Jasper defended thee; he spake so loud and gesticulated so wildly that knives were drawn, and thy poor Jasper would have been vanquished by the number or treachery of his enemies, when, aided by my men, I put them all to flight. This small service rendered to the brave lad, I gave him five pieces of gold to drink with, and I invited the fugitives to make acquaintance with the cask of wine. As you may imagine, they did not refuse; and I brought Jasper away in order to save him from their future vengeance."

"I thank thee for having saved one of my brave fellows, my dear Knight," said Robin. "He who lends his support to my companions hath an endless claim upon my friendship. An ever thou have need of me, ask me what thou wilt; my arm and purse are ever at thy disposal."

"I shall always look upon thee as a true friend, Robin," answered the Knight; "and I hope that thou wilt treat me in the same spirit."

The remaining hours of the afternoon wore merrily away, and toward evening Sir Richard accompanied Robin, Will, and little John to Barnsdale Hall, where all the members of the Gamwell family were again assembled.

Sir Richard could hardly refrain from smiling as he admired the ten charming women who were presented to him. After having directed the Knight's attention to his beloved Maude, Will took his guest aside and asked him in a whisper if he had ever seen so ravishing a face as Maude's.

The Knight smiled, and whispered to Will that he would be lacking in gallantry toward the other ladies, if he permitted himself to say aloud what he thought of the adorable Maude.

William, enchanted by this gracious reply, went over to his wife and kissed her with the firm conviction that he was the most favoured of husbands and the happiest of men.

When night fell, Sir Richard left Barnsdale, and, escorted by some of Robin's men, who were to guide him through the Forest, he soon regained the Castle of the Plain with his numerous following.

CHAPTER X

The Sheriff of Nottingham (we are now speaking of Lord Fitz-Alwine of happy memory) having learnt that Robin Hood and a portion of his band were in Yorkshire, thought it would be possible, with a strong troop of his own brave men-at-arms, to clear Sherwood Forest of these outlaws, who, separated from their chief, would find it impossible to defend themselves. In planning this clever expedition, Lord Fitz-Alwine resolved to watch the approaches to the Forest in order to catch Robin as he returned. We know that the Baron's mercenaries were not very courageous, but he likewise sent to London for a troop of ruffians and trained them himself for the pursuit of the Outlaws.

The Merrie Men had so many friends in Nottingham that they were warned of the fate in store for them and the Baron's kind intentions, even before he himself had fixed the day on which the bloody battle was to take place.

This gave the Foresters time to put themselves on the defensive, and to prepare to receive the Sheriff's troops.

Attracted by the hope of a rich reward, the Baron's men marched to the attack with every appearance of indomitable courage. But no sooner had they entered the wood, than they were met by such a terrible volley of arrows that the ground was strewn with the corpses of half their number.

A second volley, more vigorous and more murderous still, followed the first; each arrow found its mark while the bowmen remained invisible.

Having thus filled the ranks of the enemy with fear and confusion, the Foresters broke from their hiding-places, shouting loudly and overthrowing all who tried to resist them. A terrible panic spread among the Baron's troop, and in indescribable confusion they regained Nottingham Castle.

Not one of the Merrie Men was wounded in this strange encounter, and in the evening, recovered from their fatigue, as fresh and vigorous as they had been before the combat, they collected upon litters the bodies of the soldiers who had been killed, and deposited them at the Outer Gate of Lord Fitz-Alwine's Castle.

Desperate and furious, the Baron passed the night in cursing his luck. He accused his men; he said that his patron saint had deserted him; he laid the blame of the non-success of his arms on everybody, and proclaimed himself a valiant leader, but the victim of the faintheartedness of his subordinates.

On the evening of the following day, one of Lord Fitz-Alwine's Norman friends came to visit him, accompanied by fifty men-at-arms. The Baron told him of his misadventure, adding, doubtless to excuse his perpetual defeats, that Robin Hood's band was ever and always invisible.

"My dear Baron," quietly replied Sir Guy Gisborne (such was the visitor's name), "if Robin Hood were the devil in person and I took it into my head to tear out his horns, I should tear them out."

"Words are not deeds, my friend," answered the old man sharply; "and it is very easy to say, 'I could do that, an I would,' but I defy you to catch Robin Hood."

"An it pleased me to take him," said the Norman, carelessly, "there would be no need to excite myself. I feel strong enough to tame a lion, and, after all, Robin Hood is only a man; a clever man, I admit, but not a diabolical or unassailable being."

"You may say what you please, Sir Guy," declared the Baron, evidently bent on persuading the Norman to make an attempt against Robin Hood, "but there is not a man in England, be he peasant, soldier, or great Lord, could make this heroic Outlaw bow down before him. He believes in naught, he fears naught, and a whole army would not intimidate him."

Sir Guy smiled disdainfully.

"I do not doubt the bravery of your fine Outlaw in the very least," said he; "but you must own, Baron, that up to the present Robin Hood hath fought only phantoms."

"What!" cried the Baron, cruelly wounded in his self-esteem as commander-in-chief.

"Yea, phantoms; I repeat it, my friend. Your soldiers are made, not of flesh and bones, but of mud and milk. Who ever saw such fools? They fly before the Outlaws' arrows, and the name alone of Robin Hood sets them a-shuddering. Oh! if I were but in your place!"

"What would you do?" asked the Baron, eagerly.

"I would hang Robin Hood."

"My good intentions in that respect are not lacking," replied the Baron, sombrely.

"So I perceive, Baron. It is the power that is lacking. Well, it is lucky for your enemy that he hath never found himself face to face with me."

"Ha, ha!" laughed the Baron, "you would put your spear through his body, would you not? You amuse me very much, my friend, with all your bragging. Let be, you would tremble from head to foot, if I were only to say, 'There is Robin Hood.'"

The Norman bounded up.

"Know well," said he, furiously, "that I have no fear of either man or devil or of anything in the world, and I challenge you to test my courage. Since the name of Robin Hood was the starting-point of our conversation, I ask you, as a favour, to put me on the track of this man whom you are pleased to consider invincible, only because you are unable to vanquish him. I undertake to seize him, crop his ears, and hang him up by the feet, with no more compunction than if he were a hog. Where is this mighty man to be met with?"

"In Barnsdale Forest."

"How far is the Forest from Nottingham?"

"Two days' journey would take us there by unfrequented ways; and as I should be grieved, my dear Sir Guy, if you were to come to any harm through me, if you will permit it, I will join my men to yours, and together we will go seek the rascal. I have learnt from a trustworthy source, that, at this moment, he is separated from the greater part of his men; it would therefore be easy, if we act with prudence, to surround the robbers' den, carry off their Chief, and deliver his band over to the vengeance of our soldiers. Mine have suffered greatly in Sherwood Forest, and they would be overjoyed to take a fierce and savage revenge."

"I am right glad to accept your offer, my good friend," replied the Norman; "for it will give me the satisfaction of proving to you that Robin Hood is neither a devil nor invincible. And, not only to equalise the struggle between the Outlaw and myself, but likewise to show you that I do not intend to act in any underhand manner, I will don a yeoman's costume and fight hand to hand with Robin Hood."

The Baron concealed the pleasure which his guest's vainglorious reply gave him, and in a fearful and solicitous tone, hazarded some timid remarks on the danger his excellent friend would run, and on the imprudence of a disguise which would put him in direct contact with a man renowned for his strength and skill.

The Norman, bursting with vanity and self-confidence, cut short the Baron's false-hearted objections; and the latter hastened with a briskness quite remarkable in one of his age to make ready his men-at-arms.

An hour later, Sir Guy Gisborne and Lord Fitz-Alwine, accompanied by a hundred men, and with the air of conquerors, took the cross-road that would lead them to Barnsdale Forest.

It had been arranged between the Baron and his new ally that he should direct his troop toward that part of the wood agreed upon beforehand, while, guarding against any appearance of sinister motive by his yeoman's garb, Sir Guy would take another direction, seek out Robin Hood, and fight him whether or no, and would, of course, slay him. The success of the Norman (we might add that he did not in the least doubt his own success) would be announced to the Baron by a peculiar blast upon a hunting-horn. At this triumphant call, the Baron would proclaim the Norman's victory, and gallop up to the field of battle. The victory verified by the sight of Robin's corpse, the soldiers would search the thickets and copses and underground retreats, to kill or take prisoner (the choice was graciously left to them) any Outlaws unlucky enough to fall into their hands.

ROBIN HOOD THE OUTLAW

Whilst the troop were making their way secretly to Barnsdale Forest, Robin Hood was stretched carelessly beneath the thick foliage of the Trysting Tree, fast asleep.

Little John was seated at his leader's feet, thinking the while of his charming wife and his sweet Winifred's many good qualities of heart and mind, when his tender dream was disturbed by the shrill cry of a thrush, which, perched on one of the lower branches of the Trysting Tree, sang out loud and shrill.

This strident warbling woke Robin abruptly, and he leapt up with a gesture of fear.

"Why, Robin," said Little John, "what is it?"

"Naught," replied the young man, composing himself again. "I had a dream, and I know not whether I should say it, but I was frightened. Methought I was attacked by two yeoman; they beat me unmercifully, and I returned their blows with an equal generosity. However, I was almost vanquished, death stood beside me, when a bird which came I know not whence, sang to me, 'Take courage, I will send thee help.' I am awake, and I see neither the bird nor the danger. But then dreams do not come true," added Robin, smiling.

"I am not of your opinion, Captain," said John, seriously, "for part of your dream was true. A moment agone, upon the branch which you are touching, a thrush was singing with all its might. Your awakening put it to flight. Perhaps it came to warn you."

"Are you getting superstitious, friend John?" asked Robin, pleasantly. "Come, come, at your age 'twould be ridiculous; such childishness is for young girls and boys, not for us. However," he continued, "perchance 'tis wise, in an existence so adventurous as ours, to pay attention to every occurrence. Who knows? Perhaps the thrush said, 'Sentinels, beware!' and we are the sentinels of a troop of brave men. Forward, then; forewarned is forearmed."

Robin wound his horn, and the Merrie Men, dispersed through the wood, ran up in answer to his call.

Robin sent them down the road to York, for on that side alone was an attack to be feared, and, accompanied by John, he went to search the opposite side of the wood, William and two stout Foresters taking the road to Mansfield.

After searching the paths and roads toward which they had bent their steps, Robin and John made their way down the road followed by Will Scarlett. There, in a vale, they met a yeoman with his body wrapped in the skin of a horse, which served him for cloak. At that epoch, this strange garment was in great favour among the Yorkshire yeomen, the greater number of whom were engaged in horse breeding.

The newcomer wore at his side a sword and dirk, and his face, with its cruel expression, told plainly enough of the murderous uses to which his weapons were wont to be put.

"Ha, ha!" cried Robin, as he perceived him, "upon my soul, here comes a very ruffian. Crime oozes from him. I will question him; but an if he do not answer like an honest man, I will see the colour of his blood."

138

"He hath the appearance of a mastiff with good teeth, Robin. Beware; do you remain beneath this tree, while I ask his name, surname, and qualities."

"My dear John," replied Robin, quickly, "I have taken a fancy to that rascal. Let me tan his hide in mine own way. It is a long time since I was beaten, and, by the Holy Mother, my good protectress, I should never exchange a blow with any one if I listened to your prudent advice. Take care, friend John," added Robin, in an affectionate tone, "there will come a time when in default of an adversary, I shall be obliged to beat thee unmercifully; oh! only to keep my hand in, but thou wilt be none the less the victim of thy benevolent generosity. Go and rejoin Will, and do not return to me until thou hearest the sound of a triumphant blast."

"Your will is my law, Robin Hood," answered John, in an offended voice, "and it is my duty to obey, however unwillingly."

We will leave Robin on his way to meet the stranger, and we will follow Little John, who, faithful slave to his Chief's commands, hastened after William, who had started with two men on the high-road to Mansfield.

About three hundred yards from the spot where Little John left Robin alone with the yeoman, he found Will Scarlett with his two companions, occupied in exercising all their strength against a dozen soldiers. John gave a shout, and with a bound placed himself beside his friends. But the danger, already so great, became even more so as the clash of arms and the sound of horses' hoofs attracted the young man's attention to the extremity of the road.

At the end of the road, and in the half-shadow cast by the trees, appeared a company of soldiers, and at their head trotted a richly caparisoned horse.

John sprang forward to meet the newcomers, bent his bow, and took aim at the Baron. The movements of the young man followed each other with such rapidity and violence that his too tightly stretched bow broke like a thread of glass.

John uttered a curse upon his inoffensive arrow, seized a new bow handed to him by an outlaw, who had been mortally wounded by the soldiers fighting with William.

The Baron understood the archer's actions and intentions; he bent down low upon his horse until he appeared to be one with the animal, and the arrow destined for him sent a man behind him rolling in the dust.

His fall maddened the whole troop, who, determined to carry off the victory, and finding themselves in the majority, spurred their horses and advanced rapidly.

One of William's comrades was dead, the other was still fighting, but it was easy to perceive that he could not last long. John saw the danger to which his cousin was exposed, and falling upon the group of combatants, he snatched Will from their grasp, urging him to fly.

"Never," cried Will, firmly.

"For pity's sake, Will," said John, continuing to hit out at his aggressors, "go seek Robin and call the Merrie Men. Alas, rivers of blood will flow this day; the song of the thrush was a heaven-sent warning."

William went at his cousin's request; it was easy to understand its import considering the number of soldiers who now appeared in the glade. He dealt a terrific blow at a man who attempted to bar his way, and disappeared in the thicket.

Little John fought like a lion, but it was madness to try and fight so many enemies single handed; he was vanquished and fell, and the soldiers, after binding him hand and foot, tied him to a tree. The Baron's arrival was to decide the fate of our poor friend.

Lord Fitz-Alwine hastened up, attracted by the shouts of the soldiers. At sight of the prisoner, a smile of gratified hate lent a ferocious expression to the Baron's features.

"Ha! ha!" said he, relishing with unspeakable joy the triumph of his victory, "I have you in my hands then, great maypole of the Forest. You shall pay dearly for your insolence, ere I despatch you into another world."

"By my faith," said John, in a flippant tone, biting his lip furiously the while, "whatever tortures it may please you to inflict upon me, they could not make you forget that I have held your life in my hands, and that if you still have the power to martyrize the Saxons, it is to my goodness that you owe it. But beware! Robin Hood is coming, and you will not have the easy victory over him that you have had over me."

"Robin Hood," sneered the Baron. "Robin Hood's last hour will soon arrive. I have ordered his head to be cut off and his body to be left here as food for man-eating wolves. Soldiers," he added, turning to two men, the vile slaves of his wishes, "place this villain upon a horse and let us remain on this spot to await the return of Sir Guy, who will, I presume, bring us Robin Hood's head."

The men who had dismounted stood ready to leap into the saddle, and the Baron, seated comfortably upon a grassy hillock, waited patiently for Sir Guy Gisborne's bugle call.

Let us leave his lordship to recover from his fatigue, and see what has been passing between Robin Hood and the man in the horse-skin cloak.

"Good morrow, fair Sir," said Robin, approaching the stranger. "One might think, judging by the excellent bow you carry, that you were a brave and honest archer."

"I have lost my way," replied the traveller, disdaining to reply to the interrogatory supposition addressed to him, "and I fear much to stray in this labyrinth of cross-roads, glades, and paths."

"To me all the forest paths are well known, Master," replied Robin, politely, "and if you will tell me to what part of the wood you wish to make your way, I will be your guide."

"I am not making my way to any particular spot," answered the stranger, examining his interlocutor attentively. "I wish to get near the middle of the wood, for I hope to meet there a man with whom I would fain converse."

"This man is doubtless some friend of yours?" asked Robin, amiably.

"Nay," returned the stranger, quickly; "he is a villain of the deepest dye, an Outlaw who doth well deserve the noose."

"Oh! indeed," said Robin, still smiling. "And may one inquire without indiscretion, the name of this scapegrace?"

"Certainly; he is called Robin Hood. And hark ye, young man, I would gladly give ten pieces of gold to have the pleasure of meeting him."

"My good Sir," said Robin, "congratulate yourself upon the luck which hath placed you in my way, for I can conduct you into the presence of Robin Hood without putting your generosity to the proof. Only suffer me to ask your name."

"I am called Sir Guy Gisborne. I am rich and own many vassals. My costume, as you may well imagine, is but a clever disguise. Robin Hood, not being on his guard against a poor devil so wretchedly attired, will let me come right up to him. So the question is simply how to find him. Once within reach of my hand he will die, I swear it, without having either the time or chance to defend himself; I will slay him without ruth or pity."

"Robin Hood hath done you much evil then?"

"Me? I did not know him even by name until a few hours agone; and, as you will see if you will take me to him, my face is quite unknown to him."

"For what reason, then, would you take his life?"

"For no reason at all, simply because it is my pleasure."

"A singular pleasure, if you will pardon me for saying so; and moreover, I pity you greatly for having such bloodthirsty ideas."

"Well, you are wrong. I am not really ill-natured, and had it not been for that fool Fitz-Alwine, I should be at this moment wending my way quietly homeward. It was he who induced me to make the attempt, by defying me to vanquish Robin Hood. My self-esteem is involved, therefore I must bear off the victory at any price. But, by the way," added Sir Guy, "now that I have told you my name, estate, and projects, you must answer me in your turn. Who are you?"

"Who am I?" repeated Robin, with loud voice and serious look. "I am the Earl of Huntingdon, the King of the Forest; I am the man you seek, I am Robin Hood!"

The Norman leapt back.

"Then prepare to die," he cried, drawing his sword. "Sir Guy Gisborne hath but one word; he hath sworn to kill thee, thou shalt die! To thy prayers, Robin Hood, for in a few minutes the call of my hunting-horn will announce to my companions, who are near at hand, that the Outlaw Chief is only a headless, shapeless corpse."

"To the vanquisher shall be reserved the right of disposing of the body of his adversary," replied Robin Hood, coldly. "Look to thyself! Thou hast sworn to spare me not; I swear on my side that if the Holy Virgin grant me the victory, I will treat thee as thou dost deserve. Come then, no quarter for either; 'tis a matter of life and death."

And with that, the two opponents crossed swords.

The Norman was not only a perfect Hercules, but also a past master in the art of fencing. He attacked Robin with such fury that the young man, hard pressed, was forced to step back, and caught his foot in the roots of an oak tree. Sir Guy, whose eye was as quick as his hand was strong, at once perceived his advantage; he redoubled his blows, and several times Robin felt his sword turn in the nervous grasp of his hand. His position was becoming critical; his movements fettered by the gnarled roots of the tree, which bruised his ankles, he could neither advance nor retire; he therefore determined to leap beyond the circle in which he was enclosed, and with a spring like that of a stag at bay, he leapt to the opposite side of the path, but in jumping he caught his foot in a low branch which sent him rolling in the dust. Sir Guy was not the man to miss such an opportunity for revenge; he uttered a triumphant cry, and threw himself on Robin with every intention of splitting open his head.

Robin saw his danger, and closing his eyes, he murmured fervently,—

"Holy Mother of God, help me! Dear Lady of Succour, wilt thou leave me to die by the hand of this miserable Norman?"

Hardly had Robin pronounced these words, which Sir Guy did not dare to interrupt (taking them no doubt for an act of contrition), than he felt a new force in all his limbs. He turned the point of his sword towards his enemy, and, as the latter sought to turn aside the menacing weapon, Robin leapt to his feet and stood up strong and free in the middle of the road. The combat, suspended for a moment, began again with renewed vigour; but the victory had changed sides and was now with Robin. Sir Guy, disarmed and struck full in the breast, fell dead without even a cry. After thanking God for the success of his arms, Robin assured himself that Sir Guy had really breathed his last; and, as he looked upon the Norman, Robin remembered that this man had not come alone to seek him, but had brought with him a troop of companions, who were now hidden somewhere in the wood, awaiting the call of his hunting-horn.

"I think it would be wise," thought Robin, "to find out whether these brave fellows are not Baron Fitz-Alwine's soldiers, and see for myself the pleasure which the news of my death will give him. I will dress myself in Sir Guy's clothes, cut off his head, and call hither his waiting companions."

Robin Hood stripped the Norman's body of the chief parts of his costume, put them on, not without a feeling of disgust, and when he had thrown the horse's skin over his shoulders, he resembled Sir Guy Gisborne nearly enough to be mistaken for him.

The disguise accomplished, and the Norman's head made unrecognisable at a first glance, Robin Hood sounded the horn.

A hurrah of triumph answered the young man's call, and he rushed toward the spot from whence he heard the joyous voices.

"Hark! hark again!" cried Fitz-Alwine, starting up. "Is not that the sound of Sir Guy's horn?"

"Yea, my lord," replied one of the Knight's men; "it could not be mistaken; my master's horn hath its own peculiar note."

"Victory, then!" cried the old man, "the brave and worthy Sir Guy hath slain Robin Hood."

"An hundred Sir Guys could not succeed in beating Robin Hood, if they attacked him one by one and fairly," roared poor Little John, his heart oppressed by terrible anguish.

"Silence, thou long-legged dolt!" answered the Baron, brutally; "and if thine eyes be good, look toward the end of the glade, where thou wilt see, hurrying to us, Sir Guy Gisborne, the vanquisher of thy wretched chief."

John raised himself, and saw, as the Baron had said, a yeoman with his body half enveloped in a horse's hide. Robin imitated the gait of the Knight so well, that John thought he recognised the man whom he had left face to face with his friend.

"Ah, the ruffian! the miscreant!" shouted the young man in despair. "He hath killed Robin Hood! He hath killed the most valiant Saxon in all England! Vengeance! vengeance! vengeance! Robin Hood hath friends, and in Nottinghamshire there are a thousand hands able and willing to punish his murderer!"

"To thy prayers, dog!" cried the Baron, "and leave us in peace. Thy master is dead, and thou shalt die like him. To thy prayers, and try to preserve thy soul from the tortures which await thy body. Dost think thou hast a claim upon our pity in pursuing with thy vain threats the noble Knight who hath rid the earth of an infamous Outlaw? Approach, brave Sir Guy," continued Lord Fitz-Alwine, addressing Robin Hood, who advanced quickly. "Thou dost merit all our praise and consideration; thou hast rid thy country from this scourge of Outlaws, thou hast killed a man whom the popular terror declared invincible, thou hast slain the celebrated Robin Hood! Ask me for the reward due to thy good offices. I will place at thy disposal my favour at Court, the support of my eternal friendship. Ask what thou wilt, noble Knight, I am ready to do thy bidding."

Robin had taken in the situation at a glance, and the fierce look which John shot at him revealed to him even more clearly than the old Baron's protestations of gratitude, how complete was the success of his disguise.

"I merit not such thanks," answered Robin, imitating the Knight's voice to the echo. "I have slain mine adversary in fair combat, and since you are willing to allow me to claim the reward of my prowess, I ask, my dear Baron, in return for the service I have just rendered you, permission to array myself against yonder rascal whom you have seized. He sits glaring at me so that he doth quite anger me; I will e'en send him to bear his amiable comrade company in the next world."

"As you will," returned Lord Fitz-Alwine, rubbing his hands gleefully. "Kill him, an it so please you, his life is yours."

Robin Hood's voice had not deceived Little John, and a sigh of unspeakable satisfaction had lifted from his heart the terrible anxiety he was beginning to experience.

Robin approached John, followed by the Baron.

"My Lord," said Robin, laughingly, "pray leave me alone with this villain. I am convinced that the fear of an ignominious death will compel him to confide in me the secret of the hiding-place of the robber band. Keep back, and draw off your men, for I will treat any inquisitive person in the manner that I used toward the man whose head you see here."

As he spoke these words, Robin put the bloody trophy into Lord Fitz-Alwine's arms. The old man uttered a cry of horror; Sir Guy's disfigured head rolled upon the ground, face downwards.

The terrified soldiers decamped with all speed.

Robin Hood, left alone with Little John, hastened to cut his bonds, and put into his hands the bow and arrows which had belonged to Sir Guy; then he wound his horn.

Hardly had the sound stirred the depths of the wood ere a great clamour was heard as the branches of the trees were thrust violently aside to make way, first for Will Scarlett, whose face was of so vivid a red as to approach purple, and next for a body of the Merrie Men, sword in hand.

This terrifying apparition appeared to the Baron more like a dream than an actual fact. He saw without perceiving, heard without understanding, his mind and body were completely paralysed by an overwhelming terror. This moment of supreme agony seemed of endless duration; he made a step forward towards the supposed Norman, and found himself face to face with Robin Hood, who, having rid himself of the horse-skin and drawn his sword, commanded the respect of the soldiers as well as that of their no less dejected leader.

The Baron, with clenched teeth and unable to utter a word, turned abruptly, mounted his horse, and without any orders to his men galloped away with all haste.

The soldiers, carried away by so praiseworthy an example, imitated their Chief and followed in his steps.

"May the devil catch thee in his claws!" cried Little John, furiously; "but thy cowardice shall not save thee; my arrows carry far enow to strike thee dead."

"Shoot not, John," said Robin, holding his friend by the arm. "Thou canst see that by all the laws of nature this man hath not long to live; why then hasten his death by a few days? Leave him to his remorse, to his loneliness—cut off from all family ties, a prey to his malevolent helplessness."

"Hark ye, Robin, I cannot let the old thief save himself thus; let me give him a lesson, as reminder of his sojourn in the Forest. I will not kill him, I give thee my word."

"So be it, then; draw, but swiftly, or he will be out of sight round the bend of the road."

John let fly an arrow, and, judging by the way in which the Baron bounded in his saddle and the haste he made to draw the arrow from the wound, it was impossible to doubt that it would be long ere he would mount a horse again or be able to sit at ease in a chair.

Little John shook hands warmly with his rescuer. Will asked Robin to give them an account of his doings, and the latter hours of this memorable day slipped merrily away.

CHAPTER XI

Baron Fitz-Alwine looked upon Robin as the curse of his existence, and his insatiable desire to avenge himself liberally for all the humiliations he had suffered at the young man's hands did not lose one whit of its intensity. Beaten on every occasion by his enemy, the Baron returned to the charge, swearing, both before and after the attack, to exterminate the whole band of Outlaws.

When the Baron found himself forced to recognise that it was quite impossible to vanquish Robin by force, he resolved to have recourse to cunning. This new plan of conduct having been long meditated, he hoped that he had at last discovered a means of decoying Robin into his snares. Without losing a moment, the Baron sent for a rich merchant of Nottingham and confided to him his plans, recommending him the while to keep the most profound silence regarding them.

This man, who was of a feeble and irresolute character, was easily led to share in the Baron's hatred for one whom he described as a highway robber.

On the morrow of his interview with Lord Fitz-Alwine, the merchant, true to the promise he had given the irascible old man, gathered together in his house the principal citizens of the town, and proposed to them to go with him to ask the Sheriff to establish a public shooting match, where the men of Nottinghamshire might try their skill against those of Yorkshire.

"The two Counties are not a little jealous of each other," added the merchant, "and for the honour of the town, I should be happy to offer our neighbours an opportunity of proving their skill at archery; or, better still, an occasion to set forth the incontestable superiority of our able marksmen. And in order to equalise the match between the rival parties, we would hold the encounter on the borders of the two Counties, the victor's prize being an arrow with silver barb and feathers of gold."

The citizens, called together by the Baron's ally, received the suggestion with a generous heartiness, and, in company with the merchant, they went to ask Lord Fitz-Alwine's permission to announce an archery competition between the rival Counties.

The old man, delighted at the prompt success of the first part of his project, concealed his secret satisfaction, and, with an air of supreme indifference, gave the required consent; even adding that, if his presence would give any pleasure or be of any advantage to the success of the festivities, it would be both a pleasure and a duty to him to preside over the games.

The citizens cried unanimously that the presence of their liege Lord would be a heaven-sent blessing, and they seemed as happy at receiving the promise of the Baron's presence as if the latter had been bound to them by the closest ties. They left the Castle with light hearts, and made the Baron's condescension known to their follow citizens with enthusiastic gestures, and eyes and mouths agape with astonishment. Poor fellows, they were so little used to politeness from a Norman Lord.

A proclamation, learnedly worded, announced that a match would be thrown open to the inhabitants of the Counties of Nottingham and York. The day was fixed, the spot chosen between the forest of Barnsdale and the village of Mansfield. As great care had been taken to spread the news of this public joust to every corner of the two Counties concerned, it reached Robin Hood's ears. The young man at once resolved to enter the lists and sustain the honour of Nottingham. From further information which he received, Robin learned that Baron Fitz-Alwine would preside over the games. This condescension, so little in harmony with the old man's morose character, explained to Robin the secret end to which the noble Lord's wishes tended. "Oh, indeed," said our friend to himself, "we must needs attempt this venture with every necessary precaution for a valorous defence."

The eve of the day on which the contest was to take place, Robin assembled his men, and announced to them his intention of bearing off the archery prize for the honour of the town of Nottingham.

"My lads," he added, "hearken to me. Baron Fitz-Alwine will preside over the games, and there must certainly be some particular reason why he should be so anxious to please the yeomen. I think I know the cause—it is to attempt my capture. Therefore I shall take with me to the range one hundred and forty companions. I will enter six of them as competitors for the prize; the others will be dispersed among the crowd in such manner as to re-assemble at the first call in case of treachery. Hold your arms ready, and prepare for a desperate combat."

Robin Hood's orders were faithfully carried out, and at the appointed hour his men, in little groups, took the road to Mansfield, and arrived without hindrance at the place, where a crowd was already assembled.

Robin Hood, Little John, Will Scarlett, Much, and five others of the Merrie Men were to take part in the contest; they were all differently dressed, and hardly spoke to one another, in order to avoid any danger of being recognised.

The place chosen for the archery was a large glade situated on the borders of Barnsdale Forest, and a short distance from the main road. An immense crowd gathered from the neighbouring country, and pressed noisily into the enclosure, in the centre of which were placed the butts. A platform had been erected opposite the shooting range; this was for the Baron, on whom devolved the honour of judging the shooting and awarding the prize.

The Baron soon arrived, accompanied by an escort of soldiers, fifty of his men having already mingled with the crowd, clad in yeoman's dress, with orders to arrest any suspicious characters, and take them before the Baron.

These precautions taken, Lord Fitz-Alwine had hopes that Robin Hood, whose adventurous nature courted danger, would come to the joust alone, and he would have the satisfaction of taking a revenge, for which he had waited beyond the term of human patience.

The match began; three men from Nottingham grazed the target, each of them touched the mark without reaching the centre. After them came three yeomen from Yorkshire, who were equally successful. Will Scarlett presented himself in his turn, and he pierced the centre of the mark with the greatest ease.

A shout of triumph greeted Will's prowess, and Little John took his place. The young man sent his arrow into the hole made by William. Then, even before the range-keeper had had time to take it out, Robin Hood's arrow broke it in pieces and took its place.

The enraptured crowd became violently excited, and the men of Nottingham laid big wagers.

The three best archers of Yorkshire came forward, and with steady hands, hit the bull's-eye.

It was now the turn of the Northerners to cry victory, and accept the wagers of the citizens of Nottingham.

All this time the Baron, but little interested in the success of either one or other of the Counties, was attentively watching the archers. Robin Hood had attracted his attention; but as his sight had for some time been getting feeble, it was impossible for him to recognise his enemy's features.

Much and the Merrie Men selected by Robin to compete touched the mark without difficulty; four yeomen followed them, and succeeded equally well.

The greater number of the archers were so well used to shooting at a target, that it appeared as though the victory would be to none in particular, and it was decided to set up wands, and choose seven men out of the victors on either side.

The citizens of Nottingham chose Robin Hood and his Merrie Men to sustain the honour of their county, while the inhabitants of Yorkshire took as their champion the yeomen who had proved the best archers.

The yeomen began. The first split the wand, the second grazed it, and the third skimmed it so closely that it appeared impossible that their adversaries would be able to surpass their skill.

Will Scarlett advanced, and taking up his bow, he shot underhand, and broke the willow wand into two pieces.

"Hurrah! for Nottinghamshire," cried the citizens of Nottingham, throwing their caps into the air, without in the least considering how impossible it would be to recover them.

New wands were prepared. Robin's men, from Little John to the least of the archers, split them easily. Robin's turn came; he shot three arrows at the wands with such rapidity that had it not been seen that the wands were shattered, it would have been impossible to believe in such skill.

Several fresh attempts were made, but Robin triumphed over all his adversaries, although they were all tried bowmen, and it began to be said that Robin Hood himself could not compete with the yeoman in the red doublet, for it was thus the crowd had named Robin.

This supposition, so dangerous to the young man, soon became an affirmation; and the report circulated that the victor was none other than Robin Hood.

The Yorkshiremen, smarting under defeat, hastened to assert that the match was not an equal one between them and a man of Robin Hood's strength. They complained of the slur cast upon their honour as archers, of the loss of their money (the most weighty consideration with them), and they attempted, no doubt with a hope of eluding their wagers, to turn the discussion into a quarrel.

As soon as the Merrie Men became aware of their adversaries' ill-will, they rallied together, and formed, though without apparent intention, a group of eighty-six men.

While the seeds of strife were being sown among the wagerers, Robin Hood was borne to the Sheriff amid the joyous acclamations of the citizens of Nottingham.

"Way for the victor! Hurrah for the skilful archer!" cried two hundred voices. "He is the winner of the prize."

Robin Hood, with eyes modestly cast down, stood before Lord Fitz-Alwine in the most respectful attitude.

The Baron stared hard to try and descry the young man's features. A certain resemblance of figure, perhaps even of dress, led the Baron to believe that the invincible Outlaw stood before him; but torn between conflicting emotions of doubt and a faint certitude, he could not show too great precipitation without compromising the success of his plan. He held out the arrow to Robin, hoping to recognise the young man by the sound of his voice. But Robin cheated his hopes; he took the arrow, and bowed politely as he stuck it in his belt.

A moment passed; Robin pretended to move off. Then, as the Baron, desperate at seeing him thus escape, was about to take decisive measures, he raised his head, and looking full at the old man, said with a laugh—

"Words fail me to express the value which I attach to the present you have just given me, my excellent friend. I shall return with a heart full of gratitude to the green trees of my fair dwelling-place, and there I will treasure with care this precious token of friendship. I wish you a very good day, noble Lord of Nottingham."

"Stop, stop!" roared the Baron. "Soldiers, do your duty! That man is Robin Hood. Seize him!"

"Miserable coward!" returned Robin. "You proclaimed that the game was public, open to all, destined for the amusements of every one without exception and without fear."

"An Outlaw hath no rights," said the Baron; "thou wast not included in the appeal to all good citizens. Now then, soldiers, seize the robber."

"I will slay the first who advanceth," cried Robin, in a stentorian voice, directing his bow toward the fellow who approached him. But at sight of his menacing attitude, the man drew back, and disappeared into the crowd.

Robin wound his horn, and his Merrie Men, prepared to sustain a bloody combat, advanced quickly to protect him. Stepping back into the midst of his men, he ordered them to bend their bows and retreat slowly, for the Baron's soldiers were too numerous to make it possible to fight against them without risking much bloodshed.

The Baron precipitated himself before his men, and in a furious voice commanded them to arrest the Outlaws. The soldiers prepared to obey, and the Yorkshiremen, irritated by their defeat and exasperated by the loss of their money in the wagers they had just made, joined the Baron's men in pursuing the Foresters. But the citizens of Nottingham owed Robin Hood too great a debt of friendship and gratitude to leave him helpless at the mercy of the soldiers and their Lord. They opened a way for the Merrie Men, and, saluting them with friendly acclamation, reclosed it again behind them.

Unhappily, Robin Hood's adherents were neither numerous enough nor strong enough to protect his discreet flight for any length of time; they were obliged to break their ranks, and the men-at-arms gained the road along which the Foresters had fled.

Then began a desperate chase. From time to time the Foresters faced about and sent a volley of arrows at the soldiers, who retaliated as well as they were able, and in spite of the ravages made in their ranks, courageously continued the pursuit.

After this exchange of hostilities had lasted an hour, Little John, who was marching at the head of the Foresters with Robin, stopped suddenly, and said to his young Chief—

"My good friend, my hour is come; I am grievously wounded, my strength faileth me, I cannot keep up the pace."

"What!" cried Robin; "thou art wounded?"

"Yea," replied John, "in the knee; and I have lost so much blood in the last half-hour that my strength faileth me. I cannot stand on my feet." And as he spoke, John sank to the ground.

"Great Heavens!" cried Robin, kneeling beside his brave comrade. "John, good John, take courage; try to rouse thyself and lean upon me. I am not tired, and will support thy steps. Only a few minutes more, and we shall be in safety. Let me bind up thy wound, it will give thee great relief."

"Nay, Robin, 'tis useless," replied John, in a weak voice; "my leg is almost paralysed; 'tis impossible for me to move. Do not stay. Abandon a useless wretch who only asks for death."

"I abandon thee!" cried Robin Hood. "Thou dost know that I am incapable of so cruel an action."

"It would not be in the least a cruel action, Robin, but a duty. Thou must answer to God for the lives of these brave men who have given themselves, body and soul, to thee. Leave me here, therefore, and if thou lovest me, if thou hast ever loved me, do not let that wicked Baron find me alive; plunge thy hunting-knife into my heart, that I may die like an honest and brave Saxon. Hearken to my prayer, Robin, and kill me; thou wilt spare me cruel sufferings and the unhappiness of again seeing our enemies; they are so cowardly, these Normans, that they would take a delight in insulting me in my last moments."

"Come, John," replied Robin, much affected, "do not ask me anything so impossible. Thou knowest well that I would not leave thee to die helpless and away from me; thou knowest that I would sacrifice mine own life and the lives of my men to preserve thine. Thou knowest, further, that far from abandoning thee, I would shed my last drop of blood to defend thee. When I fall, John, I trust that it will be at thy side, and then we shall depart for the next world with hands and hearts united as they have ever been here below."

"We will fight and die beside thee, if Heaven withholds its aid," said Will, embracing his cousin; "and thou shalt see that there are still brave men in the world. My friends," he continued, turning to the Foresters, who had come to a halt, "here is your friend, your comrade, mortally wounded; do you think that we should abandon him to the vengeance of the wretches who pursue us?"

"No! no! an hundred times no!" cried the Merrie Men, with one accord. "Let us surround him and die in his defence."

"Allow me," said the vigorous Much, advancing. "It seemeth useless to risk our lives without a cause. John is only wounded in the knee, he will therefore bear being carried without fear of losing blood. I will take him on my shoulders and carry him as long as my legs will carry me."

"When you fail, Much," said Will, "I will take your place, and another after me. Is it not so?"

"Yea! yea!" replied the gallant Foresters.

In spite of John's attempt at resistance, Much raised him with a strong hand, and with Robin's assistance took the wounded man on his back, after which the fugitives continued quickly on their way. This forced halt had enabled the soldiers to gain on the Foresters, and they now came in sight. The Merrie Men sent a flight of arrows among them, and redoubled their pace in the hope of reaching their retreat, well persuaded that the soldiers would never dare to follow them there. At the end of a branch road leading from the main road, the Foresters descried above the trees the turrets of a Castle.

"To whom doth this domain belong?" asked Robin. "Doth any one among you know the owner?"

"I do, Captain," said a man, who had been but lately enrolled in the band.

"Good. Dost know whether we should be favourably received by its Lord? For we are lost, an the gates be closed to us."

"I will answer for the benevolence of the owner, for Sir Richard of the Plain is a brave Saxon."

"Sir Richard of the Plain!" cried Robin. "Then are we saved! Forward, my lads, forward! Praised be the Holy Virgin!" he continued, crossing himself gratefully; "she never abandons the unfortunate in the hour of their need. Will Scarlett, go thou on in advance, and say to the keeper of the drawbridge, that Robin Hood and a band of his men, pursued by Normans, ask permission of Sir Richard to take refuge within his Castle walls."

With the speed of an arrow, William covered the space which separated him from Sir Richard's domain.

While the young man accomplished his errand, Robin and his companions proceeded toward the Castle.

Soon a white flag was hoisted on the outer wall, a horseman emerged from the Gate, and, followed by Will, advanced at full speed to meet Robin Hood. Arrived in the young Chief's presence, he leapt to the ground, holding out both hands.

"Sir," said the young man, grasping Robin's hand with visible emotion, "I am Herbert Gower, Sir Richard's son. My father wishes me to tell you that you are welcome to our home, and that he will feel the happiest of men, an you will give him the opportunity of discharging even a portion of the great debt we owe you. I am yours, body and soul, Sir Robin," added the young man, with an outburst of profound gratitude, "do with me what you will."

"I thank you with all my heart, my young friend," replied Robin, embracing Herbert; "your offer is tempting, for I should be proud to place so good a horseman in the ranks of my lieutenants. But for the present we must think of the danger that threatens my men. They are worn out with fatigue; my dearest comrade hath been wounded in the leg by a Norman arrow; and for near two hours we have been pursued by Baron Fitz-Alwine's soldiers. Behold, my lad," continued Robin, pointing out to the youth a band of soldiers who began to appear upon the road, "they will overtake us, an we do not hasten to seek shelter behind the Castle walls."

"The drawbridge is already lowered," said Herbert. "Let us hasten, and in ten minutes you will have nothing to fear from your enemies."

The Sheriff and his men arrived in time to witness the little troop defiling along the drawbridge of the Castle. Exasperated by this fresh defeat, the Baron immediately took the audacious resolution of commanding Sir Richard, in the King's name, to deliver up to him these men, who, doubtless abusing his credulity, had placed themselves under his protection.

Whereupon, at Lord Fitz-Alwine's request, the Knight appeared upon the ramparts.

"Sir Richard of the Plain," said the Baron, whose people had told him the name of the owner of the Castle, "do you know who the men are that have entered your domain?"

"I know them, my Lord," replied the Knight, coldly.

"What! you know that the rogue who commands this troop of robbers is an Outlaw, an enemy of the King, and yet you give him shelter? Do you know that you incur the penalty of treason?"

"I know that this Castle and the grounds that surround it are my property. I know that I am master here, and do as I please, and receive whom I choose. That is my answer, Sir. Will you withdraw at once, an you would avoid a combat in which you would not gain the advantage, for I have an hundred men-at-arms with the best sharpened arrows in all the country-side at my disposal. Good day, my Lord."

And with this ironical reply the Knight left the ramparts.

The Baron, who felt that he was not well enough supported by his soldiers to attempt an attack on the Castle, decided to retreat; and, with suppressed rage in his heart, as can be well imagined, he took the road to Nottingham with his men.

"Welcome, a thousand times, to the house which I owe to thy goodness, Robin Hood," said the Knight, embracing his guest; "welcome, a thousand times!"

"I thank thee, Sir Knight," said Robin. "But, prithee, speak not of the paltry service which I had the satisfaction to render thee. Thy friendship hath already repaid it an hundred-fold, and to-day thou savest me from a real danger. Hark ye, I have brought a wounded man; I pray that thou wilt kindly entreat him."

"He shall have the same consideration as thyself, dear Robin."

"The worthy lad is not unknown to thee, Sir Knight," replied Robin. "It is Little John, my first lieutenant; the dearest and most trusty of my companions."

"My wife and Lilas will look to him," returned Sir Richard. "And he will be well cared for; be easy on that score."

"If you are speaking of Little John, or rather of the biggest John, sure, who ever wielded a cudgel," said Herbert, "he is already in the hands of a clever leech from York, who hath been here since last evening. He hath already tended the wound and promiseth a speedy cure."

"God be praised!" said Robin Hood; "my dear John is out of danger. Now, Sir Knight," added he, "I am at the disposal of thyself and of thy family."

"My wife and Lilas are impatient to greet thee," said the Knight. "They await thee in the next room."

"Father," said Herbert, with a laugh, "I have just told my friend—I mean the young man, Will Scarlett—that I am the husband of the most beautiful woman in the world. And do you know what he replied?"

Sir Richard and Robin Hood exchanged smiles.

"He declared that he possessed a wife whose beauty was unrivalled. But he shall see Lilas, and then..."

"Ah! had you but seen Maude, you would not speak thus, young man. Would he, Robin?"

"Certainly Herbert would think Maude very pretty," replied Robin, in a conciliatory tone.

"Doubtless, doubtless," said Herbert. "But Lilas is marvelously beautiful; and, in my opinion, there exists no woman to be compared with her."

Will Scarlett listened to Herbert with a frown. The poor young husband's self-love was wounded. But we must do him the justice to say that, when he beheld Lilas, he uttered an exclamation of surprise and admiration.

Lilas had fufilled all the promises of her youth; the pretty child we saw at St. Mary's Abbey had become a beautiful woman. Tall, slim, and graceful as a young fawn, Lilas advanced toward the visitors with downcast eyes and a lovely smile upon her rosy lips. She raised two timid blue eyes to Robin Hood and held out her hand.

"Our deliverer is no stranger to me," she said sweetly.

Mute with admiration, Robin Hood raised the white hand to his lips.

Herbert, who had followed Robin, said to Will, with a smile of tender pride, "Friend William, this is my wife...."

"She is very beautiful," whispered Will; "but Maude..." he added, in a still lower voice.

He said no more. Robin Hood commanded him by a glance to have no eyes save for Herbert's charming wife.

After a mutual exchange of compliments between Sir Richard's wife and her guests, the Knight, leaving Will and his son to talk to the ladies, took Robin Hood aside, and said—

"My dear Robin, I wish to prove to thee that there is no man in the world whom I love like thee, and I declare again my friendship for thee, so that thou mayest carry out thy plans according to thy will. Thou wilt be secure here so long as this house can shield thee, so long as there remains a man standing upon its ramparts, and, sword in hand, I will defy all the Sheriffs in the Kingdom. I have given orders for the Gates to be closed, and for none to be permitted to enter the Castle without my leave. My men are under arms, and ready to offer a stout resistance to any attack. Thy men are resting; let them remain one week in peace, and when that time hath elapsed, we will take counsel together as to the part thou shouldst play."

"I willingly consent to remain here some days," answered Robin. "But on one condition only."

"What is that?"

"My Merrie Men will return to-morrow to Barnsdale Forest. Will Scarlett shall accompany them, and he will return hither with his dear Maude, Marian, and poor Little John's wife."

Sir Richard readily acquiesced in Robin's wishes, and all was arranged to the mutual satisfaction of the two friends.

A fortnight passed happily away at the Castle on the Plain, and at the end of that time, Robin, Little John, entirely cured of his wound, Will Scarlett and the incomparable Maude, Marian and Winifred, found themselves once more beneath the green trees of Barnsdale Forest.

The day after his return to Nottingham, Baron Fitz-Alwine made his way to London, obtained an audience of the King, and recounted to him his pitiful adventure.

"Your Majesty," said the Baron, "will find it strange, no doubt, that a Knight with whom Robin had sought shelter should have refused to deliver up this great criminal to me, even though I asked in the King's name."

"What! a Knight, and failed to show respect to his Sovereign!" cried Henry, in an irritated tone.

"Yea, Sire, the Knight, Sir Richard of the Plain, refused my righteous demand. He replied that he was king of his domains, and cared but little for the power of your Majesty."

As may be perceived, the worthy Baron lied freely for the good of his cause.

"Well," replied the King, "we will judge for ourselves of the impudence of this rogue. We will be in Nottingham within fifteen days. Bring with you as many men as you think needful to give battle, and if any untoward occurrence should prevent our joining you, act as best you can. Carry off this indomitable Robin Hood and Sir Richard. Imprison them in your gloomiest dungeon; and when you have them safe under lock and key, advise our justices. We will then reflect upon our course of action."

Baron Fitz-Alwine obeyed the King's orders to the letter. He assembled a numerous troop of men and marched at their head against Sir Richard's Castle. But the poor Baron was the sport of fate, for he arrived the day after Robin's departure.

The idea of pursuing Robin to his retreat did not commend itself to the old Baron's mind. A certain remembrance, and a certain soreness, which still rendered riding painful to him, checked his ardour in that direction. He resolved, as he could do no better, to take Sir Richard, and, as an assault of the place would be a difficult thing to attempt and dangerous to put into execution, he made up his mind to attain a more certain success by means of treachery.

The Baron dispersed his men, keeping with him only a score of stout fellows, and placed himself in ambush at a short distance from the Castle. He had not long to wait. The next morning, Sir Richard, his son, and some followers fell into the trap laid for them, and in spite of the valiant resistance they offered, they were vanquished, gagged, tied to horses, and carried away to Nottingham.

One of Sir Richard's servants succeeded in making his escape, and came, all black and blue with the blows he had received, to announce the sad news to his mistress.

Lady Gower, distracted with grief, wished to join her husband; but Lilas made the unhappy woman understand that this step would be of no help to them. She advised her mother to apply to Robin Hood; he alone was capable of judging calmly of Sir Richard's position and effecting his deliverance.

Lady Gower yielded to the entreaties of the younger woman, and without losing an instant, she chose two faithful servants, mounted a horse, and set out in all haste for Barnsdale Forest.

A Forester, who had remained ill at the Castle, was now sufficiently recovered to act as guide to the Trysting Tree.

By a providential chance, Robin Hood was at his post.

"God bless you!" cried Lady Gower, throwing herself with feverish haste from her horse; "I come to you as a suppliant. I come to ask you yet another favour in the Holy Virgin's name."

"Lady, you frighten me. For mercy's sake, what ails you?" cried Robin, overcome with astonishment. "Tell me what you desire; I am ready to obey."

"Oh, Robin," sobbed the poor woman, "my husband and my son have been carried off by your enemy, the Sheriff of Nottingham. Oh, Robin, save my husband, save my child! Stop the wretches who have taken them away; they are few in number, and have only this minute left the Castle."

"Be reassured, Madam," said Robin Hood. "Your husband shall soon be given back to you. Remember that Sir Richard is a Knight, and under this title he has a right to the law of the Kingdom. Whatever the power of Baron Fitz-Alwine, it does not permit him to put to death a noble Saxon. He must bring Sir Richard to trial, if the fault of which he is accused offer occasion for trial. Take courage, dry your tears; your husband and son shall soon be in your arms."

"May Heaven bless you!" cried Lady Gower, clasping her hands.

"Now, Madam, allow me to give you some advice. Return to the Castle, keep all the gates shut, and do not allow any stranger to enter. For my part, I will assemble my men, and fly at their head in pursuit of the Baron."

Lady Gower, much reassured by the young man's consoling words, left him with a more tranquil heart. Robin Hood announced to his men the capture of Sir Richard, and his desire to capture the Sheriff. The Foresters gave a shout, half of indignation against the Baron's treachery, half of joy at having a fresh opportunity of bending their bows, and gleefully they prepared to set out.

Robin put himself at the head of his valiant troop, and accompanied by Little John, Will Scarlett, and Much, started in pursuit of the Sheriff.

After a long and fatiguing march, they reached the village of Mansfield, where Robin learnt from an Innkeeper, that, after having rested, the Baron's soldiers had continued their way to Nottingham. Robin made his men refresh themselves, left Much and Little John with them, and accompanied by Will, galloped at the best speed of a good horse to the Trysting Tree of Sherwood Forest.

Arrived at the confines of the subterranean dwelling, Robin blew a joyous flourish upon his hunting horn, and a hundred Foresters ran up at the well-known call.

Robin Hood took this fresh troop with him, and so arranged them as to get the Baron's men between the two troops; for the men left at Mansfield were to take the road to Nottingham after an hour's repose.

The Merrie Men soon arrived at a spot, a short distance from the town, where they learned to their great satisfaction that the Sheriff's troops had not yet passed. Robin chose an advantageous position, hid some of his men, and placed the remainder on the opposite side of the road.

The appearance of half a dozen soldiers soon announced the approach of the Sheriff and his cavalcade.

The Foresters prepared to give them a warm welcome. The advance guard passed beyond the limits of the ambush without hindrance, and when they were far enough for the troop that came behind to imagine there was nothing more to fear, the sound of a horn rang through the air, and a flight of arrows saluted the front rank of soldiers. The Sheriff commanded a halt, and sent some thirty men to beat the underwood; they went to their death.

Divided into two groups and attacked on both sides at once, the soldiers were soon forced to lay down their arms and cry for mercy.

This exploit terminated, the Merrie Men threw themselves upon the Baron's escort, who, being well mounted and used to arms, defended themselves with vigour.

Robin and his men fought with the hope of delivering Sir Richard and his son; the soldiers from London, on their side, sought to gain the reward promised by the King to whoever should capture Robin Hood. The struggle was desperate and furious on both sides, and the victory uncertain, when suddenly the shouts of another band of Foresters told that the situation was now to be changed. It was Little John and his band, who flung themselves into the conflict with an irresistible violence.

Some ten archers already surrounded Sir Richard and his son, cut their bonds, gave them weapons, and, undismayed by the danger to which they were exposing themselves, fought hand to hand with men clad in coats of mail. With the heedless impetuosity of youth, Herbert, with some of the Merrie Men, hurled himself into the midst of the Baron's escort. For nearly a quarter of an hour the courageous youth held his own against the horsemen; but, overcome by numbers, he was about to pay for his foolhardiness, when an archer, either to help the young man or to precipitate the issue of the battle, took aim at the Baron, and pierced his throat with an arrow, flung him from his horse, and cut off his head; then, lifting it in the air on the point of his lance, he cried in a loud voice—

"Norman dogs, behold your Chief! Contemplate for the last time the ugly face of your proud Sheriff, and lay down your arms or prepare yourselves to meet a like..."

The Forester did not finish his sentence, a Norman broke open his head, and he rolled in the dust.

The death of Lord Fitz-Alwine constrained the Normans to lay down their arms and ask for quarter.

By Robin's orders some of the Merrie Men conducted the vanquished men to Nottingham, while, at the head of the rest of his band, he carried away the dead, succoured the wounded, and removed all traces of the combat.

"Farewell for ever, thou man of blood and iron," said Robin, throwing a look of disgust at the Baron's corpse. "At last thou hast met they death, and wilt receive the reward of thine evil deeds. Thy heart hath been covetous and pitiless, thy hand hath been as a scourge to the unhappy Saxons. Thou hast oppressed thy vassals, betrayed thy King, and abandoned thy daughter. Thou dost merit all the tortures of hell. Yet do I pray the God of infinite mercy to have pity on thy soul and to pardon thy sins."

"Sir Richard," said Robin, when the old man's corpse had been raised by the soldiers, and borne away in the direction of Nottingham, "this hath been a sorry day. We have saved thee from death, but not from ruin, for thy goods will be confiscated. I could wish, Richard, that I had never known thee."

"How is that?" asked the Knight, in great surprise.

"Because without mine aid, thou wouldst assuredly have succeeded in paying thy debt to the Abbey, and thou wouldst not have been obliged to render me service out of gratitude. I am the involuntary cause of all thy trouble. Thou wilt be banished, outlawed from the Kingdom, thy house become the property of a Norman, thy family will suffer, and it will be my fault....Thou canst see for thyself, Sir Richard, how dangerous my friendship is!"

"My dear Robin," said the Knight, with an expression of ineffable tenderness, "my wife and my children are alive, thou art my friend, what have I to regret? If the King condemn me, I will leave my Castle, deprived of all, but still happy and blessing the hour that led me to noble Robin Hood."

The young man gently shook his head.

"Let us speak seriously of thy situation, my dear Richard," returned he. "The news of the events which have just occurred will be sent to London, and the King will be pitiless. We have attacked his own soldiers, and he will make thee pay for their defeat, not only by banishment, but by an ignominious death. Leave thy home, come with me. I give thee the word of an honest man that while a breath of life is in my body, thou shalt be safe under the care of my Merrie Men."

"I gladly accept thy generous offer, Robin Hood. I accept it with joy and gratitude. But before establishing myself in the Forest, which my children's future makes my duty, I am going to try and soften the King's anger. The offer of a considerable sum of money may induce him to spare the life of a well-born Knight."

That very evening Sir Richard sent a message to London to ask a powerful member of his family to speak to the King for him. The messenger came back from London at full speed, and announced to his master that Henry II., deeply irritated by the death of Baron Fitz-Alwine, had sent a company of his best soldiers to the Knight's Castle, with orders to hang him and his son to the first tree on the roadside. The Chief of this company, who was a penniless Norman, had received from the King's hand the Castle of the Plain as a gift to himself and his descendants to the last generation.

Sir Richard's kinsman likewise sent word to the condemned man that a proclamation was to be made in the Counties of Nottinghamshire, Derbyshire, and Yorkshire, offering an immense reward to the man clever enough to capture Robin Hood and give him, alive or dead, into the hands of the Sheriff of either of these Counties.

Sir Richard at once warned Robin Hood of the danger menacing his life, and announced his own immediate arrival.

Actively assisted by his vassals, the Knight despoiled the Castle of all that it contained, and sent his furniture, arms, and plate to the trysting-place of Barnsdale.

When the last wagon had crossed the drawbridge, Sir Richard, his wife, Herbert, and Lilas rode away from their dear home, and gained the Forest without hindrance.

When the troop sent by the King reached the Castle, the doors were open and the rooms completely empty.

The new owner of Sir Richard's domains seemed much disappointed to find the place deserted, but as he had passed the best part of his life in struggling against the freaks of fortune, he readily accommodated himself to his circumstances.

Consequently he sent away the soldiers and, to the great despair of the vassals, established himself as master of the Castle of the Plain.

CHAPTER XII

Three peaceful years followed the events we have just related. Robin Hood's band had developed in a remarkable manner, and the renown of their intrepid Chief had spread all over England.

The death of Henry II. had placed his son Richard on the throne, and the latter, after having squandered all the Crown treasure, had set out for the Holy Land, abandoning the Regency of the Kingdom to his brother, Prince John, a man of dissolute habits and extreme avarice, whose feeble spirit rendered him incapable of fulfilling the high mission entrusted to him.

The misery of the people, already very great under Henry, became complete destitution during the long period of this bloodstained regency. Robin Hood, with inexhaustible generosity, relieved the cruel sufferings of the poor in Nottinghamshire and Derbyshire, and he was the idol of them all. But if he gave to the poor, he took from the rich in return, and Normans, prelates, and monks contributed largely, to their great vexation, to the good works of the noble Outlaw.

Marian still lived in the Forest, and the young couple still loved each other as tenderly as in the first days of their happy union.

Time had not lessened William's passion for his charming wife, and in the eyes of the faithful Saxon, Maude, like a pure diamond, still kept her immutable beauty.

Little John and Much still congratulated themselves on their choice in taking to wife sweet Winifred and witty Barbara; and as for Will's brothers, they had no reason to repent of their hasty marriages; they were happy, and life was rose-coloured to their eyes.

Before we leave for ever two persons who have played an important part in our story, we will pay them a friendly visit at the Castle of the Dale in the valley of Mansfield.

Allan Clare and the Lady Christabel still lived happily together. Their home, built chiefly under the Knight's directions, was a marvel of comfort and good taste. A circle of old trees shut off the garden from inquisitive eyes, and seemed to place an insuperable barrier around the place.

Beautiful children with sweet faces, living flowers in this oasis of love, enlivened the calm repose of the great House with their turbulent spirits, their laughing voices awoke the echoes, and the light steps of their little feet left a fleeting imprint on the sandy paths of the park. Allan and Christabel had remained young in heart, spirits, and looks, and for them a week seemed like a day—a day passed as quickly as an hour.

Christabel had not seen her father since her wedding with Allan Clare in Linton Abbey; for the irascible old man was cruelly determined to repulse all the efforts at reconciliation made by his daughter and the Knight. The Baron's death affected Christabel profoundly; but how much greater would her sorrow have been if, in losing the author of her being, she had lost a true father.

Allan had intended to maintain his rights to the Barony of Nottingham, and, by Robin's advice, who recommended him to make all haste in putting forward his very just claim, he was on the point of writing to the King, when he learned that the Castle of Nottingham, with its revenues and dependencies, had become the property of Prince John. Allan was too happy to risk his peace and well-being in a struggle which the superior rank of his adversary would render as dangerous as it was useless. He therefore took no further steps, and did not regret the loss of this magnificent heritage.

Robin's attacks upon the Normans and clergy became so frequent and so prejudicial to the rich that they attracted the attention of the Lord Chancellor of England, Longchamp, Bishop of Ely.

The Bishop resolved to put an end to the existence of the Merrie Men, and he prepared a serious expedition. Five hundred men, with Prince John at their head, arrived at Nottingham Castle, and there, after a rest of several days, they made arrangements to seize Robin Hood. He, however, being promptly informed of the intentions of this honourable troop, only laughed, and prepared to baffle all their attempts without exposing his men to the dangers of a fight.

He made his band take shelter, arrayed a dozen foresters in different costumes, and sent them to the Castle, where they presented themselves and offered to guide the troops into the inextricable recesses of the Forest.

These offers of service were accepted with alacrity by the chiefs of the troop; and as the Forest covered very nearly thirty miles of ground, it was not easy to take account of the turns and twists through which the guides led the unhappy soldiers. Now the whole of the troop was engulfed in the declivities of a valley, now they sank knee deep in the muddy water of swamps, now they found themselves dispersed on wild and barren heights. They cursed a soldier's life, wished the Lord Chancellor of England, Robin Hood, and his invisible band at the devil; for it should be observed that not a single green doublet had ever appeared upon the horizon.

At the close of the day the soldiers found themselves seven or eight miles from Nottingham Castle, which they must regain if they did not wish to pass a night in the open. They returned therefore, exhausted with fatigue, dying of hunger, and without having seen a thing that could reveal to them the presence of the Merrie Men.

For two weeks they renewed these fatiguing marches, and the result was always the same. Prince John, recalled to London by his pleasures, abandoned the undertaking, and returned with his escort to the town.

Two years after this expedition, Richard returned to England; and Prince John, who justly dreaded to face his brother, sought refuge from the King's anger within the walls of Nottingham Castle.

Richard Cœur de Lion, having learned of the Regent's obnoxious behavior, stayed only three days in London; and then, accompanied by a small troop, marched resolutely against the rebel.

Nottingham Castle was besieged. After three days it surrendered at discretion, but Prince John managed to escape.

While fighting like the meanest of his soldiers, Richard had noticed that a troop of lusty yeomen gave him great assistance, and that it was owing to their valuable help that he was able to win the victory.

After the combat, and once installed in the Castle, Richard asked for information concerning the brave archers who had come to his aid. But none could tell him, and he was obliged to seek information from the Reeve of Nottingham.

This Reeve was the same man upon whom Robin had played the trick of taking him into the Forest and making him pay three hundred gold crowns for his visit.

Under the influence of this poignant memory, the Reeve answered the King that the archers in question could certainly be none other than those of the terrible Robin Hood.

"This Robin Hood," added the malicious Innkeeper, "is a downright rascal. He supports his band at the expense of travellers; he robs honest men, kills the King's deer, and daily commits every sort of brigandage."

Halbert Lindsay, pretty Maude's foster-brother, who had had the good fortune to keep his place as Warden of the Castle, happened by chance to be near the King during this interview. Impelled by a feeling of gratitude toward Robin and by the natural impetuosity of a generous nature, he forgot his lowly condition, made a step towards the Reeve's august listener, and said in an eager tone—

"Sire, Robin Hood is an honest Saxon and an unhappy Outlaw. An if he despoil the rich of their wealth, yet he doth allay the misery of the poor; and in the Counties of Nottingham and York the name of Robin Hood is aye spoken with respect and eternal gratitude."

"Do you know this brave bowman personally?" asked the King of Halbert.

The question recalled Halbert to himself. He blushed crimson, and replied confusedly—

"I have seen Robin Hood, but it was a long time ago; and I only repeat to your Majesty what is said of him by the poor whom he hath saved from dying of starvation."

"Come, come, my good lad," said the King, with a smile, "hold up thy head and never disown thy friend. By the Holy Trinity, if his conduct be such as thou hast described to me, he is a man whose friendship must indeed be precious. I avow I should be charmed to meet this Outlaw; and as he hath done me a service, it shall never be said that Richard of England hath shown himself ungrateful, even toward an Outlaw. To-morrow evening I will hie me to Sherwood Forest."

The King kept his word. Early next morning, escorted by Knights and soldiers, and conducted by the Reeve, who did not find this expedition very attractive, he explored the paths, roads, and glades of the old wood, but the search was in vain. Robin Hood was not to be seen.

But little pleased at his ill-success, Richard sent for a man who fulfilled the functions of Keeper in the Forest, and asked him whether he knew of any means of encountering the Outlaw Chief.

"Your Majesty might search the wood for a year," rejoined the man, "without perceiving even the shadow of an Outlaw, if you went accompanied by an escort. Robin Hood avoids strife as much as possible—not from cowardice, for he knows the Forest so well that he hath naught to fear, not even the attack of five or six hundred men—but from moderation and prudence. If your Majesty wishes to see Robin Hood, it were best to go disguised as a Monk, with four or five of your Knights, and I will be your Majesty's guide. I swear by St. Dunstan that your lives will be in no danger. Robin Hood waylays ecclesiastics, he entertains them, he despoils them, but never doth he ill-use them."

"By the Holy Cross, Forester, thy speech is golden," said the King, laughing, "and I will follow thy wise counsel. The garb of a Monk will become me but ill. No matter! Let them fetch me a Friar's robe."

The impatient monarch was soon clothed in an Abbot's costume, and chose four Knights, who dressed themselves as Monks, to accompany him. Moreover, following another stratagem suggested by the Keeper, they harnessed their horses in such a manner as to convey the impression that they carried a load of treasure.

About a league from the Castle, the Keeper, who served as guide to the supposed Monks, approached the King and said—

"My Lord, look to the end of yonder glade; there you will see Robin Hood, Little John, and Will Scarlett, the three Chiefs of the band."

"Good," said the King, gaily. And urging his horse forward, Richard made as though he would escape.

Robin Hood leapt on to the road, seized the animal's bridle, and compelled it to stop.

"A thousand pardons, Sir Abbot," said he; "pray tarry a while and receive my hearty welcome."

"Profane sinner," cried Richard, seeking to imitate the habitual language of the clergy. "Dost dare arrest the passage of a holy man on a sacred errand."

ROBIN HOOD THE OUTLAW

"I am a yeoman of this Forest," replied Robin Hood, "and my companions and I live upon the proceeds of the chase and the generosity of pious members of Holy Church."

"Upon my word, thou art a daring rogue," answered the King, concealing a smile. "To dare tell me to my face that thou eatest my...the King's deer, and plunderest members of the Church. By St. Hubert! thou dost possess at least the merit of frankness."

"Frankness is the only resource of those who possess naught," returned Robin Hood. "But those who have revenues, lands, and gold and silver can pass them on, when they know not what to do with them. I believe, noble Abbot," continued Robin, in a mocking tone, "that you are one of the happy number of whom I speak. That is why I ask you to come to the aid of our modest wants, and of the misery of our poor friends and dependants. You too often forget, my brothers, that round about your rich dwellings there are homes lacking bread, although you possess more money than wants for it to satisfy."

"Perchance thou speakest truth, yeoman," replied the King, partly forgetting the religious character with which he was invested. "And the expression of loyal frankness which shines from thy face pleaseth me singularly. Thou hast an appearance of being more honest than thou art in reality. Natheless, for the sake of thy good appearance, and for love of Christian charity, I make thee a gift of all the money I possess at this moment—forty pieces of gold. I am sorry that it is no more, but the King, who hath been staying for several days at Nottingham Castle, as thou hast doubtless heard, hath almost entirely emptied my pockets. This money, however, is at thy service, for I like well thy fine face and the strong countenances of thy lusty comrades."

With these words, the King handed Robin Hood a little leathern bag containing forty pieces of gold.

"You are the paragon of Churchmen, Sir Abbot," said Robin, laughing; "and if I had not made a vow to squeeze more or less every member of Holy Church, I should refuse to accept your generous offer. However, it shall not be said that you have suffered too cruelly on your way through Sherwood Forest. Your escort and horses may pass freely, and more, you must allow me to accept only twenty pieces of gold."

"Thou dost behave nobly, Forester," replied Richard, who appeared sensible of Robin's generosity; "and I shall give myself the pleasure of speaking of thee to our Sovereign. His Majesty knoweth somewhat concerning thee, for he told me to greet thee from him if I were so fortunate as to meet thee. I believe, betwixt ourselves be it said, that King Richard—who doth love bravery where'er he finds it— would not be sorry to give his thanks in person to the brave yeoman who helped him to open the Gates of Nottingham Castle, and to ask him why he and his valiant companions disappeared so soon after the battle."

"If some day I were happy enough to find myself in His Majesty's presence, I should not hesitate to reply to the latter

164

question; but at present, Sir Abbot, let us speak of something else. I love King Richard well, for he is English in heart and soul, though he belongeth by ties of blood to a Norman family. All of us here, priests and laity, are the faithful servants of His Most Gracious Majesty, and if you will consent, Sir Abbot, we will drink in company to noble Richard's health. Sherwood Forest knoweth how to be freely hospitable when it receiveth Saxon hearts and generous Monks beneath the shade of its old trees."

"I accept thy kind invitation with pleasure, Robin Hood," replied the King; "and I am ready to follow thee wherever thou dost wish to conduct me."

"I thank you for your confidence, good Monk," said Robin, leading Richard's horse toward a path ending at the Trysting Tree.

Little John, Will Scarlett, and the four Knights disguised as Monks, followed the King, who was preceded by Robin Hood.

The little escort had hardly entered upon the path when a deer, startled by the noise, ran quickly across the road; but more alert than the poor animal, Robin's arrow pierced its side with deadly effect.

"Well hit! well hit!" cried the King, heartily.

"That is not a very wonderful shot, Sir Abbot," said Robin, looking at Richard in surprise. "All my men, without exception, can kill a deer like that, and my wife herself can draw a bow and accomplish acts of skill far superior to the feeble exploit which I have achieved before your eyes."

"Thy wife?" repeated the King, in questioning tone. "Thou hast a wife? By the Mass, I am anxious to make the acquaintance of the woman who shares the perils of thine adventurous life."

"My wife is not the only one of her sex, Sir Abbot, who prefers a faithful heart and a home in the wilderness, to a faithless love and the luxury of a town existence."

"I will introduce my wife to you, Sir Abbot," cried Will Scarlett, "and if thou dost not acknowledge that her beauty is worthy of a throne, thou must permit me to declare either that thou art blind or that thy taste is execrable."

"By St. Dunstan!" returned Richard, "the popular fancy is quite right in calling you the Merrie Men. You want for nothing here— lovely women, royal game, fresh verdure, and entire liberty."

"Yea! we be very happy folk, Sir," replied Robin, laughing.

The escort soon reached the greensward, where a repast awaited the guests; and this repast, sumptuously furnished with fragrant venison, excited Richard Cœur-de-Lion's appetite by its mere appearance.

"By my mother's conscience!" he cried (let us hasten to say that the Lady Eleanor had so little conscience that it was sheer pleasantry to appeal to it), "here is a truly royal dinner!" Whereupon the King took his place at the board and ate with great enjoyment. Towards the end of the meal, Richard said to his host—

"Thou hast made me anxious to meet the beautiful women who people thy vast domain. Introduce them to me. I am curious to see if they are worthy, as thy red-headed companion assured me, to ornament the Court of the King of England."

Robin sent Will to find the beautiful woodland nymphs, and to tell his men to prepare the sports in which they engaged on days of rest.

"My men will endeavour to amuse you a little, Sir Abbot," said Robin, again taking his place beside the King; "and you will see that there is naught really blameworthy in our pleasures and the wild fashion of our lives. And when you find yourself in the presence of good King Richard, I ask it as a favour that you will tell him that the Merrie Men of Sherwood are neither to be feared by brave Saxons, nor unkind to any who have compassion on the inevitable hardships of the rough life they lead."

"Rest assured, brave yeoman, His Majesty shall know of all that hath happened here, as surely as though he himself had partaken of thy repast in my stead."

"You, Sir, are the most gracious Abbot that I have ever met in all my life, and I am very glad to be able to treat you as a brother. Now be pleased to direct your attention to my archers. There is nothing to equal their skill, and, in order to amuse you, I am sure they will accomplish wonders."

Robin's men then began to draw the bow with such extraordinary steadiness of hand and aim, that the King complimented them with an expression of real surprise.

The exercise lasted about half an hour, when Will Scarlett reappeared, bringing with him Marian and Maude, arrayed in Amazon costumes of Lincoln green cloth, and each carrying a bow and quiver of arrows.

The King opened his eyes in astonishment, and gazed speechless at the charming faces that blushed beneath his gaze.

"Sir Abbot," said Robin, taking Marian by the hand, "allow me to present to you the Queen of my heart, my dearly loved wife."

"Thou mightest well add the Queen of thy Merrie Men, brave Robin," cried the King; "and you have every reason to be proud of inspiring a tender passion in such a charming creature. Dear Madam," continued the King, "allow me to salute you as the Queen of Sherwood Forest, and to render you the homage of a faithful subject."

So saying, the King knelt upon the ground, and taking Marian's white hand, touched it respectfully with his lips.

"Your courtesy is great, Sir Abbot," said Marian, modestly; "but I pray you remember that it doth but ill become a man of your holy character to bow thus before a woman. You should render to God alone that token of humility and respect."

"That is a very moral rebuke for the wife of a simple forester," murmured the King, again taking up his position under the Trysting Tree.

"Sir Abbot, here is my wife," cried Will, leading Maude up to Richard.

The King looked at Maude, and said laughingly—

"This lovely lady is without doubt the one who would do honour to a King's palace."

"Yea, Sir," said Will.

"Well, my friend," replied Richard, "I share your opinion, and if you will allow me, I will implant a kiss upon the beautiful cheek of her you love."

William smiled, and the King, who took this smile for a reply in the affirmative, embraced the young woman gallantly.

"A word in your ear, Sir Abbot," said Will, approaching the King, who listened with complacency to the young man. "You are a man of taste," continued Will, "and you will never have anything to fear in Sherwood Forest. From this day forth I promise you a cordial reception every time a happy chance brings you amongst us."

"I thank you for your courtesy, good yeoman," said the King, gaily. "Oh! oh! but what more do I see?" cried Richard, with his eyes upon Will's sisters, who, accompanied by Lilas, appeared before him. "Truly, my lads, your dryads are real fairies." The King took Lilas' hand. "By our Lady!" he murmured, "I did not believe that so beautiful a woman as my sweet Berengaria existed; but, upon my soul, I am forced to confess that this child equals her in purity and beauty. My pretty one," said the King, pressing the little hand he held in his own, "thou hast chosen a very hard life, deprived of all the pleasures of thine age. Dost not fear, poor child, that the stormy winds of this Forest will destroy thy frail life, as they destroy young flowers?"

"My father," replied Lilas, gently, "the wind is tempered to the strength of the plants; it spareth the feeble ones. I am happy here; one who is dear to me lives in the old wood, and I know no sorrow by his side."

"Thou art right to acknowledge thy love if the man whom thou lovest is worthy of thee, my sweet child," returned Richard.

"He is worthy of even greater love than I give him, my father," replied Lilas. "Albeit, I love him as tenderly as can be."

Saying these words the girl blushed. Richard's big blue eyes were fixed upon her with such a burning look that, seized with an undefinable fear, she gently drew her hand away from the King's clasp, and sat down by Marian.

"I own to you, Master Robin," said the King, "that there is not a single Court in Europe that can boast of gathering around the throne so many young and beautiful women as we see around us. I have seen the women of many countries, and I have never met anything to compare with the sweet and tranquil beauty of Saxon women. Curse me, if any one of the fresh faces that meet my gaze be not worth an hundred women of the East or of any foreign race."

"I am pleased to hear you speak thus, Sir Abbot," said Robin. "You prove to me once more that pure English blood flows in your veins. I cannot presume to judge of so delicate a point, for I have never travelled, and know no lands beyond Derbyshire and Yorkshire. Natheless, I am strongly disposed to say with you that Saxon women are the most beautiful in all the world."

"They are certainly the most beautiful," cried Will, decidedly. "I have travelled over a great part of the Kingdom of France, and I can certify that I have not met with a single matron or maid who can compare with Maude. Maude is the pick of English beauty, that is my opinion."

"You have served as a soldier?" asked the King, looking at the young man attentively.

"Yea, Sir," replied Will, "I have served King Henry in Aquitaine and Poitou, at Harfleur, Evreux, Rouen, and in many other places."

"Ah, ah!" exclaimed the King, turning his head for fear that Will would end by recognising him. "Robin Hood," he continued, "your men are preparing to continue the games. I shall be very pleased to witness some fresh exercise of skill."

"It shall be as you wish, Sir. I will show you how I set about forming my archers' hands. Much," cried Robin, "place garlands of roses upon the wands."

Much executed the order given him, and soon the top of the wand was seen above a circle formed by the flowers.

"Now, my lads," cried Robin, "take aim at the wand; he who misses his stroke will have to give me a good arrow with which he shall receive a blow. Attend, for, by Our Lady, I shall not spare the maladroit. It is well understood that I take part with you, and, in case of unskilfulness, I submit to a like punishment."

Many Foresters missed their aim and received with good grace a sturdy blow. Robin Hood broke the wand in pieces; another was put up in its stead. Will and Little John missed their aim, and amid shouts of laughter from all the onlookers they received the reward of their awkwardness.

Robin had the last shot; but wishing to show the supposed Abbot that in such a case there was no distinction made between himself and his men, he purposely missed the wand.

"Oh, oh, Master!" cried an astonished yeoman, "you have missed the mark."

"'Tis true, i' faith, and I deserve the punishment. Little John, thou art the strongest of us all, and thou wilt know how to strike hard."

"I do not hold with it in the least," replied John; "the mission is a disagreeable one, for 'twould set me at variance with my right hand for ever."

"Very well, then, Will, I ask you."

"Thank you, Robin; I refuse entirely to do thee this kindness."

"I refuse too," said Much.

"I too," cried another man.

"And so do we all!" exclaimed the Foresters with one accord.

"All this is ridiculous childishness," said Robin, severely. "I did not hesitate to punish those who did wrong, you must do the like to me, and as severely. As not one of my men will lay his hand upon me, it is for thee, Sir Abbot, to settle the dispute. Here is my best arrow, and I pray you, Sir, to serve me as I served my unskilful archers."

"Nay! I dare not take it upon me to satisfy thee, my dear Robin Hood," cried the King, laughing, "for I have a heavy hand, and I hit hard."

"I am neither tender nor delicate, Sir Abbot; so be easy."

"Thou dost really wish it?" asked the King, baring his muscular arm. "Well, thou shalt have thy wish."

The blow was so vigorously applied that Robin fell to the ground, but he soon rose again.

"I confess before Heaven," said he, with smiling lips and a red face, "that you are the most powerful monk in all merry England. You have too much strength in your arm for a man who doth exercise a holy profession, and I would wager mine head (it is valued at four hundred gold crowns) that you know more about stretching a bow and wielding a cudgel than carrying a crozier."

"It may be so," cried the King, laughing; "and let us add likewise, an thou wilt—handling a sword, a spear, or a shield."

"Your conversation and manner reveal rather a man accustomed to the adventurous life of a soldier than a pious servant of Holy Church," returned Robin, examining the King attentively. "I should much like to know who you are, for strange thoughts have come into my head."

"Dismiss those thoughts, Robin Hood; and do not seek to discover whether or no I am the man I represent myself to be," replied the King, quickly.

The Knight, Sir Richard of the Plain, who had been absent since the morning, appeared at this moment in the midst of the group and approached Robin. Sir Richard trembled when he perceived the King, for Richard's face was well known to him. He looked at Robin, but the young man seemed completely ignorant of his guest's high rank.

"Do you know the name of him who wears the garb of an Abbot?" Sir Richard asked in a low voice.

"Nay," replied Robin; "but I think I discovered a few minutes agone that those russet locks and those large blue eyes could only belong to one man in England, to..."

"Richard Cœur-de-Lion, King of England," cried the Knight, involuntarily.

Robin Hood and Sir Richard fell upon their knees.

"I now recognise the noble countenance of my Sovereign," said the Outlaw Chief; "'tis our good King Richard of England. May God protect your gracious Majesty!" A benevolent smile played upon the King's lips. "Sire," continued Robin, without changing his humble attitude, "your Majesty knoweth who we be—Outlaws driven from the homes of our fathers by unjust and cruel oppression. Poor and without shelter, we have found a refuge in the solitude of the woods. We have lived by the chase, on alms—exacted by force, no doubt, but without violence, and with the most engaging courtesy. These alms were given with good or bad grace; but we never received them before we were quite certain that he who refused to come to the help of our distress carried a Knight's ransom at the least in his wallet. Sire, I implore your Majesty's pardon for my companions and their Chief."

ROBIN HOOD THE OUTLAW

"Rise, Robin Hood," replied the King, kindly, "and tell me the reason why thou didst lend me the help of thy brave archers in the assault on the Castle of Nottingham."

"Sire," returned Robin Hood, who, while obeying the King's command, still held himself respectfully inclined before him, "your Majesty is the idol of all true English hearts. Your actions, so worthy of general respect, have won for you the gracious title of 'bravest of the brave,' 'the man of the lion's heart,' who, like a loyal Knight, triumphs personally over his enemies and extends his generous protection to the unfortunate. Prince John earned your Majesty's displeasure, and when I heard of my King's appearance before the walls of Nottingham Castle, I secretly placed myself under his orders. Your Majesty took the Castle which sheltered the rebel Prince, my task was accomplished, and I retired without saying anything, because the knowledge of having loyally served my King satisfied my inmost wishes."

"I thank thee cordially for thy frankness, Robin Hood," Richard replied; "and thine affection for me is very gratifying. Thou dost act and speak like an honest man. I am pleased, and bestow full and entire pardon on the Merrie Men of Sherwood Forest. Thou hast had it in thy power to do wrong, but thou hast not taken advantage of this dangerous power. Thou hast only levied courteous contributions upon rich Normans, and then only in order to supply the needs of thy band. I excuse thy faults—they were only natural in such an exceptional position; but, as the Forest laws have been broken, as Princes of the Church and noble Lords have been obliged to leave bribes out of their immense treasures in thine hands, thy pardon needs be set down in writing so that thou mayest live henceforth in safety, free from all reproach and all pursuit. To-morrow, in the presence of my Knights, I will proclaim aloud that the ban of proscription, which hath placed thee below the meanest serf of my kingdom, is entirely removed. I restore to thee and to all those who have participated in thine adventurous career the rights and privileges of free men. I have said it, and I swear to keep my word by the help of Almighty God."

"Long live Richard Cœur-de-Lion!" cried the Outlaws with one voice.

"May the Blessed Virgin protect your Majesty for ever," said Robin Hood, in a tone of emotion, and kneeling upon one knee on the ground, he respectfully kissed the generous Monarch's hand.

After this token of gratitude, Robin rose, sounded his horn, and the Merrie Men, who had all been variously occupied, some in drawing the bow, others in wielding the quarterstaff, at once abandoned their respective occupations to group themselves in a circle around their young Chief.

"Brave comrades," said Robin, "kneel, all of you, upon the ground, and bare your heads; ye are in the presence of your legitimate sovereign, of the well-beloved Monarch of Merry England, of Richard Cœur-de-Lion. Do homage to our noble Master and Lord." The Outlaws obeyed Robin's command, and while the troop remained humbly bowed before Richard, Robin made known to them their sovereign's clemency. "And now," added the young man, "make the old Forest ring with your joyous hurrahs. A great day hath dawned for us, my lads; ye are free men by the grace of God and of noble Richard."

The Merrie Men did not need fresh encouragement to express their inward joy; they gave vent to such a formidable hurrah, it were easy to believe that the echo of it was heard two miles off from the Trysting Tree.

This noisy clamour stilled, Richard of England took up the thread of the conversation, and invited Robin and all his troop to accompany him to Nottingham Castle.

"Sire," replied Robin, "the flattering notice that your Majesty deigns to show me, fills my heart with unutterable joy. I belong body and soul to my Sovereign, and if he will permit me, I will choose from among my men an hundred and forty archers who will humbly serve your most gracious Majesty with absolute devotion."

The King, as much flattered as surprised by the heroic Outlaw's humble demeanour in his presence, thanked Robin Hood cordially, and making him send his men back to their momentarily suspended games, took a cup from the table, filled it to the brim, drank it to the dregs, and said with an expression of friendly curiosity—

"And now, friend Robin, tell me, I prithee, who is that giant over yonder; for it is difficult otherwise to describe the huge lad whom Heaven hath likewise blessed with such an honest face. Upon my soul, I thought until to-day that I was more than ordinary tall, but I see now that if I stood beside that jolly dog, I should look but an innocent chicken. What breadth of limb, what vigour! The man is magnificently made!"

"He is likewise as good, Sire," replied Robin, "as his strength is enormous; he could stay the march of an army with his single arm, and yet he will listen to a touching story with the simple innocence of a child. The man who hath the honour to attract your Majesty's attention is my brother, my companion, my dearest friend. He hath a heart of gold, a heart as true as the steel of his invincible sword. He wieldeth the staff with such wonderful skill that he hath never once been beaten; moreover, he is the best archer in the county, and the finest lad in all the world."

"Truly, these be praises right pleasant to hear, Robin," returned the King, "for he who inspires them is worthy to be thy friend. I should like to speak with this honest yeoman. What is his name?"

"John Naylor, Sire; but we call him Little John on account of his small stature."

"By the Mass," cried the King, laughing, "a band of such Little Johns would greatly terrify those dogs of infidels. Ho there, fine tree of the forest, tower of Babylon, Little John, my lad, come to me; I would fain look at thee nearer."

John approached with bared head, and awaited with an air of quiet assurance for Richard's commands.

ROBIN HOOD THE OUTLAW

The King asked the young man several questions relating to the extraordinary strength of his muscles, tried to wrestle with him, and was respectfully vanquished by his gigantic adversary. After this trial, the King took part in the games and exercises of the Merrie Men as naturally as though he had been one of their companions, and finally declared that it was long since he had spent such an enjoyable day.

That night the King of England slept under the protection of the Outlaws of Sherwood Forest, and the next day, after doing justice to an excellent breakfast, he prepared to take the road once more to Nottingham.

"My brave Robin," said the Monarch, "could you place at my disposal some clothes like those worn by your men?"

"Yea, Sire."

"Well, then, give me and my Knights costumes like thine own, and we will have a diverting scene upon our entry into Nottingham. Our men of office are always extraordinarily active, whenever the presence of a superior puts them on their good behavior, and I feel certain the good Reeve and his valiant soldiers will give us proofs of their invincible courage."

The King and his Knights donned the costumes chosen by Robin, and after a gallant kiss bestowed upon Marian, in honour of all the ladies, Richard, accompanied by Robin, Little John, Will Scarlett, Much, and a hundred and forty archers, gaily took the road to his lordly dwelling.

At the gates of Nottingham, Richard commanded his suite to give vent to a shout of victory.

This formidable hurrah brought the citizens to the thresholds of their respective houses, and at sight of a body of Merrie Men, armed to the teeth, they imagined that the King had been killed by the Outlaws, and that the robbers, whetted by their bloody victory, were going to descend upon the town and massacre all its inhabitants. Distracted with fear, the poor creatures rushed about in disorder, some into the most obscure recesses of their dwellings, others straight before them. Others pealed the bells, besought the aid of the town guard, and went to find the Reeve, who by an extraordinary miracle had completely disappeared.

The King's troops were about to make a dangerous attack upon the supposed Outlaws, when their Chiefs, little desirous of entering upon a contest without knowing the cause of it, put a check upon their bellicose ardour.

"Behold our warriors," said Richard, with a sly look at the cowardly defenders of the town. "Meseemeth the citizens, as well as the soldiers, cling to life. The Reeve is absent, the leaders tremble; good Heavens, but these cowards deserve exemplary punishment."

The King had scarce arrived at this by no means flattering conclusion concerning the citizens of Nottingham, when his own personal body-guard, led by a Captain, left the Castle in all haste, in line of battle and with spears at rest.

"By St. Denis, my fine fellows joke not," cried the King, putting to his lips the horn that had been given him by Robin. Twice he sounded a call betokening the advance to the Captain of his Guards, and the latter, recognising the signal agreed upon by the Monarch, lowered his arms, and respectfully awaited the approach of his Sovereign.

The news of the return of Richard of England, triumphantly accompanied by the Prince of Outlaws, spread as quickly as the news of the approach of the Outlaws with murderous intent. The citizens, who had prudently retired into the recesses of their houses, sallied out again with pale faces, but with smiles upon their lips; and as soon as they learnt that Robin Hood and his band had won the King's favour, they pressed round the Merrie Men, complimenting this one, shaking the hand of that, vying with one another in proclaiming themselves the friends and protectors of them all. From the midst of the multitude cries of felicitation and joy arose, and one heard these words repeated on every side—"Glory to noble Robin Hood, glory to Robin Hood, the tender and true!"

The voices growing more and more emboldened, proclaimed the presence of the Outlaw Chief so loudly and enthusiastically, that Richard, tired of the increasing clamour, cried at last—

"By my crown and sceptre, meseemeth that thou art King here, Robin."

"Ah, Sire," replied the young man, with a bitter smile, "do not attach any importance or value to these tokens of apparent friendship; they are but the vague result of the gracious favour with which your Majesty doth overload the Outlaw. One word from King Richard could change the admiring shouts which my presence here excites, into howls of hatred, and these very men would pass at once from praise to blame, from admiration to scorn."

"Thou speakest true, my dear Robin," laughed the King; "rogues are the same everywhere, and I have already proved the heartlessness of the citizens of Nottingham. When I came here with the intention of punishing Prince John, they greeted my return to England with a profound reserve. For them, might is right, and they did not know that with thy help it would be easy for me to capture the Castle and expel my brother. Now they show us the fair side of their ugly faces, and plaster us with their vile flattery. Let us leave the wretches, and think only of ourselves. I have promised thee, Robin, a noble reward for the services which thou hast rendered me. Put thy request; King Richard hath but one word, to which he ever holds, and he aye fulfils the promises he doth make."

"Sire," replied Robin, "your gracious Majesty hath made me happy beyond expression in renewing your generous offer of support. I accept it for myself, for my men, and for a Knight, who, disgraced by King Henry, hath been obliged to seek a refuge in Sherwood Forest. This Knight, Sire, is a warm-hearted man, the worthy father of a family, a brave Saxon, and if your Majesty will do me the honour to hearken to the history of Sir Richard of the Plain, I am sure you will grant the request I am about to make."

"We have given our kingly word to grant any favour which it may please thee to beg of us, friend Robin," replied Richard, affectionately. "Speak out fearlessly, and tell us by what chain of circumstances this Knight fell into disfavour with my father."

Robin hastened to obey the King's command, and recounted as briefly as possible the history of Sir Richard of the Plain.

"By our Lady," cried Richard, "this good Knight hath been cruelly treated, and thou hast acted nobly in coming to his aid. But it shall never be said, brave Robin Hood, that in this case again thou hast surpassed the King of England in large-heartedness and generosity. I will protect thy friend in my turn; bring him to our presence."

Robin called the Knight, who, with a heart beating high with hope, presented himself respectfully before the Monarch.

"Sir Richard of the Plain," said the King, graciously, "thy valiant friend, Robin Hood, hath just told me of all the misfortunes that have occurred to thy family, and the dangers to which thou hast been exposed. In doing thee justice, I am happy to testify to the sincere admiration and profound esteem which his conduct inspires in me. I restore to thee possession of thy goods, and for one year thou shalt be freed of all imposts and taxes. Besides this, I annul the decree of banishment proclaimed against thee, in order that the remembrance of this act of injustice shall be entirely effaced both from thy memory and from that of thy fellow citizens. Return to thy Castle; letters of full and entire pardon shall be delivered to thee by our command. As for thee, Robin Hood, ask something more from him who feels that he can never repay his debt of gratitude, even after having granted all thy wishes."

"Sire," said the Knight, kneeling upon the ground, "how can I express the gratitude which fills my heart?"

"By telling me that thou art happy," the King replied gaily; "and by promising me never again to offend against members of Holy Church."

Sir Richard kissed the hand of the generous Monarch, and discreetly retired among the groups standing a short distance from the King.

"Well, brave archer," continued the Monarch, turning toward Robin Hood, "what dost desire of me?"

"Naught at present, Sire; later on, if your Majesty will permit me, I shall ask one last favour."

"It shall be granted thee. Now, let us return to the Castle. We have received generous hospitality in Sherwood Forest, and it is to be hoped that Nottingham Castle can furnish resources for a right royal feast. Thy men have an excellent mode of preparing venison, and the fresh air and fatigue of the march had singularly sharpened our appetites, so that we ate greedily."

"Your Majesty had the right to eat your fill," Robin laughingly replied, "considering that the game was your own property."

"Our property or that of the first hunter that comes along," the King returned gaily; "and if all other folk make out that the deer of

Alexandre Dumas

Sherwood Forest belong exclusively to us, there is a certain yeoman whom thou dost know very well, Robin, and three hundred of his companions forming a merry band, who reck mighty little of the prerogative of the Crown."

Talking thus, Richard proceeded toward the Castle, and the enthusiastic acclamations of the populace followed the King of England and the famous Outlaw to the gates of the old fortress with their noisy clamour.

The generous Monarch fulfilled the promises he had made to Robin Hood the very same day; he signed an act annulling the ban of proscription, and restored to the young man possession of his rights and title to the wealth and dignities of the Huntingdon family.

The day after this happy event, Robin assembled his men in the Court-yard of the Castle, and announced to them the unhoped-for change in his fortunes. This news filled the hearts of the brave yeomen with sincere happiness; they loved their Chief devotedly, and with one accord they refused the liberty he wished to give them. It was decided forthwith that for the future the Merrie Men were to cease from levying contributions even on Normans and Churchmen, and that they should be fed and clothed afresh by their noble master Robin Hood, who had become the rich Earl of Huntingdon.

"My lads," added Robin, "since ye wish to live near me and to accompany me to London, if I be commanded to proceed thither by our well-beloved Sovereign, ye must swear to me never to reveal the situation of our cave to any one. Let us reserve this precious refuge in case of fresh misfortune."

The men loudly took the oath demanded by their Chief, and Robin urged them to make their preparations for departure without delay.

On March 30th, 1194, the eve of his departure for London, Richard held a council at Nottingham Castle, and amongst the many important matters that were then discussed was the establishment of Robin's right to the Earldom of Huntingdon. The King peremptorily announced his wish to restore to Robin Hood the property held by the Abbot of Ramsey, and Richard's councillors formally promised to carry out to his entire satisfaction the act of justice, which was to make amends to the noble Outlaw for the misfortunes he had so courageously borne.

CHAPTER XIII

Before leaving, perhaps for ever, the ancient Forest that had so long sheltered him, Robin felt such an intense regret for the past, and such apprehensions for the future, but little in keeping with the prospect which Richard's generosity had opened up for him, that he decided to await under the protecting shelter of his leafy home the definite results of the arrangements made by the King of England.

It was a lucky decision that kept him at Sherwood, for Richard's coronation, which took place at Winchester shortly after his return to London, so much absorbed his thoughts that all proceedings tending to restore the recognised but still unproclaimed rights of the young Earl of Huntingdon, were rendered inexpedient.

The coronation festivities ended, Richard departed for the Continent, to which he was summoned by a desire for vengeance upon Philip of France, and, relying on the promises of his Counsellors, he left the re-establishment of brave Robin Hood's fortunes to their care.

Baron Broughton (Abbot of Ramsey), who enjoyed the wealth of the Huntingdon family, set in motion all his influence and the resources of his immense fortune, to retard the execution of the decree made by Richard in favour of the true inheritor of the titles and domains of this rich Earldom. But all the time he was gathering to himself friends and protectors, the prudent Baron did not attempt openly to oppose the edict issued by Richard, contenting himself with asking for time, and loading the Chancellor with rich presents; and thus maintaining quiet possession of the patrimony he had usurped.

While Richard was fighting in Normandy, and the Abbot of Ramsey gradually winning over the entire Council to his cause, Robin Hood confidently awaited the message that would inform him of his having entered into possession of his father's estates.

Eleven months of fruitless waiting lessened the young man's patience. He plucked up courage, and trusting in the kindness shown him by the King during his sojourn at Nottingham, he addressed a request to Hubert Walter, Archbishop of Canterbury, Keeper of the Great Seal of England, and Lord Chief Justice of the Kingdom. Robin Hood's request reached its destination. The Archbishop was aware of it. But if this very just demand was not openly repulsed, it remained unanswered, and was treated as though it had never been made.

The ill-will of those who had to do with restoring Robin Hood's possessions, manifested itself in this inactivity, and it was not difficult for the young man to guess that an underhand struggle was going on against him. Unluckily, the Abbot of Ramsey, who had become Baron of Broughton, was too strong an adversary to make it possible for Robin to revenge himself upon him in Richard's absence. He therefore decided to shut his eyes to the injustice of which he was a victim, and prudently to await King Richard's return.

Acting on this decision, Robin Hood sent a second message to the Lord Chief Justice. He confessed to great dissatisfaction at the evident protection accorded to the Abbot of Ramsey, and declared that, hoping for prompt justice on Richard's return to England, he would again place himself at the head of his men, and continue to live in Sherwood Forest as he had done before.

Hubert Walter apparently paid no attention to Robin's second message; but, while taking strong measures to restore peace and order throughout England, while destroying numerous bands of men who had gathered together in different parts of the kingdom, the Archbishop left Richard's friend and his Merrie Men in peace.

Four years went by in the false calm that precedes the storm of revolutionary disorders. One morning, the news of Richard's death fell upon the kingdom of England like a thunderbolt, and filled all hearts with fear.

The accession to the throne of Prince John, who seemed deliberately to have undertaken the task of making himself universally hated, was the signal for a series of crimes and acts of reckless violence.

During this disastrous period, the Abbot of Ramsey, accompanied by a numerous suite, passed through Sherwood Forest on his way to York, and was waylaid by Robin. The Abbot and his escort were taken prisoners, and could only obtain their freedom at the cost of a considerable ransom. He paid, storming and promising himself a fierce revenge the while; and this revenge was not long delayed.

The Abbot of Ramsey addressed himself to the King, and John, who at that time greatly needed the support of the nobles, lent an ear to the Abbot's complaint, and forthwith sent a hundred men under Sir William de Grey, the eldest brother of John de Grey, the King's favourite, in pursuit of Robin Hood, with orders to cut the whole band to pieces.

Sir William de Grey, who was a Norman, hated the Saxons, and moved by this feeling of hatred he swore ere long to lay the head of his insolent adversary at the feet of the Abbot of Ramsey.

The unexpected arrival of a company of soldiers of warlike appearance and clad in coats of mail, caused a panic in the little town of Nottingham; but when it was understood that their destination was the Forest of Sherwood, and their purpose the extermination of Robin's band, terror gave place to discontent, and

ROBIN HOOD THE OUTLAW

some of the Outlaws' friends hastened to warm them of the fate in store for them. Robin received the news as a man on his guard, who awaits the reprisals of a deeply injured enemy, and he did not doubt for an instant that the Abbot of Ramsey had lent his assistance to this sudden expedition. Robin assembled his men, therefore, and prepared to offer a stout resistance to the Norman attack. He at once sent out a skilful archer, disguised as a peasant, who was to meet the enemy and offer to conduct them to the tree known throughout the county as the rallying-point of the band of Merrie Men.

This simple trick, which had already rendered Robin such good service, again succeeded completely, and Sir William de Grey accepted the offices of Robin's spy without hesitation.

The genial Forester then put himself at the head of the troop and took them through bushes, thorns, and thickets for three hours, without noticing, apparently, that their coats of mail rendered the progress of the unhappy soldiers very difficult. Then, when they were overcome by the crushing weight of their armour and spent with fatigue, the guide led them, not to the Trysting Tree, but to the middle of a vast clearing surrounded by elms, beeches, and century-old oaks. On this spot, where the turf was as fresh and as green as the lawn before a country house, was gathered, some sitting, some standing, the entire band of Merrie Men.

The sight of the enemy, to all appearances disarmed, revived the soldiers' spirits. Without giving a thought to their guide, who had slipped into the ranks of the Outlaws, they uttered a shout of triumph and threw themselves upon the Foresters. To the great surprise of the Normans the Merrie Men hardly quitted the listless attitude they had taken up, and almost without a change of position, they raised their immense cudgels above their heads, whirling them round and round with shouts of laughter.

Exasperated by this derisive reception, the soldiers rushed confusedly, sword in hand, upon the Foresters, who, without manifesting the slightest emotion, knocked down the threatening weapons with lusty blows of their cudgels; then, with dazzling rapidity, they dealt a shower of deadly blows upon the heads and shoulders of the Normans. The clatter of the coats of mail and helmets mingled with the cries of the terrified soldiers and the shouts of the Foresters, who did not appear to be defending their lives, but merely exercising their skill upon inanimate bodies.

Sir William de Grey, who was in command of the soldiers, saw with rage in his heart, the best of his troop falling around him, and he cursed the folly that had made him load his men with such heavy accoutrements. In a combat with men of such superior strength, and where the victory was so uncertain, bodily skill and agility were the first elements of success, and the Normans could hardly move without an effort.

Terrified at the probable result of a total defeat, the Knight called a truce, and thanks to Robin's generosity, he was able to take back the remnants of his troop to Nottingham.

It is needless to add that the grateful Knight promised himself secretly to recommence the attack on the following day with men more lightly equipped than the Normans he had brought from London.

Robin Hood, who had guessed Sir William's hostile intentions, arranged his men in order of battle on the same spot on which the combat of the previous day had taken place, and awaited calmly the appearance of the soldiers, who had been met some two miles from the Trysting Tree by one of the Foresters sent as scouts to different parts of the Forest in the neighbourhood of Nottingham.

This time the Normans were clad in the light garb of archers, and armed with bows and arrows, small swords, and bucklers.

Robin Hood and his men had been at their posts for about an hour, and the soldiers had not yet appeared. The young man began to think his enemies had changed their minds, when an archer, who had been posted as sentinel, ran up in all haste to announce that the Normans (who had lost their way) were now marching directly upon the Trysting Tree, where, by Robin's orders, the women had assembled.

This news struck Robin with a fatal presentiment. He turned pale, and said to his men—

"Let us intercept the Norman dogs; they must be stopped on their way. Woe to them and to us if they get near our women!"

The Foresters rushed as one man to the road taken by the soldiers in order to bar their way or to reach the Trysting Tree before them. But the soldiers had advanced too far for the Merrie Men either to stop them or even to be in time to prevent a terrible disaster. The manners, or rather the want of manners, of this lawless period, made Robin and his companions fear cruel retaliation upon the group of completely isolated women.

The Normans soon reached the Trysting Tree. At sight of them the women rose in terror, uttering cries of anguish, and fled distractedly in every direction open to them. In the weak and forlorn position of their terrified wives, Sir William saw at a glance a means of satisfying his hatred against the Saxons; he resolved to seize them, and by their deaths to avenge the ill success of his first attack upon Robin Hood.

At their Chief's command, the soldiers halted, and for a second Sir William followed with his eyes the tumultuous movements of the poor distracted women. One of them ran forward, and her companions endeavoured to join her, and to protect her flight. This evident solicitude conveyed to the Norman the superior position of her who headed the retreat; he also considered that it would be according to the rules of war to strike her first, and seizing his bow, he fixed an arrow to it, and coolly took aim. The Knight was a good marksman; the unhappy woman, struck between the shoulders, fell bleeding in the midst of her companions, who, without a thought of their own safety, knelt around her, uttering piercing cries.

A man had seen the miserable Norman's murderous action, and hoping to arrest the fatal stroke, he took aim at the Knight. His arrow reached its mark, but too late, for Sir William had shot Marian before he met his own death at the hand of Robin Hood.

"Lady Marian is wounded—mortally wounded!"

The terrible news flew from mouth to mouth; it brought tears to the eyes of all the Saxons, who dearly loved their young Queen. As for Robin, he was mad with grief; he did not speak, he did not weep, but he fought. Little John and he leapt like tigers thirsting for blood upon the Normans, and scattered death through their ranks without uttering a cry, without even opening their livid lips. Their active arms seemed endowed with superhuman strength; they avenged Marian, and they avenged her cruelly.

The bloody battle lasted for two hours; the Normans were cut to pieces, and shown no grace or mercy. One soldier alone escaped, and went to tell Sir William de Grey's brother of the fatal result of the expedition.

Marian had been removed to a clearing some distance from the scene of the combat, and Robin found Maude there, weeping as she vainly tried to staunch the blood which gushed from a frightful wound.

Robin knelt beside Marian, his heart torn with anguish; he could neither speak nor move, and felt as though he must choke. At Robin's approach Marian had opened her eyes and looked tenderly at him. "Thou art not wounded, my dear?" she asked, in a weak voice, after a moment's mute contemplation.

"Nay, nay," murmured Robin between his clenched teeth.

"The Holy Virgin be praised!" added Marian, smiling. "I have prayed to Our Dear Lady for thee, and she hath heard my prayer. Is this terrible combat over, dear Robin?"

"Yea, sweet Marian, our enemies have disappeared; they will never come back again. But let me speak of thee, think of thee; thou art...I...Holy Mother of God! This grief is more than I can bear."

"Come, come, courage, my well-beloved Robin; lift up thy head, look at me," said Marian, still trying to smile. "My wound is not deep, it will soon be cured; the arrow hath been withdrawn. Thou knowest well, my dear, that if there were anything to fear, I should be the first to perceive that mine hour was come....Look, look at me, Robin dear."

As she spoke, Marian tried to draw Robin's head towards her; but her last strength was spent in the effort, and when the young man raised his weeping eyes to her, she had fainted.

Marian soon came to herself, and after having sweetly consoled her husband, she expressed a wish to rest a little, and soon fell into a profound slumber.

As soon as Marian was asleep upon the mossy bed in the shade of the trees, that had been prepared for her by her companions, Robin went to inquire into the condition of his band. He found John, Will Scarlett, and Much occupied in tending the wounded and burying the dead. The number of the wounded was very inconsiderable, for it resolved itself into half a score of men seriously hurt, and there was not a single death to deplore amongst the

Outlaws. As for the Normans, we know that they no longer existed, and several large ditches were dug in the glade to serve as their sepulchre.

On awaking after three hours' deep sleep, Marian found her husband beside her, and the angelic creature, still wishing to give some consoling hope to him she loved so dearly, began softly to say that she felt no weakness at all, and would soon be well.

Marian was suffering, she felt a deathly depression creeping over her, and she knew there was no hope; but Robin's anguish wrung her heart, and she sought to soften, as much as lay in her power, the fatal blow which must soon be dealt him.

Next morning she was worse, inflammation had set in in the wound, and all hope of recovery faded even from Robin's heart.

"Dear Robin," said Marian, laying her burning hands in those of her husband, "my last hour approaches; the hour of our separation will be cruel, but not insupportable to such as have faith in the mercy and goodness of Almighty God."

"Oh, Marian, my beloved Marian!" cried Robin, breaking into sobs, "hath the Holy Virgin abandoned us, that she can permit this desolation of our hearts? I will die at thy death, Marian, for it will be impossible to live without thee."

"Religion and duty will be the support of thy weakness, my Robin," replied the young wife, tenderly. "Thou wilt resign thyself to bear the sorrow that overwhelms us, because it hath been imposed on thee as a Heavenly decree; and thou wilt live, if not happy, at least calm and strong, amidst the men whose happiness depends on thy life. I am going to leave thee, but, ere I close mine eyes to the light of day, let me tell thee how much I have loved thee, how much I do love thee. If the gratitude that fills all my being could be clothed in visible form, thou wouldst comprehend the strength and the extent of a feeling that hath no equal but my love. I have loved thee, Robin, with the confident surrender of a devoted heart; I have consecrated my life to thee, only asking of God the one gift of pleasing thee."

"And God hath granted thee that gift, dear Marian," said Robin, trying to moderate the violence of his grief; "for I can tell thee truly that thou alone hast filled my heart, that whether at my side or far from me, thou hast ever been my only hope and sweetest consolation."

"If Heaven had permitted us to grow old together side by side, dear Robin," replied Marian; "if a long succession of happy days had been granted to us, the separation would have been still more cruel, for then thou wouldst have had less strength to support the crushing sorrow. But we are both young, and I leave thee alone at a time of life when solitude is crowned by remembrance, perhaps even by hope....Take me in thine arms, dear Robin, so...let me rest my head against thine. I would whisper my last words in thine ear. I would have my soul take its flight lightly and happily. I would breathe my last sigh upon thy heart."

"Beloved Marian, speak not so," cried Robin, in heartrending tones. "I cannot bear to hear that fatal word 'separation' upon thy lips. Oh, Holy Mother of God! Holy Protectress of the afflicted! Thou who hast ever granted my humble prayers! Grant me the life of her whom I love! Grant me the life of my wife, I pray thee, I beseech thee with clasped hands and on bended knees!"

And Robin, with his face bathed in tears, raised supplicating hands to Heaven.

"Thou dost address a vain prayer to the Divine Mother of the Sorrows of Mankind, sweetheart," said Marian, laying her pale face against Robin's shoulder. "My days, or rather mine hours, are numbered. God hath sent me a dream to warn me."

"A dream! What dost say, dear child?"

"Yea, a dream; listen to me. I saw thee, surrounded by thy Merrie Men, in a vast clearing of Sherwood Forest. Thou wast evidently giving a feast to thy brave comrades, for the trees of the old wood were twined with garlands of roses, and purple streamers waved merrily upon the perfumed breath of the breeze. I was seated by thee; I held one of thy hands clasped in mine, and my heart was full of unutterable joy, when a stranger, with a pale face and black garments, appeared before us, and beckoned to me with his hand to follow him. I arose in spite of myself, and, still in spite of myself, I obeyed the dark stranger's summons. Natheless, before leaving thee I questioned thee with a look, for my lips could not even give vent to a sigh from my anguished bosom. Thy calm and smiling looks met mine. I directed thine attention to the stranger; thou didst turn thy head toward him and didst smile again. I made thee understand that he was leading me far away from thee. A slight pallor spread over thy face, but the smile did not leave thy lips. I was desperate, a convulsive trembling seized my limbs, and I began to sob with my head buried in my hands.

"The stranger still led me on. When we found ourselves a short distance from the clearing, a veiled woman appeared before me; the stranger stepped back, and this woman, raising the veil that hid her features from me, disclosed the sweet face of my mother. I uttered a cry, and trembling with wonder and fear, I held out my arms to her.

"'Dear child,' said she, in a tender and melodious voice, 'weep not, submit with the resignation of a Christian soul to the common destiny of all mortals. Die in peace, and leave without sorrow a world that hath only vain pleasures and passing joys to offer thee. There exists beyond this earth an abode of infinite bliss. Come and dwell there with me. But ere thou follow me, look!' Uttering these words my mother passed her hand, white and cold as marble, across my forehead. At this touch the veil fell from mine eyes—till then obscured by tears—and I saw around me a resplendent circle of maidens of supernatural beauty and with a divine smile upon their fresh and shining faces. They did not speak, but they looked at me, and seemed to convey to me how happy I should feel in coming to augment their numbers.

Alexandre Dumas

"While I was admiring my future companions, my mother leant toward me, and said tenderly, 'Dear child of my heart, look, look again.'

"I obeyed my mother's tender injunction. All around me was spread a vast garden of sweet-smelling flowers, trees laden with fruit—crimson apples and golden-tinted pears—bent their branches to the thick grass, which was all enamelled with the blossoms of the white Easter daisies. The air was full of a sweet perfume, and a multitude of many-coloured birds fluttered and sang in the balmy air. I was enchanted. My heart, which late was full of grief, gradually lightened, and my mother, smiling at my happiness, said to me again with an expression of caressing tenderness, 'Look, dear child, look!'

"I heard the sound of light footsteps behind me. The sound was scarce audible, yet it seemed like music in mine ears, and without understanding the feeling that redoubled the beating of my heart, I turned round.

"Oh! then, Robin, my joy was complete, for thou wast running down the garden path; thou wast running to me with shining eyes and open arms. 'Robin! Robin!' I cried, trying to run to thee. My mother held me back. 'He will come,' she said. 'He comes—here he is.' And taking both our hands she joined them together, kissed me on the brow, and said, 'My children, you are here where joy is everlasting, where love is never ending; you are in the abode of the elect—be happy!'

"The end of the dream escapes my memory, dear Robin," continued Marian, after a short silence. "I awoke, and I understood that Heaven had sent me a warning and a hope. I must leave thee, doubtless for many years, but not for ever; God will re-unite us in the blissful eternity of the next world."

"Dear, dear Marian!"

"My beloved," continued the young wife, "I feel that my strength is exhausted. Let me rest my head upon thy heart, entwine thine arms around me, and like a tired child that falls asleep upon its mother's bosom, will I sleep my last sleep."

Robin embraced the dying woman feverishly, while his burning tears fell upon her brow.

"God bless thee, my beloved," repeated Marian in a more and more feeble voice. "God bless thee in the present and in the future. May He extend His Divine mercy over thee and over all whom thou dost love. All grows dark about me, and yet I would fain see thee smile once more. I would fain read in thine eyes how dear I am to thee. Robin, I hear my mother's voice. She calls me! she calls me! Farewell!"

"Marian! Marian!" cried Robin, falling on his knees beside his young wife's couch. "Speak to me! speak to me! I cannot let thee die! No, I cannot! Almighty God, come to my aid! Holy Virgin, take pity on us!"

"Dear Robin," murmured Marian, "I wish to be buried 'neath the Trysting Tree....I want my grave to be covered with flowers...."

"Yea, dearest Marian—yea, my sweet angel, thou shalt sleep beneath a carpet of balmy verdure, and when my last hour is come, I swear it by all I hold sacred, I will demand a place beside thee from him who closes mine eyes...."

"I thank thee, my beloved. My heart's last beat is for thee, and I die happy, for I die in thine arms....Good-bye, good—"

A sigh and a kiss fell from Marian's lips; her hands feebly clasped Robin's neck, around which they were entwined, then she grew quite still.

Robin remained bending over her sweet face for a long time. For long he hoped to see the closed eyes open again; for long he waited for a word from the pale lips, a tremble from that dear form; but alas! he waited in vain. Marian was dead!

"Holy Mother of God!" cried Robin, laying the motionless body of the poor girl upon the bed, "she is gone; gone for ever! my beloved, my only joy, my wife!"

And, maddened with grief, the unhappy man rushed from the spot crying wildly, "Marian is dead! Marian is dead!"

CHAPTER XIV

Robin Hood religiously performed his wife's last wishes. A grave was dug beneath the Trysting Tree, and the mortal remains of the angelic creature who had been the guide and consolation of his life, were interred beneath a bed of flowers. The maidens of the County hastened to attend the funeral ceremony, strewed Marian's tomb with roses, and mingled their tears with poor Robin's sobs.

Allan and Christabel, informed by messenger of the sad occurrence, arrived early in the day; they were both in despair, and bitterly bewailed the irreparable loss of a well-beloved sister.

When all was over, and Marian's body had disappeared from sight, Robin Hood, who had presided over the heartrending details of the burial, gave a piercing cry, trembled from head to foot like a man wounded full in the breast by a murderous arrow, and without listening to Allan, without answering Christabel, who was frightened by his fierce despair, he escaped from their hands, and disappeared into the wood. Poor Robin wished to be alone with his grief, alone with God.

Time, which calms and softens the greatest griefs, had no such effect upon the open wound in Robin's heart. He wept ceaselessly, he mourned continuously, the wife whose sweet face had brightened their woodland home, who had found happiness in his love, who had been the only joy of his life.

Life in the forest soon became insupportable to the young man, and he retired to Barnsdale Hall. But there, the distressing memory of the past was livelier than ever, and Robin Hood fell into a gloomy apathy that numbed all his moral faculties. He seemed to be alive neither in mind, spirit, nor memory.

This splenetic sorrow, if it may be so described, threw a shadow of the deepest melancholy over the band of Merrie Men. The grief of their young leader had quenched the light of their mirth, and they wandered through the old Forest like lost spirits. No longer did Friar Tuck's loud laugh echo through the greenwood; no longer was heard the sound of the nimble quarter-staves striking against each other with vigour and skill, amidst a chorus of bravos. Arrows remained idle within their quivers, and the butts were deserted.

Want of sleep and a distaste for food wrought a visible change in Robin's features; he grew pale, his eyes were encircled by dark rings, a dry cough shook his frame, while a slow fever finished the work commenced by sorrow. Little John, who silently watched this cruel transformation, at last succeeded in making Robin understand that he must not only leave Barnsdale, but even Yorkshire, and seek to assuage his grief in the distractions of travel. After an hour's resistance, Robin had taken Little John's sage advice, and before leaving his companions, he had placed them under the command of his excellent friend.

In order to run no risks of being recognised, Robin dressed himself as a peasant, and in this simple garb he arrived at Scarborough. Here he stopped to rest at the door of a small hut occupied by the widow of a fisherman, and claimed her hospitality. The good dame gave our hero a kindly welcome, and as she served him with food, she related to him all the little sorrows of her life, adding that she owned a boat manned by three men, whose support pressed heavily on her, although they were insufficient in numbers to row the boat to shore when it was fully laden with a full catch of fish.

Eager to kill time in any way whatever, Robin Hood offered, for a small wage, to complete the number of boatmen, and the peasant woman, much taken with her guest's kindly disposition, gladly accepted the offer of his services.

"What are you called, fair lad?" asked the woman, when the arrangements for Robin's installation in the hut were complete.

"I am called Simon of Lee, good dame," replied Robin Hood.

"Well, then, Simon of Lee, to-morrow you will begin your work; and if the trade suits you, we shall long live together."

Early next day, Robin Hood embarked with his new companions, but it must be owned that, despite his will, Robin, who was ignorant of the most elementary details of the work, was of no use whatever to the experienced fishermen. Luckily for our friend, he had not to deal with evil comrades, and, instead of grumbling at his stupidity, they only laughed at the idea of his bringing with him his bow and arrows.

"If I had these fellows in Sherwood Forest," thought Robin, "they would not be so ready to laugh at my expense; but there— every one to his own trade. I certainly am not their match in the one they follow."

After loading up the boat to the gunwale with fish, the men unfurled the sails and made for the jetty. As they sped along, they saw a little French corvette making for them. The corvette did not appear to have many men on board, but none the less the fishermen seemed terrified at her approach, and cried out that they were lost.

"Lost, and wherefore?" questioned Robin.

"Wherefore? Simpleton that thou art!" returned one of the fishermen. "Because the corvette is manned by the enemies of our nation; because we are at war with them; because, an they board us, they will take us prisoners."

"I trust indeed that they will never do that," replied Robin; "we will e'en try to defend ourselves."

"What defence can we offer? They are fifteen, we are three."

"Then you do not count me, my man?" asked Robin.

"Nay, my lad; thy hands have never been blistered by handling oars. Thou art no sailor, and shouldst thou chance to fall into the water, there would be one fool the less upon the earth. Nay, never take offence, thou art a pretty fellow, I bear thee no ill will; but thou art not worth thy keep."

A half smile hovered on Robin's lips.

"I am not very sensitive," said he; "however, I will prove to you that I am some good in the presence of danger. My bow and arrows will help us out of this difficulty. Bind me to the mast, for my hand must be sure; then let the corvette come within range."

The fishermen obeyed; Robin was firmly lashed to the mainmast, where he waited with bended bow.

As the corvette drew nearer, Robin took aim at a man standing in the bows, and sent him rolling on the deck with an arrow through his throat. A second sailor met a like fate. The fishermen, overwhelmed with wonder and delight, uttered a shout of triumph, and the foremost among them pointed out to Robin the commander of the corvette. Robin killed him as quickly as he had killed the others. The two vessels placed themselves side by side. There were only ten men left upon the corvette, and soon Robin had reduced the numbers of the unhappy Frenchmen to three. As soon as the fishermen perceived that only three men were left alive on board the boat, they determined to seize her, and this was made still easier because the Frenchmen, seeing that all opposition was dangerous and useless, had laid down their arms and surrendered at discretion. The sailors were given their lives, and allowed to return to France on board a fishing smack.

The French corvette was a fine prize, for she was carrying a large sum of money to the King of France, twelve thousand silver pieces.

Needless to add, that, in taking possession of this unlooked-for treasure, the gallant sailors made excuses to him at whom they had been poking fun so short a time before; then, with heartfelt disinterestedness, they declared that the whole prize belonged to Robin, because he had won the victory by his skill and bravery.

"Good friends," said Robin, "the right of settling this question is mine alone, and thus will I arrange matters—half the corvette and her contents is to be the property of the poor widow to whom this boat belongs, and the rest will be divided betwixt the three of you."

"Nay, nay," said the men; "we will not allow thee to deprive thyself of the wealth thou hast acquired without our aid. The vessel doth belong to thee, and if thou wilt, we will be thy servants."

"I thank you, good lads," returned Robin; "but I cannot accept this testimony of your devotion. The division of the prize is to be according to my wishes, and I will employ the twelve thousand pieces in building for you and the poor inhabitants of the village of Scarborough healthier houses than you possess at present."

The fishermen tried, but in vain, to change Robin's plans. They tried to persuade him that in giving a quarter of the twelve thousand pieces to the widow, to the poor, and to themselves, he would still be acting very generously. But Robin would not listen to a word, and ended by imposing silence on his honest companions.

Robin Hood stayed for several weeks with the good people who had been made so happy by his generosity. Then one morning, tired of the sea, hungering to see the old woods and his dear companions once more, he called the fishermen together and announced his departure to them.

"My good friends," said Robin, "I leave you with a heart full of gratitude for all the care and kindness ye have lavished upon me. Probably we shall never meet again; but I hope that ye will preserve a pleasant memory of him who hath been your guest, of your friend Robin Hood."

Before the wonderstruck fishermen had recovered their power of speech, Robin Hood had disappeared. To this day the little bay, upon whose shores stood the hut which sheltered the noble Outlaw, bears the name of Robin Hood's bay.

It was in the early hours of a beautiful June morning that Robin Hood reached the confines of Barnsdale Forest. With a spirit stirred by deep emotion he entered a narrow path, where often, alas! the dear creature, whose absence he must ever mourn, had awaited him with merry heart and smiling lips. After some moments' silent contemplation of the spots which bore witness to his lost happiness, Robin breathed more freely. He lived again in the past, and the memory of Marian stole lightly and sweetly like a perfumed vapour along the dim alleys, on the flowery meads, and into the glades shaded from the sun's rays by the foliage of the old oaks. Robin Hood followed the beloved shadow, with it he penetrated into the thick groves, in its steps he descended into the vales, and, still accompanied by the sweet vision, he arrived at the cross-road where the greater part of the Merrie Men were usually to be found.

To-day, however, the large open space was empty. Robin raised his hunting-horn to his lips and made the old wood resound with a vigorous call. A cry, or rather a sort of clamour, answered the notes of the horn; the branches of the surrounding trees were abruptly pushed aside, and Will Scarlett, followed by the whole band, threw himself upon Robin Hood with open arms.

"Robin, my dear, dear Robin," murmured Will in a broken voice, "so thou art returned at last, the Lord be praised! We have awaited thee with much impatience, have we not, Little John?"

"Yea, 'tis so indeed," replied John, whose eyes were sadly contemplating the traveller's pale face; "and Robin hath pitied our anguish and anxiety, since he is come back to us."

"Yea, good John, and I trust never to leave thee again."

John took Robin Hood's hand and wrung it with a violence so full of tenderness, that he had not the heart to complain of the pain which the too ardent pressure caused him.

"Be welcome among us!" cried the Foresters, joyously; "be welcome a thousand times!"

The transports of delight induced by his presence shed a refreshing balm upon our hero's incurable heart wound. He felt that he must no longer give himself up to his grief, and leave helpless the brave men who had attached themselves to his evil fortunes.

This courageous resolution caused the blood to mount to poor Robin's face. His heart, alas! revolted against his will; but the latter was the stronger, and after addressing a mental farewell to Maid Marian's memory, he held out his hand to his faithful followers, saying in a strong, calm voice, "Henceforth, dear friends, ye will have in me your friend, your guide, your chief, Robin Hood the Outlaw, your captain, Robin Hood!"

"Hurrah!" cried the Foresters, throwing their bonnets in the air; "hurrah! hurrah!"

"Be my Merrie Men once more," said Robin, "and let happiness once more reign supreme here. To-day we will rest, to-morrow the chase, and let the Normans beware!"

Robin Hood's new exploits soon became the subject of men's talk through the length and breadth of England, and the rich Lords of Nottinghamshire, Derbyshire, and Yorkshire contributed to the needs of the poor and to the support of the band.

Long years slipped by without bringing any change in the condition of the Outlaws. But before closing this book, we must acquaint our readers with the fate of some of our characters.

Sir Guy Gamwell and his wife died at very advanced ages, leaving their sons at Barnsdale Hall, to which they had retired on ceasing to form part of Robin Hood's band.

Will Scarlett had followed his brothers' example; he lived in a charming house with his dear Maude, already the mother of several children, and still as tenderly loved by her husband as in the first days of their union. Much and Barbara settled down near Maude; but Little John, who had had the misfortune to lose Winifred, having no reason to desert the Forest, remained faithful to Robin's commands. Besides, let us hasten to add, John loved Robin too dearly to have ever thought for a single moment of leaving him, and the two companions lived side by side, thoroughly convinced that nothing but death would have the power to separate them.

Let us not forget to mention good Tuck, the pious chaplain who had consecrated so many marriages. Tuck remained faithful to Robin; he was still the spiritual adviser of the band, and he had lost none of his remarkable qualities; he was still the dignified drunken monk, noisy and boastful.

Halbert Lindsay, Maude's foster-brother, appointed Warden of Nottingham Castle by Richard Cœur-de-Lion, fulfilled the duties of his post so well that he succeeded in keeping it. Hal's wife, pretty Grace May, retained her charms in spite of passing years, and her little Maude promised to be the living image of her mother later on.

Sir Richard of the Plain lived quietly and happily with his wife and two children, Herbert and Lilas. The honest Saxon preserved an affection and gratitude for Robin Hood which would only end with life; and there was merrymaking in the Castle whenever the gallant

ROBIN HOOD THE OUTLAW

Outlaw, drawn by the magnet of affection, came there with Little
John to rest from his fatigues.

Shortly after signing Magna Carta, King John, after a series of
monstrous actions, started personally in pursuit of the young King of
Scotland, who fled before him, and marched towards Nottingham,
scattering desolation and terror in his path. John was accompanied
by several generals whose exploits had earned for them pithy
surnames, such as Jaleo the Ruthless, Mauléon the Bloody-Minded,
Walter Much the Murderer, Sottim the Cruel, and Godeschal of the
Iron Heart. These wretches were the chiefs of a band of foreign
mercenaries, and their footsteps were marked by rape, fire, and
death. The news of the approach of this robber band fell like a
funeral knell upon the ears of the terrified populace, who fled in
dismay, leaving their homes at the mercy of the Normans.

Robin Hood heard of the odious conduct of the soldiers, and
resolved thereupon to inflict upon them the same tortures to which
they forced their unlucky victims to submit.

The Foresters responded to their leader's appeal with an
enthusiasm which would have made King John's men tremble, for all
the old hatred of the conquered for their conquerors, of Saxon for
Norman, remained unappeased.

The band prepared for battle; Robin Hood awaited his
opportunity.

In approaching Sherwood Forest, the Norman chiefs sent a
small body of scouts in advance, and when the greater part of the
army penetrated into the wood, they saw, hanging motionless from
the branches of trees along the roadside, or expiring in the dust, the
men whose return they had vainly looked for. This terrifying
spectacle chilled some of their warlike ardour; but as they were in
large numbers, they continued their march. Robin could not openly
attack a whole army; he could only hope to succeed by stratagem;
and he therefore skilfully turned to advantage the agility and
inimitable dexterity of his men. He harassed the soldiers, killing
them with arrows that came they knew not whence; he pursued
them, slaughtering the stragglers, and pitilessly massacring all those
who had the ill-luck to fall into his hands. A general terror paralysed
the movements of the army; it had quite lost its bearings, and the
superstitious ideas of the age led the men to believe that they were
the victims of some infernal witchcraft. One of the foreign leaders,
Sottim the Cruel, endeavoured to put an end to a massacre which
threatened to cause terror and confusion throughout the army. He
called a halt, conjured his men in the interests of their own safety to
overcome their fears, and at the head of fifty determined Normans,
he started to explore the underwood. But scarcely had the little band
plunged into the inextricable windings of a by-path than a volley of
arrows descended from the treetops and arose from the depths of the
thickets, striking down Sottim the Cruel and his fifty companions.

The disappearance of these scouts and their intrepid leader,
redoubled the terror of the Normans, and lent them wings to fly
through Sherwood Forest to Nottingham. Arrived there, spent with

fatigue, and furious with rage, they abandoned themselves with fresh zest to the unqualified excesses which had signalised their sojourn in the valley of Mansfield.

On the morrow of these fatal reprisals, the army, still led by King John, made its way into Yorkshire, burning and massacring at will the unoffending inhabitants of the villages through which it passed.

Whilst the Normans thus ploughed for themselves a furrow of tears and blood and fire, the Saxons, some of whom had been despoiled of their wealth, others violently torn from their wives and children, joined themselves, drunk in their turn with murder and carnage, to Robin's band, and our hero, at the head of eight hundred brave Saxons, started in pursuit of the blood-stained cohort.

A providential chance protected the peaceful dwelling of Allan Clare and the Castle of Sir Richard of the Plain. Neither of these two houses was in the way of the pillagers, for it goes without saying that John did not spare the rich Saxons. He chased them from their dwellings, and permitted his favourites to instal themselves as masters in the homes of the unhappy gentlemen. But then Robin and his formidable companions would arrive, and the new owner and the soldiers whom he had paid to help him to maintain by force the rights of this unjust usurpation, fell into the hands of the Outlaws and were mercilessly put to death.

The King learned from the public outcry, and the complaints of his men, of the Saxon's triumphal avenging progress, and sent against him a small portion of his army, hoping that it would succeed in investing Robin Hood's band, which was said to be encamped in a little wood. It is hardly necessary to say that John's soldiers had not even the satisfaction of returning to announce their defeat to the King; they were killed without having so much as reached the supposed camp in which they were to surprise Robin Hood.

Our hero's prowess made a great noise throughout England, and his name became as formidable to the Normans as had been that of Hereward the Wake to their predecessors in the reign of William I.

John reached Edinburgh, but not being able to capture the King of Scotland, he returned to Dover, leaving orders to his scattered troops to rejoin him. But the greater part of these troops were captured by Robin Hood's men, some in Derbyshire and some in Yorkshire. In the mean time King John died and his son Henry succeeded him.

In the reign of this Prince, Robin Hood's existence was not so adventurous or active as it had been during the blood-stained reign of King John, for the Earl of Pembroke, tutor to the young King, set to work seriously to improve the condition of the people, and succeeded in maintaining peace throughout the kingdom.

The sudden suspension of all physical and mental activity depressed Robin and weakened his powers. It is true our hero was no longer young; he had attained his fifty-fifth year, while Little John was gently nearing his sixty-sixth. As we have already mentioned, time had brought no solace to Robin's grief, and the memory of Marian, as lively and fresh as on the morrow of their parting, had sealed Robin's heart to any other love.

Marian's tomb, piously tended by the Merrie Men, was covered every year with fresh flowers; and many a time, after the return of peace, had the Foresters surprised their Chieftain, pale and sad, kneeling upon the greensward which extended like a green girdle around the Trysting Tree.

Day by day, Robin's sorrow grew deeper and more overpowering. Day by day, his face took a more dejected expression; the smile left his lips, and John, the patient and devoted John, could not always succeed in obtaining from his friend a reply to his anxious questions.

It came about, however, at long last, that Robin was touched by his comrade's care for him, and he consented, at his prayer, to seek the assistance of a Lady Abbess whose convent was a short distance from Sherwood Forest. The Abbess, who had already seen Robin Hood and knew all the particulars of his life, welcomed him heartily, and offered him every assistance in her power to bestow.

Robin Hood showed himself sensible of the frank welcome of the kindly Nun, and asked her if she would be good enough to bleed him immediately. The Abbess consented. She led the sick man to a cell, and with wondrous skill she performed the wished-for operation; then, as skilfully as a clever physician could have done, she bandaged up the invalid's arm and left him, nearly worn out, stretched upon a bed.

A strangely cruel smile played about the Nun's lips when, coming out from the cell, she locked the door and carried away the key. Let us say a few words about the Nun in question.

She was related to Sir Guy of Gisborne, the Norman Knight who, in an expedition, attempted with the aid of Lord Fitz-Alwine, against the Merrie Men, had had the misfortune to die the death which he had hoped to give Robin Hood. However, it would not have occurred to this woman to avenge her cousin, had not the latter's brother, too cowardly to expose himself in an honourable combat, persuaded her that she would be doing both an act of justice and a good deed in ridding the kingdom of England of the too celebrated Outlaw. The weak-minded Abbess submitted to the will of the miserable Norman. She committed the murder, and cut the radial artery of the unsuspicious Outlaw.

Having left the sick man for an hour to the overpowering sleep which was the inevitable consequence of so great a loss of blood, the Nun went silently to him again, took off the bandage which covered the vein, and when the blood had again begun to flow, she crept away on tip-toe.

Robin Hood slept till morning with no feeling of discomfort, but when he opened his eyes and tried to rise, he felt so weak that he thought his last hour was come. The blood, which had flowed ceaselessly from the wound, flooded the bed, and Robin Hood then grasped the full danger of the situation. By an almost super-human effort of will he managed to drag himself to the door. He tried to open it, found it was locked, and, still sustained by the strength of his will—a will so powerful that it succeeded in reviving his exhausted body—he got to the window, opened it, and leaning out, tried to leap from the sill; then, failing in this, he made one last appeal to Heaven, and, as though inspired by his good angel, he took his hunting-horn, raised it to his lips, and with difficulty made some feeble sounds.

Little John, who could not be separated from his well-beloved comrade without sorrow, had passed the night under the walls of the Convent. He had just awakened, and was preparing to take measures to see Robin Hood, when the dying echoes of the hunting-horn sounded in his ears.

"Treachery! treachery!" cried John, running like a madman towards the little wood where a party of the Merrie Men had encamped for the night. "To the Abbey, my lads! to the Abbey! Robin Hood is calling to us! Robin Hood is in danger!"

In an instant the Foresters were on their feet and hastening in the wake of Little John, who was hammering at the gate of the Abbey. The attendant refused to open. John lost not a second in prayers, which he knew would be of no avail. He smashed in the door with a boulder of granite lying at hand, and guided by the sound of the horn, he gained the cell where, in a pool of blood, lay poor Robin Hood. At the sight of Robin dying, the strong Forester felt his strength fail him; tears of grief and indignation rolled down his bronzed cheeks. He fell on his knees, and taking his old friend in his arms, he said to him amid his sobs—

"Master, my well-beloved master, who hath committed the infamous crime of striking a sick man? Whose is the sacrilegious hand which hath committed this murder in a Holy House? Answer me, for pity's sake, answer!"

Robin slowly shook his head. "What boot it," he said, "now that all is over for me? Now that I have lost to the last drop all the blood in my veins—"

"Robin," replied John, "tell me the truth. I ought to know; I must know. Must I accuse this cowardly assassin of deliberate treachery?"

Robin nodded his head.

"Well, beloved friend," continued John, "give me the supreme satisfaction of avenging thy death. Permit me in my turn to bring murder and sorrow where murder hath been committed, where for me hath arisen the most cruel sorrow. Say one word, make one sign, not one vestige of this hateful house shall remain. I will have it destroyed stone by stone. I still have the strength of a giant, and I have five hundred brave men to come to my assistance."

"Nay, John, nay! I do not wish thee to lift up thy clean and honest hands against these women who are vowed to God; that would be sacrilege. She who hath slain me obeyed, doubtless, a will stronger than her religious feelings. She will suffer the tortures of remorse in this life, an she repent; and she will be punished in the next world, an she win not from Heaven the pardon which I accord her. Thou dost know, John, that I have never harmed a woman nor permitted one to be harmed, and for me a Nun is doubly sacred and to be respected. Let us speak no more of that, my friend. Give me my bow and arrow. Carry me to the window. I would breathe my last where my last arrow falleth."

Robin Hood, supported by Little John, took aim, drew the string of his bow, and the arrow, skimming the tree-tops like a bird, fell some distance away.

"Farewell, good bow; farewell, trusty arrows," murmured Robin, in a trembling voice, letting them slip from his hands. "John, my friend," he added, in a calmer tone, "bear me to the spot where I have said that I wished to die."

Little John gathered Robin in his arms, and laden with this precious burden went down to the Court of the Convent, where, by his orders, the Merrie Men had quietly assembled. But, at the sight of their chief lying like a child against John's strong shoulder, at the sight of his white face, they uttered a cry of fury, and wanted to punish forthwith those who had struck Robin.

"Peace, my lads!" said John; "leave vengeance to God. For the moment the state of our well-beloved master should alone occupy our thoughts. All of you follow me to the place where the last arrow shot by Robin is to be found."

The troop divided in two to make a passage for the old man between them, and John walked on with a firm step, and soon gained the spot where Robin's arrow was stuck in the ground.

There John spread upon the turf some garments brought by the Merrie Men, and on them he laid, with infinite precautions, the poor sufferer.

"Now," said Robin, in a weak voice, "call all my Merrie Men. I would be surrounded once again by the brave hearts that have served me so well and so faithfully. I would breathe my last in the midst of my gallant, my life-long comrades."

John sounded the horn three several times, for this call, while warning the Outlaws of an imminent danger, hastened their progress.

Among the men who came in response to John's bugle-call was Will Scarlett; for although he had ceased to belong to the band, he paid them frequent visits, and he rarely passed a week without coming to greet his friends and bringing down a stag, which he would share with them.

We will not attempt to depict William's despair and stupefaction on learning Robin's condition, and seeing the distorted countenance of that dear friend who was so worthy of the love that he inspired.

"Holy Virgin!" said Will. "Ah! my poor friend! my poor brother! my dear Robin, what hath happened? Tell me all; art wounded? Doth he who laid his cursed hand upon thee still live? Tell me, tell me, and to-morrow he will have expiated his crime!"

Robin Hood raised his aching head from John's arm, upon which it had been resting, looked at Will with an expression of lively tenderness, saying, with a sad, wan smile—

"I thank thee, good Will, but I do not wish to be avenged. Put from thy heart all feeling of hatred for the murderer of one who dies, if not without regret, at least without pain. Doubtless I had reached the term of my existence, since the Divine Mother of the Saviour, my Holy Protectress, hath abandoned me at this fatal moment. I have lived long, Will, and I have been loved and honoured by all who have known me. Painful though it be to leave you, good and dear friends," continued Robin, with a tender look at Little John and Will, "that grief is sweetened by a Christian thought, by the certainty that our separation will not be for ever, and that God will unite us in a better world. Thy presence at my death-bed is a great consolation to me, dear Will, dear brother; for, indeed, we have been good and loving brothers. I thank thee for all the tokens of affection with which thou hast surrounded me. I bless thee with heart and with lips; I pray the Holy Mother to make thee as happy as thou dost deserve to be. Thou wilt tell thy dear wife Maude from me, that I did not forget her when praying for thy happiness, and thou wilt embrace her for her brother, Robin Hood."

William sobbed convulsively.

"Weep not, Will," said Robin, after a moment's silence; "thou dost grieve me too much. Has thy heart then become as weak as a woman's that thou canst not bear sorrow more hardily?"

William did not reply; he was choked with tears.

"Old comrades, dear friends of my heart," continued Robin, addressing the Merrie Men grouped silently around him, "ye who have shared my toils and my dangers, my joy and my grief, with a devotion and fidelity beyond all praise, take my last thanks and my blessing. Farewell, my brothers; brave Saxon hearts, farewell. Ye have been the terror of the Normans; ye have gained for ever the love and gratitude of the poor. Be happy, be blessed, and pray sometimes to our dear Protectress, the Mother of the Saviour of Mankind, for your absent friend—for Robin Hood."

Stifled groans were the only reply to Robin's words. Distracted with grief, the yeomen heard these farewells, but refused to realise their cruel significance.

"And thou, Little John," resumed the dying man, in a voice that grew weaker every moment, "thou of the noble heart, thou whom I love with all the strength of my soul, what will become of thee? To whom wilt thou give the affection thou didst bestow on me? With whom wilt thou dwell beneath the grand old forest trees? Oh, John! thou wilt be very lonely, very desolate, very miserable; forgive me for leaving thee thus. I had hoped for a sweeter death. I had hoped to die with thee, beside thee, bow in hand, defending my country. God hath willed it otherwise. Praised be His Name! My hour approaches, John. Mine eyes are failing. Give me thy hand; I would die holding it in mine own, John. Thou dost know my wishes; thou knowest where my mortal remains are to be interred—beneath the Trysting Tree, beside her who awaits me—beside Marian."

"Yea, yea!" sighed John, sadly, his eyes brimming with tears; "thou shalt be—"

ROBIN HOOD THE OUTLAW

"I thank thee, old friend. I die happy. I go to be with Marian for
ever. Farewell, John—" The great Outlaw's dying voice became
inaudible. A light breath touched Little John's face, and the soul of
the friend he had so dearly loved took its flight from earth.

"To your knees, my children!" said the old man, crossing
himself; "the noble and generous Robin Hood hath ceased to live!"

All heads were bowed as William uttered a short but fervent
prayer over Robin; then, with the help of Little John, he carried the
body to its last resting-place. Two Foresters dug the grave beside
Marian, and there Robin was laid upon a bed of flowers and foliage.
Little John placed Robin's bows and arrows beside him; and the
dead man's favourite dog, which might never serve another master,
was killed upon the grave and interred with him.

Thus ended the career of one of the most extraordinary
characters in the annals of England. May he rest in peace!

The possessions of the band were loyally divided among its
members by Little John, who wished to pass the remaining days of
his sorrowful life in some peaceful retreat. The Outlaws separated,
some going to live in Nottingham, others settling down here and
there in the neighbouring counties, but none had the heart to
remain in the old green wood. Robin Hood's death had rendered that
abode too painfully sad.

Little John could not decide to leave the Forest after all. He
stayed there for several days, wandering about the deserted paths
like a soul in pain, and calling aloud to him who would never answer
him again. At last he decided to go and seek shelter with Will
Scarlett. Will received him with open arms, and sad as he was
himself, he tried to afford some consolation to this inconsolable grief;
but John would not be comforted.

One morning William, seeking for Little John, found him in the
garden, standing upright, his back against an oak, and his head
turned toward the Forest. John's face was very pale; his fixed and
staring eyes appeared to have no sight in them. William seized his
cousin's arm in terror, and called to him in a trembling voice; but
the old man made no reply—he was dead.

This unexpected blow was a great grief to William. He carried
Little John into the house, and the next day the whole Gamwell
family followed this second dearly-loved brother to Hathersage
Churchyard, situated six miles from Castleton in Derbyshire.

The tomb containing the remains of Little John still exists, and
is remarkable for the extraordinary length of the stone that covers it.
This stone presents to a curious eye two initials, J.N., very artfully
engraven in the heart of the granite.

A legend recounts that a certain antiquary, a great lover of the
curious, had the gigantic tomb opened, removed the bones, and bore
them away as worthy of a place in his cabinet of anatomical
curiosities. Unhappily for the worthy man of learning, from the
moment that these human remains entered his house, he knew no
repose; he was visited by sickness, ruin, and death. And the grave-
digger who had helped to profane the tomb was equally afflicted in

his tenderest feelings. Then the two men understood that they had offended against Heaven in violating the secrets of a tomb, and they piously reinterred the old Forester's remains in holy ground.

After which the antiquary and the grave-digger lived quietly and happily. God, who grants remission to all repented sins, had pardoned their sacrilege.

THE END.

Find other classic restorations from
the Reginetta Press...

The Prince of Thieves
&
Robin Hood the Outlaw
Alexandre Dumas
1872 & 1873

The Virgin of the Sun
H. Rider Haggard
1922

Peter and Wendy: The Restored Text
J.M. Barrie
1911

...and more.

www.ReginettaPress.com

Return to Neverland with **The *Hook* & *Jill* Saga**
by Andrea Jones.
Award-winning novels of Neverland,
for "grown-ups."

REGINETTA
PRESS

www.ingramcontent.com/pod-product-compliance
Lightning Source LLC
La Vergne TN
LVHW090838131224
798956LV00015B/374